Thank you

I would like to acknowledge the assistance of a number of people for their insightful contribution towards progressing the manuscript of this story to its completion.

In particular thank you to Julie for taking the time to go through the entire document producing a comprehensive report on its condition from the smallest detail to an overview of the entire concept.

Also Graham for his review with words of encouragement and pointing out a few major aspects for re-thinking.

Thank you also to all the members of our local writing group, including Susanna, Gwen, Susan and Lara for their unique insights into so many detailed aspects of the narrative.

I don't want to forget Helen MacKinnon for her special contribution. Helen is a poet and after reading just a few chapters she wrote "On The Edge of Darkness" as an introduction to 'Fugitive Reality', expressing exactly what an elusive component actual reality is in our daily lives.

The intelligence foundation of the author of this work has come into existence as a result of the combined biological blueprint of his parents.

Unlike an artificial construct of pre-manipulated data it has evolved to possess faculties such as knowledge, as distinct from data; of understanding and the ability to find connections between unrelated elements of memory when creating solutions.

He has relied on his own spontaneous creativity to the exclusion of the use of any AI.

FuGiTiVe ReAliTy

Index

Facet 2 – Space Reality

Iluska, From Siberia to the Stars
An Unintentional Stowaway
Migration of the American Golden Butterfly
City of Apollonia
Dangerous Liaisons
Redundant Reality
Back to the Butterfly
Nano-bots Back in Action
Peter Returns from the Dark
Preparing for the Jump
Iluska and Bee-Bee Disinfected
Crossing into Dark Matter
From Mars to Jupiter to Saturn

Facet 3 – Titan Reality

Titan Mindscape Project
The Plains of Rui Regio
A Mutiny Brewing
The Last Picnic
Schrödinger's Box

Reality Check

John can run.
'Run John, RUN.

Betty is coming!'

Betty can run.
Betty can run faster than John.

'Run John, Run!'

Renunciation

Je pense, donc je suis.

If I think about this for too long I may disavow my
existence altogether.

The diabolical imagination machine resident in my skull
has not only the capacity to question its own existence
but to convince those who are a part of my reality that
they are figments of their own imaginations, as am I.

In which event my experience of existence, that which
constitutes my reality, and others experiencing my reality
may become nothing more than a matter of
philosophical debate.

On The Edge of Darkness

I live on the edges of darkness.
In the daylight of today and tomorrow, life beckons
I feel the space that spins across the waves,
I touch the light and tremble in its brightness.

Through the night I anchor my thoughts.
Slipping through time that tugs at my being
This cavity of life stirs my heart,
A pulse that stretches across years.

The light that shields me from now,
Its strength caresses my soul.
I see the map unfolding my future,
Rising – disappearing – beyond my horizon.

I am forever captivated.
This day, this life, this minute,
It sweeps across my being, and delivers me life.
Feeling for what is – and what can be.

> I see
> I feel
> I am

Helen McKinnon 2024

When a child attains the age of comprehension it knows intuitively without any doubt it is immortal. The risks taken throughout life, particularly in the early years, are an affirmation of that conviction.

The child, adolescent and young adult can conceive of one reality only; the imperative to survive. It is not a philosophical position of not dying but one impressed on the mind by the brain of not doing anything that would injure its biological support unit.

Eternal continuity is a possibility which so entertains the brain's imagination machine that it seeks to devise constructs to make that possibility a certainty within its core belief structure. When those theories become too embroiled in complexity, surpassing even the childlike faith in a life beyond the physical, this sentient entity creates alternate realities.

It puts forward the question, 'What if nothing exists at all?' What if we are all figments of imagination? This theory may have its foundations in a reality construct we know as virtual reality. To the brain immersion in virtuality becomes as valid a reality as any other.

For those whose lives are so well organised as to make their reality within the framework of existence stable to the point of not having to exert themselves in order to survive, reality becomes elusive. Escape mechanisms have become abundant, to be indulged in freely or by allowing social pressures to nudge them into a variety of parallel membranes of reality.

Prologue

When are we?
Depends –
Common Era 2200 years, more or less.
Homo Sapiens 300,000 years.
Behavioural Modernity 65,000 years.
Hominin 6,000,000 years.

John and Betty are in about the Twenty Second Century
of our Common Era.

Aside from the above uncertainty there is one physical reality neither of them can challenge and remain reasonable.

Under a microscope, an impartial instrument of science without bias regarding the objects seen through its eyes, John possesses an XY chromosome pair, and Betty the XX version for life's blueprint. This foundation is a challenge to the minds which will emerge from the cocoon of their diabolical imaginations fermenting conspiracy theories about all things, including the nature of their very own existences.

This confronting condition of sentience isn't unique to these two people, thought it may well be outside the realm of reality for lesser consciousnesses, regardless of the theories of panpsychism. A rock, in all probability, doesn't need to ruminate on whether it exists, and if it does then agonise over the nature of that reality.

Having pondered, regardless of what size it may or may not be, its collision with another heavenly body, which itself may or may not exist, would have little significance in the matrix of its existence.

John and Betty have the most unfortunate condition not only of sentience, but of intelligence. This compels them to consider their reflections in the mirror with deep introspection.

Such contemplation can lead to either the acceptance or denial of the characteristics of their reality. In either case the mental exercise is generally inadequate in preparing for either sudden or slow changes in the nature of their existence.

Their individual realities can become fugitives to the reality they may desire for themselves, or fugitives to a past reality they may want to recapture.

Facet 1

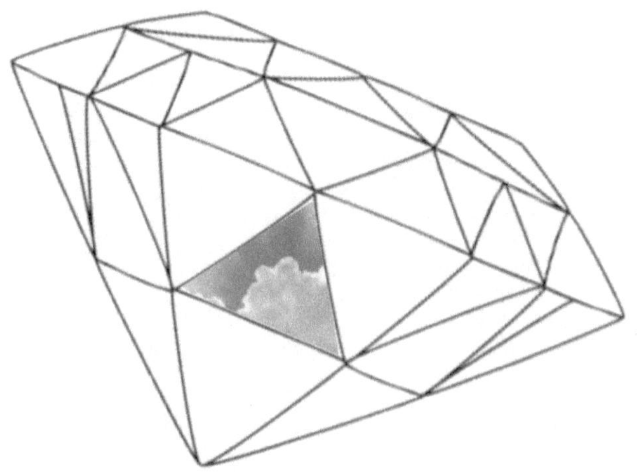

Earth Reality

John and Betty

John became John one day, suddenly.

It didn't happen when he met Betty. He was still a human animal then, a young animal with instincts still intact. It happened well after when he tried to run into his bedroom. The door wasn't there. He bounced off the wall. His bleeding nose did not seem as important as an answer to his question; *Why can't I run through the wall?*

That's when John realised something fundamental. It dawned on him he really did exist. His presence in physical reality became a conscious acceptance. He wasn't just a name his mother screamed from the kitchen in his direction ... 'John! Stop torturing that cat.'

'John' until then was nothing more than a sound he had become accustomed reacting to - not 'Peter'. Peter was the other, the father other. So he reacted by letting go of the cat's tail and running upstairs and bouncing off his bedroom wall and bloodying his nose and becoming aware of existence; of 'I' as a self, separate from the animal body. There was no reasonable explanation for why this young, sentient animal should not be able to walk through a wall. Perhaps if he wasn't in terror of his father - and if the lights had been on upstairs - and if he didn't hear his father's heavy footsteps on the stairs - and if he wasn't in such a hurry he might not have missed the door.

Already at age eight he tried to remember important things. Like why he had to run. It only became obvious when he thought about it. Betty could run faster. Most of the kids he knew could run faster. Running became a matter of survival, a basic indisputable aspect of continued existence.

'Don't! Don't!' he half pleaded, half warned his tormentors.

But Veronique pushed him anyway when she'd caught up to him at the side of the stream. He could swim better than he could run. He remembered having to swim to the other side to get away from the meanie Veronique. It was the only way to survive. Every time the gang caught him John would get hurt. He remembered very well. It was one of the most painful realities of his young life.

Betty was different, though scary in other ways. She was an animal too at an early age. The two of them played like animals; hide-and-seek, pretending to be hunting each other. What do you do when you catch your prey? You have to kill it and absorb its life force.

John didn't know how to kill. Nor did Betty, yet they both pretended and took it in turns to be dead. She would punch him hard in the stomach and he would pretend to die.

'You thought you could get away!'

John remained lifeless on the ground. 'I can catch anything. Now I'm going to devour you!' Betty threatened with eyes devoid of empathy.

There is an art to dying. John had near perfected it.

He did it so well one day it really scared Betty.

Having cornered her prey she brought it down by punching him as hard as she could. As John hit the ground he thrust his arms and legs about then became perfectly rigid. He even closed his eyes and held his breath - and held his breath - and held his breath ...

'John! John! Get up John! Stop it, you're scaring me!'

He continued to hold his breath. John was extremely good at pretending anything, especially being dead. As a skinny kid he definitely could look dead, particularly with his arms and legs all over the place. Playing possum had saved him in the school yard a few times already. The other kids got bored with him when he did that.

'John! Cut it out!' She kicked him again, hard.

John came back to life. What do kids know about the true reality of existence? One thing was certain - he had to breathe eventually. He didn't know that to make his pretence an absolute reality he would have to let his consciousness slip away and allow his body to entropy into atoms, dissipating into the heat energy of the cosmos. That was not a reality young John aspired to, let alone imagine or have a theological perspective about.

Jumping up so suddenly he unintentionally bowled Betty over.

'Oops!' He held his breath again. This was trouble! Betty got that look in the eye animals get when they mean business. John was already halfway down the hill when Betty began her pursuit after tidying her hair and smoothing out her skirt.

'You'll never get away!' She shouted. 'I can run faster than you.'

Run John run. Betty is coming after you!

As John grew into adolescence his body filled out, the stick insect legs gained muscle and strength. He could run as fast as Betty if he really tried. That's when instinct began to dictate it was time for her to start chasing him. John wasn't quite ready to start chasing her, though she'd given him plenty of subtle hints. In time, which didn't take very long at all, John realised an objective worth pursuing more than scoring goals on the football field.

One day, quite unexpectedly, without making a conscious decision, he began thinking a lot more about Betty. A facet of his existence morphed into a realm that seemed to gain control over his life. His hormonal awakening turned the once young human animal into a predator within a realm unfamiliar to him, banishing his boyhood reality altogether. The other kids on the football team couldn't understand why John had lost that 'edge'. He used to be one of the best on the field. But try as he might John couldn't recapture the thrill of scoring the winning goal when thinking about Betty.

'Betty?' He said, or rather used her name to pre-empt a furtive question. They were sitting on the grass in a park across the street from Betty's place. She glanced up from her mobile phone. His eyes had a different look in them.

Run Betty, Run!

The childhood relationship between John and Betty couldn't have been more ordinary because both their parents were conventionally, boringly ordinary. Except perhaps for Peter, his father, in one respect; his work within the realm of theoretical quantum unreality. In that world of quantum improbability he was a recognised genius. A casual glance at the man would not have betrayed that. Balding at an early age with a body build more suited to a couch potato did not inspire closer scrutiny.

Peter didn't think about ordinary things too much. Therefore he was generally happier than many other people who pondered the meaning of their lives, sometimes wondering whether they existed at all. Peter accepted his reality of work, family, his car and his sport. That's all there was to existence until you got snuffed out. The meaning of life for Peter was uncomplicated. Work. Science, experimentation, discovery and lately putting his knowledge to practical use.

'Dad, why is the sky blue?' An annoying question from young John the answer to which was simple yet with considerable philosophical depth.

'Because it just is.' Peter knew the answer to that one. But the other question from his son somewhat vexed him because he never considered the time taken to explain it to John would be of any use to him. John was just a kid; like any other kid running after girls. Yet most kids didn't ask these kinds of questions.

'Why is water wet, Dad?'

John didn't ask himself why he felt so amorous towards Betty. He just did. Anyway - why was Betty running away?

'Wait Betty, Wait!' He shouted.

The question of why he couldn't walk through the wall to his bedroom was never resolved within the realm of mundane reality. It had to wait until John was old enough to look at trees so they would come into conscious existence. The bloodied nose healed and the next time he went towards his room the door was there. At that age he knew nothing about quantum superimposition, about electrons being everywhere around a nucleus at the same time, yet being nowhere simultaneously. It didn't seem relevant to study up on the phenomenon even several years later when perhaps he could have understood, especially not when confronted with the tail feathers of his Betty bird.

Unlike John's dramatic enlightenment Betty became Betty gradually over a few short years.

A more domestic scene couldn't be imagined; Shirley her mother in her favourite lounge, Betty playing with her doll on the carpet, the aroma of dinner infiltrating the sitting room.

'What do you want to be when you grow up darling?' Shirley asked for no apparent reason while knitting and occasionally glancing at her phone. The mechanism seemed to give her some nebulous reassurance all was right with the world just by it being turned on.

'I want to be exactly like you Mummy.' Betty didn't stop getting her doll Harry ready for bed. She answered without thinking about it, although she must have considered what her life would be like with children after experiencing her aunties' kids. 'I want to have three babies, all boys. Boys are much nicer than girls.'

'Why do you say that dear?'

'My girlfriends are so mean to me.

They say I don't look nice. They say I should stop wearing girl clothes because I'm not really a girl.' She adjusted Harry's pillow while Shirley continued her knitting without looking up.

'Whatever do you mean my sweet?' Shirley knew perfectly well many of the children at Betty's school had problems; gender identity issues. At least Betty was normal. She liked playing with John.

'They keep trying to tell me I'm a boy.' Betty blushed. She knew about boys and what *they* looked like. John was definitely a boy. I'm not a boy, am I mummy?'

'Well ...' Mummy hesitated for a moment. What was reality now could be quite different as the years rolled on. 'It depends honey ...' and left the question unanswered. The situation had developed into an uncomfortable realm so Shirley left the knitting to see to dinner. Betty continued getting Harry ready. As she began pulling Harry's pyjama up she noticed something that didn't match her understanding of how things ought to be; Harry doll didn't

have the funny little dangly bit between its legs like all boys
had.

...

A few revolutions of the Earth around the sun had come
and gone. Betty's hair grew longer and she began to care
about how it looked. John got taller, more handsome and
smellier. That's one thing about boys Betty definitely
notice. Chasing one another was replaced by other games.
Actually, it was during one of those other games when she
couldn't cope with his closeness to her any longer.

'John. Will you do something for me?'

'What's that Betty Boo?'

'Go have a wash!'

She pushed him away so hard he hit the ground bum
first, tripping over his undone shoe laces. So he did as he
was told. The next day their games became much more
interesting.

Even more interesting was that Betty never had a
bouncing off the wall experience. Her doors were always
exactly where she expected them to be. Not a single one
took a quantum leap in order to change position in order
to annoy her understanding of how the world should be
organised. It was John's job to figure out his own problems.
He became rather good at that as time went on.

'Mum?'

Shirley lifted her glasses off her nose, turning her head
towards her daughter. Her image of Betty had become a
little fuzzy whenever she didn't use her glasses to look at
her. That had nothing to do with her mind being unable to
focus during her advancing years. Nor did she think for one
second her daughter had started to disappear because she
wasn't consciously thinking of her every second of the day.
Just a sad fact of life; her body wearing out.

Wishing or making believe it was otherwise didn't help at all.

Shirley had noticed the changing relationship between John and her daughter.

Betty took advantage of another opportunity at home to talk seriously to her mother. Shirley was relaxing, knitting one thing or another and Betty having spread herself on the ground at her mother's feet lazily scanning her mobile, asked her mum,

'What do you think about John, Mum?'

'That's a strange question. What brought this on? You've known Johnny all your life - practically all your life.

You know what I think. He's a very nice boy.'

'Actually, that's exactly what I mean. He's nice to me. He's soft to cuddle. He's nothing like all those other rough boys who can't think of anything other than motorbikes and sport and doing stupid risky things and those *other* things.'

'Oh yes? ...' A slight suspicion crept into Shirley's mind. Betty had become a rather beautiful young girl. It was only natural she should be thinking about boys differently to when she was a child.

'I know - I know ...' she blushed '... he's a boy. But what if - you know - he is a bit different.'

Shirley thought about it for a moment, remembering it seemed not all that long ago Betty had asked her a similar strange question - about herself.

'Do you want him to be - different? You don't mean - perhaps ...,' how to say this, '... you'd like him to be a girl? Would you prefer him to be a girl?'

Betty blushed crimson this time. It was so hard to decide what she wanted. She sat up, crossing her legs on the carpet. This time her mum didn't escape into the kitchen. She knew that although she'd tried to raise Betty to be a good girl, to have good morals and to understand what life was about it was time to impress on her daughter the truth about life, about its ultimate purpose.

John didn't have such complicated thoughts about reality. His hormonal problems didn't give him much of a chance to consider Betty within such an opaque, theoretical framework of gender possibilities. She always smelt so good. Her long blond hair and dark intense eyes warped his capacity to see the world as it really was. Any thoughts he might have had about quarks and their contribution to disappearing bedroom doors had long ago found a safe little niche in the back of his mind in which to hibernate until he came of an age to ponder those type of mysteries.

In the meantime he just wanted to spend time with her, as she did with him. Weekends were the best when they could visit each other at their respective homes. Helping Mrs Johnson to prepare dinner didn't qualify intrinsically as an activity worthy of sustained effort. However, being with Betty after dinner had become the incentive to sacrifice a minuscule part of his adolescent life to kitchen duties.

'You be careful with the knife young Johnny boy,' warned Mrs Johnson. It's not that Betty's mother was the controlling type. She had firsthand experience, literally 'first hand' what a chef's vegetable chopping knife could do if not treated with caution and respect. John didn't take much notice of course. Mrs Johnson always worried too much about what could happen. But the sky never did fall.

He noticed Betty watching his masterful skills with carrot and the knife. Time to show her what a real man could do. In John's mind knives were definitely a man's tool.

'Hey Betty, can you do this?' He'd been guillotining carrots. He stole a look at Betty as she peeled a potato, executed a twirl on one foot simultaneously flipping the knife into the air. The plan was to catch it by the handle as his pirouette resumed the starting position.

His eyes were on Betty, not the knife which had devised a plan of its own.

The knife sliced across his lifeline without stopping to consider the neatness of the cut, continuing its spin as dictated by the forces of gravity. Betty could not only run faster than John she also had better reflexes. Her lunge to catch the knife resulted in the predictable outcome.

John bled profusely.

Betty bled profusely.

John instinctively reached out with his cut hand to help Betty. She'd screamed out as the sharp knife slashed deeply into her skin. John didn't think about his own stupidity in the heat of the moment. He saw the blood flowing out of Betty's hand and he knew immediately the blood flow had to be stopped. He grabbed hold of her hand, rolling it into a tight fist, folding his own hand over hers. Blood oozed and dripped everywhere as Mrs Johnson rushed into the kitchen on hearing Betty scream.

Mrs Johnson couldn't work out how serious the situation had become. She panicked as she heard the knife come to a clanging stop on the tiled floor.

Heartbeats of the two youngsters synchronised then gradually returned to normal as they continued clutching each other's hands. Adrenalin still coursed through their veins giving them a few minutes of respite from the pain soon to come. It was time enough for their eyes to meet, hands still warm from the rush of blood.

John offered no apology. Betty asked for none. This was the very first time in their young relationship they'd come face to face with a simple reality of life; the possibility of mortality.

Reality Template

'Before you know it you'll be out of university.
What then?' commented Peter.

He was a pragmatist. His beer had gone flat, and the football game had just ended. With a fresh beer in hand he confronted his son, who to some small extent turned out to be an idealist.

John didn't look up from his keyboard. Part way through his thesis he'd finally got a good rhythm going. Anything his dad had to say could be dealt with later. He tried ignoring the man sitting on the aged, frayed couch. Peter had a highly paid job in space craft propulsion research yet never thought of spending the money on the ordinary simple comforts of life. His thoughts existed in a different realm.

'I'm talking to you, son.' He'd almost forgotten what he wanted to say as he fiddled with the technology so he could replay the last game. 'Are you listening to me?'

John's mind couldn't withstand the barrage of his dad's croaking old voice on top of the inane sounds emanating from the football game crowd. After his mother died his father's reality crumbled. It seemed to John that Peter's only respite came from being on his son's case. He just couldn't realise John wanted to build his own life. Though eternally grateful for having a roof over his head, leaky as it was, John wanted his own space after he graduated; he wanted his life to be different.

'Can't you see I'm working Dad. If this thing isn't finished on time I'll have no chance of getting into the Amerasian Space Academy.' He swivelled away from the desk. His screen went blank, the work automatically saved by Reggie his AI buddy.

Peter would not let up. 'You think you're going to have a better life floating around in space between planets? What's the matter with having that lovely girl by your side, a couple of nice kids and a good job with both feet firmly on the ground.'

'I'm not you Dad. You just don't understand. Even when Mum was alive you seemed to have nothing to live for apart from your booze and sport and those experimental machines at the Institute.'

It happened every time he tried to concentrate on his thesis when Peter was in the same room with him. 'I don't want your kind of life where everything is so boring and predictable.' Without warning an old memory flashed into John's mind. He saw himself on the floor, upstairs, with a bloodied nose, unable to get into his room because his door had disappeared. The image of his dad walking over to him, sipping on another cold beer, completely faded as John remembered why he couldn't dash through his door into his bedroom. *I want to know why,* he had said to himself.

'John, are you listening to me?' Peter was almost on top of him. Apart from his work at the laboratory Peter couldn't motivate himself on his weekly one day off. He used to take time off regularly to take Margie places; such as the Star Camp. On the occasions when they took John with them to camp out for a week at a time John became absorbed in another universe. Normality had to be out there somewhere else, not here on this third rock where everything was catalogued, everything was known, everybody seemed to know exactly how things should be.

The camp was made up of several huge interlocking hemispherical domes. They covered under one hundred acres of open spaces and wooded hills in which the periods of day and night were managed, making days only long enough not to break the circadian cycle. Every waking moment during the artificial nights John's imagination blossomed with the images of the greater universe being shown to the audience in breathtaking clarity. Nebulae and star systems and super novae became the garden of his reality, which he never wanted to leave.

'Don't you remember where you used to take me? It's actually your fault I don't want to end up being buried on this rock so close to the sun.'

Peter chose not to hear *it was his fault*. 'Boring? What do you mean boring and predictable? You know perfectly well our work on ant-grav systems is the world's most important evolution in transportation. Why Hell son! - it's the very thing that'll help your crazy idea of getting out of our solar system a reality!' Peter's voice had escalated to the point where John had to get his ear away from his father's booming.

Those halcyon days were truly over when John, Peter, Margie, his mum, and sometimes Betty enjoyed a common reality of wonderment laced with flights of imagination into realms far beyond the Milky Way. In John's mind imagination was only the first step in achieving another actual reality.

Was it only time which robbed them of happiness, though quite insubstantial? The transition to life without his mother made no sense to John. New sensations of affection for a stranger, who for all practical purposes looked exactly like Betty and acted exactly like Betty, were different to the emotions he'd felt towards the other woman in his life whom he called his mother.

And it was all changing too fast. Yet it all changed so slowly, like sand sifting through the closed fingers of the palm of his hand. John became impatient to get on with life; his version of what life could and should be. He didn't become aware how this warp and weft of his ideal reality always had a missing element. Betty occupied a prominent space in his life now. Her presence didn't quite complete his tapestry of the future though he never imagined being alone.

Betty's understanding of an ideal life was ruined at quite an early age. John wasn't the only boy she chased, though he was the one running behind her most of the time. She chased all the boys at her school. They all wanted the challenge of who could outrun her. One or two of the fastest did manage this extraordinary feat. It all started innocently enough as a game to outdo each other. Within two years a deviation in hormone induced reality changed the innocent fun to a subtle but a more important reason for running and chasing. It used to be to outrun each other. The new paradigm had become to catch, capture and subdue.

All Betty knew was that danger gilded the fun of being caught. She decided she didn't want to be caught. Not by those mean, smelly, leering, groping boys. She tried to explain her growing confusion to Shirley.

'Mum?' It was during the last year of her secondary education when she arrived home late from school, somewhat dishevelled.

'Whatever have you been doing dear? You're all dirty.' She turned her daughter around to better gauge her well-being. 'Why is your skirt torn?'

'I hate them! I hate them all!' The sobbing started as she fiercely hugged her mum.

Mrs Johnson, being the kind of person whose personality happily accepted the common blueprint of life, within the correct framework of course, suddenly understood.

'They didn't try to do something?' Her note of deep concern made Betty sob even louder. 'I hope nothing happened.' Shirley couldn't think beyond the obvious. She'd lived her entire life not questioning the template for normal existence. Yet all 'normal' things had to happen at the right time under the right circumstances. What appeared to have happened to her daughter didn't satisfy either of those criteria.

'No Mum!' Betty cried out between sobs. She'd known for some time what boys wanted. She knew what she wanted, or thought she knew and how it had to happen that way, but only when *she* wanted.

'Come and sit with me dear. It's time we had a very serious talk.' Betty let go of her mom, searching for her handkerchief between sobs.

Her open palm displayed a bright purple scar, the wound healed over not so very long ago.

'Do you remember telling me when you were much younger what you wanted?'

Betty wiped her eyes and blew her nose. It gave her time to think. 'Yes I do and I don't want to have boys anymore.' She said this with such a sense of finality Shirley decided not to follow that avenue of discussion.

'Well then, what do you want? You're almost seventeen. You should start thinking about having a family, find a nice boy.' Betty smirked as if to say there were no nice boys in existence. 'Don't you think John is a nice boy.'

'Oh Mum!'

'You did say you wanted to be just like me.'

'Yes, I remember. But things change. Life doesn't have to be the same for everybody. I mean - suppose I want to join the United Nations Security Council or something.'

Betty said it on the spur of the moment then immediately wondered at herself for having said it with such energy. Her mother was so stunned she couldn't find the words to respond. Her eyes widened at her baby girl having such strange ideas. She had raised her daughter to understand what was important in life. Like having a nice home, several lovely children - a good man to look after her. What kind of life could she possibly expect to have by working for the United Nations? It could be dangerous. She would have to travel all over the world. It was a reality for her daughter she could not possibly come to terms with.

'That's exactly what I'll do. I bet they're looking for smart fearless people all the time.' Betty blurted out with faux enthusiasm.

Yet having said the magic words a whole new world opened up for Betty, a world in which John no longer played a prominent role. Not that she'd had any firm ideas he would be the father of her children. That just seemed to be the grey background smudge of a reality their respective parents had painted on a canvas which wasn't hers. And as far as she knew it wasn't John's either.

He'd gone off to university. Thinking about it now Betty realised how often John talked about the future in which her name didn't play an important part. The last time they cuddled he'd said something about going to some Space Academy somewhere.

'Anyway, John's got his own plans,' she said aloud to Shirley as if her mother had been a part of her inner dialogue. 'We can still be friends. I really do like John.' Betty let out a little giggle. 'He can run so much faster now. Sometimes I let him catch me.' Another giggle and a slight blush.

'Don't be too hasty my darling. Just remember - you two are almost joined by blood.' She said this as if fate had already decided everything for her daughter. Shirley couldn't imagine not having John as her son-in-law.

The statement didn't make any sense to Betty. 'Oh,' she remarked and looked down at her hand, remembering.

'Yes, dear. I know he was being completely silly, but then he could actually have saved your life. You remember how badly you started bleeding.' Betty remembered very well. She also remembered how he had held her hand and how warm it felt. It all seemed like a strange dream now, both wonderful and yet quite frightening.

'That was so long ago Mum.'

'You think barely a year and a half is a long time?'

It made Betty think. So many things had happened since then. Like for instance she'd worked out how her life would not follow the same pattern as her mother's ... like for instance understanding how boys were so very much different from girls and not only physically ... like how John never seemed to include her in his plans for the future.

Yet on the other hand John had some qualities she still liked very much. He didn't want to do the ordinary things everybody else did. John had big ideas and big ambitions. She could see her own life becoming extraordinary. Maybe she and John could travel down that path together, for a while at least. It could be fun. It could be exciting.

Dreams
and
Aspirations

Six years isn't the same length of time as when you've just turned twenty four years old from eighteen, compared to turning eight from a child of two.

In some respects adolescence doesn't last long enough. They had the luxury of enjoying its tribulations and joys together. John and Betty's parents lived close to one another. Not quite walking distance, certainly close enough to visit with a quick bicycle ride. In the past they attended the same secondary school. Growing into adulthood together they didn't lose touch, although their tertiary education took widely different paths. John's comprehensive academic studies couldn't have been more different from Betty's dedicated pursuit of the social sciences. Her experiences with those smelly, groping, aggressive boys left a deep impression on her about the true nature of the human psyche. It may not have been an accurate picture of human nature. Nevertheless contemplation of the fate of mankind based on her observations of its behaviour developed in her a desire to do something, anything, to bring about change for the better.

In the interval of time between eighteen and twenty four years of age the Earth had orbited around its sun six times. John had come to a religious conviction it must be so. Once humanity believed the Earth to be flat. Since then it had proved to be a sphere, so we became convinced of that. Science insisted this to be true, though some still clung to the old paradigm quite openly and others secretly.

Having succeeded in obtaining master's degrees in engineering, computer science and quantum physics left little room in his neural network to accommodate a value system based on conspiracy theories or philosophy: For he suspected cosmology to be substantially a branch of philosophy. Most theories about the cosmos could neither be proved or disproved. John dreamt that one day he could turn cosmology into a science. That was one kind of dreaming; the kind which excited his fertile mind. It was not the kind to wake you in the middle of the night in a cold sweat wondering whether the event you've just dreamt was real.

Sometimes the stepping stones through life seem far apart. Occasionally the Universe shows a little kindness. Betty's academic pursuits brought her to Houston University to study biotechnology. She didn't question why her project with the United Nations Security Council should want her to study the subject as well as languages.

John had already started at NASA in a dual capacity. It seemed to be a natural progression in their relationship to move in together when Betty found out John had been accepted into astronaut training at NASA. She didn't know the details of his other job, which would become a major preoccupation for her as part of her 'duties' with the UNSC.

Some weeks after having settled into their accommodation provided by NASA, the couple could finally relax into a routine giving them the time to discuss the important things in their lives. Weekend mornings seemed most conducive to idle chatter.

'I meant to ask you, how did you manage to get this great house? I love the quiet and the privacy,' Betty began as they both stepped over the dream threshold into fully conscious reality.

'I didn't have to do anything. NASA wanted me to be close the training centre and the research labs. They found this place for me.'

'If you're going to become a space monkey you'll have to learn sign language and tell me secret things. I wonder what else.' Betty quipped seductively. He couldn't tell her his involvement with the space program extended well beyond going for a walk in space at the International Space Station. Her prompt didn't work so Betty let it slide. There would be other opportunities.

'What do you really want to do with your life when you finally get through all your highly secretive training BB,' he countered. He continued calling Betty that since their childhood, and because of other attributes she had. He knew she'd joined the UNSC - nothing about the assignment she'd been given. She was reluctant to discuss that as much as he was to talk about the research project he worked on with his father.

'I've learnt some amazing things about how the world works and it's not the way we used to imagine it to be,' she commented cynically. 'It's ... it's warped and it needs straightening out. I can't tell you anymore about how it's going to happen because then they would have to come and kill you.'

'And I'm guessing you want to do something about it. And incidentally, who are 'they' exactly?' asked John with seemingly only passing interest.

'I want to do a lot about it. Best if you don't know too much because they don't play nice.'

Even before Betty was accepted in the UNSC she was already curious about Peter's research. When they all went to the Star Park together as kids at home Peter would say interesting things, not just about space but living in space, travelling to distant worlds and how it would be possible even in his lifetime. Anti-gravity travel had been a standard science fiction concept since for ever as far as Betty could remember. Peter never actually mentioned anything about the experimental work he'd been doing. Betty just had a natural curiosity about how humanity would be able to achieve interstellar journeys. On the few occasions she'd asked Peter about ways of moving through space he either side-tracked the question or deferred to explaining standard space propulsion systems. After joining the UNSC acquiring the details of the special technology had become Betty's specific assignment concurrent with her training.

Although many of their conversations had life exploratory characteristics Betty and John never quite managed to nail down their specific aspirations into achievable positive actions. Such hopes became a layer of their shared experience of life, which never seemed to synchronise with the simple reality of living together and surviving from day to day. Perhaps one day Betty's better world would not be recognisable for the evil it used to be. Same as John's desire to understand all of creation could end up confirming the existence of a grand architect of all there is - or throw all contemporary knowledge and belief systems into complete chaos.

The fundamental nature of existence completely baffled him. He needed to tackle it one small element at a time. John could not deny one specific building block of reality, one that had disrupted his life most recently; his dreams. They had a mechanism and a purpose designed to maintain cognitive balance when in the waking state.

He understood that. Yet he couldn't cope with the random, disorganised and fanciful nature of a barrage of dreams assailing his nights in the past few months. He could find no logical reason for the unpleasant experiences.

'I can't stand it anymore,' he complained to Betty one Saturday morning while still in bed. She turned over, put a hand on his forehead and felt the beads of perspiration, as she had on numerous occasions lately.

'So I see. Are you fully awake yet?'

'I've been awake since three o'clock!' he snapped.

'That bad?' She gathered up a corner of the bed sheet to wipe his face dry.

'Sorry.'

'You want to tell me about it?'

'I don't think you'd understand. We think about everything so differently. We might as well be living on different planets.' John had tried to define the reasons on numerous occasions why they were still together as a couple. Reasonable explanations eluded him other than the obvious physical 'chemistry' between them, which had existed since their early adolescence.

Betty's brow furrowed at the one aspect of their lives together which had become quite obvious to her, more so than other driving forces. The older they became the more their concepts of life diverged. Yet here they were, living together - and taking great pains to make sure they didn't make any more little humans to encumber their futures. Betty found this puzzling when she thought about what she really wanted out of life. Was having a family with a bunch of kids really so important? She and John never delved into that aspect of their relationship to any depth, although the measures they've taken to keep their lives uncomplicated seemed contradictory to the lack of discussions between them.

John noticed Betty's thoughts had wandered off. 'I can see you're not really interested,' he said somewhat disappointed as he made a move to get up.

She came back to the present - pressed gently on his chest to get him to settle back down. Neither of them had immediate work or study commitments on the weekend. *I might as well hear him out.* 'No, no, no - I mean yes. Sorry, my mind wandered off. Please, tell me - if you think it would help.' The look on her face seemed to say she wasn't bothered whether she understood the nature of his dreams or not.

John had already retreated back into himself so Betty's obviously disinterested questioning eyebrows made little impact.

Yet for some reason he launched into it. 'It's all so real!'

'What is?'

'Don't you remember?' He took her injured hand and turned it palm out to reveal the scar. 'I couldn't stop the bleeding!' With her other hand she stroked his damp hair. 'I feel so guilty about my stupidity. Look what I've done to you.' She looked at the purplish scar. Sometimes when it was cold it did hurt. Yes, he was stupid. But so was she to reach out for the falling knife.

'Yes, what you did fooling around was stupid. But it's all in the past now.'

'Is it? Is it really? When I'm in the dream it's unbelievably real. I can feel and see everything. Then I wake up and you're here beside me. Why can't I realise they are only dreams. Like when we play virtual reality games. What if one day the dream becomes a warped reality and we start hacking away at each other with kitchen knives?'

'Not likely Johnny boy, but if you don't get over it and keep annoying me to distraction - who knows.'

He wasn't listening to her, still enmeshed in the re-dreamt experience. 'What if - what if we spent sixteen hours a day dreaming and only eight hours awake? Which would be reality then? Would we even know the difference between a dream life and reality?

Would we go on being crazy to each other with weapons?'

'An interesting thought,' Betty mused. 'Would you like me to put a couple of knives beside the bed – just as a test?'

He had let go of her hand, propped himself up on one elbow to see her eyes more clearly. 'Sometimes I don't know who you are Betty Boo. I'd love to know what actually goes on inside that pretty head of yours.'

She punched him in the stomach like she used to when they were children, but not as hard. He doubled over pretending to be dead, like he used to. The strange situation had taken a rather unpleasant, perhaps foreboding turn. 'I suspect, though I don't subscribe to the theory, our hopes and aspirations funnel reality to some extent towards making those things come true. I also believe, and this is a matter of faith though unproven, that we achieve in life exactly what we work towards, consciously or unconsciously. I mean - look at all the effort you're putting into becoming an international whatever. Sometimes you behave quite strangely. What is it you are actually training for? You've never told me.'

'Soo, you don't want the knives by the bed?' She completely ignored his question. Having secrets made her job so much more exciting.

'Come on, let's have breakfast. We can talk about something a little more serious.' He gave her a husbandly hug, which she passively reciprocated.

'Alright. You can tell me if you're ready to be a space monkey yet.' Betty tried lightening the mood.

It must have worked. 'Have we got any bananas? I'm developing a taste for them,' John grinned back, feeling a little better as the memory of the dream faded and he'd dumped some of his worrying feelings.

A suburbanised country house located by itself on the unfrequented County Road 38 Houston turned out to be an ideal temporary location for the two of them to set up house. Surrounded by small farms with cows and chickens and a few crops it seemed like an ideal location for privacy. Given their respective career choices a reasonable degree of anonymity from society in general had been enforced on each of them by their respective controllers. To some extent in a subtle way their normal realities had already begun to morph towards a realm impossible for either of them to have imagined when they were adolescents chasing each other. The chase continued; the methods and prize at the end became substantially different.

The yoke of domestic conditioning from the past had left its mark on their shoulders though the heavy burden of their parents' constant badgering had been lifted. Their individually chosen career paths had created possibilities well outside the realms of normality imagined for them by their parents or what they could have imagined for themselves at the beginning.

'You know BB, I rather fancy this,' he remarked looking out the window at open fields with a few trees along the borders. 'The open spaces I mean. The animals, the lifestyle. So different from the training centre. There we are either cooped up in enclosures no larger than a bathroom, or windowless labs. I can't wait to get out into space.'

'I suppose you also fancy a plump wife, half a dozen kids and a couple of milking cows, maybe a dozen chickens as well as an alternative to space walking from the way you're talking.'

'You know what I mean. It's like we're living two different lives, you and me. I can't imagine what you do at the Uni in Houston. You're always so secretive about it. Do you like living here, you know - in this kind of rural environment?' She actually didn't, being so sensitive to all kinds of nasty smells.

'I've told you all I can Johnny boy. But I can tell you this, learning Chinese ain't easy.

French and Russian are okay. I already knew a bit of French from school.'

John grinned at her. He definitely knew all about her athletic tongue but not that it could babble in foreign gibberish.

'What are you grinning at?'

'I wish I could be as talented with my tongue,' John quipped.

She swung a loose open palm in his direction. She liked his naughty banter - something she would definitely miss as her training entered a more serious phase requiring her to be sequestered for more lengthy periods away from their home.

'And another thing ... you know those VR games we like to play, with the two of us as co-conspirators. Not a patch on the augmented reality simulations at the Bioinformatics Centre.' Betty suddenly stopped. She'd said way too much. *Now he's going to start asking all sorts of awkward questions.*

'Right. Sounds fascinating. Anything we could use here in our cosy little domicile?'

'Is that all you can think about - and space! How about you tell me about your space monkey training.' They'd finished breakfast as the sun rose higher over their second cups of coffee, flooding the kitchen with beckoning light.

'I'll do better. Want to come and visit the Astronaut Training Centre? NASA runs Tram Tours. I might even be able to take you behind the scenes.'

NASA
Betty has
Suspicions

The visit gave Betty ideas ... and suspicions.

It might have been half hour's drive. They remained silent. Perhaps they were daydreaming about success in their chosen careers. Perhaps mulling over their strained conversation over the morning cuppas. Unlike Betty John didn't have a hidden agenda. Essentially, he was at the stage of learning how to survive in space in order to carry out experiments to help develop the anti-gravity propulsion system through application of his and his father's theoretical work. Perhaps not as huge an undertaking compared to Betty's industrial espionage training when considering repercussions on personal security.

Apart from displaying the enormous space vehicles on the outside the Centre itself did not invite visitors to explore it. The grey, bland façade gave away nothing of its extraordinary internal contents. As they went from one spectacular display to another John spoke with a constant flow of information. It was obvious he enjoyed showing off to his girl and how his dream was coming true. The little quip about country life was nothing more than a remnant of past conditioning. It was never going to be his reality. Visiting the Space Camps with his dad made sure of that. The complex architecture of a child's mind will, whether desired or not, influence the adult in all facets of its life expression. Rebelling against his parent's life-map for him would not be enough to completely erase John's susceptibility to the implanted template.

Because the Centre was an actual astronaut training facility there were limits to where he could take her.

'Through there is the pool where we train for the weightlessness environment in space. They call it the Neutral Buoyancy Laboratory.' She could see a completely uninviting area, nothing like a 'real' swimming pool. Nobody having fun splashing about there on a Sunday. Equipment of every size and function spread about, no doubt used to monitor the trainees progress and well-being.

Not very exciting for Betty. 'Oh yes. I see.' He didn't hear her lack of enthusiasm because of the noise of excitement in his own head. What she wanted to know would not be available for public scrutiny. They walked to a different building for the next treat.

'And here's the lab which most of us don't like. It's where they keep the sensory deprivation pods. They are diabolical I can tell you. You get in there and after just ten minutes you think you've been in there for hours. Your brain starts playing tricks on you. Some of the trainees have hallucinations. But I guess that's the point - to see how we would cope in unreal situations likely to be found stuck in a ship somewhere out in space with few if any companions. Or imagine being stuck in a small ship with just one other person. How long before both went nuts and tried to kill each other?'

'The pod's got possibilities!' Betty's imagination kicked in thinking of some of the interrogation methods they had to learn about in her own training and those pods could be most useful. Another one of the things she couldn't discuss with John.

'You like that, eh.' John had little idea what actually motivated Betty. They'd been friends since childhood, but somehow their relationship never managed to break through the third layer of superficiality. He'd always felt Betty kept her deeper self well hidden, or well protected. He only knew Betty seemed to have a global sense of responsibility that superseded all personal aspirations.

'Move on people, move on. Centre's about to close.' A security guard had been rounding up stragglers who'd wandered off to where they were not supposed to be.

'So - what is it they actually do to you in there?'

The guard urged them on as she got absorbed in discussing the possibilities. This was a part of John's training she wasn't aware of. 'Like - do they use drugs on you while you're isolated?'

'They don't need to. Everything changes inside your head so quickly. What we actually have to do is come to terms with our own minds. We have to accept the nature of our personal reality when confronted with it in such a dramatic way. It works by forcing you to learn to live with your own thoughts, confront who you truly are and not try to force your own imagined reality onto your crewmates. When you're confined in a small area in space there's nowhere to go. You can't afford to try and imprint your own personal reality on the others.'

'I suppose all this has been worked out by your bosses and you have to follow their rules.'

'Yes, if you want to put it that way. But it's more serious than just following protocol. Imagine, and this can happen in the pods as much as in real life, your mind gets immersed in some desire you've been nurturing. Because you're so completely isolated from sensory input it's no problem at all for the mind to jump the tracks and make you believe those desires are actually attainable in reality. Then when you emerge into the 'real' world you can't adjust to it out of your brain construct and behave as if you were still in the illusion.'

'I definitely like the sound of that. Can anyone have a few sessions in the pods? A little reality adjustment on certain people might help to make the world a better place.' She listened intently to everything he'd been saying, realizing how opposite to his her attitudes were becoming. Her dream was to make the world a much better place. And there was only one way to do it. She had to toughen up, accept some harsh realities about the world and all the nasty people in it. There had to be rules which could not be broken. Things had to be a certain way and that was the only way. Until she could achieve her dream and change the undesirables' reality to match her own template of what should be she would not be satisfied. Hers was not just a dream or a career aspiration. It had become the all-consuming goal of her life; the current assignment being one of the stepping stones to achieving that. She saw everything through that filter. All her behaviour patterns had begun to orient in that direction.

John waited till they were on the way home to ask Betty about her training and what she hoped to achieve. Her offhand remarks were in character with the Betty he'd become accustomed to, yet there was a little underlying current of something strange going on in her head. He couldn't quite define it and let it slide into the background for the time being.

'How is Bioinformatics going to help you turn the world around?' He glanced at Betty. Then something caught his eye in the rear view screen on the dashboard. A car with darkly tinted windows had been behind them since they left the training centre. 'I would not have thought genetic information to be within the realm of the UN Security Council's sphere of interest.'

Here it comes I knew he'd latch onto it. 'All information is valuable.' She noticed his eye movements and glanced at the screen also. 'Do you know that car?'

They'd just turned into their own road. The car behind them continued on without slowing. 'No. Do you?'

Another vehicle came down their road towards them. It had the same dark look about it. 'If anyone should be watched it's more likely they'd be keeping an eye on you BB, not me - I mean, who'd be interested in an ordinary astronaut?'

Betty still hadn't divulged her deepest motivations or in what direction they were driving her ambitions. She didn't want to take him into her confidence … Her supervisor made it quite clear that was not a possibility, especially not if she wanted to continue her long term relationship with him.

Within a few minutes they had arrived home. She always stepped forward to unlock the front door first. 'Why didn't you lock the door?'

'I did.'

'Then why isn't it locked?' she accused.

'Because one of us didn't lock it. So what. There's nothing valuable in there.' He remembered leaving the house after her, but not whether he'd locked the door. One generally doesn't remember things done out of habit.

Since becoming a trainee at the UNSC Betty had begun to develop a suspicious nature. Previously she took everything more or less at face value. Things were exactly as she saw them. As a young girl the only caution she had to exercise was watchfulness over ulterior motives of teenage boys. They seemed to live in a world made up entirely of their own hormone driven fantasises. She definitely didn't feel like opening up to John with a deep and meaningful exchange of life aspirations - not then anyway. As they stepped over the threshold those cars had begun to bother her, her eyes already scanning the interior for any sign of disturbance. John dumped his stuff in the corridor. Betty walked about the apartment like a hound dog on the lookout for squirrels. At this early stage of her training she had not been issued with gadgets to help her maintain secrecy by neutralising spyware.

'I can't spot anything.'

'What are you looking for?'

'Anything people in the cars with tinted windows may have left behind. I smell a skunk. What dark mysterious things have you been up to Johnny boy?'

'I might ask you the same question. You're becoming paranoid.'

Betty wouldn't let it rest. She went through the entire house, picking things up, looking behind everything. The concept of implanted nano-spies had not yet entered her consciousness. John caught up to her, put his hands on her waist from behind. Their chases were not as energetic any more.

Betty stopped, though not having quite exhausted her suspicions. She could see no signs of forced entry - nothing was missing - nothing seemed to have been left behind - nothing looked out of place. John's warm hands had the desired effect of distracting her bloodhound nose.

'You've caught me,' she managed a smile.

'How about we make some happy memories,' he asked nonchalantly as they settled in after their outing. 'It'll give me something to think about while I'm in the sensory deprivation pod,' he grinned suggestively.

'You hungry?' She asked, genuinely famished, seemingly uninterested in his suggestion. Reluctantly he released her. They went into the antiquated farmhouse style kitchen, set up with all the standard implements with which to torture food. The knives all sharp, waiting patiently in their block.

Food wasn't on his mind. Nor were those strange cars in spite of never having seen them before along their road. It had been an exciting day for him. It was a thrill to be able to show off to his girlfriend. In some strange way she always managed to make him feel a little bit inferior. Perhaps it all went back to the time they were children and he could never run fast enough to catch her. And when he did it always seemed like she let herself be caught.

Expendable Operatives

'They saw us for sure. Look at the way she's snooping around the place,' Johnson said watching the monitor.

One of the black cars with the tinted windows had stopped at the end of County Road 38 to check signal reception. Visuals and sound were both coming in clearly. These two agents from the CIA didn't feel the need to be overly cautious with this assignment. Their two targets were after all just ordinary people doing something out of the ordinary. They were not trained agents.

'Nah. Don't worry about it. Besides, the equipment's been there since they got the place. She hasn't spotted the bugs yet ...' Matthews felt confident, '... and we don't have to worry about him. He's a dreamer. If he starts any trouble there are two dozen other astronauts who could easily take his place. He'll be easy to neutralise and there won't be any ripples. I don't know what he's involved in but it must be pretty serious for NASA to get us to keep an eye on them.'

'What about the other car?' Johnson was probably right to be more concerned about that. It may have looked like an ordinary vehicle to any normal person but to Johnson it had all the signs of being 'one of them'; the opposition.

'All we have to do is get data to help build up a psychological profile of Johnny boy, you know - when he thinks no one's watching him. The girl's UNSC's problem. They're probably going to do something to break up the relationship anyway, once they've got what they want.'

'We might as well go, they're about to go into AVR. It's some stupid augmented reality hunting game. Not much for us to see when they're in a parallel reality. You know what it's like - just another world to suck you in.'

Kurt: 'You saw them, Ja?' Alluding to the other vehicle.

Auguste: 'Ouais. Et?' The layback Frenchman from the UNSC wasn't in the least concerned. Extracting her would be dead easy. 'The two crétins have chosen such an isolated place to shack up together. There's no way Betty could resist when we have to pull her out. None of the neighbours would notice if either or both disappeared.'

Kurt: 'I'm talking about the idioten in the other car. They gotta be from NASA, maybe CIA. I don't like it. What if *Betty Boo* finds out what we want while they're immersed in VR?' Kurt liked the nickname for Betty. She fitted the name well.

Auguste: 'Ouais - and ... So what if she knows. We'll get it out of her, or they will. N'est-ce pas? We've got instructions what to do with her afterwards.'

Fredrick: 'She's not a prop, Auguste.' He didn't feel as blasé about disposing of a human being as if she was only a tool no longer useful. 'If she gets anything out of him we'll see it in her behaviour. And she's not a pro, not yet anyway. In any case - we can't do anything until she does find out. The CIA might get in our way. You ready to deal with them?'

August: 'Ouais. Pourquoi?'

Kurt: 'No problemo.'

Fredrick: 'Just making sure you two fine gentlemen have no qualms about doing what has to be done. This shit going down has global implications. I don't know what he's working on, but I do know she wants that intel.'

All three UNSC special division men were larger than normal human specimens; fit, intelligent and well trained. Their instructions were clear; wait till the woman gets the information out of the guy then force it out of her if she decides to be uncooperative, which she might be if her loyalty to the NASA guy gets in the way. Do whatever has to be done, they were instructed. 'After she gets the intel for us she's expendable; no longer of any use to anybody.'

Fredrick: 'What're they doing now?' Auguste had been watching the vid-feed from their own surveillance equipment secreted in the house.

Auguste: 'They're in another one of their VR games, waving their arms about and climbing into something or another. There's nothing in their games room to get in their way.'

Fredrick: 'Right. Let's get back to HQ. We won't find out anything tonight.'

They'd been on the side of Brazoria County Road 182 waiting, watching and monitoring for at least twenty minutes. Time enough for the other vehicle to have gone on its way. Auguste had to unbutton the vest stretched across his broad chest just to get his hands comfortably on the steering wheel. They didn't need to see in real-time what the two targets were doing. They were going to be in a different world anyway for some time; a reality experienced only by themselves.

Contaminated
Virtual
Reality

It was Sunday.

John and Betty still had a free day to themselves before immersion in the harsh realities of exhaustive training. Why not enjoy their limited time together?

'Seriously Johnny boy, you never talk about your work. I'm interested. What do you actually do, apart from monkeying around in the pool and playing with yourself in those pods?' She searched in the fridge at the end of the kitchen bench while he got out the coffee.

'Like - what do you want to know?' He started hedging.

'For example, where are you planning to go? What are you going to do? How many will be going?' Betty had made herself a ham and cheese sandwich, leaving the bread knife and the sandwich on the cutting board for the moment.

'Is this some kind of interrogation?' He opened the jam jar and put the kettle on. 'Why so interested in the details all of a sudden?' John was not suspicious by nature but he'd been with Betty long enough to know when she was chasing after something. 'Titan, no secret really. It's already been made public knowledge.'

'If you must know, it's part of my training; interrogating people without making them suspicious.'

'It's not working.'

She giggled. 'Just practicing. Okay then. How about you just tell me. How are you going to get all the gear you need out into space to get you out to Titan?' She kept fishing. He seemed willing to play.

'Shuttle.'

'Come on! What I'm really interested in is how much energy it's going to take to lift all the payload up into the ISS.' Betty had worked out from snippets of passing comments from both Peter and John that some unique gravity containment and control process was being developed in secret. That's what the UNSC wanted to know. They were convinced of the value, and danger, if all nations got hold of such technology. They wanted to be in a position to control NASA's little secrets, not convinced NASA's security measures could contain the technology. Betty's relationship with John was the perfect hide from which to watch and catch.

'Not much.' John had decided to play it safe and say the minimum without going into details. He remembered how she used to get information out of him for exams at school. Not anymore.

'Oh - so - you'll just flap your wings? I thought it would take about seven years to get to Titan.'

'You've been researching. Clever girl. Don't be silly. I hope it won't take that long,' he commented obtusely. 'Coffee's ready. What did you find in the fridge?'

'Cheese.'

'Which one?'

'Gouda.'

'So now you're being evasive.'

'So how long do you think?' Betty would not give up.

Mathews and Johnson had arrived at their base in time to check the little cat and mouse game between the two lovers.

'He's smarter than I thought,' commented Matthews. 'Admittedly she's using a soft technique but he's not giving anything away.'

'Put it on his file,' said Johnson. He wasn't interested. All they had to do was collect data on him, not do a psychological analysis.'

Auguste: 'Hey Fredrick - regardez. She's trying'
Kurt: 'Dumm! She's got no idea what she's doing.'
Fredrick: He was watching the vid-feed. 'We could be here all night. I'll check later - pillow talk secrets - best time.

Over preparations for cheese, crackers and coffee Betty continued the pursuit.

'I know you're dying to tell me. I can see the excitement in your eyes Johnny boy. What do I have to do to get it out of you,' she cajoled, giving him a sideways glance through half closed eyes.

He took a sip and a bite of his cheese and cracker while still standing in the kitchen, leaning against a cupboard. 'Look BB - all I can say - it's - um - revolutionary. So much so our engines will get us to Titan in months, not years. Now, have your coffee and let's go play. Don't forget your sandwich.'

Betty tried to look unimpressed. A stupendous revelation. *The rest will come later - in bed* ... she hoped. She gulped down the rest of her drink without bothering to get her ham and cheese sandwich.

She might have choked on it. The partial disclosure was too exciting.

'So - just knives - yes?'

'What?' John realised what she'd said. He didn't actually give away any secrets but it was enough to fire up Betty's curiosity even more. And he knew what she was like. Once she got the smell of the hunt she'd not easily give up. 'What about knives?' He'd lost track momentarily of his train of thought, slightly concerned about what he'd revealed about his work.

Instead of indulging in ordinary physical reality exploring the biological pleasures of friction they chose a parallel universe where unexpected pleasures could be expected. However, Betty now wanted something a little more exciting. Her desire for the secret had been primed.

'Space Hunt,' she said. 'How about we play Space Hunt?' They'd played this one before, with many variations. A sense of urgency in her quest had also been generated by seeing those two suspicious vehicles.

Perhaps an opportunity would present itself to talk further about Peter's work. She hadn't seen or spoken to him since John moved out to live with her, almost two years ago. The UNSC Counter Security Department had made it abundantly clear that part of her job was to obtain certain information. It was essential for her to do so if she expected to graduate. They never brought up the subject of her tenuous life expectancy.

'It's not what I had in mind.' He sounded disappointed. 'But sure hon. With or without weapons? John asked as he began loading the game program.'

With a twinkle in the eye she shot back, 'With - Hon,' emphasising the term of endearment. The setup options presented choices ... weapons of mass destruction ... riot control automatics ... medieval close combat ...

'Just knives,' she answered, without elaborating.

This woman had a mean, ruthless streak he had never

fully experienced. Hunting each other as kids only left pleasant memories for John, mostly. He'd forgotten how hard she could punch, or how painful her kicks were in his side when he'd pretended to be dead. At the time he never really took notice of the expression on her face at the moment when the 'kill' instant lit up her eyes taking her out of herself.

'How are knives going to work if we're floating around in space? Besides, there's nothing out there to hunt.'

'Aliens,' she responded, though already hatching a plan to hunt something a little more rewarding.

'All set. You ready BB?'

'Have you got the aircon on?'

'I'll connect it to the program. You still haven't eaten. Not hungry anymore? Your sandwich is still in the kitchen.'

'Oh, yeah. I'll be right back.' Her hunger pang returned as soon as he mentioned the sandwich. With full gear already on she went back to the kitchen, her thoughts deep in the hunt strategy. She wolfed down several bites, absentmindedly discarding the rest, not bothering to wash up - the knife no longer on the cutting board.

Two VR headsets had already been charged, ready to deceive the wearers. Their platform on one side of the otherwise empty room already had an occupant. John didn't have long to wait for Betty to return from the kitchen. Without saying a word she planted herself in the command position, strapped on the HMD and hit the launch button.

The monitoring cameras in their house saw nothing out of the ordinary. Almost every person on the planet indulged in some form of escapism. Mundane reality had morphed into a boring drag. Life in the New Age had become essentially a struggle to survive in a different way, by keeping the body and the spirit encased in the one place without being bored to death. Augmented dreams satisfied some people but not many could afford dReams, the public version of the dream maker implant. Augmented VR systems were the most widely used as an alternative mechanism for escapism.

John and Betty's gear also connected the room's environment temperature to the game system as well as the platform's mobility control. Augmented virtual reality helped create sensory feedback to an extent actual reality couldn't match. All their sensory experience was managed by game feed impulses as well as actual environmental input, like temperature and external motion generators. From all practical perspectives they no longer existed in the normal world. System simulations had advanced to the life-termination threshold in some of the game apps. If your mind told your body it had died then a whole new reality opened up which had no connection to the world of quarks, neutron stars or soft warm sand under your feet on the beach.

They'd played this game many times, exploring many of its variations. They were familiar with the costumes and accessories. Their habit of checking everything each time was no longer necessary. Betty seemed to be in such a hurry she also dispensed with the procedures for checking the equipment and those accessories.

Their eyes only took moments to adjust to the artificial environment. The ship's control centre already appeared familiar, with Betty in the command chair. The Earth receded rapidly into the distance.

'Who or what are we hunting?' asked John to clarify, though in real life he'd already realised Betty always hunted him, even when he was running after her.

'Each other, silly. I'll go hide first. See if you can find me. You know what I'll do if I catch you,' she teased.

'Wait, Wait! Why are you such a hurry?' John turned away from her to look out the side porthole. He couldn't immediately find Earth. They had already moved far into the solar system away from the sun and the Earth. 'How did we get out here so fast?'

'That's exactly what I aim to find out.' In his distracted state John didn't register the last comment. Betty knew their VR game matrix had been enhanced beyond the capabilities of normal commercial units. She was counting on its ability to take the most prominent thoughts of a player, like their fears and desires, and incorporate them into some aspect of the unfolding adventure. She hoped perhaps this facility will help him loosen up to shed some light on her darling boy's secret project.

The transition from Earth into deep space seemed almost instantaneous. John tried to come to grips with the new paradigm of existence. He still had trouble incorporating being in space into his world concept. At the same time Betty explored their space craft after engaging the autopilot. The high res 3D eye mode had already flipped John's perceptions into another reality matrix. In his 200 degree vision horizontally and vertically his brain told him he was in space speeding away from Earth. The logical mind in him said it couldn't be possible. His senses overrode all logic. It looked like space. It was a mix of light and dark like space and he could definitely feel the chill in the air. He got up out of the co-pilot seat. The sudden movement made him steady himself against a wall to help overcome the feeling of vertigo turning his stomach as he watched the Earth fall away into blackness below him.

The simulation off button as an extra safety feature was there on the rim of his glove. All he had to do was realise the simulation was not reality. He could terminate at any time by remembering to press the button. That was the only flaw in the algorithm. The VR traveller had to realise their circumstance in case of an internal emergency.

'What are they doing now,' asked Matthews. They got bored when Betty kept digging in the kitchen and John refused to yield. You'd have to be especially weird if you found watching two people drinking their coffee to be interesting.

'They've gone to their games room, all kitted out with headsets, gloves, kneepads - the works,' said Johnson, 'she's even put a knife belt on. Now she's moving about the room while he seems to be leaning against something like a stunned mullet. Wait a minute - he looks like he's going to puke.'

'Keep watching. I'll be back.' Matthews disappeared to take care of a nature call.

At first the vehicle seemed no bigger than a normal shuttle astronauts used as a bus between Earth and the new space habitat complex being constructed. Betty took a step forward and reached out a sensory gloved hand. A portal appeared in front of her eyes. She could feel the cold of space on the silver metal surface through her glove and instinctively withdrew her hand.

'Outstanding!' she said aloud when she pushed the hatch open onto a large area which didn't look like it could have been accommodated by the external dimensions of the shuttle. At the back of a rows of seats a dividing wall seemed like the end. At her touch another hatch appeared in the partition which wasn't there before.

On the other side comfortable furniture looked out into space through numerous large portholes. Every seat was unoccupied. Betty examined the lounge more closely to make sure the place was empty of people other than herself. *That's good. I don't want any witnesses.* She pulled herself up about the strange thought. *Witnesses to what? What people?* AVR environments can do strange things to peoples' behaviour, like when you put on a mask and become someone else. She took several steps away from the entrance still thinking about the fact she had no specific plans to do anything nefarious that would make having witnesses problematic.

'What did you find?' came John's recovered voice as if from a distance. He heard the sound of a door opening. He turned and moved towards it, still feeling the effects of vomiting.

Betty searched for a small nook somewhere deeper in the structure where she could hide. She had in mind a pigeonhole not entirely hidden so John could still easily find her.

'Stay where you are. I'm not ready,' she shouted back.

The scene would have seemed strange to someone watching them from the door of their games room, with the woman only a few feet away from the guy who had just spilled the contents of his stomach onto the sensory mat under their feet, the cheese and biscuits clearly visible.

Looking to the left and right Betty saw two other hatches materialize. The one on the left turned out to be a kitchen. She moved through the other hatch opening towards an equipment locker - too small, not enough room to manoeuvre. Another hatch from the kitchen led her into a dark space that could have been a habitat cabin. *This'll do. Not too hard to find and I can swing my arm.* She patted her knife sheath on her belt - the knife was still there comfortably secured in it, with the handle protruding from it, safety clip undone. No need to check further. *No rush. Johnny boy won't find me till I'm ready.*

When setting up the game before John arrived home from work yesterday she made sure the system monitored her vital signs, programming it not to lead John to her until her pupils dilated and her pulse increased. All she had to do for the moment was to stay calm and not let her expectations prime her biometrics.

Johnson couldn't help himself. He started watching the strange reality show, enjoying the adventure being created using his own imagination, although all he could see were two people moving about making all sorts of strange movements in an almost empty room. He could see the vomit on the sensory mat, almost smelling the stench of it.

'You still watching those two idiots?' Matthews had returned.

'Yeah. Strange. Look at them. She's moved five steps away and turned around to face him. Wonder why she's crouched down in an attack pose. She just checked her knife. You're not supposed to take weapons with you into an AVR sim, are ya?' asked Johnson.

'Shit! Absolutely not. Is it real? Has he got one? I can't see.'

'Nah. He's clean, but he's started looking for her. It's like their playing hide-and-seek.'

'That's no game,' said Johnson when he saw Betty draw the real knife out of its sheath. He wasn't watching when in the kitchen Betty absentmindedly put the vegetable knife in her sheath instead of back in the block when she half finished with her sandwich. 'There's no way we could get there on time. Damn those two. She's gotta be one unstable bitch if I ever saw one.'

The goons from the UNSC were having exactly the same reaction. Both their targets could be neutralised by their own hands, and there was nothing they could do about it - except watch.

Betty heard John beginning to rummage around, obviously looking for her. She got down into an attack crouch position - knife drawn. As far as she was consciously aware it was a VR knife manifestation, not the real one. Through her VR gloves it wasn't possible to tell the difference. She was concentrating on where the noises of John's approach were coming from, not what was actually in her hand.

John found the kitchen. He'd turned the water on and off. Dropped something on the floor which made a hell of a racket. The smooth motion simulator in the mat and the realistic audio feed completely robbed John of any sense of being in a game. This was reality. He was in space, hunting for Betty inside the habitat - just playing a real life game ... not a make believe game in a virtual matrix.

His dream had come true. After years of training he was finally a fully qualified astronaut on his way to Titan, relaxing by having a bit of fun with his crew mate. It didn't enter his consciousness Betty was not an astronaut, that she had no business being on a space craft with him hurtling towards a distant moon in the solar system.

He saw the hatch leading out of the kitchen. It was slightly ajar. *Aha! Now I've gotcha!* He went into a semi crouch and moved forward with as much stealth as he could muster. He was never much good at that sort of thing. Betty always got the better of him in their childhood games.

All the racket John was making sent Betty's vital signs into the red. She held her breath ... adjusted her stance and held her breath.

John thought he heard a sound coming from the other side of the hatch. Extending one hand he pushed it open.

Betty pounced, knife drawn!

Kurt: 'I don't believe this. That bitch is gonna kill him!'

Auguste: 'Don't be so dramatic. It's just a VR game.'

Frederick: 'Yeah? well what about the knife. It's real enough.'

They watched as the woman leapt onto John, brandishing the knife. She seemed totally out of control. John yelled something unintelligible at her, which made no difference to Betty's onslaught.

They watched unbelieving as John put out a hand to protect himself, Betty on top of him wielding the knife with serious intent. The scene had become far more realistic than a simulation should have been. She slashed from right to left as he writhed beneath her, his open palm catching the full swing of the blade. The sensory glove wasn't thick enough to totally protect him from the sharp blade.

'WHAT THE FUCK!' screamed John. It wasn't the usual 'wtf' but the full blown 'I don't believe she did this to me!' version.

John didn't need to press any buttons to bring himself out of the simulation. Betty had already yanked the headset off herself and John, her eyes blazing wild with disbelief.

They both ended up flat on their backs on the mat in the games room. Space had receded back into its own multidimensional unreality leaving the two people to sort things out for themselves.

John had lifted his bleeding hand up into the air to tear the glove off. Betty lay beside him completely disoriented, with the bloodied knife between them. She couldn't utter a single word, breathing hard, heart pounding.

John looked at his cut hand. It wasn't actually so bad. The sensory glove had absorbed the brunt of the slash, not enough to prevent a substantial amount of blood still oozing out of his palm. The pain of it had not yet kicked in. He had the presence of mind to get up - to try and get up - 'SHIT!' - slipping on his own vomit: Not yet enough awareness in spite of the pain to work out where the door was. His brain was still on the spacecraft with his body wedged in the hatch between the kitchen and the darkened cabin.

It took several minutes to reorientate himself to be able to take his hand to the bathroom - back on Earth in their isolated farm house.

Kurt: 'Have you ever seen this kind of bullshit!' he exclaimed. The other two could only shake their heads in disbelief.

Auguste: 'Merd. Non. Incroyable!'

Fredrick: 'What are we going to put in the report, Eh?'

Kurt: 'Nichts. Like Auguste said, it was only a VR game. They got carried away. So what?'

Fredrick: 'You don't get it do you?' Although the other two saw the whole drama the most peculiar thing about it was the knife. 'The knife you idiots. There wasn't supposed to be a real knife. It was just a VR game for fuck's sake!'

Kurt: 'Ach So!' It dawned on the German what the real issue was. He didn't know what to do about it.

Auguste: 'D'accord. Ouais. Now we also have to keep them alive.'

Fredrick: 'Exactly - Merd - as you say mon ami!'

'John - John! Where are you? Betty had withdrawn into her panicked self as John left the games room.

'Where do you think!' he yelled back from the bathroom with a definite edge to his voice. From the sheer shock of it he hadn't had time to fully ferment his anger.

Betty had finally come back to Earth reality out of the VR game. She picked up the knife and staggered into the bathroom. John glanced in the mirror. The first thing he saw was the knife, getting such a shock he slipped on the wet floor ending up on his backside again. It wasn't the first time he found himself in such a position. Veronique from his childhood days had managed to drop him quite a few times, but she didn't have a knife with blood dripping from it - his blood.

'John?'

'WHAT IS WRONG WITH YOU!' he shouted trying to get up off the tiles, his ire rising.

'I'm so sorry,' Betty half whimpered, the knife still in hand. 'I - I - I don't know what happened. I'm so sorry.' She moved towards him, presumably to help him get up.

'Get rid of that knife, you crazy bitch!' John pushed himself up against the wall away from her approach.

The tension in the bathroom had not eased since Betty entered. She looked down at the knife, only then realising she had white knuckles squeezing it. She flung it away from herself, making John duck from the sudden movement.

'John - John ...' she pleaded, distraught at the full realisation of what she had done. 'I only wanted to frighten ... ...'

'I don't care what you wanted. Just stop it! I don't want to speak to you. Get out of the house - before *I* do something.'

He had never spoken to her like that, even when angry with her - ever. He had never intentionally set out to hurt her - ever. The incident so many years ago was nothing more than a young kid being stupid, not some deranged killer on the loose.

Consequences

The entire VR event happened so fast he didn't have time to fully assess the situation.

Betty didn't pick up the kitchen knife. She backed out of the bathroom grabbed her bag, stuffed a few clothes into it and ran out of the house. Nothing else she could do in the face of John's anger. She'd never seen him like that before. Slowly the situation filtered into her rational mind. She realised he was right to be so upset. *Where did the knife come from?* In the heat of the moment Betty couldn't even remember going back into the kitchen to finish off her sandwich let alone sheath the knife.

With her no longer blocking his view of reality he started going over what she had done. Not so much why she'd done it, but how it was at all possible for such a thing to happen in a virtual reality context. Something was definitely not right, quite apart from what might have been motivating her.

That woman's motivation ... he said the words in his head. *She's not just any woman. God damn it, she's my partner - my life partner. How could she do something like this? I've loved her since - since for ever. It's impossible.* He looked down at his left hand unable to fully believe what had happened. The throbbing pain had begun stirring rogue thoughts into his head. Even the old scar on his right hand started aching, reviving unpleasant memories.

After a few days the pain was still there. The injury, though not life threatening had curtailed his physical training, probably setting him back months. His immediate supervisors in the lab didn't believe him when he told them the knife had slipped off the kitchen bench and he tried to grab it. He had to explain himself to the Head of the Space Propulsion Project at NASA.

Not getting a greeting from his boss, or being invited to take a seat exacerbated an already uncomfortable frame of mind for John as he moved into the office. Angus Silverman remained seated behind his desk. The strong light behind him through the window prevented John from clearly seeing the exasperated expression on his face. John took several steps closer to the desk towards the unoccupied chair.

'That's far enough,' said Silverman.

John didn't have many interactions with his ultimate boss. There was no need. On the few occasions when they met at briefings and updates the man seemed approachable enough. Being stopped so unceremoniously as he was about to sit down only brought on a level of defiance and did not bode well for what was about to unfold. He had no doubt whatsoever for the reason of the interview. The incident wasn't his fault.

How could he betray Betty for such a simple, though unexplainable, perhaps even an innocent incident?

'You realise, perhaps you don't, the importance of the work we're doing and your part in it,' Silverman stated flatly and waited for his response.

'I - I didn't do it on purpose. It's not as though I've given away any secrets. It's a flesh wound. Just an accident.'

'What you and your father are involved in is highly classified.'

Silverman kept his eyes on John noting the play of emotions on his face. 'Of course you do, as does Peter. Any leaks, no matter how insignificant they may be, have serious and immediate implications. Peter will be most disappointed if you don't carry this project through with him.'

There was no mistaking the direction this conversation was going in. *I don't want to look for another job - not now, not after all the ...*

Silverman carried on through John's thoughts as if John had spoken aloud. 'Peter's work continues to be valuable to us. His mind is still good, sadly not so his body. We *were* hoping you would be able to continue on with the project after him.' Silverman didn't explicitly say Peter was on the way out, though he might as well have. It definitely sounded like Peter had had his day, in Silverman's opinion anyway.

Is he threatening dad? Who does he think he is! John adjusted his stance, as any man would suspecting an imminent attack.

A strong defiance had risen in John, though not anywhere to the same intensity he had to exercise with his father in the past. Silverman's implication took the edge right off it. 'Of course. Absolutely. I've dedicated my life to this, ever since I found out what my father was so mysteriously doing in his laboratory and ...'

Silverman cut him off. 'Enough. There's something else of concern to us.' Again he waited to see if their golden boy was astute enough to catch on. He didn't seem to be. 'Betty. You know she's with the United Nations Security Council. Do you have any idea what she does there?' John gave him a blank look. 'You should. Don't give me that puzzled look. You've been with her for - how long now?'

First Dad and now Betty. He really is pushing it!

A deep intake of breath and a straightening of the back didn't go unnoticed by Silverman.

John was about to answer as Silverman's out turned palm lifted off the desk. It said, 'Shut up John and listen!' All thought of sitting down had fled. John set his jaws as if preparing to hear the worst, ready to respond in kind.

'I can't tell you exactly what she does. We know even if you don't. Without labouring the point I can tell you this - the cut on your hand wasn't an accident. Do you understand me?' Silverman stopped short of revealing he'd seen the vid of the incident. He knew the cut to be accidental, most probably. Best if John thought otherwise. It may help him keep his mouth shut.

An electric wave surged through John's body bringing every hair on his skin to attention. Blood drained from his face with the realisation their privacy had been a fiction in his mind. He tried to work out how long he and Betty had been lab rats under constant scrutiny.

Silverman noted John's reaction but didn't want to discuss the comprehensive surveillance network around the project; an entirely different web of reality John was not aware of, though caught in the centre of it.

John is good at his job - a brilliant researcher. He can turn theory into practice. If I can keep him on track the critical propulsion technology will become a reality with his input. But I have to control him. The boy has no idea of the global implications of getting the project to succeed. No less than worldwide security - and the future of the human race depends on it. He's an idealist, a dreamer. Even if he realises the importance of his and his father's work I doubt if he understands this technology must remain the property of the US.

While watching John digest the elusive nature of his privacy Silverman let his own thoughts cycle back to the situation immediately in front of him - a man trying to puzzle out his future. He got up from his comfortable executive resting place, aware of John's eyes following him, not interrupting the implications of his smiling approach.

The ruse didn't ease John's turbulent thoughts.

'Here's what we're going to do, John,' Silverman said placing a hand on his shoulder, 'you can have a little rest, let your wound heal then we'll see you back for a medical. We'll be in touch.' Silverman waited. He waited until John finally did a double blink. 'Oh, and by the way, do the best you can to sort out this relationship with that woman of yours - Yeah?' He didn't say it but to John the implication was crystal clear. Fix it or find another girlfriend. That's not what Silverman wanted at all.

Silverman and NASA tolerated Betty's liaison with John for one reason only, which was not due to their empathy with his 'love' interest. She served a most important purpose. They were fully aware of the machinations behind the scenes of the European Space Agency's agenda. They wanted the new space propulsion technology. The only problem with that was the United States did not think it 'useful' to share the knowledge with certain other State members of the ESA. Betty was being used to wheedle the intel out of John. As long as Silverman had Betty in his sights he could control the situation.

The seemingly flippant comment from his boss destroyed John's temporary relief of not getting fired from his job. He thought that would be the best scenario he could hope for under the peculiar circumstances. *What the hell does he mean by 'sorting out the relationship'?*

On the way back to their house he'd forgotten about the surveillance and the suspicious vehicles. 'What the fuck am I supposed to do now?' he half yelled as he banged on the front door of their house, having trouble opening up the damned thing from sheer frustration.

'Shit!' He suddenly remembered what Betty had said about the open door when they arrived from their tour to the NASA space centre.

Betty had no friends, at least no one close enough in Houston she could confide it, or perhaps crash at their place for a day or two. There was only one place she could think of.

'Mum?'

Shirley heard the question her daughter didn't ask. Betty's tear strained face said it all. Something serious had happened and Betty needed her mother.

'You don't have to say anything dear.' Her arms going around her daughter only opened up the floodgates of Betty's tears as they stood by the front door. Shirley wanted to warn her the moment she saw her at the door, but Betty's condition forestalled the intention.

She also forgot for a moment those two huge men who had invaded her home just minutes before Betty arrived. They said nothing to her when they arrived. One of them stepped behind the front door and the other pushed Shirley outside to greet her daughter. He moved into the sitting room through a door two steps from the entrance. It happened so suddenly all Shirley could do was to step outside when she saw Betty.

Without thinking about the men Shirley moved back inside taking Betty with her. Fredrick appeared immediately from the side door, none too gently pushing Shirley aside separating her roughly from Betty. In her condition Betty couldn't take in what was happening. She clawed after her mother trying to hold onto her as Fredrick forced himself between them. Tears turned to terror as the large unknown man tried to grab her flailing arms.

'Mum! Mum!' There was no point in screaming. Frederick efficiently restrained her within moments.

Fredrick: 'Excuse me ma'am,' the UNSC operative wasted no time, 'we have to go.' He glared at Shirley his business-like subdued voice adding to the terrifying situation. He clamped his large paws onto Betty's arm just as Kurt stepped up behind her from behind the door, restraining her other arm.

'Let me go you bastard!' Betty continued struggling having forgotten all her initial combat training. It wasn't really necessary to send two European gorillas to bring in one woman. The performance they watched as she attacked John in the VR game suggested otherwise.

'What have you done?' Shirley called out as Betty was forcefully jostled back out the door. Betty couldn't answer through her hysterical tears reappearing from utter fear and frustration.

Fredrick: 'Ma'am, say nothin' to nobody.' He growled close to Shirley's ear threatening a clear warning of consequences if she did otherwise. 'You'll have her back soon enough.' That's all the man was prepared to say. Kurt remained silent as he stuffed Betty into the same dark vehicle which had visited County Road 38 not so long ago.

Before Shirley could realise exactly what had happened the car disappeared around the corner. *My goodness, what just happened?* She stood by the front door, stunned.

The entire incident, from Fredrick and Kurt's arrival to them taking Betty away didn't take more than five minutes. For all Shirley knew the space-time continuum had a glitch forcing her mind into a temporary reality that never even existed.

Just then the kettle screamed for attention. Shirley turned towards the sound. 'What did I come out there for?'

Perhaps it was her advancing years making her imagine something that had never actually happened. Her face brightened at the thought of finishing making her afternoon cup of tea. She went back into the sitting room, tea in hand to pick up her knitting. Nothing had been disturbed. Betty had not been in the house long enough to even sit down.

'Now where was I?' Then a thought occurred to her ... *I must find out what's happening with my little girl ... I haven't seen her for so long.* The reason for thinking about Betty had already escaped her.

59

The Target

'Why have you brought me here?' A natural question
for Betty to ask after her abduction.

It didn't look like Betty's training centre where she'd
spent most of her time when not at the University. The four
hour flight from Houston to the UNSC headquarters in
New York gave her ample time to consider her situation.
She realised soon after recovering from hysteria in the car
the whole drama must have been connected to her injuring
John. It was an act which she couldn't even explain to
herself. Her job was to acquire the sensitive information,
via the UNSC, with all the details of the new technology
being developed and hand it over the European Space
Agency. It was not *her* job to neutralise the source of that
information, especially not before she even got what was
wanted.

Betty didn't know and didn't need to know why the ESA
had to have access to that technology. She had not been
made aware of what had been happening in the past. There
was long term planning, spanning several generations,

involving the second largest moon of the solar system. Titan was the only reachable heavenly body to have an atmosphere dense enough to protect the human species from solar radiation. It also had liquid water under its ice shell. Humanity could live on this moon - if only man could get there.

It wasn't just a matter of survival for the human species. For some people it was a matter of wealth - incomprehensible riches. Competition for Titan's resources had already become so fierce there were no limits to what the competitors would do to be the first to harvest Titan's potential. The loss of a few human lives was no impediment for doing what needed to be done to achieve domination.

Betty of course had not been briefed on the finer points of her assignment. She only needed to know she had to 'cuddle' the information out of John. Force wasn't considered an appropriate MO in this situation. If she couldn't do it what use was she? Unfortunately the project needed to be as low key as possible with as few people involved as absolutely necessary. There was one last chance available for her. Being at the UNSC HQ and not in the bottom of a deep grave should have made the situation abundantly clear to her.

Life could have been so much more comfortable for Betty if only she could have accepted a normal reality. Now that was gone. No matter how many times she visited her mother it could not be recaptured. The abduction had set the new reality of her life onto an irreversible path.

Aksel Ingersen's office was more like a comfortably furnished sitting room in a home. Other than the view out the window it might have been - but not if it happened to be on the top floor office of the UNSC building. Betty wasn't aware the man she was about to meet was the President of the UNSC or that he also had a prominent role in the Europaean Space Agency. Nothing about the room could have suggested his status. Stepping from the lift corridor through an ordinary looking door into a tastefully furnished room seemed like a warp in some strange reality. Much of the retro furniture suggested 21st century taste in interior decor.

'Come in Betty,' Aksel spoke to her as if she was his life time friend. He stepped up to her to shake her hand. 'Please, have a seat - here by the window if you like. The view is magnificent.' His mouth spoke friendly words, unlike his eyes.

Lost for words at the completely unexpected nature of the encounter, so different from the one with Fredrick and Kurt on the plane, she forced a smile and sat in the nearest couch.

Although disarmingly friendly Aksel come directly to the point. 'Now, tell me Betty, what seems to be the problem?' He poured and offered her a glass of water.

Suspicion didn't take long to bring Betty back to her normal inquisitive self. 'If you don't mind my asking - who actually are you?'

'Oh, I apologise. We haven't been formally introduced. I'm Aksel.'

Betty tilted her head. The man didn't answer her question. He clarified. 'Let's just say I am the person who makes the decision.' He smiled broadly and left it at that for her to digest.

The decision about what? ... ... Oh.

She realised quickly enough this was the somewhat serious reckoning for her recent actions, which obviously had consequences well beyond her understanding. A trainee operative doesn't get to the UNSC HQ to meet the boss for any simple reason, if at all.

'I have a job to do and ...' she didn't get a chance to finish.

'Yes, yes, yes - I know.

Let's see if we can help you do it a little more efficiently, with a little less drama.'

Betty immediately understood the implication. The open door at home, the suspicious cars, the abduction ... *This guy must know everything!* She blushed at realising the extent the surveillance might have taken.

Aksel lifted an eyebrow as he watched her working it out. 'Very good. I see we understand one another. May I say we are very pleased to see you have been able to override your emotional connection with the target. Tomorrow you will begin a slightly different area of training. Good bye Betty. Thank you for coming to see me. Good luck.' She didn't get the chance to ask any more questions as Aksel led her back to the door. She'd hardly had a chance to say anything at all.

This guy has already made his decision even before talking to me, whatever it was. I wonder why he bothered.

'Target? Why are you referring to John as a target?' she protested aloud in the corridor. Suddenly a sense of ownership had been awakened in Betty for 'her' John. He was no target! Aksel had already turned to walk back to his picture window, not hearing the comment behind the closed door.

Something Isn't Right

'Interplanetary Security Consultantancy?'

'Kom, this way please.' Kurt had been waiting for her outside. So much had been going through Betty's mind that the encounter seemed to take an hour when it lasted only ten minutes.

'Who is he? she asked Kurt, eyeing him suspiciously in case he was about to 'gorilla' her again.

'The boss.' He escorted her to the lift, down ten floors, through countless corridors until she'd lost all sense of direction. It took longer to get to their next destination than the interview itself.

On a door the sign read 'Interplanetary Security Consultantancy'. 'You planning on sending me somewhere?' she blurted out with a little giggle of apprehension.

'Go in, Ya,' Kurt ordered, giving her a little unnecessary push.

Obviously he had little patience, especially for dangerously unpredictable women.

She stepped into a three metre square room.

Two chairs facing each other - suggestively.

No table.
Bare walls, no windows.
Only one door.
Not much of an office to consult from. Betty was not a person to be easily intimidated. Yet this cell began the process without having to do anything other than to exist with her in it. *Which chair?* Under the circumstances this seemed like a remarkably difficult decision, almost as if a portal to an entire new reality would open if she chose the wrong one.
She chose left.
Sat.
Nothing happened.
She waited.
As far as the universe was concerned she may or may not have existed; alone in Schrodinger's box.
She waited.
Minutes, Hours? It seemed irrelevant.
In the sound dampened space she couldn't even hear her own breathing.
She tried the other chair. It made no difference to the condition of her existence.
Nothing, not even the sound of air entering the enclosure. She'd barely fully sat on the second chair.
The door opened.

The clandestine arm of ESA had very few operatives. Simply put, J'Ark's classification was Information Technologist; her duties - to implement processes, procedures and strategies to manage information assets. Betty was nothing more to her than a conduit to exploit an information asset, called John. His only value in existing was the knowledge he possessed, which ESA wanted. Betty's only value - to get it.

'Did you see that?' asked Aksel as J'Ark entered his office from an adjoining room after Betty left. 'What do you think?'

'Still workable, though she'll have to be softened up. Her emotional attachment to John is still an obstacle. We both realise the importance ESA places on getting access to the propulsion technology. Europe cannot afford to have the US monopolise ready access to the solar system's resources.'

Perhaps J'Ark only considered the commercial implications. Aksel wasn't as cold-blooded about it. 'Not to mention the survival of the human species into the future.' No doubt he had in mind not only the mineral resources available from Titan but mankind's capacity to colonise Saturn's moon. 'If we could freely share efficient space exploration capability no doubt there would be a great deal more cooperation between nations. What has to be done, must be done.' Aksel had no illusions as to the extent to which he expected J'Ark to exercise her mandate.

So many things fell into place for John after his interview with Silverman. His achievements at university prepared him academically for the career path he'd chosen for himself. Yet his studies did nothing to help him navigate the labyrinth of changing emotional realities between two people of strong wills. Especially not of two individuals who had determined the reality of their lives would be as different as possible from the lives of the vast majority of people on the planet. Neither of them wanted the kind of life scenario being pushed on them by their parents. He was now forced to see Betty through a different filter altogether. Her actions not only utterly surprised him but Silverman's warning had put an entirely new perspective on his future with her, perhaps more aligned with the one fate had planned for him. It still didn't explain her extraordinary attack. Silverman certainly didn't shed any light on that. *The Betty I once knew is gone* - he admitted to himself. *This changes everything. How can I even think of settling down with her and having a normal life, like normal people. I want my own personal 'normal', however strange it may end up being.* Vestiges of his father's constant badgering about what constituted normality seemed to have a lingering effect on his thoughts. What John considered to be normal really meant people who had the courage and ability to follow their own self-determined paths through life. A reality of their own choosing, not one imposed by anyone else. The great challenge for Betty and John had become how to cross the bridge between an actually exciting reality and one that was only a construct of *their* imaginations.

The last thought about Betty lingered. It made John dredge through years of his life, considering each stepping stone leading him to this point. It was all wrong. *I've been living a fantasy*, he realised with a jolt. *She is not normal people.* He rolled his eyes as images of the most recent event screened across his inner vision. *Nor am I, for that matter.* Aloud he said, 'This has to stop.'

After a few days alone at home doing nothing in particular other than reviewing progress with the latest experiments he'd devised with Peter he began to think again more seriously about Betty. *Where is she? What is she doing? Probably at her mother's.* John resisted the urge to contact her. As the pain in his hand receded so did the memory of the traumatic moments causing it. With each passing day the urge to see Betty again became stronger. He wanted her back. He wanted to sort things out with her. *Maybe all she needs is a little therapy*, he mused.

The following morning did not start well.

'You're due for your medical, six am today.' The voice didn't identify itself. It made the announcement on his coms Monday, unusually early, without any introduction. The voice gave him no choice about the matter and terminated before he could respond. Being awakened at four thirty on a Monday morning didn't put him in a good mood. The night before he'd determined not to try calling Betty at her mother's but to actually go there if she hadn't returned by Monday night. *What the hell!* A normally even tempered John stomped around the house getting ready to go back to the training centre. By the time he left at about five thirty Betty had still not arrived home. Not a good start to the morning at all.

The doctor's smile was pleasant enough. John liked this particular doctor. The room wasn't the one normally used for medicals, but they were always doing new tests of one sort or another. 'Some of the procedures will be rather invasive so we'll put you under for a little while,' Dr Kathleen said quietly as she applied the intramuscular sedative. She had not bothered to check the cut on his hand. *Strange. I thought* ... Within a minute John became oblivious to the conversation above him as he lay on the operating table. Dr Harold Armbruster's assistant physician, Dr Zsuzsa, busied herself preparing the microchip for the minor operation on John.

Armbruster emerged out of a dark corner. John knew him from his work on nano-technology. The doctor was well aware of John's insatiable curiosity. He would have wanted to know exactly why this particular doctor with his specialised field in nano-robotics was needed for a simple medical examination.

'This is still in the experimental phase,' Armbruster explained to Dr Kathleen unnecessarily, 'well advanced, and of course safe in a limited application, as far as we know.'

'You are expecting AIDA to resolve John's nightmare issues. Correct?'

Dr Kathleen had assisted in developing the software to control the bots.

Armbruster was slow to respond. 'Yes - and more. Whilst he's asleep over long periods during the trip we need to ensure his dream state remains stable. We don't want random mind constructs to distort his sense of reality when he wakes up. These AI nano-bots will bring a sense of reality to his dreams. They will keep his psyche balanced.'

Zsuzsa performed the key-hole surgery to implant the control centre in his chest cavity for the Artificial Intelligence Dream Adjusting nano-bots. A robotic brain surgeon injected the bots in solution directly into John's skull cavity; a delicate operation requiring the latest in AI medical robotics to ensure absolute accuracy of the process. The two doctors watched the monitors closely as the swarm, like bees on a mission, infiltrate John's brain. Most of them headed directly for his hippocampus. Others spread out into memory and learning related contributory areas like the temporal lobe and the amygdala.

Dr Kathleen glanced down at John. His eyelids were fluttering rapidly for about ten seconds and a little bead of perspiration had formed on his forehead. She wiped it off. 'No problem,' she told Armbruster, 'just a minor reaction. We'll let him come out of it slowly, have a day's rest and tomorrow night do the first test.'

'The test - yes.' Armbruster was in two minds about telling her about those and the true purpose behind them. She had to be involved. Now that the Titan propulsion project had advanced to this stage she had to know the final details behind the real reason for the implants. 'That will be all thank you Zsuzsa.' What he needed to discuss with Dr Kathleen had to be confidential. 'You know about the bots programming ... of course you do.' He seemed a little distracted. 'What you may not be aware of are some of the finer adjustments to those algorithms we made after you completed your work, and the reasons for them.'

Zsuzsa lingered a moment or two on the pretence of clearing away some of the equipment, taking note of the conversation.

'Do tell Dr Armbruster.' They were generally on first name terms. This last little bit of information put her on guard. Her main concern was John's welfare, not some governmental high-tech interference with an astronaut's mind.

'You are aware of the sensitive nature of John's work with his father. That technology must remain within NASA's control. We may need to boost John's ability to resist any attempts to gain access to his knowledge.'

'You mean mental resistance using the bots, right?'

Armbruster nodded, no further explanation necessary.

Kurt entered the cell, remaining by the door.

'Interplanetary Security Consultantancy?' Betty asked, not really expecting a response from the gorilla. She considered the implications of the job title. Kurt kept silent motioning for her to remain seated, his deadpan face revealing nothing.

A woman came forward and Kurt closed the door with a clang.

'You've met Aksel? Hmm. Not many people get the privilege. I've had a word to him about you Betty.' The waiting experience had not put Betty in a conversational mood.

She looked around the enclosure again, so utterly different to the sitting room-office she had come from. That woman's appearance put a new perspective on the room. Her presence created a questionable new reality, the sound of the door closing still in her ear. 'Who are you? What is this place? I keep asking these simple questions and no one seems willing to tell me anything.'

J'Ark didn't respond.

She sat in the unoccupied chair and just watched Betty.

The woman's general hard edge appearance and body language didn't invite conviviality.

What is going on around here? Have all these people got some peculiar infection preventing them from being in the least bit helpful? Betty got up to walk around in the enclosure in an attempt to get a firmer grip on this unreal situation. J'Ark stepped directly in front of her.

'Nothing to be concerned about. Follow me. Here's what I can tell you. Come.'

J'Ark tapped on the door. It took a moment for Kurt to creak it open again. The woman led Betty down the corridor to another small cell, also not looking like an office; this one painted matt black. Only one recessed light in the low ceilinged room to illuminate the small table.

This austere room appeared to be designed to stifle unwanted enquiry. It had a small table close to one corner with four chairs and one other door. Betty sat, looking agitated especially after having to shuffle across the floor because it did not seem to be there at all to her eyes.

Middle aged J'Ark, with her short dark bob and severe fringe bordering directly above her eyebrows placed both hands on the table - no notes and no weapons, Betty noted.

'It seems you like games,' J'Ark's toneless voice acknowledged. The presence of two other chairs suggested more imminent interrogators. The circumstances from one room to the other were succeeding in their design to intimidate. Walls, ceiling and floor all black, including the furniture. Matt black which reflected no light and seemed to swallow sound. Betty had to adjust her stance when first stepping into the room for fear of stumbling.

J'Ark's comment made Betty cringe, a slight colour rising to her cheeks.

'Never mind about that. Regardless of whatever job you're supposed to do, about which I don't know the details, I've been instructed to help you.'

She lied about not knowing the details.

'You don't know what I'm doing, yet you're going to help me do it. Oh - Please!'

'Yes. You have a problem it seems, distinguishing between simulated reality and actual reality.'

No I don't ... then the penny dropped. Betty went positively red in the face. *Just how much has she seen? ... These people are unbelievable!*

Betty's reaction brought a bureaucratic smile to J'Ark's thin lips. 'I can help you. Do you like nice perfumes?'

'What?'

'Never mind. Ah yes, by the way ...' J'Ark mentioned almost as an afterthought, 'your training is being expanded. You will become an Interplanetary Security Consultantant. It seems you have the right skills and the correct mind-set. Though you could do with a little toughening up.'

Betty couldn't absorb any of it. She was still thinking about her favourite perfume. *How ridiculous. Interplanetary? Perhaps that's why the room is black, to give me a sense of what it's like in space. I don't want to go into space. It's too cold.*

The stress induced by the entire sequence of events caused Betty's mind to veer off centre creating reality scenarios which may never happen - but they might. It all started to unravel when John told her to leave the house.

J'Ark must have been enjoying her power over this young woman, watching the range of emotions flit across her face. She allowed Betty to flounder around for a few more seconds.

'What I am about to say you cannot repeat to anyone ... a n y o n e ... she stressed, still using the thin lipped smile. Especially not John.'

'What about John?'

'You have a dynamic imagination. Work it out.'

All I get is threats and this peculiar woman being obtuse.

'Come.' J'Ark's sudden command brought Betty back to the reality of the black room. She didn't move.

'Come!' Betty again found herself man-handle and ushered out the other exit.

This other door led to a long corridor with non-descript doors on either side of dark olive green painted walls. J'Ark nudged Betty through the nearest one. 'You will start this afternoon.' She left, locking her in the room. She had still not given Betty her name.

Rose red.

This third room was rose red - walls, ceiling and floor. Even the furniture was the same red. Betty put a hand out to steady herself against the nearest wall. Gravity still held her to the ground but her mind had difficulty determining her actual coordinates within the red environment.

A bed, an en-suite, a table and one chair. Her coms had been confiscated by Kurt. She was separated from the reality of the world she knew, with no access to it. With mind still in a daze Betty sat, then toileted, then sat, then tried to get her mind into some semblance of order. *This is unreal! John! Interplanetary what? Why do they care what perfume I like?* Her thoughts meandered into fabricated and familiar territory. Her eyes vagabonded around the room. Everything was the same colour, even all the bedding and the small en-suite. Depressing. She had to close her eyes just to be able to think, the green retinal afterimage reluctant to dissipate.

Two hours later the door opened on Betty lying asleep on the single bed, the room smelling of blossoming roses in Spring. Red roses have a unique perfume of their own. J'Ark stood by the door in a stark white dress, sniffing the heavy scented air. Shirley liked to wear white most of the time, even when gardening.

'Up!'

Betty's eyes flipped open immediately and with automatic reaction jack-knifed out of bed.

'Mum?' She stared at J'Ark wide-eyed. Shirley's favourite past time aside from knitting was her aromatic rose garden.

'Very good,' the thin lipped smile answered. 'Now focus!'

As the dream mirage of working with her mother in the rose garden faded Betty recognised the woman from their earlier meeting. 'You!' The strong perfume prevented her from following through the memory pathway to their first encounter. 'Is it - a pause, a double sniff - Armani Privé Rose?'

'Excellent. Tell me about your dream.' J'Ark sat on the only chair, leaving Betty standing by the bed, as stiff backed as a lamp post. 'Was it about John?'

That brought an immediate reaction and a flash of rage into her eyes. 'None of your business!' Then after a moments reflection, 'And no, it wasn't - it wasn't your *target*,' she spat out the last word.

Something wasn't right.

Everything had gotten mixed up. *Wasn't I supposed to start some kind of training? Their ventilation is peculiar if it comes out with the scent of roses ... Mum likes roses ... ...* her thoughts drifted again forgetting where she was ... *I was helping her prune the roses ... she was right there with me, clear as the light of day ... in her white dress ...*

J'Ark recognised what was happening. *Excellent. She's a receptive subject. We should be able to make some progress now.*

'Very good. I'll wait while you freshen up, then we'll see what we can do with you. You like gardening with your mother; pruning roses. How nice.'

Thinking about her mother settled Betty a little ... only a little as she remembered the way she was torn away from her and abducted from in front of her eyes.

Something is definitely not right.

J'Ark's job in the ESA had very narrow parameters. If she succeeded Betty would not be able to differentiate between her waking state and her dream state - under the right control triggers.

Last night's test showed she was a good subject to undergo olfactory radicalisation. Her moods could be controlled with the appropriate odours.

Betty's
Conflicting
Realities

'Tell me about being dead,' asked J'Ark.

Betty had a dozen burning questions she wanted answers for as she emerged from the shower. *Dead? What? Dead? Who's dead?*

As promised J'Ark began Betty's training the very same day. However it wasn't the kind of training Betty had imagined. Since her abduction her comprehension of reality had been challenged, no less by the transition from one strange room to another than by the peculiar question put to her by J'Ark.

'How would I know?' Betty's mind had not improved since being woken in that entirely depressing room smelling of roses. She was in no mood to answer idiotic questions. 'I think this room is stupid.' She remained standing on the other side of the small table.

'Dead is exactly what will happen to you if you don't take your training seriously and get results. Space isn't a natural environment for the human organism.' J'Ark was well aware of the strong minded, and highly intelligent woman she was dealing with. She had to present things in a way which would challenge Betty's thinking and allow her to reach conclusions of her own. It required being somewhat obtuse occasionally. Time enough to impress on her the short life expectancy of operatives who could not complete their assignments, or those who did but left a lose end by their continued existence.

Silence.

'You want to send me to Titan with John?'

'No. We hope you'll be on your way back well before you and your target get there.'

'His name's 'John'!'

'Ah - resistance already,' J'Ark said, thinking ... *Control her moods - control the person.* Betty's behaviour on the first morning was enough for her to assess Betty and to determine the strategy for managing her.

With all the confusing thoughts and emotions and the restless sleep Betty had been well primed for the first training session; hand-to-hand combat. She'd crossed her arms, tightened her gaze and straightened her back, defiant. J'Ark headed for the door. 'Come.'

Betty held her ground, narrowed her lips.

'You don't need to fight me. Your trainer is next door. Fight him.' J'Ark walked out of the room with a particular air of expectation that Betty would follow. *Even if I was dead I wouldn't tell her what it was like!* Her curiosity overcame her reluctance and Betty had to take a few quick steps to catch up.

Popovich, unshaven, smelling of three day body odour stood relaxed on the practice mat, with something in his hand she couldn't see. She could already smell him from the door, the unpleasantness only increasing as she came closer. He adjusted his stance as Betty approached and brought his right hand into view.

'Shit!' She couldn't help herself.

The man was holding a knife. That and his stink sent her into overdrive. Her lunge in his direction achieved nothing more than an instantaneous side step from Popovich and a perfectly timed arc with his knife to inflict a scalpel precise cut to Betty's forearm. He didn't bother to ground her - not necessary. Betty snapped her eyes to the wound, bringing up her other hand to stop the bleeding. Popovich remained close to her, on alert. He'd been warned about the unpredictability of this woman. Betty's furious glare didn't faze him nor did her screaming threats, some of which were directed at the other woman standing by the door of the small gym.

The first session ended abruptly after only a few minutes. Betty was still standing there overwhelmed, clutching the small wound with her other hand as J'Ark waltzed up to her.

'This is real,' she said, 'first lesson learnt. Pain is reality, reality is pain.'

During the ensuing weeks Betty was kneaded into the responsive medium ESA needed her to be for the rest of her specialist training. She was being prepared for a launch into space, to coincide with John's departure sometime in the next two years. It should not be necessary to send her out there if she did her job here on Earth. If her relationship with the target failed to lubricate the acquisition of the technology it may be necessary for her to use force on him and possibly pursue him into space.

On the morning of the second day Betty's long shower couldn't seem to wash away the unpleasantness of her dream. It started with the stinking Popovich. When she saw him for the first time she thought for a moment he looked like John. The smell assailing her was too overpowering. Then there was the knife; a small efficient, expert cut, enough to take her out of herself. It upset her ability to adjust to the changing realities she was being subjected to. And now the crazy dream.

It was so much fun running away from John. He never gave up. Betty loved that about him. That's why she always let him catch her, especially as they grew into adolescence ... ...

... She stopped under the biggest tree in the park. It had the best shade and stood well away from the sight of others enjoying the park. John staggered up to her, breathing hard. Betty leant against the trunk of the tree giving him her private smile she'd reserved only for her Johnny boy.

... It was an invitation he couldn't resist. He'd stepped up to her, raised his right arm and put it around her shoulder.

Bad smells always made Betty particularly angry.

'John. Will you do something for me?'

'What's that Betty Boo?'

'Go have a wash!' She pushed him away so hard he hit the ground bum first. It wasn't enough for her. The source of her upset had to be eliminated. What had once been playful punches of earlier childhood games became an uncontrollable desire to make the teenage boy bad smell go away ...

Betty woke after the first serious punch to John's face.

Her room reeked of adolescent male hormonal scent mingled with the reek of an unwashed, sweaty body. The scalpel cut on her arm bled during the night bring back the pain.

J'Ark walked in at the exact moment when a dream lingers before full wakefulness overrides its existential reality. Perspiration beaded on Betty's forehead. She only noticed J'Ark when she tried to find her handkerchief to wipe the blood off her cut arm.

'You had a bad dream?' asked J'Ark pleasantly. 'That was only a dream. It was not real,' adding without waiting for an irrelevant answer. 'No pain.'

She glanced at Betty's blood stained arm, then directly into her eyes.

After a week of alternating scents of aromatherapy each night Betty could hardly think straight. Her dreams on the days following were catalysed by freshly washed sun dried linen or the perfume of lavender in her Mum's vegie patch. The days following such pleasant dreams were the ones when she almost enjoyed the challenges of espionage training.

Unpleasant smell dreams, like bad breath, which John had on occasions, made her almost uncontrollable, much to J'Ark's pleasure. She woke Betty every morning with words of encouragement and reassurance - at least her contrived versions of those sentiments.

It all got to the point where Betty began to rely on J'Ark's voice to reassure her of the boundaries between dream reality and actuality to help her get through the day, especially the bad dream days.

Day eight began like every other day.

Except Betty couldn't remember her dreams on waking. The air in her red room smelled fresh. J'Ark didn't appear by the side of her bed. *What is she playing at now?* She got up, went to the bathroom and the mirror said to her, 'You're already dressed.' *Why am I already dressed?*' Something wasn't right - again. *I have to find that woman.*

The corridor with the dark olive green walls had become familiar to Betty during the week. None of the doors had signs, but she remembered J'Ark's office being the sixth from hers on the right. She ran directly to it down the deserted passage.

J'Ark sat at her desk, hands clasped together in front of her as if waiting for something. She didn't move when Betty flung the door open.

'This is a dream,' J'Ark said. 'You will have to learn the difference by yourself.'

Another two weeks went by. Each morning J'Ark asked the same question before Betty continued with her training.

'Dream or reality?'

When Betty consistently identified the correct state she found herself in J'Ark explained a simple fact of her existence, which was no longer in Betty's control.

'We will tell you when you can die. Then you'll be able to tell me what it's like to be dead.'

'That doesn't make sense. I don't want to do this anymore.'

'You think you have a choice?'

'I want to be with John.' The anger had dissipated. For the first time tears welled up. Was it nostalgia? Perhaps some deep remnant feeling for her childhood love. Maybe the glamour had dissolved out of the romantic concept Betty had of being a spy. Or this whole experience wasn't what she imagined being with UNSC would turn out to be ... such overwhelming frustration.

J'Ark took immediate advantage. 'The target is not yours to do with as you wish.'

Her comment instantaneously turned tears of despondency into rage.

Betty hurled herself at J'Ark.

A satisfied smile spread across J'Ark's face as the two attending guards restrained Betty in mid-flight.

'Job done. She's almost ready.'

___________ AIDA ___________

Artificial Intelligence Dream Adjustment

____

An insistent knocking on the front door broke the morning silence.

Images from the high resolution vivid dream he'd been woken from lingered as he tried to concentrate on the knocking ... ...

... In the second part of John's dream the construction of a chicken coop progressed quickly. He'd almost finished it. He'd allowed for plenty of wire to be dug into the ground to prevent foxes digging under it. Every detail meticulously attended to, as dictated by his approach to all things not just anti-gravity propulsion systems. Laying boxes and perches all completed - gate had the wire stretched across it's frame ready to be hung.

... He lifted it to match it against the frame, tools ready to hold it in place. *'Damn.'* Something wasn't right. The gate didn't fit square to the frame. Within the scheme of dream ultra-reality he had used the laser measure to check the entire coop structure. *'Unbelievable.'* John couldn't understand how he could have messed it up. Being so annoyed with himself he did a most uncharacteristic thing and picked up a hammer to knock the gate into shape. Bang! Bang! Bang! ...

He woke with a start, lying in his own bed at home not at the NASA medical Centre.

The banging continued for a moment. His eyes focused on the ceiling ... he thought *'chicken coop gate'* ... ceiling ... *someone at the door ... why are they knocking? Damn. I want to go back and finish the coop.*

John didn't immediately get up, continuing to stare at the ceiling.

He'd been roused from a deep sleep at home where Betty no longer slept. His mind wandered remembering Betty being with his family when they visited the Star Camp. On those few occasions they all slept in the one cabin. From the first part of the dream he could still feel the warmth of her body pressing up against him. As he lay there his eyes flicked left to right, his brow furrowed trying to remember the actual event. It eluded him. In reality, as best he could remember, his mum would never let them sleep together.

Another series of knockings.

John turned his head reluctantly towards the front door, rubbing his eyes, concentrating.

Strange, nobody comes around here.

He stood, stretched, feeling no urgency to answer the door and went to fetch his dressing gown. It was a Sunday morning. *Can't be anyone important.* He'd slept in after being at the training centre, which felt like he'd been there all of his life. So many deep, detailed dreams had the effect of blurring his perspective on the passage of time. At least it seemed as if all he did was work, though only a few weeks had passed while carrying out intensive testing on the propulsion system, working ten to twelve hours a day. John had a room adjacent to the laboratories with his father. They were restricted to the base for the duration of those secret experiments whilst in their final stages.

The work had been so consuming all sense of time and

place had morphed into a continuous stream of mundane existence. Nothing mattered, nothing existed other than getting the test craft to levitate off the ground without any visible use of energy. That was the first stage. For the second stage they had to achieve controllable propulsion; speed and direction.

John couldn't entirely remember what he'd been doing lately except he felt unnaturally exhausted, as if he'd dreamt through all of it, whatever it was. He knew from experience many of his dreams in the recent past left him feeling physically depleted. *I've been working too hard and dad is just too manic about this project.*

Something wasn't right.

Knocking.

He didn't think twice about not opening the door, although not in any hurry to do so. There was no reason to be suspicious other than for the rarely entertained fleeting thought as soon as he heard the knocking that it might be Betty. He hadn't thought seriously about her since she left. *No. It couldn't be her. She's been gone for weeks. Unlikely I'll ever see her again.* A sadness descended on him as he shuffled to the entrance putting his hand on the door knob, dressing gown hanging loosely on his shoulders.

It's probably Jack from the laboratory. Something must have gone drastically wrong with the containment field we set up to store the gravitons. All this damn secrecy - they could have called me instead of sending someone to get me. What a waste of time.

His thoughts gravitated away from the door to what could possibly have gone wrong at the lab. Still thinking about the experiment and not the front door, John opened it.

He just stood there staring, hand still on the doorknob.

Betty.

Silence.

John's open dressing gown flapped in the sudden breeze.

He tightened the cord.

Betty put her bag down.
'BB?'
He didn't recognise her get up ... her hair was too short, and the wrong colour ... a dress? Red? *She never wears red dresses. She doesn't like red.*
'Johnny boy,' a subdued, hopeful greeting.
Breakfast didn't happen.

On Monday morning before getting up John rang Silverman directly, Betty lying beside him about to wake.
'Betty is back. I won't be coming in for a few days.'
Betty heard and in her half-dream state dropped an arm across his chest.
'I know,' said Silverman and hung up. *Good. Now we'll know where we stand.* 'Johnson, keep an eye on Betty. I want a report on her by the end of the week.' *Whatever ESA had done to her I must find out. She wasn't a weapon before but if they'd turned her into one I have to know.*

An in depth conversation about past unpleasant events didn't feature prominently when Betty stepped into the house the previous night. An entirely new reason emerged for John feeling both exhausted and entirely super-charged the following morning. There was no perspiration beading on his forehead as Betty awoke to the sounds of his conversation with Silverman.
John's swarm of artificial micro-organisms were not programmed to heighten his pleasure pursuits. He could do that for himself, particularly with the help of the enthusiasm Betty displayed in being with him again. The bots had imbedded themselves into his neural net waiting for instructions. They were not autonomous, not even as much as a swarm of bees or colony of ants. These artificial creatures were primitive incapable of exhibiting any form of hive mentality.
John felt Betty stirring.

He gently lifted her arm off his chest. 'BB?'

She stroked his face with a languid hand, smoothed down his hair. 'What do we do now?' she whispered. The immediacy of tsunamic feelings that had hit her when J'Ark called her Johnny boy a target were no longer there in the bed with them, between them. Those feelings had dissipated during the night's reunion. 'Where have you been? What have you been doing?' John couldn't answer her questions. He had the same questions to ask her, and it was too hard to think of answers.

Instead he asked, 'Breakfast?'

'Later. We have to talk.'

'Yeah. Right. How's your knife handling skills?' As soon as he'd said it he regretted it. 'Sorry! Sorry! I didn't mean to say that.'

Betty had returned to him with a mind concentrated on one thing only. She didn't know exactly why but since her extended training nothing seemed to be as important as her mission. She propped herself on an elbow to face John.

She placed a finger on his lips not wanting to get drawn into an argument or recriminations.

'When we played the VR game all I wanted to do was to try and frighten you into telling me the secret of your experiments.' She wanted to tell him more but the concept of John being a 'target' kept cropping up in her mind. It had taken on quite a sinister connotation. Her experience of J'Ark told her the woman could not be trusted. She was dangerous. *If I could only get John to open up to me he would be safe.* She stroked his face again.

At least she still cared that much about him.

'You did more than frighten me. I didn't expect you to ever come back after I reacted the way I did. Why did you?'

As enjoyable as the reunion was last night John no longer felt the same deep connection between himself and Betty. Something had happened and he wanted to know what. He waited for an answer, also up on one elbow now, the two of them face to face. This had become far more serious than amorous pillow talk.

'They sent me back.'

'Oh.' The disappointment showed clearly on his face at not receiving a more personal answer. *So that's how it is*, he thought accompanied by involuntary raised eyebrows.

'I wanted to come back,' Betty added quickly. This conversation wasn't going the way she wanted it to. She needed to stay with him until she could report something very positive to her minders. Perhaps that would help keep him safe. She reached over to stroke his hair. All the touching seemed to come naturally enough. It was having an effect. Her words didn't entirely satisfy him. The need to know what had happened to his Betty Boo insisted he remain with her that day.

'I'm not going in to work today. Do you want to go for a picnic?' *Why did I say that? We've never been on a picnic before.*

'I'll unpack my bag first, shall I?'

'Yeah, go ahead.' John didn't hesitate, as Betty expected him to.

Unusual for John to take time off work for something as trivial as a picnic.

Chocolate Bayou near their place didn't feel like a hospitable enough place to take Betty. Too bushy and a bit wild. Instead they ended up at Pearson Park not more than fifteen minutes away. At least the lawns were neatly cut and it had a few comfortable benches.

Their exchange of general pleasantries, avoiding the real issues, ended up with lunch in Alvin. By tacit agreement neither of them brought up the subject of getting together again in the future; John because he was a lot more easy going and less confrontational, and Betty by design. The night had gone well, she'd unpacked her bag, they were having a nice picnic. No reason to muddy the undercurrent of feelings.

That night, after the picnic John's AIDA bots received

their instructions. John experienced another dream induced false reality ...

... 'How's lunch going? I've finished the chicken coop. We'll go get a few layer chooks this afternoon.'

... 'We're only having sandwiches so come in when you're ready,' Betty called back.

... After a few minutes John went up to the kitchen window from the outside to watch Betty fussing about with something or another. She'd changed and put on her favourite dress, the one with the soft pastel colours John particularly liked. Earlier in the morning she'd reluctantly helped him repair the back paddock fence.

... 'Go wash your hands, Johnny boy,' she ordered as he stomped in with dirty shoes. 'And take those boots off.'

... He didn't mind being ordered about. It was turning out to be an extraordinarily pleasant day. They'd finally made the decision to get a couple of milking cows ... as soon as the back paddock was ready for them.

... 'You make a great coffee,' John commented as he took hold of the mug.

... Bang! Smash - pieces flying everywhere. He'd fumbled with it dropping it onto the tiles. ...

John's eyes flipped open. He tried to look down at the mess but he was lying flat on his back staring up at the ceiling. He'd knocked a heavy book off the bedside table on his way to the floor, waking both of them.

'What are you doing?' came Betty's sleepy voice.

Yesterday had turned out to be a good day in spite of many things being left unsaid. An early evening to bed seemed like the most natural thing to do to prolong the good feelings that had developed during the outing.

Hidden aroma cannisters in their house were not instructed by J'Ark's people to infuse the night with dreaming aids. They saw the progress Betty had made so far, satisfied for the time being. They could see she'd been making an attempt to put John at ease.

'Let's see what the situation is this morning,' Armbruster said as he watched the vid feed from John's bedroom.

'I reran the video surveillance data where John and Betty jokingly discussed an ideal life-style and fed it into the bots. I expect he had a pleasant dream.' Dr Kathleen eagerly ran the nano-bot program to carry out the first real live opportunity to see how John would react to the bots programming.

'AIDA must have painted a very pleasant picture of domestic bliss in his dream for the night,' said Armbruster. 'Just look at him, all smiles. I would say the picnic implant idea worked as well.'

'Sorry. I didn't mean to wake you.' John climbed back onto the bed leaning over to plant a kiss.

She reciprocated, without passion. She needed a shower, badly. Hanging in the cupboard her favourite dress called to her, the one with those soft pastel colours. Sunlight filtering into the kitchen brought out their deeper tones. She'd just finished making the coffee as John appeared carefully taking the offered mug from her.

'You know BB, you make the most excellent coffee. Shall we go and get those hens this afternoon?'

'What are you talking about?'

'The chooks, don't you remember ... and ... ... the ... cow.' As he said the words it slowly dawned on John what he was saying. He stopped, sipped on his coffee and turned to the window. The neighbour's cows ambled by towards the milking shed in the distance. Betty couldn't see the confusion playing out on his face.

Armbruster reported directly to Angus Silverman. 'It's working. I'm pretty sure with a few more pleasant episodes our John and his Betty will be happily back together and you will be able to keep track of both of them.'

'Has Betty changed?' Silverman asked.

'Yes. She seems more settled, more affectionate. Perhaps more focused. At least she's not deliberately aggravating him.'

'That might not be a good thing,' Silverman mused. 'I want you to strengthen his immunity against coercion. Betty hasn't come back to play house with him. She'll try to pump him again soon enough.'

Following the AIDA implant and subsequent testing John didn't have the luxury of enjoying normal randomly generated dreams. Empirical reality experiences needed to be filtered, catalogued, cross-referenced and prepared for future use. His dream concierge could no longer operate in isolation. AI bots under instruction from Doctor Armbruster and Dr Kathleen controlled its ready content.

'Give them a few days, let them settle then send John's bots an edited version of their picnic.'

Their lives reverted to a tenuous semblance of normality as Betty resumed some of her studies at the University and John checked with Jack at the lab about any issues with the graviton containment field, finding none. John became less clear about what was real and what were dreams and what were his random thoughts of possible issues with the antgrav technology. Undercurrents had begun to develop which flowed deeper than Betty's once playful attempts at industrial espionage. The next weekend John woke on Saturday morning feeling oddly unsettled.

He couldn't remember his dream ...

... 'It's too nice a day to stay at home. I can see you're a bit tired too. Let's have a picnic. What do you think?' He asked. ... 'Where shall we go?'

... 'Suggestions?'

... Pearson Park. Not too many people there. We can have some privacy.' His tangential thinking had taken the wrong tangent.

... 'Sure. Privacy - Eh?'

... Betty had already started preparing a few things to put in the picnic basket. He sat and watched her swishing about the kitchen in her favourite dress.

... *She's not who she was John. You have to be careful* ...

... The female voice in his head was soft, quiet, confident. John couldn't identify who it might have been. For a moment he thought it was a real person's voice other than his own thoughts vocalising. Those words came flooding back as Betty spread the blanket well away from the playground and the basketball courts.

... She glanced up at him, feeling his eyes on her. 'We don't have to think about anything today. Forget work. Forget your problems at the laboratory. Just enjoy.'

... Natural enough things to say when having a picnic. *But why bring up the lab at all. Odd.*

... *Betty is so beautiful. Just look at her dress. What if she asks you that question? You know she can't be trusted.*

... John could feel the breeze from across the park.

... 'Here's your treat Johnny boy. It's your favourite.' She handed him a big fat sandwich. Three tiers of bread with lettuce, ham, mayonnaise and chicken on the second layer. She let him take a couple of bites. 'What are you going to give me Johnny boy?'

... The voice in his head came back. *She can't be trusted. Don't answer any questions.*

... 'Just don't ask me any questions about work.' His mood had changed rapidly. John couldn't ignore the voice in his head telling him about Betty. He already knew she could be downright dangerous. ...

He woke with that thought prominent.

'Betty. Are you awake?' She wasn't. He tried to remember his dream. Nothing. Except for feeling like he was about to have a confrontation. He had to relieve himself. Betty had stirred by the time he returned. She awoke thinking about the very strange thing he said a week ago. Something to do with an idealistic concept of what life could look like.

'John, tell me something.' Betty wanted to ask how serious he was about chooks and cows.

'Are you still on about that? When are you going to stop?' *She's dangerous - she can't be trusted.* The subliminal message combined with memories of a previous dream - was that a dream? - He wasn't sure anymore. 'I'm not answering any of your questions!'

'All I wanted to know was whether you still wanted those cows and chooks.'

'What are you talking about?'

Betty had come back into his life, but so have a bunch of bothersome uncertainties.

Dr Kathleen started to develop some qualms. She knew about the subliminal voices and what they were doing with John's mind. Changing his behaviour had shown most promising results as far as resisting Betty's digging. *Should we be doing this at all?*

Saving humanity was no longer a lofty theoretical consideration. It had become the kind of reality no amount of philosophising could ignore or spin into quantum ideologies. The mind bending had started twisting a man's reality. The consequence could conceivably end in the man turning up dead somewhere. Once you were dead you could no longer enjoy a three tiered sandwich.

'Dr Armbruster, are you satisfied with progress?' asked Dr Kathleen.

'Indeed, indeed. Such a brilliant man and yet so far out of touch. He's got a job to do and so have we.'

'Doesn't the ethics of what we are doing bother you?'

'Look, once he's finished we can give him his life back. We will reprogram him. Maybe he'll find a nice farm girl, get his cows and chickens and be a perfectly happy man.'

Dr Kathleen revelled in the AIDA technology and its untapped capabilities. She was at the exciting leading edge of developing this kind of technology, apart from being a medical doctor. However she did have some concerns. 'I'm not sure it's in our long term interests to blur the boundary between realities too much - or his for that matter.'

The   Diabolical
Imagination
Machine

'I just don't trust myself anymore. What am I supposed to
do Dad?'

Who could he possibly confide in other than Betty? But
she seemed to have changed so much. The only other
person he could think of happened to be one of his
doctors; Dr Kathleen. But she was on the Titan team. If
she knew of his problems it might affect his chances of
exploring the solar system. *But I have to do something.*

John knew without any doubt Peter wasn't exactly the
right person to confide in. Unfortunately, he didn't have
too many choices. There had to be some way to ditch these
monkeys in his head.

His dad had completely immersed himself in developing
the anti-grav propulsion system to the exclusion of
everything else in his life, especially after the death of his
wife. What could he possibly know about the world of
actual reality? Even his own dreams were a mess. He
suffered from rebound insomnia causing him serious

dream disturbances. His sense of reality would have been utterly compromised had he not had his intense work to focus his mind.

'What are you talking about son?' They had to step out into the open sunshine away from the lab to get any privacy at all. The lab constantly buzzed with technicians and scientists. Most of their eyes looked inwards at seas of formulas as if they were fields of vibrant, enticing flowers. They might still hear what he had to say. *Anyway, what would they know? Their lives are probably not complicated at all.*

Except perhaps for Dr Zsuzsa Szalai. She had made it her business never to be too far from John, and through her work keeping herself within Armbruster's close orbit as well. She had joined NASA at the beginning of the Titan project, keeping a low profile, contributing to the full extent of her professional medical capacity. Armbruster noticed her diligence early in the project and seconded her to his team. Of necessity she had become aware of some of Armbruster's research into AI nano-bots, but not the specific work John was doing.

She saw John and his father make their way through the extensive laboratory as they headed in the direction of the external recreation courtyard. There was nothing unusual in people going out there from time to time. It was unusual to see John and his Dad going out there together. This all added to Zsuzsa's collection of background information on John.

'I'm talking about Betty, Dad. She keeps trying to get information out of me about our work. It used to be like a little game. It's become quite serious lately.'

'You asking me what to do? Well I'll tell you son. Depends on how far you're prepared to go to satisfy your lust.'

'It's not that. Can't you be a bit more serious? Hear me out Dad.'

'I am serious. Let me tell you what I think. That girl's been under your skin since you were kids. Maybe you should give her the flick and find someone new.'

John wanted to tell his Dad everything, including the weird episode with Betty and her expertise with a kitchen knife. But he wasn't receptive to the dramas of real life. He lived a theoretical reality unconnected to the world of intricacies within complicated relationships.

'There's something else Dad. It's not all about sex.' Peter's forehead wrinkles furrowed a little deeper. He understood sex, at least what he could remember of it. 'It's my dreams,' said John.

'I know all about that.' Peter interrupted. 'Those damned sleeping pills. I have to keep taking more and more of the stupid things. Have I told you about my nightmares?'

'This isn't about you Dad. Are you going to listen to me?'

Peter took no notice and carried on. 'Sometimes I wake up and I don't know if my head is still attached to my body. I get this feeling our gravitons escaped containment with no regard to how reality is organised. They flung everything all over the place, dismembering bodies, destroying everything. I tell you son, if the night terrors get a hold of you ...'

John listened, becoming impatient. This was exactly why he was reticent to confide in him. But his Dad had never opened up to him like that before. Besides, what he was describing wasn't so different from his own experiences lately.

'I know what you mean Dad. Some mornings I wake up and my dreams seem to bleed into the light of day. It's as if the dreams continue on and I can't tell where reality starts and the dream ends.' Having started to open up something else came gushing out. Something he vowed to himself he would never tell anyone. 'I hear this voice inside my head telling me things,' he said uncertainly. 'You'd better shut up about that if you seriously expect to become an astronaut.

They don't accept people who can't tell the difference between imagination and reality.'

'Well, thanks Dad. That's not a lot of help.' Standing out on black asphalt in the sun with no shade was no place for a deep heart-to-heart conversation.

'Dad ...' John hesitated, looked around to make sure they were alone, '... I think there's something in my head which shouldn't be there.' Peter laughed. He couldn't help himself. 'I mean it. This is utterly weird. I expected more from my father than to be laughed at.'

It was too much for Peter. First his son admits he can't tell the difference between reality and dreams, then he says he's hearing voices. And now he admitted he's not right in the head with delusions of being manipulated.

Peter slapped his son on the back in the only friendly gesture in his repertoire of interpersonal relationships. John stepped away from his Dad. *I should have known that's all the support I'd get from him.*

Peter let his hand drop, not completely oblivious to the ineffectiveness of his gesture. In a softer voice he said, 'You'd better come inside out of the sun before you go completely insane. My advice is for you to go and see one of your doctors.'

Perhaps I should speak with Dr Kathleen. She looks like she could keep things to herself, maybe even help with the strange dreams.

The stressful time stretched weeks into unrealistic intervals between waking and sleeping. Covert surveillance by NASA and the ESA continued without the respective undercover operatives making an appearance anywhere near their targets. Manipulation of the minds of these two vulnerable individuals continued. Betty became more susceptible to the effects of subliminal aromatherapy, though still unable to do what she had to. John began to get used to hearing the voice creating suspicion and escalating the imagined danger Betty represented. The voice focused on Betty's untrustworthiness. Physical danger to John at her hands remained a latent threat in the background.

A little relief came at last. Several weeks after Betty's arrival they chatted about life in general. Each had been given a short respite from controlled dreams, which seemed to make them feel much more at ease with each other.

John was looking out the window at some cows grazing in the field next door. 'BB, just imagine, I mean about our careers - you know, what if - I'm just saying ... If you and I ...'

'Johnny boy, you're babbling.'

'Sorry. See out there, those cows. And the chooks from our neighbours in the mornings ... and the calves ... they're so ...'

'What are you trying to say Johnny boy? Are you - trying to - get me to - think of a name - for a baby for instance?'

'No! No. Nothing like that. Not that drastic anyway.'

'Exactly how drastic?'

'Haven't you ever thought what it would be like to have a small farm, with animals and ...'

She didn't let him finish. 'Are you for real? Do you really expect me to go out there and milk a cow, collect eggs and wipe the snotty nose of some demented screaming child hanging onto my apron as I put out the washing? How do you imagine that would work?' The incredulous look on her face should have alerted John to change the subject.

He didn't.

'Well, no. I wouldn't expect you to milk the cows. Not everyday day anyway. We have robots to do that sort of thing.' She laughed aloud at the very notion of her Johnny boy entertaining such thoughts.

He chuckled back, casting a questioning glance.

Alright, I'll play his little game. Let's have a bit of fun with it. Perhaps it'll lead somewhere.

This was the moment when J'Ark became very interested, as did Armbruster. Though operating completely independently these two had a compelling interest in controlling these experimental lab rats, and not only out of scientific interest to gauge the effectiveness of their coercion techniques.

J'Ark gave immediate instructions to her technician. 'Get ready to activate a few nice farm aromas for Betty tonight. Something she would absolutely hate. She's getting too cosy with her Johnny boy.'

'Yes ma'am. Chicken poo and warm cow pat on John?'

'Excellent. Our installations are still working in their house I assume.

'Yes ma'am.'

I want some aggression from this woman. She has to stop playing happy families with him. J'Ark felt it was time to put extra energy into Betty's primary task.

'Have you sorted out in your mind what has to be done Dr Kathleen?' Armbruster hadn't forgotten his colleague's expression of unease about their work on John.

'As long as we don't cause him any unmanageable distress and lasting mental damage.'

'Good enough. Come and listen to this.' He reran the conversation John and Betty had. 'This is a perfect opportunity to build his firewall against this UNSC puppet. Feed some of this content back to him in tonight's dream. Let's see if we can get him to express some discontent and bolster his general opposition to Betty.'

'I'll suggest to his bots he should come in from the cow pasture without having cleaned himself up. That should get a reaction from both of them.'

'Good - good - good. The launch isn't far away now. We don't want him blabbing before he leaves.'

'Just what would you do with yourself on a farm?' Betty threw herself into the mirage.

'Finish the chicken coop for a start.'

'You haven't started to build it yet,' came Betty's flat response. *If I didn't know any better I'd say his work at the lab is starting to unravel his mind.*

'Oh. Why did I say that? But I know how to go about it.'

'How would you silly boy. You've never picked up a hammer or a shovel in your whole life.'

'I dreamt about it.' As soon as the words came out it didn't feel right. She didn't throw it back at him.

'How many chooks?' she asked.

Their conversation delved into all the intricacies of domestic life on a farm. Their respective imaginations filled in all the gaps left by lack of experience and actual knowledge. They ended up both looking out the window, their fanciful thinking of an unreality augmented by the view on the other side of a thin pane of glass. Sometimes that's all there was to separate their realities from rampant imaginings - a thin membrane of ignorance or perhaps uncertainty.

Synchronised dreaming could be triggered by something as simple as a shared vision of an ideal, if the timing was right.

Betty enjoyed their little virtual reality game played out in actual reality. In some respects it turned out to be more entertaining than VR games. Those always presented impossible scenarios, whereas imagination tantalised with the thrill of real danger. John relaxed into it, no longer feeling foolish as Betty became more enthusiastic. Surprisingly their visualisation included enjoying the sunset and watching a few cows wandering towards a distant farm house.

There is something in the rhythm of a single bovine file winding its way across a green paddock at dusk to instil in a person a sense of peace and contentment. A wave of wellbeing washed over John and Betty. It was a satisfying end to the day.

'That was great,' John said as he settled on his back after the games in the bedroom.

'Yeah - fair,' Betty quipped. 'You referring to the sex or our excursion into an improbability?'

'Both?' That made them laugh. They were feeling good for a change. He'd forgotten about the emergent problems of how to change the polarity of encapsulated gravitons. Betty relaxed into the expectation of having a holiday from her intense inquisition of a daydreaming boyfriend. She was due back at ESA HQ next week for another stage of her training. *At least I won't have to keep dreaming up ways to get John to open up.*

John's REM sleep symptoms started first. Their bedroom had a strong aroma to which Betty reacted by turning from side to side, restless.

... 'Damn!' he vocalised indistinctly, then mumbled something about too many cow pats.

... The morning was well advanced by the time he got the milkers hooked up. On his way to the chicken coop he heard Betty shout to him.

... She called out 'Coffee!' while lying on her back asleep. It didn't wake John. His arm moved about as if he had just started swinging a hammer at something.

... 'Come and give me a hand,' he called back.

... 'Look out! Cloe is behind you!' Betty turned in bed calling out 'Run!'

... John mumbled, 'Come on - I need you'.

... Betty stood by the back door, with rubber boots on - ready. 'Why did you let the chooks out?' She changed her mind about going out and went back into the kitchen to finish cutting the vegetables.

... John finished repairing the chicken coop, his hands filthy, boots smelling of hot cow dung and chook manure. He headed for the house with some sense of urgency, forgetting to clean up before he stomped in.

... Betty dropped the large kitchen knife - and sat bolt upright in bed startled from the sound of it hitting the floor.

... John slipped on the tiles, flung out an arm, 'Shit!' It hit Betty across her breasts as he woke.

He stared straight ahead for a moment before turning towards the obstacle his arm had collided with.

'BB!'

'Why did you frighten me like that?'

'You mean my arm? Sorry. I didn't mean to. I was dreaming.'

'No, not your arm. Coming into the kitchen like that without any warning, stinking the place out. You - could - - have ...' Her words faded away.

They gazed at each other mystified. Neither of them knew anything about synchronicity in dreams. John had reclaimed his arm as Betty rubbed her breast where he'd hit her so hard. Eyebrows went up, unspoken questions flew across the chasm between them, the space where reality and dream refused to pass each other across the bridge of empirical existence. Betty noticed the time first. 3:45 am.

'No point you going back to sleep. It'll be milking time by the time you're ready to get out there.' Betty couldn't

believe what she heard herself say. 'But I've already done ....
... What just happened?' asked John.

'I thought I told you to create conflict between them.'
Armbruster's clipped voice hissed at Dr Kathleen.

That achieved nothing more than getting her back up.
She did exactly as he'd asked. The nano-bots did their job.
John got his hands smelling of chook shit and his boots
reeking of warm cow pat perfume and cow piss from the
milking shed.

'There was no way of knowing he would dream of
slipping on the tiles. We can only prime the brain to visit
specific memory sectors and suggest a few simple
variations to possible realities. But we cannot control
incidental memory bleeds into any dream scenario. He
must have slipped on something in the past, the memory
of which remained in his upper recall layers.' Dr Kathleen
bristled internally at her colleague's unreasonable reaction.
'Program the bots yourself next time. You've done it before
- as you've already said.'

She began to suspect Armbruster of having few or no
boundaries when it came to dealing with John's situation.
Any limited restraints may not come into play at all if
making him resilient to data mining needed to be
considered above John's mental wellbeing. *I am not happy
about this at all. Perhaps Armbruster should suggest the removal of
Betty from the equation rather than endanger John's life. Creating an
international incident be damned.* At this stage Dr Kathleen had
not formed a workable resolution to her rising discontent.

Armbruster didn't acknowledge the taunt. 'We must be
more detailed and more specific next time.' Without
looking at her or bothering to see the remainder of the
show he left her to watch the outcome of the discussion
between John and Betty.

John had just jumped out of bed. Seeing him naked made Dr Kathleen forget for a moment why she was watching the surveillance vid. As the pair's discussion unfolded she realised the outstanding success they had achieved with controlling John's subconscious. More importantly she understood the implication of the synchronised aspect of the dream. The UNSC or ESA had done something to gain some measure of control over Betty. This substantially complicated the situation. Armbruster had to be made aware. *I hate doing this but I have to tell him. He's going to be furious. I have to think of something to protect John.*

'You had a dream, didn't you. Can you remember any of it?' Betty asked. Taking no notice of both of them being naked John got up, saw the time and moved to go to the kitchen to prepare an early breakfast, mumbling ...

'It's time to get up, and see to the milking ... Oh ... oh.'

'Coffee?' she asked following him into the kitchen.

'What did you say?'

She heard exactly what he said alluding to the milking. It didn't make sense. She glanced at the floor. There was no knife there. The smell of cow dung was weakening in the bedroom but still lingering in the kitchen which made her grimace.

'Did you drop something?' He noticed her looking intently down at the tiles.

'I'll tell you what I remember of my dream.' Betty already suspected they had experienced something quite out the ordinary, much more interesting than any VR construct could possibly be.

John started to say something else. 'Don't interrupt. I have to get it all out before I forget. You know what dreams are like. And before you say anything - I didn't make this up.'

She gathered her thoughts, her memories of the night's episode. Her dreams of the past had always been fragmented, sometimes chaotic and always elusive right after waking. This was different.

She could remember it as clearly as if the events had actually happened.

'You'd just gone outside. I heard you clearly call out, 'Damn'. She paused a moment. John started to say something else. Betty put a finger on his lips across the small kitchen table as she glanced down at the tiles again. 'I was in here. I called out to you. I asked if you wanted coffee.'

'I know, just a minute ago.'

'No, no. Hush. This was in my dream. Next minute you were stomping into the kitchen with those filthy smelly boots.'

'That's when you dropped the knife, just as I slipped on the tiles.' He remembered.

They sat there naked, mugs of coffee in front of them, unbelieving. Silent.

Minutes passed as each tried to fathom how it was possible for them to have a shared dream, so vivid, so real.

Betty was first to break the silence. 'Did you get the eggs?'

'I'll go get them now.'

'Not like that you don't.' It wasn't cold outside. She was concerned about the chooks when they saw his dangling bits.

Their minds didn't need to fill in any missing details of the dream. It was all there, in full colour, full smell, every aspect shared.

Aksel paced up and down the length of his office at UNSC HQ, refusing to look at J'Ark. 'I've given you a free hand to work with this woman.' The implication being

J'Ark had not done enough as clearly evidenced by the night's performance about not acquiring the intel. J'Ark started to say something. His palm went up. 'Don't say anything unless you know it'll produce results.'

'We have to make her angry enough to act. Pain. She's been primed to react to pain.'

'I don't want to know the details. What I want is the details of the anti-gravity propulsion technology.' He stopped pacing and fixed her with steel cold eyes.

J'Ark had no empathy for the woman. John made no impression on her whatsoever, not even seeing him on full display, her heart as cold as the steel in Aksel's eyes. There was only one thing to do if the aroma conditioning wasn't working. *I'll have to activate the Hun. John is proving too resilient, much more than his character profile suggested. They must be doing something to him at NASA. Whatever it is it will probably work on Betty as well. It may well be the experimental micro robotics everyone seems to be talking about.*

The Hungarian sleeper operative, Zsuzsa, was about to be given a chance to put her training into practice. A simple enough job as far as undercover work was concerned, though not without consequences.

The

Hun

'Face-to-face. 4:17 pm. George Bush Intercontinental Airport, Houston,' texted J'Ark.

The Hun was ordered to meet someone arriving from Paris. She received an unambiguous cryptic message at her private address, the dedicated device self-emolliating after delivering the message.

4:17:35 am
'Hello Zsuzsa. Any idea why I'm here?' J'Ark didn't bother to disguise herself. Zsuzsa, like her one-use comms unit, was needed for one job only. Any life she might have built for herself when she became a mole at NASA was a temporary fiction she may not be able to sustain much longer.

'You vant to expand the parameters of my assignment, yes?' Zsuzsa knew better than to ask this severe looking woman her name. It wasn't important. She knew where the woman came from. That *was* important.

'How are you coping living in two realities? Do you have any nightmares?'

It may have been an unusual way for two strangers to greet each other, one arriving from Paris looking every bit Parisienne. The other exuding an air of medical professionalism, both quite distinct from the look of the other normal travellers in the terminal.

Matthews and Johnson were not interested in what Zsuzsa did, where she went or who she met in her spare time. Betty was their target, not Armbruster's assistant. Even if they had overheard the conversation it would have been meaningless apart from recognising it to be a rude and impersonal way to speak to someone, unless you happened to be French.

'I know someone who does.' Zsuzsa replied.

'That,' J'Ark said with her paper cut smile, 'is most excellent. Walk with me.'

'Vat you vant? Please do not vaste my time.'

'Information. Acquiring this will not transgress on your Hippocratic Oath. You were present when they operated on John.' Zsuzsa continued looking directly ahead showing no reaction to the implication. She had already compromised her professional ethics through her secondary role at the NASA astronaut training centre. As a child she craved danger, adventure, excitement, intrigue. She saw no conflict in what she was potentially being asked to do. So far her job had been boring, mundane and repetitive. This presented an exciting opportunity to show off her capabilities and the hope of promotion within the ESA.

'You vant to know vy he has nightmares, yes?'

'Everything. Why and especially how.' They were walking side by side close enough to each other for J'Ark to drop something into Zsuzsa's handbag. By the time they reached the escalator everything that needed to be said had been said. J'Ark contemplated Zsuzsa's fate as she casually walked on to pick up her rental without bothering to acknowledge the woman any further. She did not inform this Hun mole of the consequence of either failure or success in her assignment. Either way Zsuzsa from that moment represented a liability which would require some form of attention. The realities of existence were, particularly for someone in her precarious position, so unpredictable, so prone to change at the whim of the universe. Why bother the woman with a certainty. It would only become a source of anguish.

The note in Zsuzsa's handbag from J'Ark had four words - Your source is Armbruster - It made Zsuzsa smile. *They must think I'm incompetent, but not for long.*

She worked alone, lived alone, enjoyed infrequent romantic liaisons. Armbruster had not become consciously aware of Zsuzsa's almost constant presence in the training centre. She seemed to be there all the time. No matter how early Armbruster arrived at the lab she was already there doing something useful. They had many trainee astronauts to look after so Armbruster found her dedication most reassuring, particularly when the workload seemed to consume all of his life; not that he had much of one as a middle aged bachelor with no living family and no life interests other than his work.

The inevitable only becomes inevitable when it happens. Until then it's a hope or a fear - or someone's plan to be put into action.

It wasn't her ethnicity he found attractive. There was always an aura; an impenetrable bubble of mystery about Zsuzsa. He knew nothing about her apart from her work at NASA, nothing of her background or the other facet of her life. Zsuzsa permeated the atmosphere of his laboratory, always within reach but always one nanometer short of touchable. Armbruster never progressed in his imagination beyond an occasional second fleeting thought of a possibility existing only on the membrane of the next parallel universe. Mundane reality claimed his attention to the exclusion of almost everything else; most recently the case of John and his dreams in relation to the Titan project. The other woman, Dr Kathleen, managed to stir his discontent only, not his imagination.

Dr Zsuzsa had been meticulously and subtly cultivating Armbruster's emotional landscape for well over a year before she received the special assignment from J'Ark. She became aware that this man had become the foundation of her value to an organisation which had planned out humanity's future for the next two centuries.

'You are always vorking Dr Armbruster,' Zsuzsa commented to him on one of the rare occasions he visited the cafeteria while she was also there enjoying an espresso. She'd invited him over to her table. Fortuitously it happened the day after the J'Ark rendezvous. She kept her eyes averted and her smile one level beyond professional as he happily took a seat. She let her cleavage do some of the work, her long auburn hair framing it to advantage.

'So are you Dr Szalai.'

'Are you vorking late today?' She looked up to fix his gaze.

'Er ... yes.'

'It must get lonely.' Zsuzsa took the bold step to cross the line of professional decorum. She used her soft, understanding voice. J'Ark had made the urgency of her task quite clear. Zsuzsa had to take some calculated risks to apply pressure to progress a simmering relationship towards achieving her assignment.

He responded as she fervently hoped he would. 'Yes. It does sometimes - Zsuzsa ...' Not, Dr Szalai.

'Take care of yourself Dr Armbruster.' She extended a hand wave to stir the air close to him, a thin wisp of her perfume wafting across him.

Three days later.

She couldn't afford to wait any longer. She went looking for Armbruster finding him in the same theatre where they had performed the surgery and implant for John. He was alone. She checked the corridor ... busy but no one looked like they were heading to this particular theatre.

'Oh, it's you. I didn't see you. I just came in to get something. Hello,' she said with a wider smile than on the previous occasion at the cafeteria.

'Hello.' He stopped what he was doing to look directly at her. Unusual. Previously he'd always self-consciously continued working without even looking up when she entered.

'Are you doing anything I can help vith?' Her smile widening.

'Well - er - actually - perhaps.' Most gratifying to see him not being his one hundred percent concentrated efficiency. 'We have to prepare another batch of - of micro-chips like the one you helped implant into John. You remember John?'

'Yes I do. He's one of the trainee astronauts, also vorking on a research project, no?'

'Indeed. A very clever man but a little troubled.' A sharp intake of breath betrayed the realisation he'd said more than he should have. An opportunity opened for Zsuzsa.

'He has trouble sleeping, yes?'

'Well - not exactly. Why did you say that?'

'I am doktor. I can see sleep deprivation symptoms on a man's face. How you are helping him?'

'Of course - of course.' His subsequent roundabout explanation served little purpose other than for him to spend a little more time with her. She let him chatter on, slowly edging closer to him - close enough he could smell her perfume.

Two days later.
Zsuzsa's apartment.
'How did this happen?' Armbruster asked as the night progressed towards its full moon zenith.

'Vat does it matter. This is good. You vill sleep vell.'

'Yes. Sleep and dreams,' he mused.

In Zsuzsa's moonlit bedroom he could clearly see her slightly smudged makeup. *What am I going to do? Can we continue working together?* Zsuzsa gave him a moment or two, guessing the thoughts going through his mind.

'Harold?' She paused to gauge the effect of her calling him by his first name for the first time since they've known each other. He tilted his head slightly, question wrinkles appearing on his forehead. 'I couldn't help overhearing some of vat you vere saying about John the other day when ve vere vorking on him. You are a clever man Harold. I have always admired your vork.' Without being too obvious she touched him gently on the hand which was still resting on her thigh.

Harold let out a long, slow sigh. He'd been under so much pressure over this whole John and Betty thing. He couldn't even tell her the full story, though she was an assisting physician, not until the last moment. Even then he had to hold some things back.

'If I showed you what we have achieved in AI nano-robotics you have to keep it absolutely to yourself.' Regardless of what she might have said Harold had already made up his mind. He needed to do this. Trying to bear the pressure by himself had made his life burdensome in the extreme. The simple act of deciding to share, even before he did so, already made him feel better. 'Tomorrow, after the rest of the staff have completed their shift come to the lab theatre. Everything is set up in there.'

'I am in awe of vat you're doing with robotics Harold.'

They made their way to work separately the next day, both looking somewhat tired. Armbruster was as good as his word, though somewhat apprehensive. If he were found out giving classified information to just anybody ... But Zsuzsa wasn't just anybody. She was his assistant. She had a right to know, he convinced himself.

'This is the control unit. You've seen this before when you installed it.' She nodded enthusiastically, taking the micro-chip in her gloved hand to examine it more closely.

'We have used many ICs like this before. These particular ones have been modified for a special purpose.'

'Yes - yes. Like this one? Beautiful!' Her interest spurred him on, becoming more excited to reveal the incredible advances he'd been able to achieve to control a person's subliminal thoughts. He led her to the other end of the room to a small refrigerated cabinet. It was security code locked. Eleven numerals. He didn't see how closely Zsuzsa observed the pattern of numbers as he babbled on about how long it took to develop the algorithm to control the bots. He handed her a phial of clear fluid.

'I cannot see anything.'

'That's because they are so small and inert. They have to be in order to infiltrate the neural network without causing an immune response from the patient. These little creatures are intelligent. They will do whatever the queen bee tells them.'

Zsuzsa observed the phial was well sealed and well insulated. They were no bigger than a four centimetre thin tube. *These will travel well.*

'And who is the queen bee? You, Harold?' She stroked his arm, giving him the same smile she bestowed on him last night.

'No, no, no. Dr Kathleen and I wrote the queen bee program. It tells them where to go and what to do.' Armbruster paused for a moment. This was the most exciting part of the revelation. Any qualms he might have had had been eroded by the excitement of the moment.

'Vy go to all this trouble to help a person sleep better?'

'Oh they do much more, Zsuzsa. They can control what a person will dream! Come have a look at this.' There was no turning back now. He had to show her everything.

Pride and desire drove him on ... pride in his work and desire for her.

Armbruster typed in his password to the algorithm files, mumbling it as he did so. There were so many passwords he had to remember. Vocalising them helped. He no longer considered Zsuzsa was seeing everything - access passwords, the intricate algorithm and where it resided in the directory structure. He even showed her how the command syntax needed to be structured so the bots would understand.

It felt like only a short time had passed since they entered the lab theatre and Armbruster finally took a breath to look Zsuzsa intensely in the eye. He wanted to warn her again of the absolute need for secrecy. Somehow the intention deteriorated into a degree of intimacy that could only be concluded in private.

Guards at the training centre were used to seeing employees leave the facility at all hours. Watching the two of them leave together so late did not arouse suspicion, only a little interest. Both scientists were well known - yet never observed to be walking so close together as they went home at the end of the day.

Zsuzsa didn't care about the guards. She got what she wanted. She was prepared to pay for it, without knowing the personal cost, and knew what she had to do next. J'Ark was waiting.

Auguste: 'Mon Dieu!' he exclaimed not believing what was asked of the three of them. 'We now have to do the job of a concierge and clean up after them.

Kurt: 'Not *we* mein freund - You. Just you. It doesn't take three of us to manage one woman scientist. You've been to America before. You will enjoy it. Take a few days off. Visit the NASA space centre.

Auguste: 'Très dole. I do not appreciate your humour.'

Fredrick: 'It's an easy assignment. No blood, no violence. Simply hook her up to her favourite VR sim, crank it up past the life-termination threshold and let technology do its job.'

Although outlawed some augmented entertainment systems, particularly those with extreme adventure programs, still had the capacity to end life under the most extreme simulations. Unfortunately Zsuzsa had a penchant for exactly that kind of entertainment. It was her way of releasing the stress of being a spy. She thought a life of danger and adventure would be fun - so much fun. Admittedly cultivating and seducing Harold had been most entertaining. Not so the acquisition of the technology she had been asked to acquire and deliver to J'Ark. She didn't dare take any time off work after stealing several control units, phials of bots and downloading the algorithms. Her absence would have seemed far too suspicious if NASA discovered the theft quickly - which inevitably they would. Her meeting with J'Ark went down without a word being spoken. It took less than five minutes, but in that time Zsuzsa's heartbeat must have sky-rocketed.

Base jumping over the Grand Canyon had become her favourite form of stress relief. A world where one could experience the thrill of danger without the consequences, if one was careful.

As Fredrick said it turned out to be an easy job. Auguste waited, hidden in her apartment. Zsuzsa didn't bother to have a shower when she got home after the delivery, get changed or fix her hair - nothing. She went directly to her games room. With her headset on and the program running she wasn't even aware of Auguste as he entered, adjusted the remote console and faded back into the shadows without a sound.

Zsuzsa had made this jump many times, always with near misses, sometimes even scraping against an outcropping ledge she flew too close to. A jagged peak appeared, some two thousand feet high at the North Rim. She hadn't navigated this one before. She didn't manage to do it successfully this time either. The realisation of the imminent and unavoidable impact triggered a fatal heart attack. Auguste waited to ensure the life terminating algorithm did its job. Leaving the body undisturbed on the floor he readjusted the controls of the VR game to normal operation. *Easy job, as Fredrick said.*

The disappearance of equipment and data from Armbruster's lab theatre happened so soon before Zsuzsa's sudden disappearance the authorities had no way of connecting her accidental death with any other event.

Armbruster became a deeply troubled man. It started during the second night they spent together. Inexperienced in the art of juggling a romantic liaison with a work colleague presented yet another challenge for him to manage at work. The feelings and inner glow which barely had time to nest themselves in his emotional landscape came to an abrupt end. He was never a fearful man. He had the confidence generated by excelling in his profession and the position of responsibility he'd attained at NASA.

Did any of that matter? The woman he'd revealed the most sensitive information to had suddenly died. Yes, he knew what the police said about the nature of the accident. Was it an accident? He was not convinced. It was too much of a coincidence, yet he could do nothing about it. He didn't want to do anything about it. His friends at the office might help; Angus Silverman and the bourbon? Perhaps not Angus, on second thought. He was the Head of Operations at the NASA facility. Perhaps he would not appreciate secrets being given away to the first woman who flirted with him.

John had no idea anything out of the ordinary had happened at the training centre. He didn't know Dr Zsuzsa personally and took no particular notice of her when he had to go for a medical. When news of the fatality of a staff member eventually filtered down it meant nothing to him at all. Besides, his life was complicated enough without getting involved in something that didn't concern him. He never took notice of the woman when they happened to be in the cafeteria. The reality of someone else's life didn't impact on his own even if they superficially intersected on the odd occasion.

Betty was even less concerned. Until recently she had nothing to do with the NASA training centre other than her involvement with John. Her most recent appearance there both pleased and disturbed Angus Silverman. He couldn't refuse outright her taking part in the early stage of the astronaut training program without drawing undue attention to her and her relationship with John. She and John were at different levels of training. At least having her so close meant better surveillance was possible.

Betty didn't tell John she was joining the general astronaut training program. It would be a surprise. And indeed it was.

In the middle of the day John had a break from resolving issues with the graviton containment field. Waiting in a long line at the cafeteria his eyes roamed, his thoughts meandered. Several times his eyes landed, like an Apollo butterfly on a flower; on a waitress behind the counter. Several times ... then returned again and again. When at last he received his order his eyes were on her as he turned away from the counter. He watched the waitress's movements before searching for a seat.

Oh My God! There she was - Betty in a bright yellow dress looking like a sunflower in the wrong field. She had just completed the second day of her induction. John couldn't understand why she should be there. No thought came to his mind other than to go over there. His impulsive turn in her direction resulted in a collision with a heavy set, hirsute man with a broom in one hand and a trash can in the other.

'Sorry - sorry - sorry,' he said to the man as the man uttered something he couldn't understand, but it definitely sounded Russian whatever he said. John had dropped his lunch. Some of the coffee saturated the front of his shirt, the rest ended up on the tiles.

Betty appeared in a flash having recognised John when she heard the commotion. 'John, John - what *are* you doing?' She turned to the cleaner to apologise again. 'Sorry, so sorry!'

He looked up from helping to clear the floor. 'Is okay. Da.' He was looking at Betty, not John. He said something else, which could have been an apology as he held Betty's gaze. She didn't answer him. Either she didn't hear him above the ambient noise or was trying to work out why this incredibly attractive man should be carrying a broom and a trash can and dressed like a cleaner.

'Betty! What are you doing here?'

She snapped her attention back to John. The Russian finished cleaning up and went on with his work, stopping for a moment to wave at a blond girl behind the counter. His expression saying to her ... *What an idiot!*

'What I'm doing here is the same as you Johnny boy. I'll be visiting the ISS.'

'Outstanding! Tell me everything.'

That Betty couldn't do, other than to ask him to give away the secret in return, which he would not do so easily.

'I will, I will but first I have to go away for a little while.'

They went back to the counter to get something to clean up John's shirt.

'Why don't we get you another lunch and we can talk.'

They had to stand in the queue again. Only five people ahead of them, the girl John was distracted by doing most of the serving. Betty babbled on about something or another, to which John gave the occasional grunt - all the while watching the waitress.

'John,' Betty nudged him, 'are you listening to me?' aware of John being distracted.

Over lunch they could only manage to discuss the training facility and how great it was and all the mundane everyday nonsense about space travel. They did listen to each other, superficially. John seated himself so he could still see the waitress. Betty's eyes casually roamed the area not looking for anything or anyone in particular, although the image of the cleaner did come into her mind.

The day turned out to be a long exhausting one for both of them. At home John still wanted to know why Betty was at the training centre.

'You keep everything so secret. What's the big deal? When were you told about the ISS?'

Betty countered, 'You keep secrets too. Life would be so much easier if we could only - trust each other.' John remained silent. What she wanted from him regarding his work he could never tell her. 'Like the girl at the cafeteria today.'

'Alright. Yes, I noticed her. She must be new there. She looked foreign. Rather pretty if you ask me.' He tried sounding casual about it. 'And who were you looking for? I noticed your eyes searching the place during our entire conversation.'

The
Butterfly   Effect ...
... Yuri and Iluska

It smelt God damn awful!

The East Siberian brown bear must have been eating fish and the aroma of its scat oozed up the sides of Yuri's boots as they sunk into the pile which had retained some heat. He dared not make a noise. The bear could still be close by. Yuri slowly lifted one boot out then the other. He looked to see in which direction the leaf litter had been disturbed, so he knew not to go that way. Though bearlike in his muscular and hirsuite body an altercation between himself and the bear would probably have one result only. Yuri did not stray far from the road as he took a break from the journey so early in the dark hours of the morning to relieve himself.

His home in Krivlyak along the Yenesei river in Sibera wasn't far away from his destination, only a few miles. Yet there was no guarantee he would get to Yartsevo alive if he wasn't vigilant. A reality every person in Krivlyak accepted without question and lived with when they went hunting for berries, or anything else.

Neither John or Betty knew where Yuri lived. They didn't even know he existed, let alone be concerned about his having stepped into a large pile of bear scat. The possibility he might meet an untimely death, or that he may survive had no impact on their lives. Their two realities couldn't be conceived of ever converging.

Yuri was born in Krivlyak. He'd never gone further than Zotino, about forty miles up river. Iluska lived a little closer, some eight miles down river in Yartsevo, a curvaceous girl with long blond plaited hair, a little shorter than himself. She had become his universe. Oh - the smile radiating from her face each time they met! Yuri woke with that image each morning between visits. No thought needed to exist about the reality or otherwise of John and Betty, whoever they were or wherever they might or might not be - a reality of zero consequence.

Every fortnight he made the trip by horse following the course of the river. His Yakut stallion seemed unbothered by the smell Yuri brought back to him on this ocassion. A good indication the big brown must have gone some distance by the time Yuri found its treasure.

The day was still young. He'd set out early and by the light of the Spring rising sun he could clearly see the ice had almost completely broken up in the river. It couldn't have been a more wonderful day. Thousands of Apollo butterflies, not unlike himself, were on the hunt for that one true love of their lives. Altogether an outstanding day, even the pungent scent of bear scat highlited the extraordinary beauty of existence. Yuri was on the way to propose to Iluska.

One white Apollo lighted on his shoulder for a few seconds as Yuri trotted along lost in deep thought. The hooks on the ends of its feet must have got caught in the rough weave of his overcoat. It had to flap vigorously to get away; a drama Yuri was oblivious to.

Before entering Iluska's family home Yuri made sure

his boots were clean and devoid of all unpleasant smells. Iluska had been waiting for him since early morning. The moment she saw Yuri's strong kindly face she launched herself out the door of their cabin.

'Yuri!' she breathed in relief, not loud enough for him to hear. She knew as well as every other person in the village the dangers of travelling through the woods in their area.

The wonderful smile released by her sunshine eyes greeted him as always, making Yuri's heart swell. Seeing his Iluska standing there with her long blond hair and rosy high cheek bones froze him to his saddle. Iluska stepped out onto the threshold of the doorway, breaking the magical moment between them.

Yuri dismounted slowly. Three strides up the front ramp brought him within a breath's distance of his dream. She took another step forward. As a well behaved girl should, she kissed him three times on the cheek, starting on the left. Yuri could feel her body pressing against his thick coat.

'Iluska,' he whispered to her on the third kiss, her mother standing at the door, watching.

After the long ride the filling mid-day meal was not as welcome as sitting beside Iluska. He'd decided the best time to ask Iluska's father's permission to marry his daughter would be tomorrow, Sunday, the one day of the week reserved for rest and happy events.

In the depths of the night no one in the village heard the Earth rumbling in upheaval around the Baikal region between Irkutsk and Yartsevo. Yartsevo wasn't far enough away to escape the worst of this earthquake.

Devastation hit Iluska's village. The few who survived looked out upon an unrecognisable landscape as the sun rose on Sunday morning. No two bricks had remained one on top of another. No structure remained standing. The Yenesei river had changed course.

The night had produced a reality nightmare. Yuri's eyes snapped open at the first sound. *Iluska!* To be a light sleeper meant survival amongst life's dangers in the Siberian wilderness. His bed was dancing out of its usual position, dust filtered down from the rafters and the sound of breaking windows struck fear into Yuri. *Iluska!* There was no room left in his soul to think of what this disturbance might have been. *Iluska!* Yuri flew out of bed. *Boots! Boots!* Another mechanism the survival instinct would not allow to be neglected. Outside he could see no one else in the village ahead of him as he ran from his hut near to Iluska's home trying to make his way to her. He couldn't see her crouched in her hut that seemed to be tossed about like a small boat on an ocean wave. Fissures around the entire village opened and closed within minutes of each other swallowing everything and everybody in their vicinity.

The earth shuffled under Yuri's feet as he staggered towards her. They saw each other at the same moment she began crawling towards the front ramp of her home.

'Iluska!'

Without a warning shudder the entire foundation on which her family home was build moved several meters away from Yuri's advance. Her arm reached out towards him as the ground lurched again, moving back to where it started from. He didn't falter, jumping across each crack in the earth, keeping his eyes fixed on Iluska.

Just as suddenly everything stopped, the rage of the Earth spent. Dust and silence all around them became a surreal climax to the drama. Iluska's home no longer stood to assure survival in this wilderness. For a moment, just a brief moment Yuri faltered as he lost sight of Iluska in all the rising dust. He couldn't breathe. His mind became the emptiness of the universe. Then he saw her hand rise into view, just a few meters in front of him. 'Maliska!' The void filling again to nothing else but the image of Iluska.

This reality of destruction lasted perhaps half an hour, maybe an hour. Yuri wasn't keeping track of time as he and Iluska searched the village in the moonlight to help anyone they could see. It was a miracle neither of them had disappeared underground, althought they had lost sight of each other several times. The moonlight was a blessing in some respects but not when they had to witness their friends, their families and their homes making their dramatic jouney into the afterlife.

'Yuri, Yuri, Yuri,' Iluska whispered through her tears. The joy of still having Yuri could not break through the pain of losing her parents. As the early light of the morning peered over the tree tops on the river's further shore Yuri held Iluska in a deep embrace numb to the loss of the village, loss of life, the loss of Iluska's parents, unable to say anything. He had managed to save two people only. Iluska none at all despite her strength. It was not enough to overcome the terrible force of gravity dragging her friends into the depths.

'Maliska, baby girl, we are together,' he said. What else could he say? As the sun rose on the scene of destruction what they saw would have created the terror of panic in people not as strong in themselves. She tightened her embrace. 'We have to build a shelter and find food.' This was part of the new world, as it and they struggled out of the old. 'Tomorrow we will get help.'

'What are we going to do Yuri?' Her words carried the realisation their old life had been utterly obliterated. They could never go back to it.

A few animals wandered about, as animals do, with their reactions locked in animal souls, unshaken, fully accepting of the new reality; find something to eat, some water to drink.

They, like Yuri and Iluska had no choice. Take another breath, take another step and eventually open your eyes to another day. Life's imperatives had not changed. A new world had begun, unfamilliar and utterly daunting. The reality of effort needed to survive would very soon force itself into their consciousness. Could they even get to Zotino quite a few miles north of them? Maybe they should head south to Krilyak, it was closer. Would they need to cross the river as it cut its new way through the reshaped landscape?

Authorities in Irkutsk city, capital of Eastern Siberia, wasted no time in dealing with the earthquake aftermath and despatching forces to outlying villages. News of the effects of the 7.5 earthquake even 500 kms North up the Senesei river reached them quickly. Local government had decided the only thing to do was to send many of the survivors to Vladivostok; the only city with the infrastructure to deal with so many refugees at the same time.

'They have just told me we will have to go to Vladivostok because we have no friends or family to support us here in Irkutsk.'

'Oh Yuri, how will we get there. I have no money. I have nothing ... only you.' Life had been simple for Iluska. She didn't need to think about the logistics of long distance travel. Two hundred and fifty miles to Vladivistok was like another universe to her. She hadn't even seen a real train.

The Apollo butterfly caught in Yuri's coat yesterday survived to continue flapping its wings of change.

'The government will take us. It could be four days or more to get there. They will look after us.'

Iluska was overwhelmed by the size of Irkutsk. She never imagined such a place could exist. It was magnificent, beautiful and frightening; so many people. The uncertainty of what would happen to her, the dramatic events of the last weeks, the journey to Irkutsk with so many other refugees had become too much.

'What is going to happen to us Yuri?' Iluska broke down in a torrent of tears.

He could only get general information from one of the Officials, mostly about the many stops along the way - nothing about what would happen to them in Vladivostok.

Conditions on the Trans-Siberian for non-tourists had not improved perceptibly since the 21st century. 'This is horrible Yuri,' Iluska couldn't help herself complaining. 'I can't sleep. We wouldn't serve this food to our pigs at home. Can't we go home Yuri? Please,' she pleaded, forgetting her home had no more substance than a memory.

It was the third day of their cramped conditions on the famous train. At least two more days to put up with extremely poor sanitation, loud complaining fugitives and no privacy at all.

'This is a magnificent country,' Yuri observed as the train laboured up another steep climb in a heavily wooded landscape. From the top of the rise they could see further than from the top of the tallest tree in Krivlyak. 'But we can never go home. We have to make a new life for ourselves wherever we end up. Be brave my Maliska.'

Yuri had a firmer grasp of the elusive nature of existence than Iluska. When a village sinks into a crevasse there is no way to bring it to the surface again, or to recreate a life that had become permanently denied to its inhabitants. His future life began with Iluska though far more elusive than the precarious predictability promised by the past. A reality with little more substance to it than memories from the past confused with hopes of the future.

Four and a half days of unbearable conditions later the Vladivostok train station public amenities could only be compared to heaven according to Iluska.

'Hurry up! Hurry up! Your plane leaves in three hours.

Hurry up. You there, get moving!' The refugee attendant grabbed Iluska by the arm and pulled her roughly towards the waiting bus.

'Comrade,' Yuri was there in an instant. 'Where would you like to sleep tonight, a hospital or in your bed?' He snarled at the attendant whose hand instantaneously release it's prey, leaving a mark on Iluska's arm from the rough handling.

Vladivostok didn't want them.

At the airport the same attendant didn't rush this particular pair, careful to avoid Yuri's eyes. Hospital beds in Vladivostok were not known for the comfort they offered.

It was like a fantastic dream for Iluska. She had no previous exposure to such large internal spaces. The entrance to the airport terminal smelt unwholesome, as if many people had vomitted and left the contents to rot for a few days. All the dirty glass reaching up to the ceiling, which Iluska could hardly see, robbed the sky of its cold brilliant blue. This reality provoked all of her senses, all her preconceptions of the nature of the life she knew from childhood.

'I don't know if I can cope with all this Yuri. This cannot be the real world.' The two of them stood in line waiting to be processed for the flight. No one had bothered to tell them where they were going or about travelling in an aeroplane. The speed of the train and the bus already challenged Iluska's concept of normal modes of travelling. She looked at images on posters of aeroplanes climbing steeply into the sky. What did that mean? Were there people inside those machines? 'Yuri?' she pointed at one photo, unable to express her question.

Another Russian, waiting in an adjacent line noticed how these two appeared to be completely lost and overwhelmed by their situation. He glanced at a label on Yuri's bag.

'You will like America,' he said, 'it is a place where you can do anything.'

Yuri turned to look at him. A stranger, obviously not hostile. Yuri relaxed a little. 'What is America?'

For the first of the sixteen hour flight to Houston Iluska kept her eyes closed. Then she had a meal and slept for the rest of the flight from utter exhaustion. First the earthquake, then the escape to Irkustk followed by the nightmare train journey to Vladivostok - and now being in the air so high above the ground the Earth couldn't be seen through the clouds. Flying through and above the clouds ... *only angels can do that*, Iluska thought when she awoke.

The 22nd century had heralded in a new era in Soviet - USA relationships, agreements existed but without provisions to deal with the welfare of refugees from natural disaster devastation in either of the two major powers. Yet they had agreed, for purposes of long term reciprocal benefit, to offer each other aid in such circumstances as they arose. The world with a stable climate no longer existed. Increased geological upheavals and volcanic activity contributed to the realisation life as it had been in the past could never be reclaimed. It became a matter of mutual survival for nations to help one another.

After some confusion on arrival, being shuffled from one interrogation room to another at the George Bush International Airport Yuri and Iluska saw the light of day again, both feet firmly on the ground. The city had an unwholesome smell and a tainted colour in the air they couldn't describe when they were changing buses in Houston.

'What is this place Yuri?' The skyscraper glass cliff faces of downtown Houston added another layer of incredulity to Iluska's concept or reality. Their arduous journey through Siberia to Vladivostok had already stretched their endurance capacity to the limit. They had no say at all when the Russian authorities singled them out as a couple, amongst many others, to force a new existence on them in a foreign land. They didn't consider the mental landscape of two people who had lived their entire lives in the wilderness, each day frought with danger and a struggle just to survive to the next day. Would they even understand this new reality with its highly intricate set of foreign rules for an entirely different type of survival?

'We will find no bears here,' he answered, suddenly remembering the scat smell on the day of his trek to Iluska's village. It gave Yuri such a hit of nostalgia he almost lost his balance just standing there. He saw no boots on his feet as he glanced down though he could almost feel them.

'Move along, move along!' urged Carnegie's hostile voice, an Immigration and Customs Enforcement officer. This group of ten people were after all Russians. In some respects the past animosities carried long shadows.

Carnegie didn't want this assignment. He had extremely low tolerance for any foreigners who entered Texas, be they Mexicans or anyone else. And the Russian guy Yuri really put him on edge, no doubt intimidated by the look Yuri gave him each time he pushed Iluska in his impatience to get them on the bus for the CoreCivic Houston Processing Centre.

On arrival at the ICE immigration enforcement facility Iluska clutched Yuri's arm in disbelief. Had they been brought all this way only to be put in prison? They saw the tall wire fences with razor wire on top surrounding large buildings with very few windows. Yuri folded his arms around her, confused.

A female Russian voice spoke to him from behind. 'Zdravstvuyte, Hello. My name is Charlotte.' Yuri snapped around so fast he almost knocked her over. 'I can see you are a little puzzled,' the woman said in perfect Russian.

A torrent of words burst out of Yuri and Iluska simultaneously. 'Slow down, not so fast,' Charlotte interrupted, 'I will explain everything.'

Charlotte helped them retrieve their two bags from the bus as she continued reassuring them this was not a prison but a temporary place for them to stay.

'This is only for a little while. Do you speak any English?' she asked Yuri.

'Nyet, nyet.' Of course they didn't. What use would it have been in the deep South of Siberia?

'This is the first thing you will have to do - learn a little English. Then we will find jobs for both of you and a place to live.'

'I want some proper clothes. These are rags they gave us in Irkutsk.'

'Yes of course,' Charlotte said her, 'and I will arrange for a nice haircut for you Iluska.' That brought a huge smile to her. *Perhaps life might be a little better here.*

Labour shortages all over the US probably contributed to so many foreigners being accepted into the country. Yuri and Iluska's ability to learn passable English in just a few short weeks earned them the opportunity to be taken on as maintenance staff at the NASA facility. They didn't pose a security threat, as indicated by their backgrounds and the circumstances which brought them to the USA.

'What is this world Yuri?' asked Iluska on arrival back at ICE from a shopping trip with Charlotte. A question Iluska had asked him many times since arriving in the US. She had a lot of difficulty in comprehending a world where every building was taller than their tallest trees back home.

A place of concrete and glass where there were hardly any trees at all. The human psyche had not evolved enough to remain balanced in the face of such unrealities. Yuri couldn't help her to adjust. He suffered from the same impact of a world of incomprehensible illusions.

How would these two people who knew and lived a simple life of survival, who understood actual reality, cope with seeing machines that could take people to the Moon? Would the name 'Titan' have any meaning for them at all? They didn't need AI robots in their brains to create an alternate reality. Just being in this city of monstrosities forced them to abandon the past, what to them was now fast becoming a fading memory.

After many weeks of a simple routine that also provided the necessities of survival Yuri and Iluska could at last reflect on their journey from Yartsevo. They spoke of it as if the place still existed.

'Some nights I dream of mother and father, and of the day before the earthquake when you arrived. You looked so handsome, so excited. I had the feeling you had something special on your mind. I still remember that.'

In their simple studio apartment they were begining to feel the comfort of security. They both had employment at the same place, so they were never separated from each other for very long, except when they went about their work at the NASA training centre.

'Oh yes. I was going to speak to your father about something very serious.' Iluska lowered her head and a little colour came to her cheeks.

Without stretching the moment Yuri told her what she had probably already guessed. 'I was going to ask for his blessing to marry you.'

'Yes, I know. I was expecting you to, but you waited. I was so disappointed.' Then after a long break, with the colour rising to her face again she said, 'Yes. Yes, Yuri.'

Well, that was settled. The future now had a meaning. It had a purpose. It was going to be a life so different from the past their imagination could not have painted a picture of it. Sitting on the couch close beside each other a gentle silence filled the room with happiness and joyous expectation. But the human mind is never satisfied to allow contentment to dominate for too long.

'Maliska baby girl, can I tell you something really strange?'

'What is it Yuri?' Sudden concern gathered like a grey cloud on her forehead. She had been through so much. Any little thing could upset her fragile happiness that evening.

'Oh, nothing serious. There was this idiot man at work at the cafeteria. Do you remember?' The gathering cloud cleared as she nodded, for she did recall the incident. 'He almost knocked me over. Dropped all his food and spilt coffee over himself.'

'Yes, I do remember. He must be the same man who kept staring at me when he came to get his meal. These Americans are very strange. No manners at all.'

'I was helping him pick up the mess when a woman in a bright yellow dress suddenly appeared. Well, can you believe it? She stared at me as if I was some kind of ghost.'

'These are very odd people Yuri. We have to be careful.'

Yuri didn't tell her how he returned a glance of interest with the strange girl. He'd probably forgotten all about that little detail.

Reprograming
Betty

The interrogation room had been repainted to subtly
influence Betty's state of mind.

J'Ark could not change her own character or her manner
to achieve a greater effect on Betty. Her lack of social skills
were a palpable hindrance. At least the soft green walls and
light blue ceiling would help Betty fall sleep. Immediately
after her orientation at NASA Betty had to report for a
debrief and further training under J'Ark's manipulations.

'In preparation for your short stay at the ISS we will
implant a small device to monitor your biologicals.' That
was an outright lie. J'Ark now had in her possession all the
AIDA technology being used on John, acquired through
the operative Zsuzsa. 'Do you know why you might be sent
there? No?' Betty feigned ignorance. She knew the job she
still had to do. Where John went she had to go. One way
or another she had to get her hands on every detail of this
highly secret anti-grav propulsion process.

'Of course you do. Tonight sleep. Tomorrow you train.'
Then she left quite abruptly.

Betty's room was small.

No fresh air. Eight and a half minutes after she put her head on the pillow and fell asleep the door to her cell opened. The nitrous oxide had been sucked out replaced by a nurse ready with a strong sedative.

When Betty woke the next morning she had been appropriately augmented to take on John within the altered reality state of dreaming. J'Ark sat beside the bed watching her come out of an anaesthetic dream.

'You have been dreaming.' J'Ark said as if she knew it for a fact and said it in such a way as to intimate she knew what the dream was about. 'Rural domestic bliss?'

'Not exactly. I don't like the smell of a milking shed.'

She paused. Raised herself to sit on the edge of the bed opposite the angular woman. *This bitch doesn't want to hear about my dream.* 'What have you done to me?' Betty almost whispered the question. 'How do you know about my dream?'

The thin bureaucratic smile appeared again. 'We have increased you level of efficiency.'

That rang a bell. The man who interviewed her when she first arrived at the UNSC said something about efficiency. She was still trying to work out what it could possibly mean, how they could possibly achieve that when J'Ark's smile widened.

'Do you know the opera AIDA? You don't want the same fate as the Ethiopian princess ... I assume.' The woman relished this little game of making her victim, her expendable toy, confused. Any uncertainty in Betty only made her more malleable. 'Never mind. I'll tell you about her sad story another time. Today you get to rest, sleep and think about how to get your job done. Tomorrow you can play with Popovich, your combat trainer.'

She turned to go to let Betty have a shower, discover her little wound and think things through. 'By the way ... just a little thing. There's pen and paper on the table. Please record any dreams you have during the next few nights.

This is important.'
'No,' came the immediate defiant response.

Things had been getting a little better at home. Their uncomplicated daily routine helped stabilise their relationship. Betty hadn't felt as much pressure of having to force John into revealing anything; other than perhaps explaining his roving eye in the direction of the new blond girl in the cafeteria. Nothing in it really. Betty was quite certain of that. Then, just as she was becoming excited about her new training to get her ready for the ISS in her role as an Interplanetary Security Consultant, that hard face bitch J'Ark called her back to UNSC HQ. Betty had decided to be as uncooperative as possible.

'No,' she said again when J'Ark shot a warning look at her.

'Never mind. You will remember them anyway.' The woman turned to leave.

To confront Betty with her failure, to berate her for not showing more positive results would only have resulted in exacerbating her rebellion. Much better to keep her guessing and maybe bring a little more pain into her life.

Popovich appeared at the small room with a large training mat before Betty had her shower. The mat was the same light blue colour as the ceiling.

'Dobroye utro, good morning,' he said without looking at Betty as he unrolled the training mat.

'What are you doing here? I haven't had a shower yet.' Popovich leant over and pulled her onto the mat with one powerful hand. 'Stop it. You're hurting me.'

He pushed her, hard. She almost toppled over. He circled around her and pushed her again, saying nothing. *What kind of damn training is this?* If it wasn't enough that J'Ark had made her angry with her stupid order now this Russian gorilla was provoking her.

He pushed again, harder. She fell backwards.

Blood rushed to her head, furious eyes flashed the gorilla a warning as she jumped back up.

He smiled.

'What the fuck!' she yelled.

Popovich backed up to the edge of the mat, bent over, grabbed it in two muscular hands and yanked. The shock of landing on her backside on the hard concrete floor dazed Betty for a moment as the pain lanced up her spine.

For the remainder of the next two hours Popovich used every trick to unbalance Betty with the obvious aim of inflicting as much pain as possible each time she landed on the concrete. The process wore her out physically and emotionally. Her anger having turned to rage did not help her to defend herself. Popovich offered no advice, no technique as to how she could counter his moves.

Her rage turned to screams, then tears. He didn't stop until she refused to get up off the floor.

'Tomorrow ve play again.' He left taking the mat with him.

Betty lay there spread out in the position she last fell, unable to move from the agony in every part of her body. *Is this going to be the reality of my life until they let me die?*

Already, after just two training sessions, she couldn't remember what it was like to lie in a soft bed next to John's warm body. *Am I dreaming?* She tried lifting an arm with the thought of pinching herself. Exhausted. No good. Betty closed her eyes. It was all she could do.

Sometime later she awoke, sore and stiff. Stripped, limped into the shower. *Was I out for an hour?* Walls devoid of a clock deprived her of the luxury of knowing.

Naked, still wet she dropped onto the bed.

... These beasts stink - their shit, their piss. Let me get out of here! Here arms were filthy up to her armpits. Where the hell is John? This is his job. I'm supposed to look after the chooks.

... 'Betty, where are you? Haven't you finished yet? We have to go soon. We'll be late for training.'

... 'What?' she yelled back.

... 'NASA, training. You know.'

... That made no sense at all. Dairy farmers don't train to be astronauts. She was still trying to work it out as she flung open the gate to the chook pen. The laying boxes all empty, chooks nowhere to be seen. 'What did you feed these chickens yesterday? There's no eggs at all!'

... On the way out she slammed the gate. It bounced back and got her on the ankle, inflicting pain through the rubber boots. She slipped, landing in the mud with a thud on top of a submerged rock.

The concreted floor didn't get any softer overnight. Betty landed on it impacting an already sore ankle from the previous training session with Popovich. She reached down with the intention of removing her boots to have a look at the injury.

Why am I naked? Where's my boots?

A hand reached down to drop a sheet of paper and pencil in front of her.

'What was worse? The mud with chicken shit or the milking shed with the cow piss?' the voice asked.

Betty looked up from the floor in utter disbelief.

'Jot down a couple of notes about your dream while I get your breakfast,' crooned J'Ark in as pleasant a voice as she could manage.

Betty had dragged herself into some clothes by the time J'Ark returned. The coffee smelt fantastic. She took a sip, picked up the pencil and wrote. J'Ark could see on her face that recording the dream helped. It probably made it easier for Betty to distinguish between actual reality and the dream. *I will not always give her the luxury to do that.* J'Ark smiled to herself. *At last we are making some real progress.*

Betty's respite didn't last long. By the time she finished her breakfast and a second cup of coffee the pencil had done all it could. J'Ark still sat there, silent so far. She reached over and took the sheet of paper, not bothering to look at it.

'Thank you Betty. Well done.' That was the very first time since their association Betty had heard a positive word from the bitch. She had begun to tentatively savour the feeling when Popovich appeared at the door. No mat.

'Shit.' The memory of pain hit her hard.

'Dobroye utro,' he said although the morning was well advanced.

Déjà vu.

'Oh no, not you again.'

'One strike, one kill.' Popovich didn't elaborate. A formal training session with soft punches this time.

Betty still hit the ground numerous times causing more capillary damage making existing bruising more severe.

How am I going to explain this to John? Being given the opportunity to release some of her anger and frustration by actually landing the odd blow on Popovich made her feel so much better.

'If I hit you, you die. Today we finish.' And just like that he was gone after three solid hours.

'Yes?' Aksel wasn't one to give away any information over comms, not even his name. 'What do you want?'

'I have AIDA. It's working on Betty. She will be able to use more structured persuasion methods to extract the intel from the target.' J'Ark might have been a little premature in her assessment based on the first dream result with Betty. But there it was, the evidence in Betty's own handwriting.

'Other sources indicate innovative progress with the propulsion technology. Wait until it has been tested with consistent positive results before pushing her too hard,' instructed Aksel.

'Understood.' *This'll give me a chance to ensure the dream program is working.* What had been a significant source of stress in this woman's life suddenly turned into an opportunity to exercise her more pleasure seeking tendencies.

Günther's world was entirely in code cutting cyberspace, immersing himself in all the latest advancements of the AI technological revolution. People outside his world didn't exist other than to provide him with the necessities of life. Beyond that they lived in a reality without meaning for Günther. 'Yes ma'am,' he replied to her question. 'I can do it again and will add a few enhancements.'

'Excellent. Make sure you instruct those little bot buggers to plant the seed of Betty's discontent with her mother. And find a way for her to experience another painful event.'

Günther revelled in having a cohort of obedient nano-robots to do his bidding. His boss, J'Ark, gave him a free hand to be creative with his programming. Whatever psychological issues his digital gymnastics created in the host of his nano-slaves didn't concern him in the least.

The second night of her incarceration started well enough. It took a while to find a position on the mattress causing the least pain before she fell asleep.

... 'Hello darling. I've been waiting for you. I know you like to help me prune the roses.' Shirley handed her a pair of secateurs.

... 'Weren't you worried about me Mum? I mean after I had to go away so suddenly?'

... 'Did you dear?' She neglected to give Betty the spare pair of gardening gloves. 'Oh yes,' she said after she'd snipped a couple stems, 'those gentlemen were very nice - so polite.'

... 'No they weren't Mum. They were horrible. They forced me to go to - to - I forget.' The memory had already begun to upset Betty. She reached out for a rose stem taking no particular care. As she pulled her hand away one of the thorns scratched her. 'Ouch!'

... 'What did you say dear?' asked Shirley, absorbed in her own little world not paying any attention to her daughter at all.

... 'Mum! Aren't you listening to me?'

... 'No darling. I'm a bit busy.'

... 'I've gone to all the trouble to come home and visit.' *It's not a short trip from Paris, and she completely ignores me!* Betty reached out for another stem. This time somewhat angry and disappointed her mother was being so casual about the visit and the effort she'd made.

... 'Damn!' Another thorn pricked her finger. In the impulsive move to yank it out from amongst all the other stems several thorns decided they'd had enough of this pruning ritual and let her know it in the most effective way they could. ...

What seemed like it was going to be a pleasant dream turned out rather painfully. Strangely, this time Betty was aware she'd dropped into a dream. She didn't like some of those feelings which seemed to surface by themselves to make the whole event so unpleasant.

As on other occasions she awoke suddenly. J'Ark wasn't there in the room this time. Someone else was; Shirley. Just standing there a few steps away from her still holding her secateurs. Betty could see her from the corner of her eye and smell her perfume. 'Mum?' Betty turned her head to see better, blinking in the process. Her blink, like a light switch, turned the apparition off. She raised her head to look about the room. Shirley was gone, her scent was gone.

Betty ended up sitting on the side of the bed. Something wasn't right. While still thinking about her disappearing mother she felt something sticky under her right thigh. Her hand automatically went to the spot.

Blood.

She almost fainted. Betty looked at her fingers. They were bloodied. She closed her eyes, trying to will herself to wake up, thinking herself to be still asleep. At that moment the door opened to reveal J'Ark standing there with a cold grin.

Three steps brought her to the bedside. She shoved a board with paper and a pencil at Betty. 'Write. Now!' No *please* this time.

Under the shock of it all Betty took the pencil in her bloodied hand and scribbled down what she could remember of the dream, making a mess on the paper in the process.

'Go wash yourself.' The woman waited.

It happened so quickly. Everything happened so quickly. *Was Mum even here?* Betty began to doubt if she was asleep or awake or having some sort of hallucination. *They've given me drugs!* Fear and pain and blood and sticky fingers - and the door opened again.

Popovich stood there holding two knives.

Betty fainted, slumping over the table.

J'ark had propped her against the wall in the bathroom, half sitting half standing. The wet face towel soaked in water and blood. She'd almost cleaned it up by the time Betty became fully conscious of what was happening.

'You're not hurt badly,' J'Ark said without offering any explanation of where the blood had come from.

'How much longer?' Betty pleaded.

'End of the week. Popovich is waiting.'

Betty turned to see him standing exactly where she first saw him. She saw the knives glint in the artificial light. They were small and broad like vegetable knives.

Involuntarily her eyes closed. She heard John's adolescent voice ... 'Hey Betty, can you do this?' ...

'Get out here. Stop daydreaming,' Popovich ordered. He wasn't being impatient. He wanted her to know who was in control.

Without checking if her thigh was still bleeding Betty raised herself almost as if she was an automaton, John's voice still lingering in her head. The instinct to survive straightened her back, raised her head, focused her eyes. She took two steps towards her trainer, her body going into a crouch-for-defence position on seeing the knives again.

Popovich suddenly flipped one of the knives thrusting the handle towards Betty. 'Take it. You like knives. Today you learn how to use.'

This was Wednesday. Today was kind to Betty. She had no more falls, no more bruising. Only cuts. Swift, precise but superficial. By the end of the session Popovich was smiling at her. 'Good, good.' He studied several short slashes across his singlet and one across his arm. Betty watched, dripping perspiration overjoyed to hear those meagre words of praise from the smelly Russian.

She startled herself when he'd gone. 'Shit! I enjoyed that. I actually enjoyed that.' Hearing herself saying it aloud made the pleasure real.

In just three days Betty had changed. She didn't realise it: Her awareness filled with bad dreams, pain and that bitch J'Ark. *Is there another world out there?* She began to question if the reality she once knew had escaped without giving her the slightest chance to recapture it.

'Tonight is your biggest challenge Günther. Think you can handle it?'

'Yes ma'am. And may I say thank you for your trust.'

J'Ark burst out laughing. *The poor idiot has no idea what he is doing. Unfortunately he is becoming one of those lose ends I'll need to cauterize at some stage.*

'My deluded boy.' Still grinning she took a handful of his hair turning his head towards the screen. The pain made him wince. 'Have a look at this video surveillance. I want you to make sure that by tomorrow morning Betty is so jealous she will want to put her knife training into action.'

'Yes ma'am!' The sheer exhilaration of being able to control a person's dream thoughts drove any vestiges of empathy for the plight of this experimental subject out of his thoughts utterly, completely. Only one reality existed for Günther - himself and AIDA; a perfect symbiotic relationship between an AI and a human.

Utter exhaustion and coming off the sustained adrenalin high left Betty with little energy other than to gulp down a quick dinner, and a quicker shower before flopping on the bed in the cell. Only one thought returned without warning; Johnny boy's boast, 'Hey Betty, can you do this?' he'd asked as he attempted to juggle the kitchen knife when they were adolescents. Her last mumbled words on closing her eyelids ... 'Better than you Johnny boy.' ...

... *Why is he making eyes at the girl behind the counter?* At first Betty didn't think much of John's occasional glance in that direction as he waited to buy his lunch at the cafeteria in NASA's main hall. *I'll go over and surprise him. He doesn't know I'll be going to the ISS.*

... Betty started weaving her way around tables towards John. *Is that girl looking back at him, smiling?*

... John's eyes kept roaming back in the girl's direction, seemingly oblivious of why he was in the queue in the first place. His hand went up.

... *Why is he waving to her?* Someone had called John's order number, written on a slip of paper.

Betty didn't see the paper. She saw what she didn't want to believe. *He's not a player!* What she saw next in the sequence of events which when strung together told her a different story - they'd been looking at each other - when she smiled at him he waved back - she must have called out to him to make him go over to the counter so quickly.

... John carried his lunch on a tray. *Just look at him*, Betty fabricated, *he's so concentrated on that girl he's not looking where he's going.*

... John collided with the maintenance man. Betty had closed the gap between herself and John in a flash. She notice the man before she reacted to John's misfortune. *Oh - Who are you?* she thought. But what she said was "Sorry, so sorry!' Her eyes lingered on the maintenance man.

... As she started helping John clean himself up the Betty in her dream said to herself - *He's cute! I wouldn't mind bumping into him myself.* ...

As on numerous recent occasions her brain told her something wasn't right - wake up! *You shouldn't be lusting after him.*

Wide awake in seconds she blurted out, 'What is wrong with me?'

'Indeed, that is a good question,' responded a familiar voice.

'Oh - It's you.' It took an effort to get up to face the woman. 'You still haven't told me your name.' This sounded like she meant to say ... If you don't tell me your name I will not cooperate any more.

'If you must know - J'Ark.'

'Really?'

J'Ark did her best to ignore the tone of voice. It still made her bristle. She hit back, not being able to help herself. 'So, has John found another romantic interest?'

Bull's eye. Betty's eyes dilated, disbelieving, unable to thrust back. J'Ark watched, amused. *So easy with these young people*. Then to heighten her pleasure she said, 'Yuri. The man's name is Yuri.'

J'Ark almost hugged Betty the next instant.

'Okay then - what's the name of the woman behind the counter,' she asked as a taunt.

'Iluska,' shot back J'Ark.

Betty had turned out to be an absolute treasure - smart, quick witted and so easily manipulated regardless. A unique combination of characteristics. It would be a pity to lose such a valuable asset.

With monotonous predictable regularity Popovich arrived. 'No breakfast,' he announced, 'vork first.' The light blue mat was back. Betty sighed with relief, stepping up onto the far corner of it. No more concrete floor to rupture capillaries. He didn't have the knives either she noticed as he began to advance towards her.

'Yuri. My comrade is Yuri. You like Yuri, eh?' He pounced and pushed her hard on her chest. 'You vant introduction?' Another push before she managed to fully recover. Whether it was a sense of guilt, or being pushed around made no difference to the anger which flared in Betty. *I don't want to hear about Yuri!* She wanted to push back. She wanted to hurt this man who was taunting her.

'Bastard!' she lunged at him, with clenched fists. Popovich side stepped, gave her a little nudge. She ended up face first on the mat.

'You vant talk about Iluska? I think John likes Iluska.'

This made no sense at all. How do they know about my dream? Betty staggered to her feet wiping the perspiration from her brow. She glanced at her bed for a moment. No. She wasn't lying on it. This was not a dream.

The baiting and shoving continued non-stop until all reason seemed to have vacated her eyes. Betty had become just an animal trying to survive, the names Yuri and Iluska and John getting tangled in her continuously looping thoughts. Dizzy, disorientated, out of breath and dripping sweat she didn't notice Popovich had left as she got up off the mat this last time trying to focus her eyes.

J'Ark had been watching on the vid with growing pleasure. She returned to have a word with Popovich. 'Good man, *Yuri*,' she said laughing as they stood outside Betty's cell door. He grunted amusement, understanding exactly what she meant. 'Is she ready?'

'Da.'

Just one more little thing left to do before we take her back to dear John, she thought on her way to talk to Günther.

'Sex,' can you do that?

'Pardon?'

'For Betty in her next dream - with Yuri.'

First
Confrontation

Betty swivelled around expecting the next attack to come from behind.

She twisted again and again making herself dizzier. Popovich had gone. The mat was still there, she sank down onto it. Sobbing escalating into tears. 'I can't - I can't ...' her words faded into silence as she stretched out on the mat then pulling herself into the foetal position, exhausted. ...

... 'Yuri, we shouldn't be doing this,' she protested against the urgings of her body. He took no notice lifting her as easily as if she was a bear cub. She could feel herself bounce on the mattress as he dumped her on it. For a moment she saw herself running and a man chasing her, his features indistinct. 'John,' she groaned.

... 'Nyet!' came the insistent denial. 'Nyet!' John didn't have luxuriant chest hair yet she could feel the abrasion from the movements on top of her.

... 'Stop it!' Betty began struggling. I don't want this. I don't want this - I don't want ...

A sudden dream scene change propelled a new set of images into her inner vision.

... 'John, what are you doing?' She stared at a woman with blond platted hair, naked beside John. 'Iluska?'

... John looked back at her. 'You want to know the secret, don't you. I can't tell you - I won't tell you. I will tell her.' Betty screamed, reaching out to claw at the naked woman grabbing a fist full of her hair.

They monitored her REM sleep cycles. The nurse with the sedative stood by her bed ready to inject her at the end of the last cycle. While in an induced coma she was transported back to her and John's house, dumped unceremoniously on their bed for her to finish enjoying her dreams. In the final minutes of her sleep Betty experienced again the figment created by Günther implanted into the matrices of the waiting little bots in her hippocampus. They wove the warp and weft of images and memories that were a complete fabrication, a contortion of reality, fears and desires mixed up.

She woke with eyes wild, her left hand clutching a handful of her own hair. She could see the lounge room window through the open door. It didn't register. Her other hand roamed over her belly sliding on the slick perspiration. Popovich, blue mat, cell - the only images to come to the back of her eyes.

As consciousness returned Betty looked beside herself. Yuri wasn't there. John wasn't there beside her either. 'Where the hell is John?' She couldn't immediately remember the events of the last terrible week.

He's with that blond Russian woman. No no no no! That was a dream - ? Where is he? Why isn't he in bed?

She was still sitting up in bed trying hard to understand the reality of an unaccountable rift in the fabric of her reality when she heard the front door open and close.

Early dawn light had only started filtering through the sitting room window. Sunlight; I haven't seen the sun for - for. Suddenly there was John standing at the foot of the bed, dishevelled, looking exhausted. He may have had some expectations of how he would react when Betty arrived home, or how she would react. Reality didn't match either of those expectations.

There she was sitting up naked in bed, dripping wet, hair in a mess as if someone had been tearing at it, just staring at him as if he was a ghost.

'BB.'

'Where the hell have you been?!'

'I - er - had to ...' he started to say, unsure of what was actually happening.

'Don't lie to me. You've been with *her*!'

'What?'

'Just look at you. You look like you've been having a party in your clothes all night.'

He took a couple of steps to come around to the side of the bed.

'Stay away from me!' He backed off. She covered herself with the bedding.

'Work. You know - the thing I can't tell you about.' He said lamely as he turned to go to the kitchen. 'I'll put the kettle on, make us a coffee.' A peace offering perhaps.

He could see her down the corridor through the partly open bedroom door. She was smoothing down her hair, wiping her brow, starting to get her legs over the side of the bed.

John brought the coffees in astonished to see Betty's body. She'd dropped the bed cover revealing the marks of her experiences with Popovich.

'What the hell happened to you? You've only been gone a week and you come back looking like this.' She examined herself, hands touching all the tender spots, eyes having gone blank after the fury of a few minutes ago.

'Who did this to you?' His genuine concern evident as he bent to touch her. She pulled away from him.

'Popovich.' Betty looked up suddenly with a new fear. John wasn't supposed to know about him.

'He's been a bit rough on you. Who is he? What exactly were you two doing? His voice having gone up a notch.

'None of your business!' She shouted back. Betty's emotions were all over the place. Confused by everything, not knowing what was real, what was a dream, what was perhaps only a memory.

'So it's okay for you to have a fling, to have a bit of kinky sex but it's not alright for me. Is that it?!' To Betty it sounded exactly like an admission not an accusation. The two coffees remained on the bedside table. In the heat of the moment John stormed out of the house slamming the door. A minute later he was back in front of Betty hanging her head, her silent tears streaming onto the carpet.

'Who am I supposed to have been with anyway?' Voice still loud, angry, confronting.

'Iluska,' she said without looking up.

'Right. As if I knew who that was.' He turned again and left. The door didn't slam this time.

'What is happening to me?' she whispered through tears, unheard by John.

'Excellent. Now we might be getting somewhere.' J'Ark took the initiative to invite Aksel to watch the show which she was absolutely sure was the result of Betty's mental state after the conditioning by AIDA and Popovich. 'Don't forget to keep her under control until we have some idea of progress on NASA's latest innovation to make the ant-grav actually work.'

John stopped on the porch, heart pounding. *How can I work with this going on? Why did she come back? What am I supposed to do now? I don't know any girl called Iluska.* He walked towards his car, turned around half way and returned to the front door. He entered as quietly as he could alert to where Betty might be. He heard the water running in the shower.

Five minutes later he was driving down their road with a few clothes and other possessions in a bag on the back seat. There was only one place he could go.

Iluska? I definitely don't know any Iluska. How did BB get those bruises? Who is Popovich? His eyes went immediately to the rear vision mirror, searching. No one following. For a fleeting moment he thought perhaps the people in the mysterious car that had once followed them had taken her and inflicted those injuries.

With his head so full of his own problems John arrived without any workable answers. 'Dad, do you still have the spare bed?' He didn't notice how tired and unwell his Dad looked.

Angus Silverman watched the drama unfold with considerable concern. Drs Kathleen and Armbruster were with him, Dr Kathleen no less concerned possibly for a different reason.

'It seems to me Betty has been interfered with. What we've witnessed isn't normal behaviour.' Armbruster concurred with a nod - Dr Kathleen frowned. 'I want you to step up John's treatment. He can't be running away from her every time they have a misunderstanding. He must take control of the situation. Work on him. You've got AIDA - use it.'

Armbruster understood exactly what needed to be done. He looked at Dr Kathleen. The furrows on her brow had deepened. 'Tonight. You get your little helpers on the job tonight before his confusion settles. A perfect petri dish to grow a few illusions. I want him emotionally distancing himself from her.'

Dr Kathleen remained silent during the replay of the surveillance vid and the conversation. Boundaries had begun to come into focus for her.

'What is happening to me?' Betty whispered again through tears after John had left the house. She didn't have the emotional energy to think things through. John often worked late. He often arrive home worn out, scruffy. Her guilt for her unconscious desire for the cleaner at the Café still hidden.

John strays, Betty strays

'What's your problem son?'

Peter went on without waiting for an answer. 'It's that woman you're with, right?'

'I don't want to talk about it.' Peter always had a way of making a situation more complicated. *If I tell him anything he'll just throw a bag full of advice at me.* 'All I need is a few good night's sleep Dad. May I use your spare bed?'

'Sure, sure. Get settled then I want to talk to you about the graviton containment.'

'Tomorrow Dad, I'm beat. I really need a few hour's undisturbed rest.' John had been up most of the previous night resolving the outstanding issues with containing gravitons in such a way as to make their directional activation controllable. A resolution was imperative if they were to move onto the next stage; graviton polarity reversal. *No doubt that's what Dad wants to discuss. He wasn't there in the lab last night. He can't go on at the pace NASA expects of him.*

John had arrived at Peter's apartment on the base a little before lunch time. As soon as his head hit the pillow the world ceased to exist. This state of exhaustion and internal conflict could not have been made more to order for what Armbruster needed to do.

While John slid into the early stages of his sleep cycle Armbruster closely supervised Dr Kathleen's coding to ensure those nano-bots wasted no time going into action inside John's head. Feeding images of Betty being physically confronting, including the latest exchange between them set the receptivity nerves on alert to heighten the tensions between them. *She's dangerous – she can't be trusted. Remember what she did to you in the VR game. She just wants you to betray us. Don't answer any of her questions. ...*

... Betty was sitting on the edge of the bed, the bedding in a tangle around her, all the bruising clearly visible on her body. John bent to touch her most prominent bruise. She lifted her head slowly, smiling strangely.

... 'Doesn't it hurt?' he asked, withdrawing his hand. *Why is she smiling like that. It's almost as if she was enjoying it.*

... 'You like that Johnny boy? Would you like to play rough?'

... John took a step back from the bed. The warning came back to him – *She's dangerous – she can't be trusted.* An image of her slashing at his hand hit just as Betty said something else.

... 'We can you know. All you have to do is tell me. Tell me everything and ...'

Suddenly she jumped up and lunged at him before he could even refuse her demands.

... As an automatic reaction his arms went up to protect himself. But Betty was faster, her fingernails dug into the side of his neck ploughing deep furrows.

... John shouted something as his right arm swung out catching her full on the side of her head. She crumbled back onto the bed ... still smiling.

... 'Get away from me! I'm not telling you anything!' ...

John woke sometime in the early morning to the sound of his own voice calling out. He lay there with eyes closed reliving every moment of the dream. *It was just a dream*, he told himself. *Just a dream. I saw her bruises, they were real bruises. She's been doing something crazy. Whatever's happened to her has changed her. I can't trust her anymore.*

He got up with the last thought going around in his head, rubbing his neck where a phantom pain had begun to disappear, yet his fingers could still feel several welts.

Peter was already up. He never could sleep well. He'd heard John's shout and went to his room to see what the problem was.

'Bad dream?' he asked on seeing his son standing there staring blankly into space.

'Yeah.'

'About Betty?'

'Yeah.'

'Want to talk about it?'

'No.' Peter waited. There was no strength in John's denial. 'No. But I do have to do something about her. Maybe I should go and see Silverman. I have to get some decent sleep. I can't work like this.' Then the words he'd been refusing to say, even to himself, popped out, 'I have to be alone for a while.'

There was no clarity behind the utterance. What did it actually mean? What did *being alone for a while* look like? Was he going to kick her out? Was he going to leave her? What?

'You want breakfast?'

'No thanks Dad. I'll get some at the cafeteria.'

'Do you want to ditch her?'

John turned to face his father, jaws clenching.

Armbruster and Silverman watched the latest vid feed of John talking to some woman at the cafeteria. It wasn't Betty.

'Do you know who she is?' asked Armbruster.

'A Russian refugee from an earthquake disaster in Siberia.'

'Russian? Do we need to be concerned?'

'No. She's nobody. A girl from the wilderness. No political connections. He does seem to be paying a bit more than casual attention to her.'

'He obviously finds her attractive,' observed Armbruster.

John arrived quite early at the main cafeteria on the base. Not many people around yet. The eatery had just opened. One of the female staff was busy cleaning the tables. John recognised the same girl he'd noticed the other day. He went to the table she had started on.

'Hello.' He sat. *I shouldn't be doing this.*

'Hello.' She looked up to see who it was. Just another customer. She turned back to the task. A moment later she looked up again to see him watching her. *Oh - it's the man who kept looking at me the other day.* Her face flushed for a moment.

'Have you been working here long?' John asked instead of ordering his coffee. She was very pretty - no, more than that - she had a glow about her, even in the drab uniform. *What are you doing John?* he admonished himself.

'Nyet - No.'

'You are Russian?' *Stop it John!* He could feel stirrings he should not have been having.

'Da - yes. Sorry, English not good - is learning.'

The table was clean. She'd finished, but found something else to wipe down. She looked at him again. Their eyes locked for a moment.

He heard himself say, 'My name is John, Hello.' *You've got work to do Johnny boy. Stop whatever it is you're doing and get on with it.* He flicked his eyes sideways to break the spell and stood up to go. He wanted desperately to ask her name.

'Iluska,' she volunteered, blushing slightly again. *What am I doing. Yuri will be furious. He can get so jealous.*

'Hello.'

Iluska! John didn't have breakfast. He took off in the direction of the lab. If his legs hadn't known the way he probably would not have made it there. He was already late.

His father beat him to the lab. 'It's about time son. What were you doing? We have to work out how to change the polarity of the gravitons in a controlled way to achieve ... Are you listening to me son?'

No. John was definitely not listening. A few days, weeks ago he could have painted a picture of his life with all the important elements; his training, the ant-grav propulsion system, Betty. The design of his life complete in its simplicity with all the colours in the right place and the future clearly discernible.

Today it seemed as if Picasso had waved his brush over the canvas. The focal point in his composition had shifted from quantum physics to an entity called Iluska. Nothing was in the right place. The external structure of his life had not changed. His inner reality had experienced a seismic convulsion.

Peter had to take his son by the arm to turn him so he could see the boy's eyes.

'Ah. I know that look. And it doesn't tell of a love affair with gravitational particles. Now listen to me son.' He had to squeeze John's arm to get his attention - 'I don't care what's happening in your private life, we have a job to do. We have come so far, we have achieved a revolutionary breakthrough in science. It has to be finished.

Come over here and let's go through these schematics.'

The systems to get anti-grav propulsion to work in a controlled way needed to be refined. Reversal of graviton particles polarity became critical. It was John's idea, not Peter's and Peter was proud of his son. But he had to make the final adjustments to hardware and software before their test craft would be ready for its first flight. If John still wanted to be the test pilot he had a good deal of work left to do. This wasn't a good time for distractions of a personal nature.

Peter's persistent urging finally got John to bring his mind back into the realm of quantum physics. Many days passed without John going back to the cafeteria. He couldn't face going home either. His dreams had lost their lucid clarity. Sometimes the lucidity had come from himself. On other occasions he felt quite certain he wasn't entirely in control and couldn't steer the dream events to his liking.

The morning had not started well for Betty either. She had her instructions. She was dumped back at NASA. She had to continue her training for her ISS mission. If John wasn't willing to divulge the propulsion system to her using soft tactics then the last resort had to be a confrontation in space itself.

'What is happening to me?' she whispered through the tears which the shower failed to wash away. John had left by the time she emerged. She tried going over the confrontation with him. *Why did it all happen like that. Could it have been because of a misunderstanding over some silly dreams. I'm not normally like this. He must be furious. If only he would open up everything would sort itself out. Why is he being such a stubborn man?* She'd forgotten one of John's most prominent character traits; he never gives up. A name came unbidden into the hazy recollection of her latest dream.

Yuri. She tried to think hard. Had she ever met a man called Yuri? No. *He sounds Russian. I don't know any Russians. There are a few of them on the ISS. That's what it is - just my imagination playing tricks. It must be pretty crowded up there. I wonder where they sleep. There couldn't be much privacy. What do they do when they get frisky?*

She'd finished drying herself off careful not to aggravate the most painful bruises. That distraction was all her brain needed to regurgitate some words with which to torture her; *I don't want this. I don't want this - I don't want ...*

The image of a hirsute Yuri moving on top of her hit her hard. She buckled at the knees needing the towel rail for support.

Betty ended up late on her first day back for the continuation of her astronaut training. It was around lunch time but John wasn't at the cafeteria, although she checked just in case. *I don't want to see him - I want to see him - no - damn!* It turned out to be a morning of theory so she didn't miss any of the procedures in the afternoon necessary for survival in space. The transfer from the shuttle into the ISS docking bay was potentially the most hazardous. Each person had to be individually tested on their uptake of safety procedures within the ISS living quarters. The day dragged on late into the afternoon, by which time her stomach was rumbling. No breakfast and no lunch had made it difficult for Betty to concentrate as the day wore on.

I'll have to get something before going home. What if John is at the cafeteria? She steeled herself for another possible confrontation. *I'll try to be nice.* She repeated it several times as she approached the facility. From a distance she picked out someone near one of the tables. It might have been John. On getting closer she saw it wasn't. She recognised the maintenance man from the other day when John made a mess all over himself. She heard his voice *Is okay, Da* - in that unforgettable deep, clear baritone.

Betty slipped into a subtle rift in reality finding herself standing behind the man as he finished picking up somebody's left overs. He seemed in a hurry for he turned so suddenly Betty couldn't get out of his way in time.

'Sorry - so sorry,' she heard herself say like the last time.

Again came the deep baritone reply 'Is okay, Da.'

'Yuri?' she blurted out.

'Da.' He had seen her before, with the idiot man who made a mess all over himself. He remembered her very well. 'You with man. He spilt coffee.'

'Yes,' Betty squeaked. 'Sorry, so sorry,' she repeated and turned in a daze. *This is not possible. Simply not possible. How did he get into my dream?*

Dr Kathleen watched the surveillance vid with deeply conflicting thoughts as John and Betty confronted each other resulting from her successful manipulation of his dreams.

'What *is* your problem?' asked Armbruster, concerned about his assistants reactions, which have become more obvious.

She didn't feel entirely confident Armbruster would understand her growing reticence in manipulating John's dreams. Instead she uttered an observation; a quite valid observation. 'It looks to me like there are two of us playing this game. Did you see how Betty was behaving. When she first appeared with John she was nothing like this. I'm convinced ESA must be using similar technology to ours to control Betty. And we both know why they would be doing it.'

That pushed Armbruster's thoughts onto another track. 'So what are you suggesting?'

'Would it be feasible to come clean with John and tell him how much of a danger Betty is to his wellbeing if she doesn't get what she wants?'

'No. Listen. Here's the reality of the situation. If it's not Betty the ESA will send someone else - somebody we may not be able to keep an eye on. What if they decide to harm John? We cannot take the risk of losing his expertise. He now knows more than his father. The polarity reversal idea was John's. It's the only thing that will make this propulsion system work.'

'Can't you see what's happening already?' Dr Kathleen countered. Perhaps women are more aware of these things than men. 'Didn't you see his reaction when he saw Iluska? And what about Betty and the Russian maintenance man. She could barely contain herself.'

'Again ... all we have to do is prevent John from leaking the technology to Betty.'

'What if he gets so exasperated he finds someone else to fall in love with, maybe even say things he shouldn't?'

It was a consideration Armbruster had in his mind all along. Just another reason to keep Betty close, but not close enough for John to spill the beans. 'We'll deal with that if it happens.'

It wasn't the kind of conversation Dr Kathleen wanted. *I'm glad I didn't come right out with it. I'm going to talk to John - privately. What we are doing to him isn't only impacting him emotionally it's also beginning to have an effect on his work. That's exactly what we don't want.*

'If you say so. But I suggest we give him a break; don't seed his dreams for a few days. Let's see if the relationship between him and Betty stabilises.' She knew it wouldn't. Her female intuition was crystal clear after seeing him with Iluska, and Betty with Yuri.

A week had elapsed since John left the house. He and Betty had managed to evade each other at the training centre; John by spending the majority of his time in the lab with Peter, and Betty by starting later in the day and finishing later in order to stagger their schedules. This meant they could go to the cafeteria at carefully chosen times.

'It's for you.' Peter passed the coms to John. It was late and they were still working. 'By changing the energy density of the electrical field around the graviton dispersal funnel we should be able to do more than just cancel the gravitational effect of the energy density of matter, in our case such as the mass of the Earth.' John, deeply immersed in the convoluted implications of the theory, didn't want to be disturbed.

'If it's Betty, I'm not here.' He couldn't think who else would want to call him.

'Dr Kathleen.'

'What could she possibly want at this hour?' It was close to 1:30 in the morning.

'John here. What's so urgent?'

I don't want any more women in my life. Not that I actually have any at this moment - he mused. Betty was a painful memory and Iluska an equally annoying distraction.

'As soon as you can, in my office. Tonight.'

John didn't have much of a choice. Dr Kathleen was responsible for his physical fitness and his readiness for the trip. *It must be something extremely serious if she wants to see me right now. I'm feeling perfectly fine. I hope it's not something which could stop my Titan trip.*

'I'll be back as soon as I can Dad. Please go over those formulas we've been working on. See if you can spot the anomaly.'

John used an electric scooters to go to the medical building. On the way he could see the cafeteria lights were still on. Probably cleaning staff doing their job. He knew he'd been a bit slack with his fitness training lately. The lab work took priority. There was plenty of time to get back into shape before the test flight. *It can't be my heart and I'm not overweight.* He couldn't work out why the interview was necessary and why it had to be in such a hurry like a clandestine spy operation.

He took the steps two at a time to the consulting room to prove to himself the old ticker was still in fine shape.

'Come in John. Best if you sit down. I'll come straight to the point.'

'I'm alright, aren't I Doc?'

'Please don't interrupt. This is hard for me to say as it is.'

'Oh no - it's my heart!'

'No - no. It's your dreams John.'

That took him by surprise. *Why would she want to talk about my dreams?* 'What? Are you serious?'

'We know about your dreams. Oh dear, I'm not saying this very well.'

'You know what's in my dreams? That's not possible.'

'Yes it is. We know because we have been manipulating them.'

'Nooooo!'

'Wait. Listen to me. Betty is trying to get you to tell her about your research into the new propulsion system.'

'I know. I thought it was just a crazy game.'

'No John. She's a spy for the European Space Agency.'

'What's that got to do with my dreams?'

John paced up and down in her office. The whole scenario didn't make sense to him. He stopped suddenly in front of Dr Kathleen trying to think what question to ask next. She pre-empted his enquiry.

'We had to make sure you could resist whenever she tried to get you to talk. The ESA have been controlling her dreams so she would put the right kind of pressure on you and to keep up that pressure.'

That was too much for John. He was tired and he was confused about his sudden interest in Iluska. He was uncertain about all the odd things happening between himself and Betty.

'No. I don't believe you. You're interfering in my life.

How do I know what's real anymore?' He turned and walked out without bothering to close the door.

'Well - that didn't go as I expected.' *In all probability we're both in big trouble. I hope he doesn't do something rash.*

'Angus, you're not going to like this.'

At the end of the following day Armbruster and Silverman met out of working hours. In a more relaxed atmosphere the two men resorted to first names. It seemed to make some of the serious conversations easier. Although the content of their discussion on this occasion would be anything but conducive to relaxation.

'Why not James? I hope it's not about our golden boy.'

'I'm afraid it is Angus,' replied Armbruster, 'actually, it's more about Kathleen.'

Angus went to his office bar, prepared two scotches. His face hardened as he handed a tumbler to James. *If he wants to talk about Kathleen it'll be about John.*

'Spill it.'

'I think she's going to tell him everything,' said Armbruster, taking a long swig of his drink.

Silverman was not the type of person to have knee jerk reactions in any crisis situation. This could not yet be classified as a crisis. It might become one if anything prevented John from completing the project. There was a lot more at stake than even Silverman realised.

'Let's keep a lid on this for the time being. I'll put our men Matthews and Johnson onto it. If we have to we'll confine John to the base. Betty has outlived her usefulness. I'll step up security in case ESA tries to infiltrate in some other way.'

Silverman almost drained his glass of scotch. He sat opposite Armbruster. He looked the doctor straight in the eye trying to gauge the man's resolve.

'Are you prepared to deal with Kathleen?'

It took two days for John to sort out his thoughts. And they had turned out to be a Gordian knot of problems. Betty; his past and present life with her. Iluska; how to deal with an attraction he couldn't understand - and his reality being so easily manipulated by Dr Kathleen. To complicate matters he very quickly realised she wasn't the core of the problem; it was NASA and his special project.

What I want is to go to Titan, he said to himself before contacting Dr Kathleen for another meeting. *That's all I want.*

Reality
Through
The
Fish   Bowl

John had made up his mind.

Only one thing mattered; Titan. 'Do we have to meet after midnight again, in your office?'

'Not unless you want the world to know our secret.' *At last. I thought he'd do something drastic.*

'It seems so melodramatic,' he said into his phone.

'This is a serious matter John. You've got your head buried in the project. You wouldn't know what's happening in the real world.' She'd hit a nerve and could see him flinch on the little screen.

In the early hours of the next morning John furtively glanced around at every shadow as he made his way to Dr Kathleen's office. One or two of the shadows seemed to move. *Just my imagination. This is all too unreal, worse than my dreams.*

Everything was exactly the same in her office. Why shouldn't it be? No one knew about the *private* meetings between the two of them. Everything was meant to be the same.

The surveillance bugs didn't have little flashing red lights to make their presence obvious.

On stepping into the office John began without a greeting. 'I've made up my mind. Only one thing matters to me.' Dr Kathleen waited to hear if this was a bad thing or a good thing. 'I want to finish the propulsion system and I want to use it to go to Titan.'

Dr Kathleen breathed a sigh of relief. At least the core of the issue had not changed. 'What about ...'

'Oh that. You mean Betty. There's no way she's going to get anything out of me - with or without your messing about with my dreams - which by the way, I want you to stop; immediately.' To make the point John leant in close to her face, his pupils dilated, 'Immediately.'

What he didn't say worried Dr Kathleen much more. Would he keep the secret? 'How do you feel about Iluska?' Not a question she really wanted to ask.

'Seriously?'

'Yes. This is important.'

John smiled, making a joke of the situation. 'You mean if I'm going to tell this girl, who is nothing more than a waitress in a cafeteria, all about how to use ant-gravity technology through controlling the polarity of gravitons, after a night of mad passionate lovemaking? Sure, why not? I'm sure she'd understand everything, don't you think?' He forced a little laugh. 'I'm sure she's well connected.'

There is a great deal of danger in voicing unbidden thoughts bubbling up out of the depth of one's being. That's how Betty ended up being a spy for ESA. She had no idea a random statement to her mother out of the blue while she was still an adolescent would become her reality.

John's unstable emotional condition might turn out to be an issue, and if it did it would be because of Dr Kathleen. *Maybe I should have waited a little longer before telling him.*

He's probably right though about the Russian girl.

His meeting didn't entirely go according to plan. The whole point of it was to impress Dr Kathleen of his unshakable resolve about Titan, and to get her to stop manipulating his dreams. That bit about Iluska and a night of mad passionate love wasn't on the agenda. Worryingly the other issues slipped to the background while Iluska filtered to the front of his thoughts.

'Armbruster, in my office, now!' growled Silverman.

It wasn't even 9 am when he extended the invitation.

Armbruster had to leave a dozen physical examinations waiting as he rushed to the summons; his virile, naked trainee astronauts, both men and women, forced to have to deal with a young, inexperienced woman doctor examining them.

'You said you were ready to deal with Dr Kathleen.' The accusatory tone did not sit well with *James*.

'I did. She's under surveillance now, *Angus*.'

'So I see. Listen to this.' Silverman ran the entire conversation between John and Dr Kathleen for his benefit.

Armbruster closed his eyes trying to visualise the scene - trying to imagine what needed to be done to stabilise the situation.

'Iluska can tell the difference between tea and a coffee. That's all,' he said. This was an effort to calm himself more than to convince Silverman of the harmless threat from John, who was clearly under stress. 'It can't seriously be considered to be a threat. That peasant from South Eastern Siberia couldn't possibly know anything about John or what he is doing.' He tried to emphasize the improbability to Silverman.

'You think so?'

Angus showed James how John and Iluska behaved when they met in the cafeteria. Then reverted to the situation at hand. 'Kathleen's obviously told him about the treatment. You were right about that.'

'My psychological assessment, if you're interested,' said James holding his ground, 'is that John is so dedicated to his trip to Titan it's unlikely anything could deter him from completing it; neither Betty or Iluska. He'll complete the propulsion system and he'll go to Titan. Don't worry about that.'

'I don't doubt it for one minute. I just don't want him telling the rest of the world about it.'

'So you think it would be safer if John transferred his romantic interest from Betty to Iluska.'

'Yes,' came the considered response from Silverman. 'Instruct Kathleen to help John move in that direction. I don't care if she has to lie to him, but she must continue with the AIDA seeding to that end.'

That night and the next couple of nights John had random dreams free of terrorist nano-bots agitating in his neural backyard. Dr Kathleen refused to push him. John could have a few nights relief at least. Even at his father's place he slept better, his work progressed to the point where he could see the first test flight becoming a reality. He felt much better overall. He began to relax into a false sense of normality. It takes more than a few nights of restful sleep to change one's view of a distorted reality which had almost become the status quo for John.

'I think I'll go home and see what's happening with Betty,' he told Peter. It was Friday night. He had the next two days free if he wanted time off work. The adjusted graviton polarity reversal software had been uploaded to the test craft in the large hangar laboratory. It would do no harm to approach the next phase with a clear mind and go over everything with the team on Monday before activating the system.

Betty's bruises had mostly healed. She had time in John's absence to assess her situation. J'Ark had not recalled her, giving her respite from the trauma of her unorthodox training methods. The last controlled dream was days ago. Betty had to endure seeing flashes of images of John speaking with Iluska, though briefly, and seeing him suddenly turning away from the woman in a rush to get away. Yet the residual effect of the encounter, as innocent as it may have been, left unpleasant, vengeful thoughts in Betty's mind.

I suppose it had to be expected after the way I treated him last time. Thoughts of reconciliation mingled with her concern she still hadn't managed to break through his mental brick wall to get the information. *How many more chances will I get from Aksel and J'Ark?*

In spite of her determination not to stir things up a naughty little gremlin put words into her mouth when she saw him standing in front of the open door on Saturday morning.

'Did you have breakfast, at the cafeteria?' As soon as she'd said it guilt threw an image of Yuri at her. She looked down at the ground noticing right away he didn't have his bag with him. 'Sorry. Want to come in?'

'Hi Betty.' His normal *BB* greeting to her had vanished. *This isn't looking good.* They must have had the same thought because Betty apologised again. He stepped inside. The awkward moment of not giving each other the usual hugs and kisses passed quickly, though not unnoticed.

'Coffee?' She went directly to the kitchen to make it without waiting for an answer. He followed, sat at the small kitchen table and waited. Betty turned. She didn't sit. Something about sitting at a small table with just two chairs brought out an odd feeling of discomfort.

'We need to talk,' John said. He looked at her closely. No bruise from my whack across her face ... another dream moment leaking into his reality. *She actually looks more like the Betty I used to know.*

'Yes.' Then an afterthought, 'What about?' Again that gremlin ... 'Yuri?' she added after a moment. In her confusion and the conflicting misinformation being fed into her dreams she didn't realise John knew nothing about Yuri. He'd only alluded to an anonymous person she might have been looking at once during an argument they had at the NASA cafeteria.

'Who is Yuri?' John was no slow witted hillbilly. The creative mind will make connections between unrelated bytes of data in a flash. His flash was *Iluska*, for no other reason than her being a Russian also.

'No one you know.' Betty responded far more quickly than was natural. 'You want to tell me about your work?'

'Yes - er, no. And, and now that you mention work tell me about Yuri.'

'Well in that case I want to know about Iluska.'

There it was. The cat had managed to escape out of Schrödinger's box. It was sitting right there in front of them on the table sharpening its claws.

'Right. Right.' The project - Titan. *Keep your mind on the priorities.* As much as the image of Iluska kept pushing itself in front of his eyes John still had the presence of mind to try and control the direction of this encounter. It was beginning to look less and less like an amicable solution would present itself to the serious gulf that had developed between them. *But I love this girl. I've loved her all my life. What in blazes is going on?* 'Can we start with all the bruising I saw a week ago? Where did they come from?'

'My trainer. He gets rough sometimes.'

'This hasn't got anything to do with you going up to the ISS has it?' 'Not exactly. Part of my job as Interplanetary Security Consultant.'

No harm in my telling him that.

'When did you get promoted? Before or after you attacked me in the VR game?'

'Better that job than to be a chicken farmer.'

The conversation gathered momentum like a tropical cyclone. They always left destruction in their wake.

'That's what you wanted to do, John.'

'Your dreaming Betty. I said no such thing.'

'Yes you did. You told me after coming in from repairing the chook pen.' That made her think. *Did he? or was it only a dream? I've had too many weird dreams lately.* 'Was Iluska just a dream?'

She saw him clench his jaws. *That was no dream. I saw the woman at the cafeteria. I saw him eyeing her off.*

John couldn't deny it. Nothing had happened between himself and the waitress. All he knew was her name - and he knew she was Russian. He hit back.

'Talking about dreams - what about Yuri? John remembered the brief encounter between the maintenance man and Betty when he dropped his lunch. It didn't mean anything at the time, but now he remembered the lingering look between the two of them. And the man certainly sounded like a Russian.

'So - I've had some bad dreams. Haven't you?' Betty diverted.

John considered that in light of what he'd found out from Dr Kathleen about being manipulated. *Maybe Betty is being influenced as well.* 'When have you been having, shall we say, unusual dreams?' He had to ask.

She looked at him, puzzled. *Is it possible all these problems between us, these twists in our perceptions of reality are nothing more than bad dreams. My last dream, with Mum, that was definitely strange. She's always happy to see me.*

Betty was still in deep thought when John confided in her about something important. Something which dramatically changed his attitude to certain things.

'BB - I have to tell you this. You might be involved in some way as well - I don't know.' Betty's attention sharpened at being called BB again. 'I've been told my dreams have been manipulated. I've been having the kind of dreams they've been wanting me to have. Maybe someone is doing the same to you.'

'Is that so. And why would *they* want you to be dreaming about that woman Iluska? Tell me that!'

Against The Laws of Nature

'I don't trust you anymore,' announced John.

'I can tell you that much. Not after all the things that've happed.' He ignored the mention of Iluska. 'You just don't let up trying to get me to tell you about my work. Why are you doing this? Who is making you do it?'

Her face seemed to harden, possibly because of the trust issue.

It's hopeless. I can't get through to her.

As soon as she brought up Iluska again she could see the change in his face. John had made up his mind about something. *He doesn't trust me. He doesn't trust me. Damn, damn, damn.* That hit Betty hard, but not the way it should have from a person she'd been with for so many years. *What am I going to say to J'Ark? What am I going to say to Aksel? Damn!* She wasn't thinking about her relationship with John since their time together from adolescence. She was thinking about her career, about what would happen to her since she'd effectively failed her mission. *Maybe there's some other way I can get it out of him.*

John kept talking but she'd missed most of it, being too absorbed in herself.

' ... If I say anything about the propulsion system to anybody it won't be you.' She heard that part. He continued. 'I don't know what world we've been living in but it sure seems pretty much an alien reality from where I'm seeing it now.'

A long silence stretched between them. John's latent animosity remained under his sudden silence. Betty had finally sat down. She'd definitely said things she should not have. At least it was all out in the open, whether real or unreal.

Both coffees remained untouched.

John was looking out the window over her head, Betty minutely examined the grain of their wooden kitchen table. Knots of imperfection everywhere. A reflection of true reality.

'Are you looking at the cows?' she asked after a long pause. 'Do you still want to be a farmer with chooks and cows and pigs and ...?

'No. That was a dream, a fantasy. I can't see you being enthusiastic about collecting eggs and cleaning dung off your boots.'

'So that's it then?'

'Maybe,' though he felt certain their relationship had run its course.

Nothing had been resolved. Neither of them understood the extent to which AIDA had influenced their perceptions of reality. Consequently they couldn't decide on a course of action to get back to the relationship they had when they first moved to Houston.

John left, as an unwelcome stranger might leave after having overstayed their welcome.

'I need to discuss something with you J'Ark.' Betty wasted no time contacting the woman who'd been the engineer behind all her problems, although Betty didn't know that.

'Yes you do.' J'Ark thought it would be all about Betty's relationship problems and what she should do about it in relation to her assignment.

'I've been having extremely concerning dreams and ...' J'Ark immediately cut her off.

'I'll see you tomorrow,' she said and terminated the connection. This was a matter needing to be discussed face-to-face.

'Understand this - you will remain at NASA to complete your training to go to the ISS. You have yet to complete your mission regardless of how disturbed your sleeping might be.' Unlike Dr Kathleen this woman had no empathy for someone who was no more than a tool.

'But my dreams. They seem to be all mixed up. I know when I'm awake and when I'm asleep, yet ...'

'I told you at the beginning what your problem was - you can't tell the difference between reality and dreams. Pain, that's what makes the difference.'

Betty's discussions with John had created so much confusion she didn't know how to respond to something that seemed to make so much sense.

'Go back to your house and get yourself a bed of your own.'

Maybe that's exactly what I should do. Maybe that'll make John think about things a little differently.

J'Ark cut into her thoughts abruptly with something completely unexpected. 'What you do with Yuri is up to you. Don't forget - he's a Russian.'

John stood in front of Armbruster, Silverman and Dr Kathleen.

'Sit, Sit John,' Armbruster invited with strained conviviality. Dr Kathleen was already seated and had only glanced at John once when he first entered.

Silverman began. 'Your controlled dreams have been an attempt to ensure your mental stability if and when you go on the extended journey to Titan.'

'If I go to Titan?'

'You must face reality John. Many things can happen between now and the launch. The most important being to get the propulsion system working reliably. Wouldn't you agree?'

'Of course.' John stole a look at Dr Kathleen whose face continue to be impassive. It had to be. She couldn't betray herself in front of Armbruster and Silverman.

Armbruster's mechanisations had been concerned with fortifying John's mind against infiltration by his childhood sweetheart, not the reason he gave John. He saw no reason to desist from that endeavour. However he did recognise an interesting opportunity to strengthen John's resilience by channelling his emotional involvement to another possible love interest thereby diluting the pressure from Betty's endeavours.

'We want you to go back to your house. See how Betty settles for a while as you become busier with your work,' Armbruster couldn't have said it more directly. Even more poignantly he said, 'If you want to pursue a friendly relationship with Iluska at the same time that's entirely up to you.'

It took Dr Kathleen by surprise considering her covert involvement so far in that realm. Her concern surfaced immediately about what John had said to her in jest. 'John, take care and stay alert,' she warned him.

John made faces at the suggestion Iluska could play a part in his life. It seemed completely unnatural these people should even suggest it while at the same time telling him to go home to Betty.

'I'll tell you people something ... When I get to Titan I might decide to stay there just to get away from you lot. Now, if there's nothing else you want to throw at me I have work to do. I'll even learn to breath methane just to get some peace.'

As he closed the door on the way out Silverman reminded Armbruster and Dr Kathleen, 'Lie to him if you have to but keep the AIDA treatment going. He can have his rest on Titan - if he makes it. We're only interested in using his knowledge until we get there.'

Iluska was running behind cleaning up after a busy day at the cafeteria. They'd only just started getting ready to close when a late customer arrived. He sat down with purpose fully expecting to be served. With hands on her hips she went up to the table to tell him they were closed.

'Privnyet tovarishch, hello comrade.' Popovich didn't bother to look up at her. He didn't see her utter amazement though he could see her arms suddenly drop. *Comrade* was no longer in general use except by the military. Before Iluska could gather her wits the *comrade* warned, 'We have to speak English in this country.'

'Hello,' Iluska squeaked. She was alone. Yuri had already gone home to start their dinner. 'Vat you vant?'

'We will talk about that another time. Bring me espresso.'

Popovich, the hulking Russian gorilla who seemed to enjoy pushing Betty around so much, hadn't finished with Betty. Being a member of the KSB, once known as the KGB, he'd been quietly going about his work in the European Space Agency mostly at the beck and call of J'Ark. Her association with UNSC fitted his undercover status seamlessly with his role as trainer of ESA operatives.

Betty was easy. Iluska might be harder. She was an innocent. But what the Russians had in mind for her wasn't the ability to kill with a single blow. Yuri he could handle easily enough if he got in the way of what needed to be done.

Popovich's orders came straight from the Director of Counter-intelligence. 'Time for Iluska to do something for Mother Russia. See to it.'

Popovich from Irkutsk, Siberia though not Iluska's cousin but definitely a compatriot. He knew the country where Iluska came from and what kind of people lived in Eastern Siberia. He'd arrived at NASA as part of the ESA away team to help with the ESA astronaut contingent. His intel for the special assignment suggested he may not have to work hard on the girl to get her to form a relationship with John, with a purpose in mind other than romance.

Apples should not fall up into the tree.

Yet that's exactly what John and his father had been working on for some years. It went against all the laws of nature that gravity should become a tool of repulsion as well as attraction.

Their test vehicle, constructed to scale, did not resemble an apple or indeed a sphere. It was a perfect cube.

'Do you realise my boy what we are about to do is not possible,' grinned Peter as the final checks were taking place on the test vehicle.

'If that's the case Dad what is a six meter cube doing in front of us?'

'Just sitting on the platform until we release it.'

A hundred and twenty technicians and scientists gathered in the control room to manage and observe the first test. Actually operating Cube #1 wasn't complex. Understanding the quantum labyrinth mechanics behind it needed many intellects, organic and artificial, to perfect its propulsion system.

'Have the atomic caesium clocks been synchronised?' John was referring to the one in the Cube and the one in the control centre. Gravitational time dilation may well have an effect on the life expectancy of an astronaut. An unknown quantity in relation to anti-gravity propulsion systems which could conceivably achieve the speed of light. He need not have been fussing about that during the last minute of instructions. Everyone knew their job.

His and Peter's role was to watch what would happen - and understand it.

Is it possible for a climax to be anticlimactic? After so many years of experiments and failures they had finally arrived at the critical stage to see if the expenditure of the time by so many dedicated scientists was justified. Success was considered to be as revolutionary as the invention of the wheel.

The hum of voices in the control centre finally ceased. All eyes turned to Peter. The technology was his brainchild. He had dedicated his life to realizing this dream. He had earned the right to flick the switch.

'Launch,' Peter said without any histrionics.

Media were prohibited from observing this moment. Earth's population could not possibly cope with having a basic tenet of the religion of science turned up-side-down. Peter and John had not taken their eyes off the Cube for the last ten minutes. Perhaps it was a peculiar form of eye strain that comes with concentrating too long on a single object making them doubt what their eyes witnessed next.

In the deafening silence in the control room no one noticed the Cube move at all. Its mirror polished outer surface reflections appeared unchanged.

Lift altitude was set to only three millimetres - not a height difference easily discerned by the human eye.

'It's gone!' shouted one of the technicians.

'Abort! Abort! Abort!' the shout went out from the head controller.

'Aborted!' responded the launch technician. The cube settled noiselessly reducing the three millimetre altitude to zero, the motion once again unnoticed.

The one millimetre thick aluminium foil, only an area of two square metres, had disappeared. It was tensioned against the bottom edge of the Cube so it would slide under the Cube if the Cube rose off the surface.

Pandemonium broke out in the control centre as people danced about, shouting, hugging each other - overflowing champagne bubbling congratulations. The utter anticlimactic climax was overwhelming.

'Well - that's that then,' Peter said infuriatingly calmly as he turned slowly towards his son. Celebrations didn't stop in spite of Peter's statement. Was he disappointed or just relieved his life's work succeeded? How could he be so dispassionate?

'What just happened? Did it fail?' John thought perhaps a peculiar effect of reducing the insulation of the gravitons had destroyed the aluminium foil.

'Don't look so concerned son. The apple has fallen back up into the tree. The most natural thing in the world.'

'The polarity reversal worked!' John still couldn't believe it. 'We have to check.' He never could understand his father's sense of humour.

The entire crew spilled out of the control room into the main body of the hangar where the Cube now rested quietly as if nothing at all had happened. They surrounded this magnificent spacecraft as the overhead crane inched its way over the top of it. The lifting process felt to be more exciting than the launch itself. Tediously the suction grips were attached to the four sides of the Cube. A quiet whirr of the crane motors put all nerves on edge. Breathing had stopped until the Cube had been lifted a full meter off its platform.

The aluminium foil lay there unwrinkled, undamaged.

Again it was Peter who spoke first. 'There you are. When do we go for a flight?' He asked John as though the most natural thing in the universe had happened, with no effort at all. 'Anyone got an apple?'

John should have been elated, he should have been bubbling out of his skin. Perhaps the moment had been too overwhelming for him to realise the true implications of what he and his father had achieved. Between them they had created a layer of reality that had not previously existed on their Earth, perhaps not even in the entire known universe.

Maybe he was shaking with excitement somewhere deep inside himself. But the reality he wanted to pursue was to be able to show Betty everything. That was a reality John knew without having to dwell on it, one which had escaped all realms of possibility.

It could never happen.

The   Bears
From   Siberia

I could just ignore him, thought Iluska.

After the early morning breafast crowd had dissipated Popovich appeared at a corner table of the cafeteria and waited.

'Tovarishch.' Iluska greeted him flat voiced. She'd noticed him the moment he arrived. An uneasy feeling came over her as she went up to his table. She told herself she could ignore him. Not true. His statement at the first meeting sounded like a veiled threat. When a thing like that came from a *comrade* it could not be ignored. Whatever he wanted she had to know so she could tell Yuri.

'English,' he replied, sounding like an admonishment for her failure to remember and obey.

'Vat you vant?' Iluska didn't look directly at him as she wiped down the table, trying to behave naturally. 'Espresso. Bring it out to the patio.' Popovich got up and went outside.

Under cover with the dappled shade of nearby trees the patio seemed like a pleasant enough space. That depended entirely on the state of mind of those who went out there.

Iluska's apprehension became so strong her mind drifted back to Yartsevo. *Why couldn't we have stayed at home? We should have stayed home. Yuri could have built another house for us. We would have been safe there.* The horrible reality of the deaths of her parents, her friends and the destruction she lived through had faded even over the short time she'd been in America. Perhaps she had not realised until that moment their past lives could never be recovered. Tears welled up impatient to burst through her fear of this man.

'Iluska, wake up, what's wrong with you?' Another waitress asked. Iluska blubbered something through the cascading tears needing only a human voice to be released. 'You have a customer - hurry up. What is wrong with you?'

Her hands continued shaking after delivering the espresso.

'Sit, sit,' the Russian bear urged with a faux friendly smile. 'I have something to ask of you. Nyet, nyet - it is Mother Russia who asks you.'

Iluska glanced around hoping no one was watching as she sat on the edge of the chair. 'I tell husband, Yuri.'

'Yes, yes, yes. Of course. Yuri will not be a problem. But ... you are not yet married.' Whether he meant to upset Iluska or make her feel somehow inadequate didn't matter. It achieved both those things. She waited to hear what else he had to say. She had to. Her willpower and courage would not let her do otherwise.

Popovich finished off the last of his espresso in silence then stood to go, which surprised Iluska. He mentioned as he turned, with only the slightest emphasis, 'You know a man called John, da?' He neglected to say, probably on purpose what it was Mother Russia actually wanted of her.

The blush Popovich didn't see wasn't the same as the one she reserved for Yuri when he came to visit her in Yartsevo.

The astronaut training centre at NASA had the most extraordinary facilities not only for the training but for all the experimental work going on to push the boundaries of technological development for space exploration.

The cafeteria had become a microcosm of intrigue, informal meetings, exchange of ideas and budding relationships.

Yuri was fastidious. His previous life had taught him to attend to all the little details of existence. It could mean the difference between life and death in the Siberian wilderness. Conditions around the training centre were not as precarious as his past life environment. Nevertheless he carried out his maintenance duties with the same mindset.

He had noticed Betty more than once. The second time when John brought her for a sightseeing tour. Why he noticed her and not the hundreds of other women who frequented the place ... well, he never asked himself.

'Oh my stars!' Betty whispered almost loud enough for others to hear. She caught a glimpse of Yuri through the slightly open door of his maintence room on the side of the cafeteria as he started to change. Her senses lit up as the memory of his body odour percolated to the surface from their previous contrived accidental meeting. She heard his baritone voice in her head. She remembered the dream!

Completely self-conscious Betty reluctantly turned her gaze back to her lunch, not daring to continue watching in case he noticed. His sense of personal space, well tuned to predators who may have been been watching him in the past, felt a disturbance. Yuri glanced up, as one does, and saw the woman look away from him. *What she vant?* He asked himself, being somewhat dishonest with his true thoughts. *I will ask.*

She should have got up and walked away. Her legs refused to move. Her fingers dabbed at the crumbs still on the plate, ears alert to every sound. She should have looked up when she heard the other chair scrape the tiles.

She knew who it was.

'Me, Yuri. You?' Yuri sat. Both hands on the table in front of him. Hirsute arms bare, partially buttoned shirt more revealing.

'Betty.'

'So.' Now that he knew her name, which is what he wanted in the first place, the crystal clear waters of the tiny stream of change began to trickle downhill gathering momentum.

'You work here?' *Stupid question! What is wrong with me?*

'Da. You?' He seemed to be a man with very few words, or just efficient with his search engine.

'Trainee astronaut.'

'Is good. Important job. Me - I push broom. Plenty dust on moon.' That broke the ice instantaneously. They both laughed. The waters trickled on picking up speed.

It gave Betty the opportunity she needed to get away, whether she wanted to get away or not. Her other Russian was waiting for her to continue into the next phase of her physical training. Yuri jumped up energetically and completely naturally and unselfconsciously extended his hand for a handshake.

Betty took his hand. Her's got lost in the size of it. It was warm and soft and gentle. *Damn, damn, damn.*

At the end of the day she went home with turbulent thoughts. *I have a mission, I have a mission* - she kept saying to herself. *This situation is ridiculous. I have to put a stop to it.* As an afterthought John entered the equation - only as an afterthought. *What am I going to do about John?*

When John left the house last time things were very much up in the air between them. Neither of them could exercise enough self control at the time to come to some understanding of what the true reality of their relationship had become. Afterwards, during her discussion with J'Ark the woman had said two things which stood out ... Betty remembered them now. *I'll get my own bed. Yes, that's it.*

Maybe I'll sleep better. But she knew that wasn't the reason. A much more disturbing thing J'Ark said: 'What you do with Yuri is up to you. Remember - he's a Russian.' *So what - so is Iluska.* The lightning bolt struck hard and fast.

As far as Betty knew the only people interested in the anti-grav propulsion drive were NASA and the ESA.

Détente

'May I come home?' asked John.

Once again Betty and John found themselves facing each other at their front door. John badly needed a comfortable place to stay, to get away from his father and to get some sleep. Success with the propulsion system test came at a price. He was overworked. Peter continued the badgering of his son as he always had and he couldn't get good rest. Although some uneasiness had developed between himself and Betty he'd been convinced by Silverman to make an attempt to smooth things out with her.

'You look happy.' Betty seemed surprised. 'So what's happened in your life?' Perhaps it was a double edged question - like who's managed to make you happy? - but then again it sounded like a genuine question. John took it as such.

'It shows? A major breakthrough with the project.' In spite of his weariness John had a considerable sense of achievement.

'Do tell.'

'Can I come in?' he asked again, still holding onto the bag with his clothes in it. Betty saw it and stepped aside to let him in. They settled in the sitting room.

Everything appeared to be the same as when he left. 'It's all the same,' he remarked meaning the house although he'd not been absent for very long.

'Not quite.' Her expression made him think.

'Are we talking about the same thing?' They both realised the conversation was heading down two different runways.

'Alright,' Betty took the initiative. 'Without revealing any secrets what can you tell me about this breakthrough?'

Ah. A new tactic. Okay. John was bursting with incredible pride in the success of his concept. He desperately needed to share it with someone. Talking to the techs in the lab just wasn't the same. There were of course many things to check and adjust; like the storage chambers holding the gravitons. 'We had one most peculiar thing happen ... the cesium clocks went out of sync.'

'I'm no scientist Johnny boy. You'll have to use language I can understand.' It wasn't much but the soft approach elicited a tiny, tiny trickle of information.

'We put a clock in the Cube and one in the Control Centre. We adjusted them to be exactly the same before the experiment. They were different afterwards.'

'That is fabulous!' Betty exclaimed. 'Isn't it?'

'Well - yes, in a way because the propulsion drive worked. But we didn't expect this side effect. It could have serious consequences.'

'Like time dilation as in Einstein's theory of general relativity?'

'BB! You surprise me.'

'An astronaut about to go to the ISS has to learn many things,' she replied grinning.

'It turns out to be a major problem you see. We simply didn't know how changing the force of gravity is going to affect what happens in real life. Theoretically if I was to travel away from Earth for a long distance by the time I got back you'd be - well, dead. Reality for you and for me would be quite different.'

'It is now, isn't it?' Betty couldn't help herself, yet again.

John thought about it. Her statement had broken his flow of thought and had literally brought him back to Earth. *Yes, things are different. I don't think we can get back to where we were. It all started with that knife incident in the VR game, then all our stupid dreams. I'm sure she's been manipulated as well.*

But John didn't say any of that. 'I see all your bruising has healed. Are you getting plenty of rest?'

'Yes. And so will you. My room's over there now.' She pointed to the other side of the corridor away from where their bedroom was before, with the double bed. 'You can have the double bed.'

Popovich had become as much a part of the crowd at the astronaut training centre as the rest of the normal crew. Inevitably he and Silverman passed each other during the course of their routine day's activities, as did Yuri and Betty and John and Iluska. They all knew of each other. In unique ways their realities converged to create eddies in the fabric of their individual existences. These relationship vortexes imperceptibly carried every one of them to realms beyond their control. Through no mechanism other than a tenuous familiarity Iluska became less concerned about Popovich. After planting the initial seed he didn't put pressure on her.

'Hello,' Iluska greeted him as she had on numerous occasions lately when he ordered his espresso.

Each time she wanted to ask the all important question. This time she did as no other patrons were near his table. 'Vat Mother Russia vant from me?'

'Iluska, Iluska - no need to worry. It's such a simple little thing. It is something you have already done. You are friends with John. I can see it from the way you speak with him.'

Popovich had touched a nerve. He knew it and she knew it, only because that developing relationship was something more than a blossoming friendship between casual acquaintances. Other customers had arrived to sit at nearby tables so Iluska didn't get a chance to elaborate on the matter, not that she really wanted to.

Life in the house of John and Betty became quite boring for those two teams of watchers from NASA and the ESA.

J'Ark experienced a moment of elation when she examined the record of John and Betty discussing the results of the first test flight. It fizzled out so quickly it was hardly worth the effort to get hopeful. Stupid Betty just couldn't keep her emotions under control.

'Günter, I need you to do something special. Can you plant one or two interrogation techniques into her dreams? She's finally getting some results.'

'Something a little more subtle than wielding a knife at him?'

'Good man. Exactly.' She gave him a slap on the back.

Silverman and Armbruster had their own surveillance systems set up at the house. At least the incident settled their concern about John's belligerence when he was told what to do about his Betty relationship.

'I am not happy James,' Silverman made it quite clear he didn't appreciate their man starting to divulge details about the project. 'It's not much I know. There's no reason for him to say anything about the clocks for instance.'

Armbruster agreed. 'What do you expect me to do about it? I can't tie him to a chair and gag him.'

'No. Get Dr Kathleen to have a word with him about divulging national secrets etc. You know the drill.'

'You're not concerned about his growing relationship with the Russian woman?'

'No. She wouldn't understand what he's talking about. Besides, who would she tell?'

In the following months John and Betty both spent more time away from the house, often nothing to do with their training or John's work at the laboratory.

Both Yuri and Iluska finally developed a few friendships of their own as they became imbedded into life in a new world. For Iluska a couple of things emerged; Yuri seemed to have changed and of course there was John in her mind.

Iluska didn't know how Yuri could maintain his fitness. Life in Siberia did it most naturally. The comfort of city living; the food, transport and poor air quality began to show their effects on his physique, and from Iluska's observations also his state of mind. Was he going out to meet some of these new friends? Fortuitously his absences gave her a little extra freedom as well.

'I'm going out,' he announced again one day after work. No details, just - going out. Iluska wasn't the kind of girl to ask her man to account for himself. Her culture and her upbringing didn't encourage such behaviour towards men in general. She did notice his evening excursions had increased over the last few weeks. He'd always returned home smelling of perspiration - and was there a hint of another scent? Too elusive to dwell on it.

'Hello Betty,' he said as he ran up beside her on the athletics track.

'Yuri!' Her friendly tone made him feel quite welcome.

An easy conversation sprang up between them about nothing in particular, just day's events, progress with her training - the weather. They never spoke about John or Iluska. Those two people belonged to another reality.

After about twenty minutes and a few cooling down stretches they generally found a bench and continued their friendly banter, sitting close to one another. The few others out on the field didn't know them so the need to be discreet didn't arise, not like around the cafeteria. Their interactions there had dwindled to nothing more than an occasional nod.

John wasn't the kind of man to go window shopping. For Iluska downtown Houston was a threatening world of light and colour and activity and noise. She only got a tiny glimpse of it when she first arrived in Houston; being so completely intimidated she resolved never to go there by herself. Circumstances eventually compelled her to consider doing some important shopping. Clothes she received on arrival in America had outgrown their usefulness. Yuri always seemed to be too busy to take her anywhere after the novelty of their first few months in a new country began to wear off.

'Privet, Hello,' Iluska greeted John and brought him his black coffee, taking time to be extra attentive to the hygiene of his table.

'Hi Iluska.' He reached out to take the mug, feeling the warmth of her hand.

She started wiping down the other two chairs. After weeks of nervous little interactions the undeniable attraction between them couldn't progress very far in the public space. Besides, they were constantly on alert for Yuri or Betty. It made things difficult. She looked around after the lunch crowd had dispersed before moving closer to John so she could quietly ask the question. This was an enormous effort on her part, so much so she started blushing even before asking.

'John, I go shop after vork. You come, help?'

Never in his entire life had John looked into so many shop windows or entered so many womens' fashion boutiques. At first it all made his head spin with the incomprehensible variety of choices. Not something a man like himself could cope with. So John resorted to concentrating on Iluska enjoying herself.

He arrived home quite late that night. Betty was already in bed.

First thing in the morning she asked, 'Enjoy yourself last night? You were late getting home.'

'Yes. Things to do, people to see.' All true. She didn't delve deeper.

'Sleep well?' he countered.

'Yes actually. Would you mind if I asked you a question?'

Immediately John's mind jumped to women's fashions and how good some of it looked on Iluska. *She's going to ask me what I did. She's going to ask me why I was so late. She's going to ...*

'You called the thing a Cube,' Betty continued without waiting for him to agree to be interrogated.

The relief on his face surprised Betty. She didn't comment on it. His clothes had a slightly different aroma about them lately, more than just his aftershave.

Feeling so relieved he didn't have to account for himself he launched into more detail than was necessary. 'We call the spacecraft a Cube because it is actually a cube. It has mirror polished sides, all six of them. There are no port holes. And the walls are thick but hollow.'

Betty leaned a little closer to him at the kitchen table genuinely interested. *It's about time this nut cracked! Just don't push him. Take it easy. Let him ramble.* Techniques surfaced which seemed to come into her mind from nowhere. Tilting her head slightly and raising an eyebrow proved to be enough to keep him going.

'Actually the hollow sides are the tanks for holding the gravitons. You know what they are?' She feigned ignorance. 'Just like photons that transmit or propagate light, gravitons are like particles doing the same for the energy of gravity. Understand?'

'How extraordinary. So this is what makes your cube fly.'

John realised he'd come close to the limit of what else he could divulge. Perhaps he'd already gone a little further than he should have.

'This is becoming serious.' Silverman was beside himself as he tuned in to the surveillance feed. 'We have to stop him.'

'Outstanding!' Exclaimed J'Ark and Aksel together. 'It seems we've made the right decision to keep her on the job.'

J'Ark of course couldn't keep their progress to herself. Popovich had played such a prominent part in getting Betty's mind into the right shape she felt it almost mandatory for the man to be advised of the developing situation.

'Yes, this is excellent. Tell me - apart from general descriptions has he revealed any of the important operational details? Have we any specs on the process, any of the software?'

'No, not yet. You seem very keen Mr Popovich. I didn't realise you were so interested.' J'Ark's elation seemed to smooth out any suspicions she should have had about a trainer being so fascinated in such a complicated quantum scientific enterprise.

'Of course I am interested. We both know the importance of this technology - for the welfare of humanity.'

J'Ark let it go at that. He was right. He should be involved. *He's done a magnificent job on the woman. So had Günter for that matter. Pity I'll have to remove him from the equation. Günter knows far more than he should.*

A renewed sense of urgency forced Popovich to do something about moving the relationship along between Iluska and John. If John was about to divulge the details of his research it became imperative he did so in Russian's direction not to the ESA.

Iluska worked every day at the cafeteria, starting early and often finishing late.

'Nyet! Nyet! Nyet!' She was adamant and appalled by the suggestion made by Popovich. Worst of all was her sense of guilt. Hadn't she already flirted with John? Hadn't she already invited him out with her? They'd already had intimate meals together in Houston under the pretence of her going shopping. 'I vill not do this for you!'

Iluska stormed away from his table. She wasn't angry at him, she was angry at herself. The anger exacerbated by Yuri's neglectful behaviour towards her. He seemed to have lost interest in her, always finding excuses to go running or training or whatever it was he was doing so often. Then she remembered a number of occasions when she saw him stop his work to talk to the other woman; the one she used to see with John. *I don't see them together very much anymore.* They used to meet here so often she thought as she automatically began preparing the extra shot espresso. *Why should I be sitting at home alone while Yuri goes out enjoying himself?*

It started as a sense of guilt which quickly changed to disillusionment then to anger. *Popovich is not asking me to kill anybody. He just wants me to get some information. What's the harm in that. It's not like I have to marry John and spend the rest of my life with him.* Justification came easily - justification to balance her suspicions and her growing jealousy.

Iluska found herself back at Popovich's table, espresso in hand. *What has happened to my life?*

'What you do is not for me Iluska. Remember that.' Her hands went up to her hips. She glared at him daring him to continue. 'You don't have to sleep with him if you can get the information any other way. Up to you. But we must have everything you can get about his special project. You don't need to know what it is as long you get all the software, all the plans, all his documents.'

'Vat this *software?*'

Popovich seemed to have forgotten this girl came from the deep wilderness of Siberia. Of course she would not know anything about computers, how they are used, their storage systems and so on. He had to re-think his strategy. He couldn't leave it up to an uneducated person like Iluska. She wouldn't even know how to turn on a computer.

She remained standing there confronting him. He looked around the cafeteria mainly checking to see if Yuri was within sight of them.

'Sit, Sit. Calm down. This will not be hard for you. I will get everything we need. All you have to do is get me the access code to his laboratory.' Another puzzled look from Iluska. He sighed, almost beginning to doubt the wisdom of getting her involved in the first place. 'It's like a key, except it's a group of numbers - and we'll need his ID card. You know what that is. You've got one around your neck.' Her hand went up to touch her ID. *I've seen John wearing his all the time. What am I going to do? I like John. I don't want to get him into trouble.*

This clandestine reality for Popovich had become natural, normal, one which he understood very well. He'd completely forgotten how his life started back in Irkutsk as a garbage collector. His life now was like a different universe. So was Iluska's. She had yet to come to terms with it.

John rarely had his main meal of the day at home any more. Betty still cooked for herself, no longer making allowance for John. Life had settled down to an uneasy truce between them, living more as house mates than as partners. Lately few opportunities presented themselves where she and John could have discussed his work, prompted by Betty's devious expressions of interest. Her training had intensified sometimes requiring her to spend whole days at the training center. As had John's. His astronaut training coming to an end but not the work on the propulsion system. Some of his days stretched to the point where he didn't bother going home at all, chosing to crash at Peter's place.

The pretend domestic reality of their home life had morphed into a mixture of convenience and inconvenience. There was no more talk of milking cows or gathering eggs. Time simply dribbled away into the abyss of meaningless infinity as their lives' foci turned away from Earth to their immenent excursions into space. Their intimate relationship no longer involved VR games or sharing the details of synchronised dreams. Sleeping in separate bedrooms became the norm when they were both home. Betty's personal life, as well as John's had developed a new dimension, both with an international flavour.

On a particular Saturday morning, on one of those rare occasions when they found themselves face to face in the kitchen making their individual breakfasts, somehow the atmosphere between them widened the rift in their growing estrangement.

'Morning Betty. Been sleeping well? You look like you have.' That was true. AIDA manipulations had been suspended for the time being. Her training regimen had reduced intensity giving her a little more private time. And her emotional needs appeared to have been serviced somehow. John didn't know that for a fact, only suspected it from seeing her a little happier than normal.

'Yes I have. But I can see you've been working yourself too hard.'

'True. Yeah - it's been pretty intense with one thing and another.'

'You feel like telling me about it? Is it the Cube?'

'Yeah.' He paused wondering how much he could say. *Oh well, she already knows about the spacecraft. She probably wouldn't understand if I said anything else.* 'We've had another important breaktrough.' In fact John was itching to again tell someone and let out his excitement. *Why not Betty? What's she going to do? Run off to the Russians?* 'Remember How I explained to you about the hollow walls of the Cube?' Betty nodded, casting an encouraging smile in his direction, the kind of *private* smile John was quite familliar with from the past. He didn't consciously notice it, though it had the desired effect. 'We can now accurately contol how the Cube levitates. We can also control motion in full four directions.'

Betty stepped up to him giving him an enormous hug as if nothing in the world had disturbed their tranquillity during the year. 'I know how hard you've worked on this. I know how much of your life you have dedicated to realising your father's dream.' Betty stepped back to arm's length, looked deeply into his eyes, 'I am really, really pleased for you.'

Her sentiment sounded completely genuine. It must have felt that way to John because it embolden him to say what he said next.

'We're finished, aren't we.' It was a statement, not a question. 'You don't even try to pump me for details about my work anymore.' Betty just looked at him, the special smile she used to have only for him having found some happier place to be. She probably knew what was coming. 'You're seeing someone else, aren't you.'

'Aren't you?' Betty's voice didn't betray any emotion about the matter.

He couldn't tell if she was sad about it, or relived it had come out into the open.

Questions with self-evident answers didn't need to be responded to.

'So what do we do about it?' he asked.

The solution didn't need elaboration either.

The American Golden Butterfly

Cube #2 had more ample proportions than the small test model.

It was difficult to imagine a fifteen meter cuboid structure being able to lift itself off the ground without any visible means of doing so.

As well as the additional storage tanks for gravitons, with enhanced partitioning to enable better multi-directional control, it had accommodation for two people and provisions for several months.

This was designed as a survival unit as well as for testing the ant-gravity propulsion unit with the enhanced graviton polarity reversal capability.

To some extent John's new living quarters resembled the interior of Cube #2. It had instrumentation which could detect his body temperature and measure the extent of his pupil dilation, not just what he may say to any visitors at his studio apartment. Silverman had become paranoid after John and Betty split up.

'I want to be able to see the pimple on his arse! I want to see what he does 24/7. I want to hear everything he says, even to himself if he's sleep. Do I make myself clear Johnson?'

Dr Kathleen had to listen to her boss's raving, somewhat concerned about the extent to which John had effectively become a lab rat. Armbruster could see her face getting a pained look to it. 'And don't you give me any shit about his privacy. He gave up his right to that when he started to blab to that Betty woman of his.' He knew about Iluska, John's new romantic interest. As far as Armbruster was concerned the blonde Russian girl could barely speak English let alone understand any of John's work if he'd decided to tell her about it. 'I want him under control, total and absolute control. You make sure your AIDA bot hive keeps his mind from wandering all over the place.'

Dr Kathleen interrupted his raving. 'We don't need to interfere with him any longer. He's left Betty. She was your main concern.'

'I don't give a damn! Just do it. If you won't, I'll find someone who will.'

Dr Kathleen had always liked John, though no chemistry existed between them. *It's my job to look after him and all the other astronauts. I will not seed his dreams while he's out there in space with the test Cube.*

'One thing worries me my boy,' Peter voiced his concern about the effects of gravitational time dilation on spending extended time in space.

'Dad, you worry too much. We're only going out there for a short round trip. If we come back a few micro seconds younger than the rest of the world - well, that can't be a bad thing.' John was thinking about Peter and his advanced age. 'Anyway, we're not going far. Just zipping around a bit to test the steering - Right?' John seemed to be in a particularly good mood. As far as Peter was concerned it could only be because of one thing. He didn't know about Iluska, or how far the relationship had developed. But it had to be a new girlfriend. Peter couldn't relax.

'Come on Dad, Earthlings will not see us as aliens when we get back. It'll still be the same reality for all of us - Right?'

'And this is the Apollo 17 command module,' explained John to Iluska during a tour he'd organised for her. Betty hadn't been around for days. She must have gone back to Uni for some reason, John thought. Not that he would have been too upset if they'd bumped into her at the training Centre.

That's the way things were. Life changes. One simply has to live with the new reality. Their decision to separate was mutual.

'You say Apollo? Ve have butterfly at home called Apollo. This not look like butterfly,' Iluska giggled. John enjoyed Iluska's innocent pleasure in all these strange machines. 'Vat this machine do?'

When she first arrived at NASA she had tried to read the descriptions on a whole range of displays. It was all too fantastical, completely unbelievable. It was not possible to fly to the moon. She was firmly convinced of that in spite of everything she saw at the Space Centre.

'Inside this module there were three people when they went into space. NASA controlled everything from the Earth for the astronauts who landed on the moon.' He could see her lips part slightly and her eyes open wide in innocent wonderment.

'People have gone to Moon!?'

'Not only gone there but they came back home as well.'

'Vat vonderful butterfly!'

She jumped up in her excitement to give him a huge bear hug - a lingering bear hug.

John had not enjoyed himself so much for a very long time. Things had changed for the better since he and Betty had separated. He didn't even think much about her any more, or being slashed with a knife, or being interrogated at every opportunity. Iluska filled all his spare thoughts. *I'm going to do it.* In that moment he decided to show her another extraordinary butterfly.

It hadn't been too difficult to gain access to the hangar. It came down to a matter of timing. The main laboratory was generally empty between 2 am and 4 am. He'd often turned up to work on a difficult problem during those hours, so the guards didn't worry about his movements. Iluska, dressed as an assistant, whispered something as she watched him present his ID to the scanner and punch in his ten digit access code. Numbers in Russia were the same as in America - she only had to remember ten of them. She had a good mind. As he punched each number on the pad Iluska sang a Russian children's folk song to herself; Chunga-Changa. It rhymed with the numbers she watched. *Popovich was right. This part isn't hard at all.*

They had the place to themselves as John took her down a series of corridors to a long high balcony outside the control centre's windows. From up there it didn't seem as large, yet still magnificent in its simplicity. She couldn't take her eyes off it as they went down to ground level, one hand up to her mouth in disbelief.

'Look! Is me!' Iluska could see herself reflected in the golden skin of the American butterfly, for that's how she came to think of it; a wonderous golden butterfly capable of flying to the stars. 'Zis butterfly no wings, how it fly?'

If ever John needed a catalyst this was it. Betty would never have appreciated his excitement about the revolutionary propulsion system. Iluska would even if she didn't understand any of it.

Just seeing her enjoying the spectacle gladdened him.

'I will explain everything. You will not believe the magic.'

'I touch?'

Iluska ran a hand along the golden mirrored surface lost in wonderment. So did John feeling her joy at the touch.

They couldn't stay long in the laboratory. The guard patrol came by every hour. They just had enough time to sneak out, hand in hand, through the labyrinth of training facilities.

'Ven you vill tell me?' She cast her eyes down, blushing a little at the veiled suggestion. Instead of responding John took her by the hand to his vehicle. Iluska didn't resist. *I don't know where Yuri is. I don't know what he is doing. He never tells me anything anymore. But I know who he is with.* The justifications for things she was about to do came quickly and with immediate impact. Her temperature went up, logic could not stand in the face of such jealousy. Life was never this complicated in Yartsevo. Competition for partners was limited. So if a girl found a boy - that was it. The American reality with John swamped what was left of the memory of her old life.

They stopped on the way home at an all-night diner, oblivious to the time of the morning. She guessed where John was taking her but she was determined to enjoy this American adventure. It had not been an adventure with Yuri, only a struggle to survive in a strange country. They ordered, John asked for some fruit including a couple of apples.

'Take this apple Iluska, hold it up in the air and drop it.'

'It vill hit ground!' No one ever wasted food where she come from.

'It's okay. Do it over the table. What will happen?'

'It vill hit table.'

'Yes it will.' He grinned as she dropped it. 'Keep your hand in the air.'

This was the exciting part. 'Watch.'

Nothing happened. Iluska looked at him strangely. 'Vat?'

'What did you call the Cube? Oh yes, the American Butterfly. Imagine I have a little box and inside the box there is special magic that controls the American butterfly. When I turn the machine on inside the box the golden cube will fly up into the air, just as if the apple on the table flew back into your hand.' He lifted the apple bringing it back into Iluska's raised hand. 'This Cube has no rockets to make it fly, it has no wings but it can change gravity to work the other way around.' Iluska's hand still hovered in the air above the table as she looked at it and then at the apple, then at John.

'Zis not possible,' she said with absolute certainty John was only telling her a strange joke.

'This is true.' John said with unreserved conviction.

'Is true?' Iluska may not have been well educated but she could tell when a person was lying to her or telling a joke at her expense.

Seven o'clock in the morning in John's apartment showed nothing unusual on the surveillance record. Two people sleeping in bed. A completely normal situation regardless of who the two of them might have been.

Betty was away. Yuri was away.

It gave John and Iluska a little freedom, especially Iluska. When she was with John an entirely new life possibility opened up for her. She was unwilling to think about it so early in their relationship because that reality felt utterly elusive. She actually managed to almost forget what Popovich wanted her to do. It didn't matter. Just some complicated information about the American Butterfly. It couldn't be very important at all. There have been many machines to go into space. This was just another one. A very beautiful one, but it couldn't be all that important - really.

It had been a long and eventful night. Miraculous magic, a marvellous blossoming of new feelings and a glimpse at a new life reality which seemed to unfold before Iluska. As she awoke the first image to flash into her memory was the golden cube. Then she turned to the spot where John had put his ID when he undressed.

A few days later the world was about to experience an extraordinary event. The third one since the dawn of history. The first, when an apple landed on the ground from Eve shaking the tree of knowledge. The second, when another apple revealed a secret to Isaac Newton. The third, when the apple was about to fall back up into the tree.

Laboriously the roof of the experimental laboratory wound open. A dark universe with a complex spider web of gravitational forces waited for this puny little man creature to fly into its trap. With the control room fully staffed and John and Peter installed in Cube #2 everything was ready. The first manned flight of a vehicle that could defy the universal law of gravity was about to make history.

'The cube is yours,' announced the launch commander after he checked all systems were nominal.

'Clocks synchronised,' responded John.

'Graviton tanks full,' added Peter.

That's when John announced the name of the golden cube, 'Ladies and gentlemen, you are about to see The American Golden Butterfly have its maiden flight.' To the sound of copious cheering and clapping the craft began its ascent; majestic, soundless, a stunning example of the potential of the human mind. This was hoped to be the gateway to the cosmos - if it worked.

It seemed odd to John to have to be strapped in like a normal astronaut with all the standard gear on. If they could control gravity was there any need? G forces could be maintained at Earth standard. They didn't need to fly at extraordinary speeds to escape Earth's gravitational pull.

They could just float like a balloon. As a simple test Peter suggested they put a small foam sphere on the floor and see what it would do. Everything else had been secured against floating about inside the Cube. He looked around to see where they had put it. John noticed it first.

'What's the apple doing in here?' he exclaimed.

It had ended up near John's feet somehow. He nudged it with the cumbersome space boot.

'Ha! It's not an apple Dad. Someone's made a foam model and painted it to look exactly like an apple.'

'We'll have to dedicate it to Isaac Newton to debunk his theory; What goes up, must come down.'

Peter had a most peculiar sense of humour, unfathomable to John.

'Are you ready Dad?'

Like the ascent of a hot air balloon neither of them could feel the moment when the Cube separated itself from Mother Earth. Flying by instruments became their only connection to reality. Without portholes they had to rely on cameras to feed visuals to their screens. Without the shuddering caused by rocket boosters it wasn't possible to even feel the launch.

At six meters, John the pilot, hovered. His joystick had been designed exactly like that of a normal aircraft. He moved it to port. An image of the windows of the control centre came onto their screen. Everyone had crowded up against the window, waving, shouting.

Smooth with no sense of motion at all John toggled to starboard. They saw the closed hangar doors of the laboratory. Only one way left to go.

'We're directly below the roof aperture,' advised Peter, getting a little impatient.

'Yes Dad, I can see.' Instead of ascending higher into the darkness of the night John set them down on the pad.

'What are doing boy?'

'Just making sure this American Golden Butterfly knows how to land gently on a flower.' The procedure had been laid out as the mandatory pre-flight test procedure. Peter had chosen to ignore it or forget it.

'Here we go Dad. Keep your eye on the clock and the gravimeter.'

Relativistic
John

Wet week time is too slow.

Fun time is much too fast. Betty and Yuri time; that had another dimension altogether. They were somewhere doing what they were doing known only to the two surveillance teams headed by Johnson and Kurt. Yuri became engrossed in learning a few American customs - Betty learning a few things Russian; they were not nuances of their respective languages.

Time for Iluska dragged. She wanted 'Ivan' back, unharmed by his strange experiment he'd tried to explain to her. She now thought of John as her Ivan. Getting entangled with another Russian lover was perhaps not as bad as betraying Yuri for an American. A delusion which helped Iluska ease her qualms about the attraction she felt for 'Ivan'. *Ivan will never force me to leave my life and go to a strange foreign country*, she told herself. *Ivan has a good job and a good life - Ivan is intelligent* ... and many other little gremlins of semi-truths contributed to Iluska's warping reality. Once she lived a simple, predictable life in the wilderness, one she realised could never become real for her again. This new land of America promised so much for her and Yuri.

Within a short time a sense of normality created the tentative foundation for a new future, a reality still so fragile it wouldn't take a seismic event to crumble it. Perhaps meeting John could qualify as a such an event.

Real time for John and Peter became a rather fluid entity. By ground time they'd been airborne no more than half an hour. Constant communication with Houston made it impossible for the two scientists to enjoy their achievement. Without any sensation of movement John and Peter's appreciation of their position in the Earth's atmosphere became a matter of trusting their instruments. Reality became relative to the mechanisations of technology. They'd risen to over twice the height of Mt. Everest.

'I'm not going to exceed 2G external,' John said more to himself than Peter.

'That's too slow son. At twenty two miles per hour acceleration it would take us at least twelve hours to get to the ISS.'

'Is that where you want to go on our first flight?'

Houston cut into their conversation again. 'This is Houston. Looking good Butterfly.' They'd decided to contact Cube #2 to ensure they followed the pre-determined test protocol. 'Please advise expected return. Over.'

'Not for a while yet. Over and Out,' came Peter's clipped voice.

'Butterfly, do you copy?' Peter ignored the call.

'Are you serious about the ISS?'

'Until I see our space station I will not believe we are anywhere other than sitting on the platform in the laboratory.'

John could understand his father. Walking around in the Butterfly felt no different to being in a room on Earth. Without their cumbersome gear, which they'd removed after the uneventful launch everything felt even more normal. He had to admit to himself the reality of the situation escaped him as well. John kept checking the instruments and the screen view to the outside. Earth's curvature couldn't be denied. But it didn't *feel* like they were so far above the Earth. Over such a short period he couldn't tell if the clock had the right Earth time either.

'Houston - John. We're going to do a little sightseeing. Keep an eye on us. Out.'

'That's my boy.' Peter took up position directly in front of the big screen. His breathing had become a little laboured. Probably nothing more than the excitement coming from achieving success of an entire life's work. His dreams had finally become a reality. *John can't possibly appreciate what we've achieved here. He's still a young pup, with half his mind on girls.* 'John, when we get to thirty miles per hour crank up the speed. Let's see what this cube of ours can do.'

There really wasn't much else to do other than sit back and enjoy the ride, one much smoother than any anything else they experienced on Earth. They wouldn't run out of fuel, as they were surrounded by it and could harvest gravitons whenever their tanks got low. Mechanically the complexity of moving parts within the Cube turned out to be less than that of a Rolex, other than for the intricacies of managing the positively and negatively charged electric fields to control the gravitons.

An hour later John was interrupted in his daydreaming. 'Butterfly - Houston. We are tracking you on radar. Report on status. Do you copy? Over.'

'All nominal. We're going to take a peek at the ISS. We'll be in touch on the way home.'

'You are not authorised. Abort - repeat - Abort. Do you copy?'

Silverman was furious beyond belief. Mostly because there was nothing he could do to control John and Peter. He should have been ecstatic at the success of the propulsion system. Even more so because so far the technology had not filtered out to America's rivals. His main worry, that Betty woman, had taken up with the Russian maintenance man and had stopped pressuring John for the intel. *Exactly what I suspected. Yuri is more her speed. She can get all the intel out of him she wants on how to push a broom or wrangle a bear.*

While Silverman fumed J'Ark was beside herself, pretty much for the same reason - distraught at how Betty had let her down. And all it took was the first hairy man that came into her life. *I should have let Popovich do more than run a few training classes for the bitch. I'll sort her out when she'd had her little fling with the Siberian bear. She doesn't even know John is out in space! Bitch.*

Dr Kathleen didn't like the risk John was taking. Actually more concerned about Peter and his advanced age and the rigorous work routine he'd subjected himself to in getting their project to this stage of completion. *I should never have let him go on this first flight. He's just as likely to do something he shouldn't giving no thought to his wellbeing at all. He's worse than his son.*

Of all the people personally involved with the major characters of this drama Iluska must have been the one most affected by the current events. Betty may not have known where John was but Iluska knew exactly where Ivan would be. Her 'Ivan' had told her everything about the flight. How could he not? She had named the Cube, she had shown more excitement about it than anyone else on the development team. Certainly more genuine interest than Betty. Her love for this American was still fresh and exciting, giving her hopes of a life that had not the slightest chance of becoming a reality if she had remained a peasant girl in Siberia. John couldn't help but feel some of the exuberant excitement radiating from Iluska.

No media outlet knew about the mission. All Iluska could do was go to work at the cafeteria and wait. Alone at home she could do no more than pace the length and breadth of her studio apartment. At least Yuri wasn't there. She didn't care where he was anymore.

Peter, asleep in the couch, didn't respond when John told him it was time to reverse the graviton polarity a little more and let the Earth's gravity give them a bit more of a push. If he could increase their speed every hour it wouldn't take them twelve hours to get to the ISS orbital altitude. That would please Peter for sure. He let his Dad sleep. He seemed comfortable enough and he definitely needed the rest after their big push to finalise the software to improve the directional control of polarity reversal momentum.

One test they'd determined to carry out was the making of a meal. Internal gravity for the Butterfly had been set at 1G. They'd achieved it by controlling the insulation of graviton energy as a separate mechanism to the propulsion system. They could walk around the enclosure without using velcro boots. Their foam apple remain exactly where it was on the floor, not even bothering to roll around.
Making a cup of coffee turned out to be no more complicated than in the house he used to share with Betty.
'Come on Dad, time for a cuppa.' He had trouble waking Peter. He seemed to have gone into a light coma. He'd opened his eyes without saying anything after John gave him a little shake on the shoulder.
'Dad, are you alright?' Peter reached out to take a hold of John's arm, still silent. 'You must have had a pretty good dream,' John commented. Peter squeezed his son's arm several times, examining it intently.
'No - yes - John?' The words faltered.
'What's the matter?'

'I've been ...' he started to explain as the time on the clock caught his attention.

Peter fixed his eyes on the large internal clock.

He seemed to zone out as if he'd lost touch with reality. The time on it seemed to puzzle him. 'Is it correct?' he asked suddenly, making an attempt to stand up, unsteady on his feet.

'Houston - Butterfly. Advise Earth time please,' John called to base.

'Houston. Copy that. Exact time 03:00:15:46. Butterfly, you were told to abort and return to base. Confirm.'

'Negative Houston. We are experiencing a time anomaly. On board real time is 3:00:15:11. Clock mechanism does not appear to be faulty. Out.'

The Golden Butterfly approached ISS orbit at considerable speed. If John didn't slow it down they would end up well beyond the space station within a couple of minutes. Peter hadn't touched his coffee, intent on watching their approach, no longer interested in the clock. He'd forgotten to finish explaining what had happened to him.

'Dad, we may have a problem. Our clocks have gone out of sync.'

'I know that! We're getting too close. STOP!' Peter shouted suddenly.

John glanced at the screen to see the ISS hurtling towards them at over 26,000 km/hr. With lightning reflexes John hit the booster button instead of stopping.

The ISS disappeared from view instantly.

The Earth disappeared from view instantly.

The clock stopped.

John and Peter stood side by side looking at the big screen which showed them exactly - nothing.

'What ...?'

Instead of slowing down the Cube continued gathering speed the further it travelled away from Earth. Peter came to his senses first. 'Look at the clock son.'

John did. Then he checked the accelerometer. It must have been wrong. Houston monitoring via radio waves feeding the craft information had ceased transmitting the data, or the Cube had stopped receiving their signal. 'Where are we?' he asked himself more than Peter. His Dad was busy grinning at something or other.

'Dad!'

'I heard you son. We have crossed over. We are in another reality. That's what I was trying to tell you before. Somehow I became partially immersed somewhere else.

'What the hell are you talking about?'

'Sit down son. It's alright. We didn't discuss this possibility back in the lab.' While Peter started explaining the event the Cube continued increasing speed without having any effect on the internal environment of its structure or anything inside it. Perhaps John should have slowed it down, but he didn't. All he could think of was that he was in another crazy dream and all he had to do was will himself to wake up.

Peter went on, 'Dark matter, son. The only thing we know linking normal matter with dark matter is the force of gravity. We have crossed over.' Peter couldn't stop himself from grinning like a Cheshire cat. 'We are now in a reality that is more real than the one we've left. The universe is 85% dark matter.'

Hearing *science talk* brought a small degree of normality back to John's mind. It was a world he understood, a world he felt comfortable in.

'Have we jumped into the dark matter universe?' At that point John's mind took another leap - into the distant past when he bounced off the wall of his bedroom. His bedroom door seemed to have disappeared.

'Dad!' his mind returned to full functioning as he checked their speed. 'We're travelling at .05% light speed Dad!' He'd returned to the controls to begin slowing down. Time still hadn't moved, at least not recorded on their cesium clock. *If I reduce speed slowly will that return us to normal reality? Are we still alive?* From one questionable reality to another dubious one - not at all a reasonable scientific approach to resolving their problem. Instead he made a snap decision. John literally slammed the brakes on. He put graviton polarity reversal into neutral in a single move instead of incremental stages keeping his eyes shut as he did so. He used to close his eyes at school when the bullies were about to lay into him. Reality was doing its best to escape his comprehension of it. Neither of them could feel any change inside the Cube.

'Son, open your eyes,' Peter stood beside him with his hand on John's shoulder.

'We're back ...

... and I know where we are.'

The two men gazed in incomprehensible wonder at something John couldn't accept. They had been in a state of limbo, not entirely in one realm yet not fully in another for no more than a few seconds according to the time lapse on their clock, which had started again. Perhaps if they'd stayed in the dark matter universe any longer they may not have been able to return at all.

On the screen their Moon was behind them, Mars in front - if the external camera feeds could be believed.

Comms crackled into life with the frantic voice of Houston. 'Butterfly - Houston - do you copy? Do you copy Butterfly?'

'Houston - John - we are here. Situation normal.'

'What do mean normal! You disappeared. You've been gone over twenty hours!'

Voice of mission control cut the chatter short. 'Butterfly - are you aware of your location? Over.'

'Houston - Peter. Indeed we are. It might take us a while to get home. Earth is a long way from Mars. Over and Out.'

Peter and John alighted from the Cube as if they were getting off a bus. Technicians poured over the Cube inside and out. Silverman and Armbruster glared at the two self-satisfied looking men. *No discipline whatsoever! What can you expect of a couple of egg-heads?*

Dr Kathleen, being less invested in the technology and more concerned with the wellbeing of her charges bundled them off to her examination centre to run some serious tests. They'd been out in space far longer than the original plan. They had gone much further than they were supposed to, exposing themselves to all kinds of danger. Far more worryingly they had disappeared out of this universe. Neither Houston, the ISS or any other tracking facility could find them for many hours.

'Did either of you get any sleep during your escapade?'

'Dr Kathleen, I doubt if you'll need to help me have strange dreams after this,' quipped John.

'You will remain in quarantine until I'm finished with you. I don't care if it takes days or weeks. You two boys will not be playing with your toy for a while. Especially not you Peter. You're lucky I agreed to pass your physical for what was supposed to be a short test flight. Your vital signs had me worried. It looked like you were about to have a heart attack just before you disappeared.'

'I'm feeling fine Doc,' Peter started to protest.

'You look fine. In fact you look great, and I don't like it.'

A   New
Paradigm

A new way of looking at existence opened up for Peter.

It reinvigorated his entire outlook on the meaning of his life. 'I don't care what you say Doc, it is we who are living in the dark. Do you have any idea what we saw out there?' Dr Kathleen was in the middle of analysing the data from an examination of a DNA string taken from Peter. All his other tests showed the constitution of a sixty year old person. Peter, now in his eighties, should have shown different results. He continued, 'We saw nothing. Not a galaxy, or a sun or any planets. Simply nothing. And I realise why. We don't have the right eyes with which to see in that dimension.'

'Can you just stop for a minute. I don't know what to do with you. Should I stuff you into a jar of formaldehyde until we work out what happened to you, or cut you up into little pieces and put them into a TEM electron microscope.'

'Alright Doc, tell me what's wrong with me. I want the truth. Things need to be done and I want to get on with it.' Peter no longer acted and talked like a tired, worn out man in his eighties.

'Nothing is wrong with you. That's the problem. You have stopped ... er ... having health issues.' She wanted to say *stopped ageing* but at the last moment something prevented her with coming out with it.

J'Ark sat at her desk exactly the same as on a previous occasion, with hands clasped together in front of her as if waiting for something. The déjà-vu moment was so real to Betty she had to pinch herself to check if this was a dream, like last time. She didn't have any confusing dreams during her tryst with Yuri. J'Ark noticed her hand movement. *This is good. She still can't tell the difference.*

'How have you been sleeping?' J'Ark asked, her initial fury with Betty having abated. Perhaps I can use her Russian Bear to some advantage.

'I needed a break,' spoken as a challenge to whatever complaint the J'Ark woman might have had in mind.

'You don't know what's been happening, do you?'

After her last conversation with John, Betty didn't find it difficult to work out the probable shift in the dynamics of changing personal relationships. *Well, I don't care anymore who he's with. John's too much hard work. He has no sense of adventure.* She started comparing him to Yuri, a man who had experienced such an incredible upheaval in his life and had the courage to start a new one in a strange land. The idea of flitting about in space didn't have as much impact on her imagination as Yuri's exploits with bears.

'He's not my target anymore.'

Laboriously a smile fought its way across J'Ark face. 'Oh yes, he is still your target. You might get the opportunity to finish what you started in your little VR game. Remember that? You will complete your training here with ESA. I'm sure John can find something to amuse himself with while you're away.'

'So - are you going to tell me?'

'You want to know about his test flight in space with that ridiculous Cube of his, or perhaps how he's getting along with Iluska?'

The bitch was right. Pain is reality, I'm definitely not dreaming.

Dr Kathleen would not let John or Peter go even after having completed the full spectrum of tests on how their bodies responded to the space flight, about which she knew none of the details yet. What Peter had already said made sense to her.

She'd half hoped and half dreaded the possibility John's and Peter's results would correlate with each other. Medical technology had advanced to the stage of being able to measure the most minute changes to the capped ends of DNA strands; changes of deterioration with the aging of the organism, yet not sufficiently advanced to be able to prevent it. If that could be achieved it would mean extended life spans for human beings. The very thought of discovering a clue to making it a reality made Dr Kathleen quiver with anticipation. *If only John's telomeres had been affected the same way - if only ...*

'Sit down John,' she tried to be as calm as she could, sitting herself down and pulling herself up close to him.

'I don't know what this means for the present, or the longer term future.'

'You're doing it to me again. Just tell me. Have I contracted some exotic disease out there and only have a few days left to live?'

'No, no. Nothing like that. It might actually be worse.' *Perhaps I shouldn't have said it like that.* John jumped up from the chair slapping his two palms against his forehead. She suddenly remembered why she was so circumspect with Peter - her rooms were bugged. 'Come for a walk with me.

It'll calm you down. We can have a coffee.' She took him by the elbow to lead him out. John didn't resist. For days he'd been exuberantly pleased with the test flight, in spite of a few peculiarities to be sorted out. Being told dying wasn't the worst thing that could now happen to him managed to take the smile away that had settled comfortably in his mind. Perhaps he would never be able to recover happy feelings after hearing what Dr Kathleen had to say to him.

'You and your father have been somewhere incredible. I only say that because of what has happened to you both. Put your coffee down for a moment.' He did, close to the other cup, and put his hands on the table, palms flat to the surface. 'I'm ready. Hit me with it. Anything. Just say it.'

She did. 'You stopped getting older.'

The cups went flying as John suddenly jerked his hands across the table. The contents and one of the cups went flying to the ground. The chair toppled backwards as he stood, arms going up in the air.

'John! Sit - sit. Let me explain.' Perhaps Dr Kathleen could have introduced her discovery by giving it a context. The implications of the anomaly didn't surface until she was actually face-to-face with John.

'For the twenty hours or so you had disappeared we knew your on-board clock had stopped. What we don't know is whether the mechanism had developed a fault in the environment you became a part of, or if time itself had stood still.' John sat down again, crossing his arms. The duration of only a few hours, so he thought, in the dark universe wasn't something he would ever easily forget. 'Our instruments tell us your telomeres experienced a temporary freeze in their normal functioning. In addition there has been no chromosomal degradation in your system during those hours. Same with your father.'

He remained motionless, staring at her. *What was that she said? Time had stopped? Dad's been infected? I've been infected!*

'Are you trying to tell me our normal reality was suspended?' Some defiance in his voice betrayed disbelief in her theory.

'In practical terms you might be twenty hours younger than we are.'

'Oh. Not good.' They remained seated staring at each other both lost in myriad implications of trying to survive in a new paradigm of existence. One cup was still on the table tipped over into the spilt coffee, the other on the ground, shattered. John looked down at the broken cup, the condition of being destroyed assumed a meaning beyond the actuality of it ... remembering the smashed coffee mugs in his dreams.

Iluska wasn't at work that day.

Yuri wasn't there either to clean up the mess.

They were at home in their apartment.

'We are not married,' Iluska said during a lull in the strained discussion, words dripping with icicles.

'She is gone,' he stated matter of factly, as if the kitchen sink had finally been fixed. Perhaps he'd exhausted his capacity for expressing emotions after the interlude with the other woman. What did it matter if he and Iluska weren't married? America was a different world, with different rules - for everything. You didn't have to be married. You were free. Anything was possible.

'Why did you come back? Is it because she's become tired of you?' He had never admitted his unfaithfulness to her with Betty. Yuri might have had the strength to fight a Siberian bear, but not the cunning of a fox to be able to respond to a questions like that without putting his tongue in the jaws of a steel trap. 'I told you these were very odd people Yuri. You were not careful.' Back in Yartsevo she would never have been so bold as to speak to her man like that. Things were different here. She could be herself. John had shown her that.

'What did you do while I was - away?' Yuri didn't ask as if he really wanted to know - but he knew. The conversation was going in an unfamilliar direction. Perhaps a defence mechanism, like finding a different track to travel on so you didn't come face to face with the bear. Iluska had responded with something but Yuri didn't hear her. A sense of frustration, anger and helplessness in the face of this new world situation had started to bubble to the surface. He could no longer hear. Blood pounded in his temples.

Iluska recognised the signs. She'd seen it in other men of her village. Yuri clenched his jaws and his fists looking down at the floor for a moment.

'I will make some coffee,' Iluska offered in a quiet but firm voice, getting off the couch and moving towards their front door instead of the kitchen.

Whether it was self-restraint or indicision which stalled Yuri from lashing out didn't matter. It gave Iluska that critical moment to get away.

He didn't run after her. Did he have the capacity for violence if he'd realised the hypocrisy of such an action? Hadn't he been unfaithful also? Wasn't he the one to take the initiative by running up to Betty on the athletics track? Yuri was, after all, a good man trying to live in a reality alien to everything he knew about life. He couldn't run after Iluska.

What will my life be without Iluska?

Yuri turned up to work at NASA's training centre the next day, and the next and the next ...

Dr Kathleen submitted her medical report on the two astronauts without expressing any repercussions concerning the anomaly she'd discovered. Decisions about their condition would have to come from higher up the command chain. Certain facts were indisputable regardless of what view of reality one entertained.

Angus Silverman and Dr James Armbruster reclined in silence in Silverman's office, drinks ready to hand. They went directly to the summary; < The telomeres' DNA caps showed no change during the period of the disappearance of the Cube. They should have. The two astronauts are younger than the Earth's population by twenty hours. They shouldn't be. In addition Peter Frazel's health condition has improved to match that of a sixty year old healthy male.>

They didn't bother reading all the data supporting the summary. No point. They had to come to terms with the elephant in the room first.

'This is pure science fiction James,' commented Angus, taking a long sip of his bourbon. 'How're we supposed to deal with this shit?'

'Are you doubting Dr Kathleen's competence?' asked James.

'It sounds like science fiction, it smells like science fiction and it reads like science fiction. NASA does not operate on sci-fi fantasy.'

'Kathleen's a thoroughly competent, professional physician. It's not the kind of mistake she'd make. But I can't disagree with you there. If it is true consider the benefit to mankind. Can you imagine sending a colonisation team to - say Titan - and not have them get older during the trip. Think about it my friend.'

Both men were worried and excited at the same time. This little jaunt into the void by their two most prominent scientists had opened up a world of paradoxes for which the science of the day had no answers. They thought by creating the ant-gravity propulsion system the majority of problems associated with solar system exploration would be solved.

'It's not that simple James. The clocks on the craft and in the control centre had desynchronised. They should not have. That's a fact. A damned annoying fact. We as human beings cannot function without time, or at least an understanding of the passing of it and being able to measure it. It anchors our comprehension of reality and how we survive in it. From what the techs have said our clocks are useless - at least useless in this Dark Matter Universe Peter's been going on about. And that's another thing. How does he know that's what's happened? It's only his word; the word of an eccentric scientist whose best years are behind him. For all we know he might have been dreaming during the entire voyage. Er - James - you're not playing a massive joke on us here? I mean, you haven't used AIDA on Peter to *dream* up all this malarkey?'

By way of a response James picked up his glass indicating a desire to *toast* the brilliant idea. They clinked glasses. 'That would be a great prank.'

'Right. Okay. Let's get back to reality.' Angus took the gesture good naturedly, not for a moment thinking there might have been any truth in the idea. 'Another issue, and I think this is a major one for future consideration; they disobeyed mission parameters. They disobeyed a direct order to return to base.'

The two men lost track of time trying to unravel this knot of problems and how to close the lid on Pandora's box. James poured them another drink. What they didn't need was clear thinking. It was time to loosen up the gates of imagination to let hitherto impossibilities claw their way into the old reality paradigm.

'We should debrief Peter,' suggested James.

'Would you know what to ask him?'

'We'll let him talk to start with.'

Peter arrived buzzing with energy. It was obvious from the way he entered the room, from the way he purposefully walked over to the unoccupied seat, from the short sharp mock salute he gave the two sitting men. This wasn't the Peter they'd been used to.

'So what do you two learned gentlemen want to know Eh?'

'You're in a good mood,' commented James, leaving the door open for Peter to speak freely.

'Absolutely! Do you realise what we've achieved? We have opened up the Cosmos to humanity!'

'In what way?' prompted James. Armbruster relaxed, happy to cast his medical eye over this anomalous specimen of humanity.

'Without putting too fine a point on it cosmology has just taken a leap into empirical physics. The dark matter universe is no longer a theory but a reality. We now live in a world where all the philosophies about the nature of existence have to re-calibrated.'

Silverman let him ramble on in generalities a little longer to gauge whether the man's mind had unravelled or if one could still reason with him. It was worth a try.

'To be more specific ...'

'Yes, yes - you want to know if it's all true. Let's start at the core of the mystery. Gravity. You know about that. I know about it and so does John. What we didn't know was that the intrinsic characteristics of normal matter and dark matter are connected by gravity - that it was possibly to cross from one universe to the other across this gravitational bridge. Without looking for it we have found how to do it.'

'But you say you saw nothing there,' interrupted Silverman.

'Let me finish. How do we know we exist? It is through our senses. These senses evolved in a specific environment enabling us to survive in it. These senses can't operate in another dimension, just like we can't breathe underwater.'

Silverman liked the sound of that. It made sense.

If the man could develop the anti-grav propulsion drive he may be able to create the tools to see in the dark matter universe.

'Tell me Peter, are you up to creating the tools to help open our eyes in the dark matter universe?'

'On it. I thought you'd never ask!'

'Unreal,' commented James quietly. This was not the same man they both knew before he went into space.

'It must be out there,' said Angus. 'We lost the Cube, the ISS lost it, every installation on Earth tracking it lost it. And now it's come back. It has to have come back from somewhere.'

The situation called for another bourbon. After the first couple of drinks a degree of loosened thinking allowed a few imponderables to escalate into the realm of unlikely possibilities. Another drink would undoubtedly contribute to helping them suspend disbelief. And that was science fiction territory. Wasn't going to Titan to set up a colony science fiction? The horizon between the possible and the impossible is imagination.

As long as neither of them fell into the trap of making rash decisions, a good dose of imagination could help expand their scientific knowledge boundaries.

That's exactly where John felt most comfortable. After his interview with Dr Kathleen his thoughts veered off into something he'd never entertained with any degree of plausibility. Immortality could not be taken seriously by any stretch of mental gymnastics. Yet John felt his atrophied philosophy muscles continuing to work hard when he was called into Silverman's office.

'We've had a chat with your father, John. For the moment we'll not dwell on your disobedience of a direct order. What happened out there?' Silverman asked, with genuine interest in his voice. The bourbon was doing its job.

'Something happened to me when I was a kid. I had never forgotten it. You might say it's the reason I became a scientist. The fundamental nature of reality has completely baffled me since then. I decided to tackle it one small element at a time. Discovering the actual existence of a major component of the universe is a hell of a large chunk of the mystery.'

'What happened when you were a kid?'

'I bounced off the wall of my room and couldn't get in - because my bedroom door had disappeared.' John didn't say it as if it was a joke. Silverman and Armbruster looked at one another then at their drinks - and took another sip.

'He sounds about as sane as his father, James,' Silverman said to Armbruster as if John wasn't in the room in front of them.

James said, 'You don't think it's an insane idea to be making plans to go to Titan. Is that what you're saying?' also disregarding John's presence.

'How many drinks have you two had? Are you going to be able to understand anything I'm about to explain to you?' Raised eyebrows and crooked grins didn't inspire John to consider the interview with the seriousness it deserved. 'If you two gentlemen can't accept the reality of what happened to us ...'

'Relax John. Relax. For the sake of argument let's accept everything you say about your experience. Here's what I want to know,' said Silverman, 'how far could we go and how fast can we get there?'

'Do you want to dream or be realistic about it?' John saw nothing but booze haze in their eyes. They probably won't remember anything I tell them today. 'Now here's the biggest *if* of your lives. If we can travel at .05% light speed it would take about seven and a half months to get to Titan. If we could jump into the dark matter universe again ... If our biology could survive not functioning for so long ... If ... Do you want me to go on?'

Silverman waved John out of his office. It was time to do some serious drinking. Was controlled immortality even possible? The bourbon thought so.

She had a key to his new apartment.

'Iluska! What're you doing here?' For a horrible moment she thought John didn't want to see her anymore from the way he said it. The man hug from him dispelled that nightmare scenario immediately. 'What's happened?' Her outburst of tears made him think the worst.

'I left him,' she finally managed to say through the sobbing.

Johns experience in the Cube had left him with a rather loosely meandering imagination machine. *I'm going to have to take her with me. Would she want to live on Titan? Would they let me take her? Maybe we could have some children on the Titan colony? There are no cows or chickens on Titan - maybe we could take a few.*

'John! John ... you not listen!' Iluska had to shake him back to Earth. 'I said, I left him.'

His eyes focused with difficulty. The world as he had known it since he bounced off his bedroom wall was in a state of considerable flux. His reality anchor couldn't hook onto anything to stabilise his thoughts. 'What do you want to do?'

'I vant be viz you.' Not a moment's hesitation from the girl from Siberia.

'For ever?' As soon as he said it the new paradigm of existence he'd revealed during the space flight began to take solid shape in the real matter universe. *A farm on a moon of Saturn.*

'You not vant me?' Life as Iluska knew it threatened to collapse in that moment. Her home and family in Siberia were gone - for ever. She'd left Yuri because he'd been unfaithful. A new chasm had opened up, as deep and as wide as the one that swallowed her village. Iluska's hand dropped off John's arm. His response seemed to take an eternity.

'Only if you will come with me.'

'Vere ve go?' Life came back into her eyes.

'Titan.' Whether he had the authority to extend the invitation or not didn't matter. The idea of making a life with Iluska suddenly seemed much more like a possibility than the tentative day-dreamed reality of it with Betty.

'Zat moon in space?!' John had painted a mindscape of Saturn's moon for her soon after their first intimate encounter. She knew where it was. She knew how unimaginably far away it was. She didn't know John had planned to go there. 'How it possible?'

Any safeguards he may have had about revealing the secrets of his many years of research and its fruitful conclusion dropped away the instant Iluska asked her question - *She didn't say no!*

'You know where I have been the last few days Maliska,' he used the name of endearment she had taught him, 'the experience was bigger than imagination. In just a few hours we were able to fly close to Mars. Of course we can go to Titan - if you want.' Iluska understood the words. She understood the concept of long distance travel. But the reality of living on another cosmic world escaped her.

For John too it was only a theory, an imagined existence still without substance in spite of his recent achievement.

John explained everything that happened in simple words so Iluska could understand. They sat side by side on the couch, her eyes getting wider each minute - except he didn't mention the anomaly of his interrupted ageing. That surprise had to wait.

After John fell asleep Iluska remembered Popovich. When she pondered her ties to Earth only one thing surfaced. She remembered the children's folk song she sang to remind herself of the code to enter John's laboratory where the American Golden Butterfly rested. She had to give his ID card to Popovich. She didn't care what he did with it. He would never be able to harm her when she went to Titan. *All I have to do is make sure John doesn't wake up in the middle of the night.* Over the next few nights she tested how soundly he slept. He was a deep sleeper. Unlike those living in the Siberian wilderness he didn't have to sleep with one eye open to danger.

'You are a true tovarishch, Iluska,' Popovich whispered the following week as Iluska handed him John's ID and told him the access code as they stood in the street in the dead of night. The rest was up to him. 'Mother Russia is proud of you.'

'I not care about Mother Russia anymore. I have been abandoned in zis strange place. I vill go viz John. Give back ID. I be out here 4 am. If you not back I vill tell him everyzing,' she threatened.

Popovich could see the fire and desperation in her eyes. She was not an agent. She didn't have the sophistication to enable her to lie or bluff. The man knew she'd abandoned Yuri. NASA and ESA were not the only ones bugging John's new apartment. He also knew Iluska was in survival mode and would do everything a good Russian woman would do regardless of whether she was in Siberia or the American jungle of Houston.

'It's time you left Houston. The way J'Ark said it gave Betty no illusions about having a choice in the matter. 'We may still be able to use you. I assume you want to live a bit longer.'

'What the hell does that mean? I told you you'll be the last person to know what it's like to be dead - unless you want to join me.'

'Very good Betty.

You will finish your training here at the ESA. We have time. They are building a larger Cube. The technology you were not able to 'love' out John was successful. Unfortunate - for John and perhaps for you if you fail again.'

How did I manage to get myself tangled up in this mess? It's not fun anymore. I want my old life back. J'ark kept talking as Betty's thoughts wandered off into a realm that had never existed. As little as she might have contemplated a life on a farm with John tending cows and chooks that was never going to be a reality - not for her. Now that day-dream assumed an appeal far greater than the certainty of spending another hour with this despicable woman in front of her. *John dreamt of letting lose his imagination on all of the universe but I want my feet planted firmly on Earth. I don't want to go to the ISS or anywhere else out there.*

'When you are on the ISS I will give you your new assignment. You might even enjoy rewarding the traitor to the free world.'

Facet 2

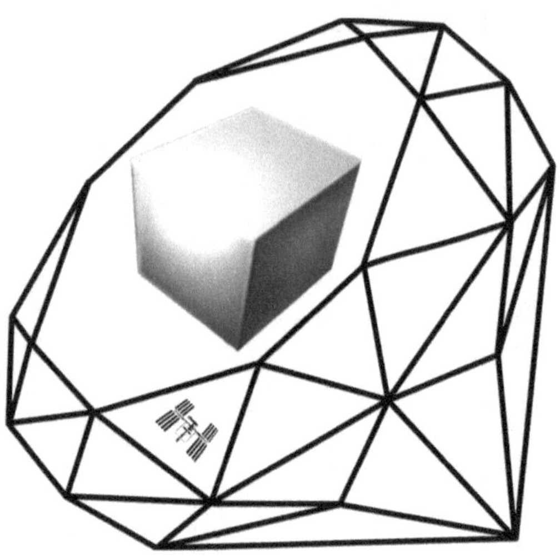

Space   Reality

Iluska
From Siberia
To the Stars

Peter stayed on Earth only long enough to help work out
the general design of upscaling the Cube concept to
version #3.

It had to have the capacity to carry 1800 people, life
support and all the infrastructure to set up a base on Titan.
This six hundred meter cuboid structure dwarfed the
International Space Station. Peter didn't get to see it
completed. Silverman had issued the greatest challenge of
his life, far more stimulating than working out the ant-grav
propulsion system. He'd asked Peter, 'Are you able to
create the tools which to see in the dark matter universe?'
Peter realised the enormous impact upon the human
psyche of creating the ability to expand the horizons of its
capacity to comprehend the true nature of cosmic reality.

The world of quarks and gluons and quantum
chromodynamics occupied Peter's imagination from the
moment of being given the challenge. He tried to discuss
his theories with John. But his son's life had become
complicated which hampered his ability to deal with

abstractions. Once John wanted one thing only; to unravel the mystery of the universe. Stumbling into the thick soup of dark energy helped that quest. Then he somehow became enmeshed in another mystery; her name was Iluska. Trying to manage those two mysteries left little patience for John to listen to his father's theories of making friends with WIMP's and baryons and all manner of outlandish speculation to understanding dark matter.

Two years later Peter had disappeared with Cube #2.

Houston received one communication from Peter an hour after his departure. 'I've taken the smaller Butterfly, Silverman. I'm doing what you asked. Only one place to go to develop the technology. I'll be in the dark universe - somewhere. I hope you're all still alive when I get back.'

Peter had served his purpose as far as Silverman was concerned. 'I assume you don't want to go after him,' he said to John fully expecting a negative response. Silverman's horizons were like most people's; about three miles. Internally even less and somewhat materialistic. The remainder of his imagination left a stain on the bottom of his bourbon glass.

'Why would I want to? Perhaps I'll catch up with him on the way to Titan.'

Silverman let it go at that. Peter had become history. 'Cube #3 is most impressive. You've got another two years to complete it. Our selection process is well underway for the colonists. A woman from the Finnish Space Committee will head the Titan operation; Helmi Järvinen.'

'Wonderful. Can we talk about Iluska?'

'We can. But what's the situation with Betty? Don't you want to meet your Captain?'

'Betty's gone. Didn't you know? I want Iluska to come with me to Titan.' John couldn't care less about who would command Cube #3.

'Dr Kathleen is one of the doctors on the expedition. She has the final say. Talk to her.' *Iluska might be useful.*

She may even get John back on an even keel. We still need him. 'There's also that little matter of your ID being used; without you being the one to use it.' It never hurt to keep individuals like John slightly off balance.

Not surprisingly the Titan project didn't attract a huge number of volunteers. That moon was too far away to be seen, so it may as well not have existed. Many of the hopeful volunteers had to be rejected outright.

I am not going without her. She doesn't pull a knife on me. She likes chickens and cows. An extensive list of other reasons came to John's mind as to why she would be an asset to the project and why he wanted Iluska to be with him - for personal reasons as well. He expressed none of them to Silverman. *If she doesn't go, I don't go.* With that last decision he went in search of Dr Kathleen. Only then did he consider Silverman's allusion to his ID. *Why would Iluska want to use it? It couldn't possibly have been Iluska. I've already shown her the Cube.* John found many reasons why Iluska would have no interest in his ID card. It must have happened over a year ago. *If Silverman knew about it why would he wait so long to bother me with it?* He tried to put it out of his head.

John found himself back in Silverman's office instead of continuing on his way to Dr Kathleen's rooms.

Silverman wasn't surprised to see John again so soon. 'We've known about her activities for some time. She's not actually a Russian spy. Popovich is the one who put her up to it, to get him access to your laboratory using your security details,' explained Silverman.

John went white. It seemed his entire world had turned inside out. Nothing seemed stable anymore. His Dad had disappeared, Betty had disappeared, Iluska's turned out to be ... whatever she was. *What about the life we've made together over the past two years? What about our plans? Why haven't I been fired or executed for treason?*

Silverman watched and let the storm blow itself out on John's face. 'We let her do it.'

'What!' John dropped into the nearest chair, incredulous.

'We wanted to see what she was doing, how far she would go and if you were involved.'

'Damn it! I am not involved!'

'Yes. We know. The Russians are now involved.' Silverman had a bourbon in hand, sipping at it nonchalantly.

'You don't seem too worried.' John's total confusion was clearly evident.

It was time to bring their brilliant scientist into the real world. 'Peter changed the specs before he left. Popovich's got a load of garbage. The Russians will be trying to sort it out for years.'

'You devious bastard!'

'Yes. That's what happens when I have to deal with people like you who can't control their partners. While Betty was still on the scene we could manage the situation. Without putting too fine a point on it, she was incompetent. We're not sure what she's doing now; still working for the ESA I believe. Iluska's an innocent. She might well turn out to be an asset on the project. Do you know why?'

Betty had become a distant figment of his imagination. And yet a twinge of some deep memory of her rose to the surface. The entire scenario had put John's thoughts into turmoil. Nothing was what it seemed to be any more. 'You bastard,' he said again more calmly.

'It's because Iluska lives in the real world. She doesn't have quarks and gravitons and God knows what else coursing through her veins. She's a survivor from the wilderness. She knows how to be self-sufficient; how to manage cows and chooks and pigs. You'd like that wouldn't you John?'

All those times he and Betty talked about such things came rushing back. They might only have been day-dream desires or fanciful thinking, yet here he was looking at the absolute reality of what it might be like to survive on a strange inhospitable world like Titan.

'Go ahead, talk to Dr Kathleen about Iluska. I have no objections.'

It infuriated the rest of the scientific world, not to mention leaders of countries with a vested interest in finding resources off the planet. The Americans had embarked on an extraordinary construction exercise in space. It looked like an enormous cube of six hundred meters in every direction. Its six flat faces betrayed nothing of its propulsion system, nothing of its internal structure. It managed to maintain a stable orbit unaffected by the pull of gravity. They also had the ability to transport all the building materials into space using a propulsion system which defied their understanding. Every effort the Russians made to duplicate the technology from the stolen information ended up in dismal failure. The graviton propulsion science developed by John and his father remained a closely guarded secret by NASA. The ESA didn't even get a sniff of the secret.

'Maliska, do you still want to come with me?'

John received a provisional approval from Dr Kathleen. First Iluska had to be trained, her mental stability established and she had to agree to having children; a condition required of all colonists.

'Your children? Da,' Iluska confirmed grinning. 'How many you vant?' she asked as she snuggled into him at their apartment.

John could imagine a machine capable of flight to the stars without using rocket fuel. He could even come to terms with the possibility of suspended ageing while on route to Titan. The dark matter universe was now a proven reality. Being a father? Having how many children clamouring for his attention? These unfamiliar concepts defied the limits of his credible reality construct.

'Ivan?' Iluska now consistently called him by the name she'd chosen for him; the Russian equivalent for John. John turned to face her. He'd learnt his new name. So far it had become a veneer only on his existence. He liked it. Once there was the past when he identified himself as *John*. That John existed in a world he no longer wanted to be a part of. In the present he was *Ivan* to Iluska and *John* to everyone else. *Perhaps I should become Ivan when we get to Titan.* A new world, a new life, an entirely new reality.

'I like it when you call me *Ivan*, Maliska. How many children? How big was your family in Russia?'

A sadness came into her eyes. Images of the past had dimmed. It was the only way to survive. She could only remember the feelings of having a family. 'I not vant talk about.' Yuri had been the only link to her past. He was gone. He had abandoned her. Her past was buried in the earthquake. 'I give you beautiful childrens.'

Understandably John held a prominent role in the hierarchy of Project Titan Management, which carried with it a few privileges. He was given permission to take Iluska on a picnic; a little further than Pearson Park in Alvin. It was an impromptu decision like his excursion with Betty. He didn't think about that. The man who made that decision was called John.

Iluska's hesitancy to step into a completely alien structure, though she'd christened the original one herself, soon dissipated.

Dr Kathleen agreed it would be an appropriate test to take Iluska to Cube #3 to help establish her mental capacity to deal with a possible future so completely alien to her previous life. Iluska, a person with no comprehension of the world of space flights, who had no understanding of the Earth as a sphere isolated in the cosmos, had to be exposed to a new reality.

'Ven do ve fly?' The cargo cube had been going through standard pre-flight checks, which only took a short time. She couldn't contain her excitement. Her first surprise came when she did not have to put on the kind of space suits she had seen at NASA in Houston.

She asked her Ivan myriad questions about the Golden Butterfly; about breathing in space; about eating and even going to the toilet. Her imagination, intellect and attention to detail already showed her suitability to undertake the experiment.

'Ven ve go?' she asked again after quarter of an hour of constant babbling.

'Close your eyes.' John led her to the control centre of the cargo cube. It had the large screens which displayed the outside view as if it had been a windscreen. 'Open your eyes,' he whispered, also overcome by the sight of his home world.

As Iluska turned her eyes up to the screen her knees began to buckle. John already had his arm around her, suspecting the effect the sight would have on her. He turned to look at her face.

Her hands cradled cheeks wet with tears streaming down her face.

She tried to say something. John's throat had also constricted and his mouth gone dry. He couldn't release her from his embrace, nor she him from hers. The emotions generated by their combined awakening welded these two people together making them capable of facing a new future.

By the time they'd arrived at Cube #3 Iluska's concept of reality filled to overflowing. She was able to say, with a voice still weakened by the emotion of the experience, 'Home.' Iluska had not broken down. She had not refused to accept what her eyes told her. John indicated the images on the other screens.

One of them had a full view of the ISS, not far in the distance. The other showed Cube #3 in its golden magnificence, settled motionless as if it had alighted on an enormous invisible flower petal. On their approach a section of the Cube opened into an aperture large enough for them to enter, then closed behind them. The Earth was no longer visible.

Iluska never let go of John. They waited together until ready to disembark.

'Vere ve go now Ivan?'

The unloading supervisor expected two passengers to arrive with this new shipment; a woman called Iluska, and her partner John. 'What was that?' he snapped in their direction when he heard the woman call the man's name. There wasn't supposed to be an 'Ivan' aboard. He singled the guards who immediately took the two into custody.

'She called me *Ivan*. I'm John, but you can call me Ivan.' He made the snap decision to initiate his new reality by using his new name.

It took a little time for Security to establish his identity. With that John/Ivan was recognised for his status on the Project and afforded every attention.

'I would like to take Iluska to Farm-level One.'

'Yes sir, Mr. Ivan. This way to the lift.'

'Farm? Zere ees farm here?' asked Iluska unbelieving.

'Not just one, Maliska. There are eight farms each on their own level. This Golden Butterfly has many levels and a lot more people will live here than there were in your village.

Cube #3 was close to departure. It had been ready for weeks with only a few last minute provisions and accommodation arrangements to be finalised. Many of the

1800 residents were due to arrive any day. They would have ample time to settle in. Captain Järvinen, head of the Titan project spacecraft wasn't due on board until they were ready to depart.

'Zis is dream!' She exclaimed as they stepped out of the personnel lift into a fairly standard looking living space. A floor to ceiling window revealed a grassy field under a slightly overcast sky. The clouds threatened to rain on a small herd of cattle. She went to the window. 'Zis is dream!' she repeated, noticing a row of trees along one of the borders of the paddock. 'How zis possible?'

Instead of answering Ivan took her to another room, which looked more like an office. Instead of windows it had a number of large screens. Three of them showed the field from different angles. One displayed the image of Earth. For all the world it looked like an enormous holographic image; something artificial, something quite unreal. Iluska fixed her eyes on it for a few minutes. The Earth turned. The clouds moved. 'Is zis ... ?'

'Yes Maliska. You are looking at Earth. It's not a picture.'

Her mouth had opened slightly, eyes wide, full colour in her cheeks. She turned back to the image of the cows in the field. 'How many childrens you vant?'

For some peculiar, incomprehensible reason they both burst out laughing. They staggered back to the first room they'd entered, dropping onto a couch to observe the animals moving about. Occasionally Ivan checked his watch. They'd have to go back to Earth soon. But he waited. He wanted to enjoy one more reaction from his Maliska. He hoped the on-board environment control AI would not disappoint them.

The enormity of the experience took its toll on the girl from Siberia. Her head eventually dropped onto Ivan's shoulder. She let herself fall into a light sleep. He had to rouse her after a little while for it was soon time to go. 'Come. Coffee?'

She followed him into a small well outfitted kitchen. The cooking area window looked out onto another view of the field. Iluska concentrated on something that seemed to be changing. She turned to Ivan with a questioning look. He knew exactly what she had noticed.

'Yes. We have night and we have day.' In her utter delight she ran up to him throwing her arms around his neck. She didn't dwell on the artificial sunset. It all seemed so natural.

'If you decide to come with me this will be our new home.'

'How many rooms for babies?'

John's last thought as they entered the lift to go back to the transport cube, only a momentary thought ... *Why is it Betty couldn't be a part of this?*

Iluska's last reflection strangely involved a man called Yuri, who had taken her away from her home to a foreign land to live with very strange people. She had said to herself not so very long ago - *Ivan will never force me to leave my life and go to a strange foreign country - Look where I'm going now!* She tightened her grip on Ivan.

An Unintentional Stowaway

J'Ark's words about rewarding a traitor to the free
world worried Betty.

Not so much the enjoyment she might derive from the
act but who the traitor might have been. A *new* assignment?

'Don't you know you stupid woman? Can't you guess?'

Enlightenment came in an instant. 'John! He'd never
betray his country!'

'Perhaps not directly. The result amounts to the same
thing when by negligence he's allowed the technology to
get into the hands of the Russians. They are working
furiously trying to get the ant-grav propulsion system to
work. Everything they try fails. Which gives you one last
chance *Betty Boo*.' J'Ark said with a sneer.

'It was the peasant girl from Siberia, wasn't it?'

'She had a hand in it, with an accomplice. We don't know
who. I don't care. Aksel Ingersen doesn't care. Tomorrow
you're going to meet him in Noordwijk at the ESA
Research and Technology Centre. You will complete your
training there before going up to the ISS.

Aksel turned out to be deceptively friendly, like the time of her first encounter with him.

'Betty, come in - come in. Have a seat. I believe it's time we had a serious discussion. Would you like a drink?'

Betty found his demeanour utterly threatening. Her life since their first discussion had progressed into high octane stress. Her career path with the UNSC turned out to be a dead end down a side alley. She'd lost her partner, fell into an affair with no future in it and had spectacularly failed in her job.

'No. I don't want a drink.' With more self-assurance than at the beginning of her glamorous assignment she looked directly at Aksel. 'How do you expect me to reward the traitor?'

'I see J'Ark's had a word to you. She's a hard one that one. The pleasure will be entirely up to you. Your primary assignment has not changed. Get the technology - the correct intel, if I might add. The Russian's have managed to get their hands on the wrong details somehow. Do what you have to.' He let Betty digest the situation and the implications. Then to ensure they understood one another he added, 'I'm still the one who makes the decisions. I am quite capable of making the hard ones.'

Do what I have to? As Betty thought about it she realised that in this new phase of her life choices based on personal inclinations no longer played a valid role. John no longer existed, only her target. *I still don't want to go wandering around in space. When the job is done I want my old life back.* Aksel's last comment amounted to a dismissal. On her way out Betty turned back and in a quiet voice stated the reality she wanted reinstated.

'When this job is done I want my old life back.'

His regretful smile in response didn't make her feel at all comfortable about the prospects of her future. Nor for that matter John's ... get from him what the UNSC wants then neutralise him for being a traitor to the free world.

An Interplanetary Security Consultant launched from Kourou two weeks after receiving her orders. Her destination; the ISS with its contingent of thirteen people on board at any one time. Her overt job; to establish convivial relations between the representatives from a variety of nations working on the ISS and to ensure cooperation between the ISS and the Golden Butterfly on its inaugural mission to Titan. Some tension had arisen between a Russian scientist on the ISS and a few of the Butterfly crew. It may well have been a situation engineered by the Kremlin considering the problems the Russians were having in resolving issues with the stolen propulsion technology.

Her covert task; get aboard the Butterfly, find her target and complete her assignment; both facets of it.

'Welcome aboard Ms Johnson.' The women faced off, neither in a particularly good mood given the circumstances created by certain individuals. Captain Järvinen resented the interference to her schedule prior to departure. This woman from the UNSC could achieve nothing useful. As soon as the Butterfly was on its way the conflict between the two crews would automatically resolve itself. It was only as a matter of international courtesy she allowed this woman's intrusion. She didn't smile at Betty Johnson. It wasn't necessary.

'Call me Betty,' Ms Johnson said.

'This is not a tea party Ms Johnson. We shall observe protocol. Please follow me. I'll introduce you to the troublesome trio.'

Awestruck might express Betty's reaction as she approached the Butterfly in a small shuttle from the ISS. *So this is what Johnny boy's been working on for so many years.*

Unbelievable. Seeing the enormity of it from a short distance made her queasy. Her new found understanding of his strength of character to resist all her efforts did not engender respect for her ex-lover. It only made her think of everything she had to endure in order to try getting the technology out of him. Especially that reprehensible J'Ark. *Popovich was a bad smell I could have done without. All I got out of the assignment so far has been a lot of pain and being jilted for another woman.*

Her mind wasn't on ways of achieving a reconciliation between crew members. *Yes indeed: The pleasure will be all mine* - as she contemplated how best to reward the target for its betrayal - of his country, no less than of his Betty.

For security reasons Captain Järvinen led Ms Johnson up to the third level to an observation room overlooking a recreation park. Those three troublesome technicians had been waiting. Captain Järvinen began introducing them. Ms Johnson didn't hear a word. She'd walked over to the large, partly open French window. A few maintenance crew were busy putting last minute touches to benches and tables under several large trees. She stepped outside, her foot landing on soft, short grass. A few small clouds drifted across what looked like a perfectly clear blue sky.

Captain Järvinen could understand a person's reaction if they'd never been to the ISS; if they've never experience space; if they'd never been exposed to a miracle. She could only watch as Betty collapsed, crying hysterically. Betty kept slapping her own face, crying out 'This is a dream! - this is dream! Wake up! Please God wake up! All the memories came flooding back of everything J'Ark had done to her: Everything Popovich had done to hurt her: Everything John had done to make her so unhappy and to feel so useless.

'Mum! Mum?' Betty reached out to the hands trying to lift her off the grass.

'No, Ms Johnson. I am Captain Järvinen aboard the Golden Butterfly.'

Betty pulled one hand away, smearing the tears away from her face. 'Butterfly?'

Captain Järvinen terminated the interview with the technicians for the time being. *Either this woman is inherently unstable or her mind cannot cope with the reality of seeing the park in the context of her awareness of it being in space on an artificial structure. Never mind. It'll just make my job easier to get her off my ship.*

Captain Järvinen asked her assistant to take Ms Johnson to get medical help. 'While you're at it ask Citizen Franklin to meet me in my office immediately.'

Betty allowed herself to be led away, glancing back at the unreality of the scene behind her. She couldn't reconcile seeing the tree in the context of where she thought she was.

'How are you feeling Ms Johnson?' asked Dr Kathleen. She knew immediately who this woman was. She also knew the circumstances under which Betty and John were no longer together. 'What are you doing here?' she asked casually. Betty had been given a mild sedative, weak enough to still enable her to focus on the voice - not leaving her lucid enough to answer difficult questions.

'Yes, I understand how you could be confused,' said Dr Kathleen. 'Just rest for a little while. I'll be back shortly. You are safe. You are amongst friends.' Dr Kathleen went directly back to Captain Järvinen. Whatever complications might arise if Betty happened to come across John while still on the Butterfly the Captain had to know of their past history.

Franklin arrived before Dr Kathleen. As the Chief Personnel Officer his responsibilities included a degree of security oversight where people of suspect behaviour were concerned. The Captain wanted to discuss this strange woman with him.

'We have a person aboard, an Interplanetary Security Consultant, who may become a problem. I need you across this.'

Within a few minutes Dr Kathleen arrived, her partially closed eyes inwardly focused.

'It was quite extraordinary, the way the woman reacted. No one on board this vessel has had that kind of reaction. If you ask my opinion she's mentally unstable and I want her off my ship as soon as possible,' Captain Järvinen stated as a matter of fact when Dr Kathleen entered her office.

'You may be right Captain. There are some things you should know about this Ms Johnson.' Dr Kathleen explained about the relationship between John and Betty, but nothing about the undercover procedures that had been carried out by NASA and the ESA, or the reasons behind them. 'In my opinion it would be best if any interaction between them could be avoided.'

Captain Järvinen listened to the words and she listened between the lines. 'Is there anything else I should know?'

'Nothing of relevance to our project anymore. Citizen Franklin, perhaps you could arrange a little sightseeing tour for Ms Johnson, to get her adjusted to this new reality. It may make it easier for her to do what she came here for and then get back to Earth. I'll find John - sorry, Ivan, and occupy him for the rest of the day.'

'Thanks for your help Dr Kathleen. I had a feeling we would work well together.' *I'll give the woman an hour. In the meantime I can look into John's past.*

Franklin listened with interest to the conversation without contributing. He hadn't met Ms Johnson yet. She definitely sounded like someone who needed help to adjust to the Butterfly even if she was only going to be aboard for a short time.

'Citizen Franklin, I need you to keep an eye on Ms Johnson for an hour or so. Don't show her any sensitive areas.'

Franklin responded immediately to Captain Järvinen's summons. A rather tall, friendly looking young man who seemed more than happy to give Ms Johnson a limited tour of the Butterfly upon meeting her.

'I'm told you've been to one of our recreation parks. Isn't it amazing! I still can't get used to it and I've been aboard for over two months and before that helped to set her up. Would you like to see our main accommodation complex?' he asked more pleasantly than was his normal manner. Betty had that effect on many people.

Franklin led her through a maize of passages, down several levels past what looked like a shopping complex.

'Where are we?' asked Betty.

'As you can see this is one of our retail hubs.'

'I can see that. But I don't understand. Where actually are we?'

'Oh - I see. We get that a lot when people first arrive. Come and have a look.'

He led her to several display screens attached to the wall of one of the buildings. Betty turned her eyes from one screen to the other scanning the images briefly on each one. The moon appeared far more spectacular than viewed from Earth. A close-up image of the ISS was difficult to fit into her sense of scale about orbiting satellites. The curvature of Earth needed to be processed by another part of her brain. 'They are magnificent photos,' Betty commented, 'When were they taken?'

'Excuse me ma'am? They are not photos. You're looking at what's outside our ship.' He let the woman hold onto his arm for a moment. 'It's quite out of this world, I know. Could you have imagined such a thing as this spaceship could exist in cold, dark space. And just think, we'll soon be on our way.'

Betty gradually let go of his arm. *This isn't a dream. Where is the pain? J'Ark said reality was pain. Where is the pain?* She was still contemplating the impossibility of her experience when a small crowd jostled past her eager to explore the shops. She could easily have been swept along if Franklin hadn't steadied her.

'Shall we go on? Would you like to see one of our farms?'

'You have a farm?' Betty had only just begun to formulate a possible way to hide away on this ship when Franklin once again jolted her back to the present.

'Not just one. Quite a few. We need to be self-sufficient on our journey even though it'll be less than a year. And when we get to Titan we'll have to continue looking after ourselves.' He seemed very proud to be part of this astounding enterprise. 'You will not believe where we're going to live. Did you know there'll be well over a thousand people going to Titan?'

'Cows?'

'Yes ma'am, and chooks and every other farm critter you can think of.' Betty didn't notice they had to use another lift. Images assailed her mind mixed with memories of discussions she'd had with John.

The moment they stepped out of the lift the noisy crowd they encountered drowned out everything else Franklin tried to say. People seemed to be moving about in a hurry as if not sure where they should be going. She cast a questioning look at Franklin. The farm was up another level.

'They're looking for their new home.' Betty scanned over the heads of the throng gazing at what could have been any well kept urban environment. Buildings of various heights and sizes crowded on either side of narrow thoroughfares.

'You said over a thousand passengers. There seems to be too much accommodation.'

'We've allowed for population growth. It's anybody's guess how long we'll be on Titan, possibly generations. This isn't the only district on the Butterfly.'

Generations? Possibly generations! She couldn't grasp what he was saying.

Ideas had started to solidify in her mind. 'Do you know anybody called John?' He was her only link to actual reality.

'No ma'am. One more stop before I have to take you back.

Betty had already experienced a considerable shock. The unreality of this world away from Earth insisted on becoming a reality in her mind. A reality where she could imagine herself surviving for a time, at least long enough to carry out her task.

At the next lift exit, which was a goods carrier and much larger than the ones they'd used before, opened onto an enormous farm shed. It had all manner of farming equipment. She guessed that's what they were although somewhat different from the ones on Earth.

'Franklin, do you believe all this?'

'With difficulty ma'am, with difficulty.'

'I can smell honey. Do you have bees?' She spotted a few bee hives near the edge of the field. 'Ah - I see.'

'Not only bees, but birds and butterflies and worms. It's just like being on Earth, ma'am.'

If they have bees they have flowers. I wonder if they have roses. It pained Betty to think of her mother. At moments like this a sense of loss swept over her as she thought of the life she'd left behind. For a horrible moment she thought, *Could I live like this on Titan?* She crushed the thought immediately. Instead her mind turned to more practical matters, like survival on this spaceship long enough to get away. *With this kind of infrastructure they must have some form of barter system.*

'What do you use for money when you go shopping?'

'That's a strange question ma'am. The same as everyone else. The same as you. The good old American dollar.'

Good, good. That'll make things so much easier. She checked her financial status. 'What if I don't have enough cash?'

'We have a bank. What are you planning to buy ma'am?'

Betty's plan involved much more than purchasing a few souvenirs to take back Earth-side.

It felt quite late to Betty by the time Franklin took her back to Captain Järvinen 's office. Her biological clock told her the sun should be setting at about that time.

Strangely the general lighting ambiance on their way back to the office confirmed the feeling.

'Can I interview those people now Captain Järvinen?'

'No. They are back on duty. You have recovered? It's somewhat of a shock to many people to experience such a natural environment when they know it's nothing more than a construction floating in space. Are you sure you're alright.'

'Yes, yes. Your man, Citizen Franklin did an excellent job on the sightseeing tour. These interviews will take a while. I need to get to the bottom of the problem. Would it be possible for me to stay here overnight?'

'I suppose so. The ISS will be back near us in the morning to pick you up. You will have to leave. We are due to depart very shortly.' Captain Järvinen didn't sound happy about the woman inviting herself like that. For some reason this person rubbed her the wrong way.

'Perhaps Citizen Franklin can show me to my room.'

I suppose there's no harm in it. I'll be rid of her in the morning. She definitely would not have passed the selection criteria to be a part of this expedition.

Captain Järvinen recalled Franklin, instructed him to organise the accommodation for Ms Johnson and with that put the unstable woman out of her mind. *I'll be too busy with the boarding parties and last minute supplies to have time to worry about a useless highly strung peacekeeper.*

Migration of The American Golden Butterfly

Franklin and Betty walked down a tree lined narrow avenue to Betty's accommodation for the night.

'Tell me again where we are Citizen Franklin?' She asked. The avenue existed. She was sure of it. They'd just walked under one of the trees. Then the aroma of freshly brewed coffee wafting across from a small café on the corner insisted on it. *But where does it all exist; the farm, the park, the cafe and this avenue?* She slipped out a pen from her bag as they walked along, gritted her teeth and stabbed her thigh with it. The pain made her wince and stumble. This must be real.

'This is the accommodation centre for new arrivals until they go to their permanent homes,' he said. Betty turned to him, asking the question again with her eyes.

'Oh - I see what you mean. No. It's not a dream. We are in space, not far from the International Space Station.

It's pretty fantastic, isn't it Ms Johnson?'

He led her to one of the smaller complexes, close to the street-corner café.

'Room twenty four. It's like a hotel room. There's everything you need.' Franklin left her standing in front of the entrance. He wasn't instructed to pick her up in the morning.

Being suddenly by herself brought on a paralysis of mind and body. Street lighting had come on. She managed at last to turn her head in the direction of the sound of light music coming from the café. All those years of training at the ESA didn't cover strategies to cope this kind of situation. The smell of fresh coffee and music brought her back into herself. The only place she'd ever had coffee with John was at the cafeteria at NASA. *I have to find him!*

Betty went to her room. It was on the second floor, with windows giving a clear view of the park she saw when she first arrived. Her analytical brain kept insisting none of this was real. Her mind told her otherwise: The long shower told her otherwise.

A clear head - that's what I need. I need a coffee. The only possession she had with her was her largish handbag with a few necessities. The visit to the Cube was meant to last only a few hours at the most. She took her handbag with her down to the café which was still open.

The air was most pleasant. Almost a faint breeze as she sipped on the coffee. *If I close my eyes maybe I'll wake up and I'll be with John at home - before all this happened - before ...*

Nothing seemed to have changed when Betty woke, except she wasn't in room twenty four. It was a similar room, with a different number. It didn't have a view to the park.

The dreamless night left Betty confused. She couldn't immediately remember what happened the previous day. The unpleasant taste of strong, stale coffee started her path back to life. This room wasn't as well appointed as the first one. It was smaller, with a single bed and pale walls. She caught her breath. A sudden memory of a cell with one table, two chairs and an unpleasant person sitting opposite her came into sharp focus. J'Ark!

That brought everything back. She neglected having a shower in her hurry to get dressed and go outside. No café on the corner. Immediate confusion - She thought she'd understood; ISS then over to the Golden Butterfly, interviews, Citizen Franklin, accommodation, coffee. But she hadn't seen this building before. What's happened to the café? It was morning, definitely - it was late morning sunlight. There were a few people walking around, happy, smiling.

'Excuse me. Where are we?' A perfectly normal question, especially considering the change that had taken place.

'We've left the Moon behind and are heading towards Mars,' the man said.

Reality exploded inside Betty's head.

She managed to make her way to a nearby street bench. It was in front of a few shops one of which had a large screen.

But we're not moving!

Two young adults stopped by the screen.

'I still can't believe it Hudson. Back in the Bronx I could never have imagined living like this.'

'Back in the Bronx?' mused Hudson. 'Without your application to be a part of the Titan project we'd still be struggling in South Bronx, Sarah. Look at us now, five hundred thousand miles from Earth.'

That got Betty's attention. She jumped up to stand beside Sarah. 'Excuse me. What did you just say?'

'Hi. I said we must be five hundred thousand miles from Earth, and getting further away every minute.'

'But we're not moving,' Betty exclaimed.

'Feels like that doesn't it. Have a look,' said Sarah.

Betty stared disbelieving as the Earth visibly receded from view.

'When are we going back?' she said half to herself.

'We thought everybody knew. We're not going back.'

Betty sat back down, put her head in her hands. It didn't help feeling the warmth of the artificial morning sun on her hair.

Captain Järvinen knew John. He was the only person with the detailed knowledge of how their unique propulsion system worked. She'd met him many times to discuss the project. She particularly wanted to be certain of the behaviour of the ship while under power. Of specific concern to her was the effect of weightlessness in space and how it would affect her colonists. It took numerous trips on cargo cubes to the main construction site to accept how Earth reality conditions would be duplicated in the Butterfly, including 1G the human organism had evolved in.

She knew all about the technical side of John's life. His private life was of no concern, not until her chat with Dr Kathleen. Any and every situation that could threaten to become a potential flash point for conflict had to be dealt with expediently.

'Good morning you two love birds.'

'You wanted to see me urgently Captain. What's happened? Why did you want to see Iluska?'

'You've changed your name to Ivan. It might take me a while to get used to it John - sorry, Ivan,' she grinned.

'I geeve him name,' said Iluska in a way suggesting the matter wasn't open to negotiation.

'Nothing technical. Everything is running perfectly. With the design you and your father created for the Butterfly to replicate Earth aboard her people will accept this reality in no time at all. Give them enough time and they might even forget the Earth ever existed. I can imagine them telling their children a fairy tale one day about a magic place in the night sky where so many people lived.'

Iluska cut in. 'I give name to spaceship.'

'It is a beautiful name. How did you think of it?'

'Ve have beeg butterflies at home een Russia.' The memory brought a shadow across her face.

'Well, I think it's a wonderful name for my ship, Iluska. I hope you will be happy here. But ... Ivan ... there is something we have to discuss. A woman came aboard yesterday. I was advised by our Dr Kathleen it was best if she and you didn't meet. Is there anything from your past I need to know about?'

Iluska looked at Ivan immediately. He'd told her all about Betty and the many strange things that happened between them. 'Betty,' John said thinking aloud.

'Yes, that was her name, Betty Johnson. A rather troubled person I gather. But not to worry. She left to go back to the ISS early this morning.' A disturbing thought occurred to her. 'Excuse me for a moment.'

Captain Järvinen went over to her secretary in the adjoining office. 'Remember the woman we had trouble with yesterday? Can you find out if she left this morning before we departed?

Ivan couldn't help overhearing through the open door. An immediate flashback hit him; the VR game in a simulated craft in space where Betty attacked him with a virtual knife - except it wasn't a virtual knife. 'Shit.'

The Captain was back. She heard that. 'Something worrying you Ivan?'

'You can forget whatever reason she gave you for being here. I'll tell you what she's after. It's what she's been after since - well, for some time. She wants the technology behind our anti-grav propulsion system. The ESA recruited her. I can tell you this much about her; she's persistent and can be unpredictably dangerous. I know from personal experience.'

Captain Järvinen 's secretary poked her head in the door. 'There's no record of anyone by that name leaving us this morning before we got under way.'

City
of
Apollonia

'Do you think she would try sabotaging the ship?'
Asked Captain Järvinen.

'You've spent a little time with her. What's your opinion?'

'I don't know what she's capable of. I don't know this person.'

Franklin, an efficient looking thirty-something man stood his ground as Captain Järvinen questioned him. He definitely remembered Ms Johnson - and where he'd left her the previous night.

'How did she look to you Citizen?'

'She looked good - I mean lost,' replied the man responsible for knowing where every Citizen was located at any time of day or night.

'Not agitated?'

'Only in so far as most people who've had trouble adjusting to this environment. If this looked more like a normal spaceship they might have been less confused. But this place could be some idyllic holiday place on Earth.

Very hard for most people to come terms with its location.'

'Find her. She may still be aboard. I've just been informed she might become a major nuisance.'

The Captain's command was clear enough and the tone suggested some degree of urgency. She didn't want to get into an in-depth conversation in front of Ivan and Iluska about security and the danger a rogue individual represented. Franklin didn't waste any time asking questions about why it was important to find this one individual. *She didn't look dangerous to me. Järvinen must have her reasons. Anyway, it gives me a chance to see her again.*

'Come, sit. Tell me about yourself Iluska,' asked Captain Järvinen when Franklin had left. She'd made a point of familiarising herself with all her Citizens. Whatever any of them left behind would have to stay on Earth. All their worries, all their prejudices, all their preconceptions about the meaning of their lives. Iluska had been added late to the list of colonists - and she wasn't an American like almost everyone else.

'I come from Russia. Ve have earthquake. Escape to America.' She didn't want to dwell on the upheaval to her life the traumatic event and subsequent journey caused. She put her arm through Ivan's. 'Now I stay viz Ivan.' She definitely didn't want to reveal her involvement in the secret little espionage incident with Popovich. 'You call zat man - er - Citizen. Vy?'

'Ivan, you have chosen a very observant Iluska to spend your life with.' Then turning to Iluska - 'This is a new world on this ship. When we get to Titan it will continue to be our home. This will be our city and all people here are its Citizens.'

'Vat name of zis city?'

Ivan remained silent. As far as he was concerned they could call it Potato. However Captain Järvinen realised that for her population to have a sense of place, a sense of home, she would have to give the new city on Titan an identity. This bizarre new reality demanded to have it's own uniqueness to separate it from a world they left behind.

'You've given our spaceship a wonderful name. Do you have an idea for our city?'

'Da. Da.' She forgot herself for a moment as an exciting thought came to her. 'Da. You have Apollo spaceships. Ve have Apollo butterflies. Apollonia is name for new city!'

An intuitive idea by Iluska which had immediate appeal to Captain Järvinen. It couldn't have been more appropriate.

'I love it. What do you think Ivan?'

'The Apollo missions have carved a permanent niche into the American psyche. They are a part of history and not only for the US. Apollonia is a perfect expression for the extension of the American desire to have a permanent presence in space.'

'Iluska, do you know any ancient Greek history?' She continued as Iluska obviously felt self-conscious about her lack of general education, let alone in the Classics. 'There was a city once in Greece a very long time ago. It started as a trading colony which later grew into a city. It was called Apollonia. What a wonderful idea Iluska.'

The distance the Butterfly will cover in the time Captain Järvinen estimated it would take to find Ms Johnson put any chance of returning the stowaway to the ISS out of the question. It was obvious to her the woman was unstable making her unsuitable for any position of responsibility in the management of their ship. Did she represent any imminent danger to the enterprise? Not unless she had plans to sabotage the project as well as steal the technology. Then Captain Järvinen had to consider the relationship between Ms Johnson and Ivan. Was that going to interfere with his ability to carry out his work?

Too many questions which could only be resolved by a face-to-face confrontation with the woman. Captain Järvinen realised at the very beginning of her appointment as Captain that she would be much more than a Captain of a spaceship. She would be the leader of an entirely new society with all the implied responsibilities.

People's sense of existence, their concept of their place in the fabric of the cosmos would be challenged by the very idea of colonising Titan. The journey itself presented a reality out of context with their normal perceptions of the nature of existence. In some respects it was going to be more difficult for many individuals to accept their current situation in isolation from Earth because of the Butterfly being set up as a replica of the Earth environment.

'Don't you have something to do in Engineering Ivan?' It sounded like a dismissal. 'Apollonia ... very good Iluska. I hope you'll be comfortable in your new home.'

Day 1 out.

Franklin decided to look for Ms Johnson by himself to start with instead of using some of his team. There weren't too many places on the ship where a person could hide for any length of time. They'd either have to find a sympathiser to stay with or come out in the open to get food. He went back to the hostel, deciding to wait at the Café after finding her room empty.

Dream or reality - Dream or reality ... these words kept hammering at Betty's mind as she sat with face in her hands. *J'Ark was right all along. I have to know!* She was about to stand when Hudson and Sarah sat down on either side of her seeing the woman obviously in some distress.

They were only a little younger than Betty out for a morning stroll. They were not scheduled to be at their work stations for another hour.

'Hi, I'm Citizen Sarah. This is Hudson. Can we help?'

'Where am I?' Betty asked.

'Don't you know? We're on the way to Titan. What's your name?'

Just having human contact brought back some sense of reality to Betty. She remembered her mission. She remembered she had to disappear until she acquired the specs on the ant-grav drive. *That's what must have happened last night! I went looking for a place to hide.*

'Citizen Bee-Bee,' She said. It was the only name to come to mind on the spur of the moment, 'Citizen Bee-Bee.'

'Shall we get you to Dr Kathleen, Citizen Bee-Bee?' asked Hudson.

Alarm bells rang immediately. Dr Kathleen already knew her. She'd be taken into custody on the spot.

'No. That's Ok. I'll be fine. I'm just a little disoriented.'

'Oh we know about that,' replied Sarah. You should have seen Hudson when he first saw where we were.'

Betty's agent training began to assert itself. 'What do you two do if you don't mind me asking?'

'I'm assigned to a farm on level 6. Citizen Hudson here is a very clever man. He works in Engineering.' Sarah took a liking to Bee-Bee. There was something about the way the woman spoke; obviously intelligent, well dressed. She liked that. 'Look - er - Citizen Bee-Bee. Do you want to come and visit with us while we sort out where you're supposed to be?'

At last, something going my way. He's in Engineering - perfect ... and I'll have a place to stay for a day or two while I get my job done. 'You are sweet - Citizen Sarah, Citizen Hudson. Maybe just for a day. I'll go and look around. I'm sure it will all work out very quickly.'

The three of them went off together as the sun appeared to rise a little higher in the sky. If Betty hadn't kept telling herself the sun wasn't real it wouldn't have taken her long to accept this strange place as an absolute reality and to be as convinced of its validity as she had been of everything she'd left behind.

Within fifteen, twenty minutes they had walked through a small park area, strolled past another little retail conclave before turning a corner to see a few buildings in front of them.

Betty could smell it before she saw it; the Café she'd been to yesterday. Already a few people relaxed at the outdoor tables, friendly conversations in progress. Suddenly she turned her face away, hoping one of the patrons hadn't recognised her.

'Do you live near here?' she asked Sarah.

'Yes, the building over there. Come on, let's go up.'

More than happy to comply Betty couldn't take the chance to turn back to see if Franklin was watching her.

'This is District #1. There's only three others. They haven't given them proper names yet. The Captain said that would be up to us. Isn't this just too exciting Citizen Bee-Bee! Floating cities in deep space!'

Not exciting at all as far as I'm concerned. All she could think of was her assignment. How she was going to get off the spaceship and how she was going to get back to Earth had not yet emerged as immediate problems to solve. Maybe if she stayed on the Butterfly long enough the Earth would recede into a distant memory with not all that many happy memories to regret having left behind.

Franklin smiled over his coffee as he watched the trio emerge from around the nearest corner. He recognised Ms Johnson immediately. So as not to alarm her he tried to look as if he hadn't spotted her. No need to scare her away. Anyway, where could she go? Step outside for a walk on the dark side? *I suppose I'll have to tell the Captain sooner or later. No rush.*

He didn't know anything about this woman. He didn't know the potential danger she posed to the project. And most of all he didn't know how proficient she'd become with a knife.

Dangerous Liaisons

Apollonia and its Citizens had become *life* present in outer space ...

... With Earth no less a haven for life. The Citizens of Apollonia had the capacity to initiate a continuation of life when reaching a suitable environment. Titan promised to be their future if they managed to get there.

Captain Järvinen considered the presence of this stowaway woman to be the greatest threat to their enterprise, which had presented itself so early on their journey. If Ms Johnson intended to engage in industrial espionage then any information she may acquire needed to be transmitted to her controllers.

The Captain would not let that happen.

'Listen to me very carefully Citizen Carlos,' she said to her Chief Communications officer, 'no message is to get off this ship until further notice.' By removing the capacity to transmit Captain Järvinen hoped it would negate the usefulness of acquiring any information in the first place. 'Inform me immediately of any attempt to contact Earth.'

Day 2 out.

The two friendly Citizens' apartment felt like a prison. She had been given her own room, the freedom to come and go as she pleased. But they didn't know her situation. What freedom? The urgency of her circumstances played havoc with Bee-Bee's thinking. What to do first? *I can't stay here all day. All I need is the details of their drive system. The structure of the ship isn't important.* In her ignorance she didn't realize where the gravitons had been stored - within the partitioned shell of the cuboid structure. John had told her once but she didn't remember it.

'Citizen Hudson, can I ask you a question? You work in Engineering, yes?'

'That's my assignment. I've been up there already. Fantastic set up. I've met all the other people. I start work in about an hour.'

'Sounds very exciting. In fact, I have this feeling I might be involved in that area somehow. Would you mind if I came along with you. People there would surely recognise me. What do you think?' Bee-Bee had sat down next to him while Sarah was busy in their small kitchen. Hudson jumped up self-consciously as she returned to the sitting room.

'I have to go.' He glanced up at the analogue clock on the wall. 'Sarah, I'm taking Citizen Bee-Bee with me. She thinks she might be part of the Engineering crew.'

Sarah glanced from one to the other. 'Sure. No harm in that. I'll be going in a minute too.' She looked at Bee-Bee, holding her gaze for a moment. 'Good luck Citizen Bee-Bee.'

'About time you got here Hudson.' the good natured ribbing started as soon as they arrived. 'Been settling in, have we?' Attention turned to Bee-Bee.

'Who's this,' asked Citizen Levi, head engineer.

'Oh - so you don't know Citizen Bee-Bee?' commented Hudson.

'Not yet.' Giving her a big welcoming smile.

'We found her wandering around, lost. She thought she might be part of the crew up here.

Bee-Bee extended a hand towards Levi, which he promptly accepted. 'So how can we help?' he asked over an extended handshake. She saw one of the screens showing their position in reference to the Earth, which had shrunk to a small bright blue sphere. Her stomach turned over at the thought of her precarious situation. It must have shown on her face.

'Remarkable isn't it,' said Levi, 'we've come so far in such a short time.'

'Extraordinary,' agreed Bee-Bee. 'How is it possible?' she fished. Levi warmed to the subject, keen to show off and impress this woman. Any thought of security or who she might actually turn out to be not entering his mind. She wouldn't be on the ship if she didn't belong.

'Our entire system depends on three things. The gravitons stored in the shell of the ship, capturing those little particles of gravity and some extremely clever software to control them. What do you think of that?' he grinned.

'You must be very smart Citizen Levi,' Bee-Bee crooned back. The others in the room watched the two performances highly amused, knowing Levi was up to his usual tricks.

'I didn't invent this stuff. Another man called Citizen Ivan did. It's all his work.

He'll be on the ship somewhere. Maybe you'll get to meet him.'

Ivan? I thought it was John's work and his Dad's. Maybe I should meet this guy - and soon. Bee-Bee's mind worked furiously to find a way to get her hands on the software. *So close and this time I don't have to play stupid games with John.*

'Er - Citizen Levi? Could I come and talk with you again?' she cajoled.

'Sure. Come visit us anytime. Perhaps when I'm not so busy.' What he actually meant was ... when there are not so many people around. Levi seemed extremely keen to become better acquainted with this lost Citizen.

Bee-Bee could see the situation becoming awkward if she tried to extend the acquaintanceship with Levi while they were being observed so closely. 'When would that be Citizen Levi?'

Before he could respond Hudson felt the urge to intervene. 'Will you be able to find your way back to the apartment Citizen Bee-Bee?'

'Yes, yes, of course. 'You must work long hours Citizen Levi.'

'Not so bad. I should be finished by four this afternoon. It's a short shift for me this week.' He knew exactly what Bee-Bee wanted to know ... or thought he did.

It wasn't difficult to get around. All the public lifts were in predictable locations and everything seemed to be a few minutes' walk away. This one's entrance faced away from the Café where she'd spotted Franklin earlier. He was still there when she emerged. *Doesn't that man do anything other than watch women all day? Me!* She made her way to the apartment building trying not to be seen. *Why isn't he following me?*

Time dragged as Bee-Bee waited for four o'clock to come around. She checked many times, finally realising the clock wasn't the normal digital time keeping mechanism. A mystery not needing an immediate solution.

At half past three Sarah arrived back. 'Aren't you home early?' asked Bee-Bee.

'We were doing a stocktake of seedlings. The vegetable planting doesn't start till tomorrow.'

'What a strange thing to say Citizen Sarah. I'm just thinking of where we are, where we're going and how this island in space is set up. Extraordinary.' Then on a completely different track Bee-Bee asked, 'Could you go back home if you wanted to?'

'I suppose so. But why would you want to? Although at the moment I'm not so sure. I wanted to send a message to my Mum to let her know we were on the way. They wouldn't let me. They said all communications back to Earth were restricted until we landed on Titan. That's months away. Mum will be so worried.'

Suddenly a seemingly insurmountable hurdle faced Bee-Bee. It would be hard enough to get her hands on the technology and now there was no guarantee she could transmit it. *What am I supposed to do now? Catch a bus ride back to Earth?*

Day 3 out.

Sarah was on for a chat. More than that she wanted to find out as much as she could about Citizen Bee-Bee. She could see no reason why this woman had to be sitting right next to her husband.

Four o'clock came and went, then half past four. 'Citizen Sarah, so sorry to interrupt your cooking but I have to meet with Citizen Levi from Engineering. He - er - thinks he may be able to help me. And with that lame excuse Bee-Bee hurried out the door and out into the street. This time when she glanced in the direction of the Café Franklin acknowledged her with a friendly wave.

Damn! He must be looking for me. Why else would he wait around? Instead of waving back she walked briskly to the lift. *I hope Levi's still there. I think he'll be easier to manage than John.*

'Citizen Bee-Bee! I thought you might have forgotten.'

'Not at all,' she replied nonchalantly, 'so far you're the only person who seems prepared to help me.'

'Whatever I can do Citizen Bee-Bee.' Levi stepped up close to her grinning broadly.

'Why don't you call me Bee-Bee, Citizen Levi. Wouldn't it be easier? Does everybody have to call each other Citizen?'

'Well Bee-Bee it's like this ...' Levi launched into the long version of the official protocol behind the directive, making a particular point of emphasising that partners and close friends didn't have to adhere to it.'

'In that case I'm Bee-Bee to you.'

'Soo, what happened to you Bee-Bee?'

Flirting with a purpose is well and good if it gets you closer to what you have to do.

She wanted to cut all this banter down to a minimum. *The software, that's all I want.* 'I must have fallen, lost consciousness and when I woke I'd forgotten almost everything. Like where I actually was for instance.'

'I can help you there. Come over here. Check this out.' He'd turned on one of their largest screens. It was like a huge picture window. The cameras showed the view behind them. Bee-Bee caught her breath. She couldn't see Earth. To show off Levi switched to the view forward. Mars! Huge, red, coming directly at them. Bigger than she had ever seen it before.

Bee-Bee took a step back from the sudden surprise, colliding with Levi behind her in the process. He caught her around the waist to stop her from falling. She quickly disengaged herself from him, though not indignantly.

Instantly regaining her composure she said, 'Gravitons. You mentioned something about gravitons this morning.'

Levi, pleased at being able to extend this fortuitous meeting, saw an opportunity to show off his expertise. 'They are important of course and without them, which is essentially our fuel, we couldn't do a thing.

Equally important is the technology, the software, which lets us control them.'

'How does it work, what does it look like?' She'd moved up closer to him. 'I don't know anything about these things. Science has always fascinated me.'

Levi didn't need too many prompts. *What harm can it do if I show her something? She doesn't know any of this stuff.* 'Let me show you something.' He took her to the other side of the control centre. Apart from the many screens showing a full 360 degree of the void around them and a group of monitors, the controls seemed remarkably simple; almost like the controls for flying an aircraft.

Stepping close behind him, accidentally on purpose bumping into him, she looked over his shoulder as his hands went to the controls.

'Now, I can't actually show you how the Butterfly responds, but I can show you some of the software. This is really exciting.' She was close enough for him to feel her warmth. He sat in front of a console. His fingers punched out several code sequences.

They brought up a screen scrolling through something looking like absolute gibberish to Bee-Bee. The access code was not complex. They didn't need to be; uncomplicated enough for Bee-Bee to remember. Aside from Ivan only one other person could comprehend the algorithms and that was Peter, who was somewhere out there in the vast dark matter universe surrounding the Butterfly.

'Is that it?' she asked doing her best to sound overwhelmed.

'Amazing isn't it!?'

Time had got away from them. When several people appeared at the entrance Levi's fingers blanked the display on the console immediately. What he'd just shown Bee-Bee would have been the most sensitive piece of technology on the entire ship. Bee-Bee stepped back from him slowly saying something along the lines ... 'You must be very proud to have the opportunity to go on an adventure like this.'

'Yes, yes. It's been my dream since childhood to travel into space.'

It all sounded very innocent to the crew arriving for the next shift. 'You still here Citizen Levi?'

'Oh, only for a few minutes. This lady seems to have gotten herself lost and I was going to help her.'

Bee-Bee extended the pretence. 'Thank you Citizen Levi. I think I'll be able to find my way now. Thanks for showing me the map.' She left feeling utterly dissatisfied.

All that pussy-footing around and I still don't have the intel. She was concentrating on what to do next to either get Levi to give her a copy, or to get it herself. Stepping automatically into the lift to take her down her mind still lingered on a vague possibility - getting more vague each day.

'There you are Citizen Bee-Bee,' Franklin appeared in front of her as she exited the lift. 'I've been looking for you. Seems like you've gotten yourself lost,' Franklin commented with easy friendly words not giving the slightest hint of how serious her sudden disappearance had become.

Shit! Bee-Bee forced a smile. 'Thank goodness you found me. I didn't know what to do. Seems like I've missed my ride back to the ISS. Is it too late?' she asked innocently.

'Well ... let's see. Not impossible. We have come a long way. Perhaps we could have a chat. The Café's still open. Hungry?'

Doesn't sound like he's in a hurry to lock me up. What is it with men on this space tub? Are they all starved for female companionship?

'Absolutely. I haven't had a decent meal since - since I arrived. By the way - can I call you Franklin? This *Citizen* business isn't strict is it?'

'Franklin it is. What would you like?'

He placed a menu in front of her, which although didn't present a huge choice the meals were adequate.

It must have been nearing six o'clock Bee-Bee guessed on seeing the daylight fading and sunset colours beginning to paint the walls of the surrounding buildings.

She closed her eyes, both hands going up to her face. Bee-Bee felt an irresistible compulsion to check if she had a Virtual Reality headset on.

Nothing there.

Franklin relaxed in his seat watching her antics, having a pretty fair idea what she was doing. Their eyes met as she returned to the new reality. His gaze wasn't that of a VR construct of a male. 'This is - not a dream, is it?' she said.

He could see she was trying to convince herself of something. Perhaps she'd realised the serious trouble she was in. Or maybe the idea of being on an Earth simulation, flying through space couldn't find a nesting place in her concept of how comprehensively the nature of existence could change so quickly. It wasn't a simulation.

Franklin on the other hand had a pragmatic approach to all experiences in life. If fate had decreed he should travel in the cosmos for who knew how many months then he would make the best of it. If he was destined to see out the rest of his life on some remote moon in Earth's solar system - well and good. None of it meant he should not seize any opportunity that came his way to help make his life more - fulsome, more enjoyable, more exciting. This lady sitting in front of him needed help. Absolutely no reason why he shouldn't oblige, quite apart from her presence offering the chance to fulfil all his core requirements from life.

'No. I am definitely real. This ship is real. Don't let this air you breathe and the sunset you see fool you into thinking we're not in space travelling at incredible speed. Why don't you go back to Citizen Sarah and Hudson's place, have a good sleep and I'll see you down here tomorrow morning.'

'Are you going to help me?' a question asked with intent and expertly masked.

'I'll do my best.'

'Call me Bee-Bee,' Franklin.

How did he know about Sarah and Hudson?

Redundant
Reality

Time to adopt another reality.

The last time Bee-Bee was in space was only three days ago. Her transition from the ISS over to the Butterfly took less than twenty minutes, most of it concerned with manoeuvring the cube shuttle safely away from the space station. She didn't have much time to dwell on the comprehensively thought numbing nature of the short space bus ride.

Now, standing in brilliant morning sunshine everything seemed normal, though she knew it wasn't. The weather perfect - perfect for going on a picnic. No sign of rain. Bee-Bee stood in front of the building, waiting for Franklin. John had promised her things in the past, often letting her down because of work. She half expected Franklin to do the same.

Looking around at the few buildings, the café across the road, the trees and the sun slowly rising Bee-Bee lost her balance for no apparent reason. Blood drained out of her head and fainted. Perhaps it was the shock of realising her situation. Maybe it was knowing she could do nothing about it.

With head pounding from the rush of returning blood she felt herself being lifted by strong arms. This was the first time Franklin had been so close to her. Bee-Bee could smell him. Her nostrils dilated taking a deep breath. In spite of the queasiness she smiled when she saw his face.

'You came.'

'Yes, Bee-Bee. I keep my promises.' He steadied her letting go of her arm eventually. Do you want to go on a picnic?' *What is it with guys and picnics?*

'How many parks on this space ship?' A day ago she could not have asked such a question and make it sound completely normal. *Parks on a space ship*, the idea had begun to solidify in her mind. The fainting may have been the turning point in coming to terms with a new model of existence.

'We have a few, but we're going outside.'

Bee-Bee wobbled slightly. He had to reach out to steady her. Park, picnic, Pearson Park, John ... memory.

'Outside?' She shuddered, aware of Franklin's steadying hand still holding her arm.

Day 4 out.

This early into the journey Captain Järvinen had initiated short excursions in small shuttle cubes, carrying no more than five to ten people at a time. Dr Kathleen insisted on it. Bee-Bee wasn't the only person having trouble comprehending the true nature of their new existence. Some people verged on complete denial setting the conditions for substantial breakdowns.

'It's our fault if you want to be completely truthful about it,' she'd said to Captain Järvinen. 'If this space ship had looked like any normal space ship everyone would've immediately understood the seismic shift in their reality. But this place is just like Earth - better, more beautiful.

How can any reasonable person think such an Earthly paradise would be speeding through space? The vast majority of the population on Earth still couldn't come to terms with Earth itself being just a huge life-supporting space ship floating in space.'

'So what do you suggest?' Captain Järvinen asked.

'Take them outside. They have to understand that unlike on Earth we are living inside this bio-sphere, not hanging onto it on the outside like on Earth.'

Franklin booked a seat for the two of them, and he brought along a picnic lunch. Not that they'd be outside for long but it might take the edge off the drama of it.

Bee-Bee could hardly believe it. She hadn't thought of her 'assignment' all morning. It only came to mind when they stepped out of the lift on the top level of the Butterfly and she saw several dozen shuttle cubes with people already milling about them getting ready to board. She remembered her idea of possibly stealing one of them and trying to fly back to Earth.

By the fourth day on the Butterfly the urgency of what she had to do had diminished. She hadn't thought about J'Ark at all. She'd forgotten the scent of John. Sarah and Hudson had offered her sanctuary, which though temporary still offered a sense of safety. The one person who represented any danger for the time being was Franklin. *He's been watching me since I boarded. Why hasn't he turned me in? What does he want from me?*

Bee-Bee and Franklin were last to board shuttle Cube #4, the largest of the excursion group. He carried the basket of provisions. From outside the Cube looked features and boring except for the perfectly smooth golden sides.

'It's like a bus except much bigger,' she couldn't help commenting about its interior.

'Are those windows?' she pointed to the large curved screen in front of the pilot, showing an image of the Milky Way.'

'Looks like a window doesn't it. But it's a screen projecting what the cameras see in space outside, just like the long screens on the sides next to the seats. Take a seat. I've reserved those in front next to the windows.'

'You said they weren't windows. I'm having trouble coping with all this as it is without you saying things like that.' Bee-Bee's hand went up to unconsciously check if she had a VR HMD on. Her brain kept telling her this was nothing more than a simulation and she had a choice to end it whenever she wanted.

No headset. No choice.

Soft babble of conversation started as the passengers settled. She could make out all sorts of comments from those nearest ...

... 'I still don't understand Frank. Are we in space or not? And if we are how come there are streets and trees and parks and farms and ...'

... 'Relax Martha. You'll see.'

Another person had a different problem.

... 'We're going to suffocate, Lucy. Find the oxygen masks.' He called out to an attendant, 'Why don't we have to put on our space suits? Isn't it dangerous out here. We could die without them!'

... 'No Citizen Spiers, it's completely safe. Nothing has happened to you yet and nothing will.' Lucy clutched his arm and pointed to the side 'window'. Everything had started to move away to the left as Cube #5 turned to the right getting ready to exit the Butterfly through the aperture.

Bee-Bee glanced in the direction Lucy was pointing. Her eyes slammed shut. Space. Stars. Noooo!

Until then their pilot had been silently going through his pre-flight routine. They were ready. The sightseeing come reality affirmation tour had begun. One of its main objectives was to give disbelievers perspective. Something for their minds to contrast against the comfortable Earth like environment within the interior of Butterfly, their cocoon of safety and a new paradigm of existence.

Without any sense of movement the passengers' only reference point was seeing the starry void slowly changing position around them. There were cameras to show a rear view but the pilot had turned that screen off for the time being. Their next view to the rear was going to be their first surprise.

Bee-Bee hadn't said a word since they started moving. She couldn't speak. Franklin reached over to softly touch her closed eyelids. The warmth and gentleness helped her to look. Her two hands plastered against the 'window' beside her framed a face with wide open eyes trying to comprehend so many stars all around her. She wasn't seeing them from the ground staring up into the night sky. She was a child floating amongst the most exquisite things she had ever seen.

Franklin remained silent giving her the freedom to be embraced by the cosmos.

Citizen Spiers and his partner were near to panic. It was hard enough for them as die-hard 'flat-earthers' to be confronted with seeing their Earth as a sphere when they were leaving it behind. Now they were confronted with incomprehensible dimensions. Lucy couldn't keep her eyes open. *I'm back on Earth - I'm back on Earth* - she kept repeating to herself. In her mind's eye she saw Level 4 in the Butterfly. It had become the Earth for both of them. It was flat. Not so much as a bump let alone hills or mountains or a vexing curved horizon. It was perfect.

'I want to go home.' Lucy's plea distressed Piers. There was nothing he could do. He wanted to go home too; home inside the Butterfly. *Maybe there is something I can do.* He needed to find a consoling thought to prevent himself from breaking down.

'Ladies and gentlemen I have a little surprise for you. We have moved about six miles away from the Butterfly. Here she is.' He turned on the rear screen, with everyone immediately straining their heads around to see.

At first - silence.

A whimper.

A sigh.

An *Oh God!* whisper escaped several people.

Cube #5 continued turning so the image of the Butterfly crept across the screens on the side and then around to the front. Behind it and around it nothing. Far, far in the unimaginable distance the rest of the Milky Way.

The shuttle cube stopped with the Butterfly on centre screen. Now they could see the tiny dots of other cubes around it like bees around a bee hive, a golden shimmering swarm.

One incredulous passenger asked, 'Is that ...?'

'Yes Citizen. You are looking at our home now.'

No one moved. They all heard Ethan the pilot, their eyes glued to the image. It was different when they first saw the gigantic golden cube parked beside the ISS. Even then it was enormous. But it was not alone in space. Below it glowed the emerald blue and green of their planet; a part of their being indistinguishable from their concept of life. It had clouds and oceans and continents all of which they could see and understand. They were a part of it as it was a part of them.

Ethan understood exactly what he had to do. This was not a sightseeing expedition to the jungles of the Amazon. He had to facilitate the earthshattering shift of their consciousness into a new dimension. Already the first scene had brought them to the plateau from which the next step into acceptance or rejection had to be taken. He changed the shuttle's angle slightly to bring into view another heavenly body.

Even without the aid of a telescope the main features of Mars could be clearly identified. This red planet was redder than when seen from a distance, redder than imagination could encompass. Only three quarters of it was visible with the Butterfly in the foreground blocking out some of it. The surreal contrast between the two challenged the brain to reject what the eyes were seeing; the cube and the sphere, and the gold and red - both floating in the vastness of dark space.

One person had bent their head down gently sobbing. Would his mind survive the next revelation? Bee-Bee had taken her hands off the window, one hand holding onto Franklin. He was solid. He was real. She could feel his warmth, an anchor against the tumultuous assault on her concepts of ... everything ... including the false reality of such inconsequential activity as espionage.

Pilot Ethan didn't want the passengers to dwell on the image of Mars. It was no more substantial than an 'idea' created by the news media with all its images and all the exploration and all the speculation about life on this remote planet. It was not real. It didn't feel real. No one aboard the shuttle had ever been there.

'May I have your attention please Citizens. You will notice Mars is no longer in front of you. Look at the screen. Tell me if you can see Earth.'

Eyes strained, people leant forward, one or two stood up to go closer. They began talking to one another, asking the obvious questions.

Citizen Spiers asked the pilot, 'When are we going to face Earth? Where is it? Show me where it is!' He'd begun to work himself up so Pilot Ethan invited him close to the main screen.

'Give me your hand Citizen. Extend your finger.' The pilot took Spiers' hand placing his finger directly on the tiny sparkling light in the middle of the screen. Spiers scrutinized the spot next his extended finger and turned around to his partner Lucy. 'I can't see anything. It's ... just a small spot of light. I can't see our Earth.'

Everyone heard him clearly. Was it a matter of fact? Was it a matter of faith? God existed, or so many of them believed even though they couldn't see the deity. Did the Earth still exist though they could not see it?

Whispers of 'Where is it? We're facing the wrong direction. He's trying to trick us ...' filled the shuttle.

Citizen Ethan had been instructed what to say next ...

'The Earth is gone.'

Without saying anything else he turned the shuttle in the opposite direction; in the direction of Titan.

One or two individuals were overcome by the inconceivable experience. They might or might not come to realise the irreversible condition of their new reality. Others had begun to open up, smiles tentatively testing the limits of their facial muscles again. Franklin had come to terms with all this some time ago because he had been intimately involved in setting up the Butterfly for the voyage. He left Bee-Bee to go through the experience at her own pace.

She held onto his hand. This time not clutching it as if it was her only life-line. She looked at the screen in the rear which still showed the Butterfly in all its magnificent golden glory. Her stomach rumbled reminding her of the promised picnic.

Turning back to look Franklin directly in the eye, 'You promised we would have a picnic.'

'You're back with us,' he smiled. Bee-Bee blushed self-consciously, being her normal self. Something that hadn't happened for a very long time. 'Excellent!' He stood up to go to the storage compartment to retrieve the picnic basket, Bee-Bee reluctantly letting go of his hand.

Pilot Ethan heard the conversation. 'Not yet Citizen Franklin. One or two more little surprises.' Franklin sat, happy to be close to Bee-Bee again - she taking back his hand.

'Now watch closely as I turn the shuttle away from our past, towards your future,' he said to the captive, fully attentive audience.

All those aboard stared at the front screen perhaps expecting something extraordinary like a supernova executing a special performance for their delight.

It showed nothing; nothing more than the previous view, nothing more than perhaps a better image of Jupiter and in the very far distance the faint image of Saturn.

Exciting but not overwhelming.

'You are now facing in the direction of your new home. You can't see Titan yet. A few more months and you'll realise it actually exists.'

Each time Ethan showed them something he gave his audience time to assimilate and come to terms with the inescapable solidity of those revelations. Then just for a bit of fun, though no less a fact of their new existence, he invited everyone to stand up.

'No, I'm not going to open the hatch and ask you to go for a spacewalk.' A few little titters broke the expectant silence. 'But I'll show you what it would feel like while you were still alive out there. Hold onto your seats, with two hands if you like.'

Even though only ten people had spread themselves around inside the shuttle it still took a few minutes for everyone to find suitable safe handholds. The flight attendant made his way between them checking to ensure no harm would come to anyone.

'Are you ready?' All ten passengers made noises; pleased, worried, excited ... 'Good. Hold on!'

Nothing dramatic happened - for a moment. Franklin being a bit more adventurous and enjoying himself enormously with his new girlfriend, gave himself a little push off the floor of the shuttle.

'He's floating!' exclaimed Lucy.

No Gravity!

Citizen Pilot Ethan had simply switched off the effect of gravitons creating the 1G internal environment of the shuttle.

Back to the Butterfly

'You could not do this anywhere except here in space,'
Pilot Ethan commented.

After a few hesitant minutes and seeing Franklin beginning to float they all got the idea, even Bee-Bee gave in to the sensation.

Satisfied about having achieved the desired effect Ethan gradually increased gravity back to the normal 1G. The entire purpose of the outing was to alleviate any residual doubt these people may have had about the nature of their new existence; to cement firmly in their minds what the future would look like for them. Life as they knew it on Earth was now in the past. Earth-like conditions on the Butterfly had been set up partly to ease the transition to their new world and to facilitate survival on a nitrogen/methane atmosphere world.

As the G force increased inside their shuttle feet touched the floor again. Yet some continued to hold on for a while longer, white knuckled. Franklin resumed with what he'd started. In the storage compartment he found their picnic basket, and the picnic rug he'd stashed there before leaving.

When he mentioned to Ethan what he wanted to do they prepared another surprise for their passengers. The shuttle had ample room for all the seats as well as a wide corridor of floor space between them, as well as between the front row and the pilot's controls.

'Come on Bee-Bee give me a hand.'

She was quite amazed to see enough picnic rugs for everyone stacked in the compartment. 'Would you mind handing these out while I distribute the other picnic baskets.'

Ethan couldn't participate, although he did receive a few treats. As the passengers overcame the utterly incongruous situation of finding themselves having a picnic in space slowly travelling around the Butterfly they gladly indulged in the delicacies organised by Ethan. They'd spread the rugs and themselves on the floor all the time keeping an eye on the Butterfly as they cruised around it.

'Is this how it's going to be?' asked Bee-Bee.

Lucy, one of the most anxious passengers commented loud enough for everyone to hear, 'I must be dreaming,' receiving numerous words of agreement. Citizen Spiers remained silent still trying to comprehend the true meaning of the experience. He hadn't touched any of the food. It may have been a conspiracy as far as he was concerned.

'How are you feeling now Bee-Bee?' asked Franklin. He'd noticed a big change in her. Something had disappeared from behind her eyes. He liked this person better than the one he first met.

'Do you want the honest truth?' This was the real Betty speaking, not the woman who'd been trained to spy, to kill with a knife. Not the same woman who'd been forced to do J'Ark's bidding out of fear for her own life.

Franklin reached over to cover her hand with his. She looked at their hands while trying to find the right words.

'Confused.'

Others looked up, knowing exactly how she felt.

Their reason for confusion was a universe away from why Bee-Bee felt that way. Franklin sensed the difference. She was no longer confused about the dramatic shift in the physical reality of their lives. There was something else. Something which had been a major driving force in her adult life.

'Do you want to tell me about it?'

The swarm of cube shuttles had formed a line in space waiting to enter back into the Butterfly. Everyone was talking excitedly, mostly about their extraordinary experience. Some were still troubled by the idea that their home, their planet, their Earth could no longer be seen. Was it truly gone? Would they never be able to return?

Franklin listened closely to the chatter making a mental note of who accepted the new reality and who didn't. One couple still seemed adamant the Butterfly was the Earth, probably only deluding themselves in order to remain sane.

'Maybe.'

'Pardon?' Franklin said. He'd become preoccupied with the return and the peoples' reactions.

'I don't know. It's all so strange. Everything has changed.'

'Yes it has indeed.' He didn't know she was actually referring to the real reason why she was aboard the Butterfly. This was coming to the end of another day and she had made no progress at all on her mission. She'd seen so much. Somehow everything had become mixed up in her mind. *I don't know what's important anymore. What if I forget about the whole thing? What could possibly happen? J'Ark can't hurt me out here.*

Franklin must have felt a complete shift in Bee-Bee. She spoke differently, her body language had changed. He decided to take a chance.

'Bee-Bee, you know I'll have to take you back to the Captain soon.' She looked up at him, brow furrowed.

Not at all sure how to respond. She didn't try to manipulate him to allow her continued freedom.

She dropped her eyes as she asked, 'When?'

That put him on the spot. He didn't want to take her into custody at all. He didn't know this woman. He knew nothing about her past. *For all I know she might have special skills we could use. Surely Järvinen won't be too worried for a couple more days. It's not as if something drastic and dangerous has happened; only a picnic.*

'Do you want to talk about what's troubling you? Maybe tomorrow?'

That'll be another day on the Butterfly. They can't catch me now. No one else has the secret of this technology. It can't be so important any more.

'If it's alright with Sara and Hudson for me to stay with them a bit longer. Yes. Tomorrow, at the Café.'

Day 5 out.

Earth Universal Time Reference would continue to be the standard until arrival on Titan, then designed to be maintained on the Butterfly afterwards. This artificial subdivision of time could be managed by the on-board AI computer to ensure circadian rhythms of all biological life were not disturbed. What was once a natural cycle of day and night had become an artificial reality.

Captain Järvinen initiated the Festival of Departure Day to be held on the seventh day after the Golden Butterfly departed Earth space. A day of celebration to herald in the future and farewell the past.

The entire population gathered in the main public space of District #1 except those with critical duties to maintain the functioning of the Butterfly and of life-support systems.

It started early in the morning with music, feasting and dancing. Towards the middle of the day Captain Järvinen appeared on the balcony of a two storey building facing the square.

'Are you enjoying yourselves?' she asked fully expecting a loud applause, which immediately ensued.

'Do you know why we are celebrating?'

All kinds of comments came floating up to her, mostly good humoured, some comical with the odd voice of apprehension. Citizen Ivan, now sporting a beard and long hair, which he'd been cultivating for some months, stood beside Captain Järvinen. Iluska fidgeted beside him.

'We are celebrating the beginning of a new life. We are celebrating the second permanent human colony to be established in our solar system.' Many cheers rang out from those who'd fully realised the commitment they had made.

Someone yelled out, 'The Second?'

Captain Järvinen ignored the question, though valid enough depending on one's beliefs. 'Standing beside me is Citizen Iluska and her partner Citizen Ivan. When we left the International Space Station we flew away in our very own Butterfly. We called it the American Golden Butterfly. You have all seen it. Many of you had been on a picnic in space and have seen its magnificence again only a couple of days ago.'

Some people didn't know about the 'picnic' in space, nor why only some members of the population had been given the opportunity. They looked about them as if trying to identify the lucky ones.

'They can tell you we are truly experiencing a whole new reality in our lifetime.'

Captain Järvinen waited for their orchestra to strike up a stirring histrionic tune, letting it sound out for a few minutes. It set the scene for the next reason for the celebration.

'This Butterfly isn't just a spaceship. It is our home.

It is our city. One of our Citizens has christened our city giving it a new name. Citizen Iluska, tell us what you named our city flying through space in this wonderful universe.'

Thinking of this moment made Iluska nervous. Yet she stepped up to the microphone without hesitation. Ivan stepped up with her. She scanned the crowd of more than a thousand people, reaching out her hand searching for Ivan and finding him. That's all she needed.

'You have beautiful Apollo butterfly. Zis is most beautiful butterfly I have ever seen! I give name this city - Apollonia!'

For a moment no one reacted. Iluska's heart missed a beat. For a second she felt the earth was going to swallow her up. She'd never even seen so many people, let alone have to talk to them. *Tomorrow I'll probably think it was a dream.*

The cheering and the shouting erupted. The orchestra joined in with the sounds of trumpets and violins and drums. Dancing, cheering hugging continued until Captain Järvinen finally managed to get control.

She raised her hands. 'Apollonia!' she shouted and everyone cheered once again. When that settled she had one more announcement. 'Next week I want each District to send me their representatives to tell me the new name of their District. Now enjoy yourselves!'

She turned to Iluska, who was grinning so hard her face ached. 'Well done Iluska, Ivan. This is exactly what they needed. I sincerely hope it helps them cross the bridge to their new reality.' The Captain dropped the *Citizen* formality to show her deep appreciation for their important contribution.

Franklin and Bee-Bee were in the crowd with everyone else. For two days since the picnic they had been getting better acquainted. Bee-Bee didn't feel the urgency to be prematurely intimate with this man. It wasn't because she felt her presence in Apollonia to be short lived, but because something had changed inside her. Not just the passing of days making the difference. It was the assault on her consciousness forcing her to consider seriously what the future could look like for her. Distance from the past, from the Earth, from the despicable J'Ark gave a new perspective on what she could be doing with her life. And in this endeavour Franklin had helped her to refocus on her current reality. It meant pain no longer had to be the defining difference between dreams and reality.

They enjoyed the feasting and the dancing. They stood in the crowd to listen when Captain Järvinen appeared. They saw the other two people emerge onto the balcony beside her. Franklin knew who the man was. He didn't recognise the woman with short black hair beside him. Ivan had also changed. His dark thick beard and long hair had altered his appearance considerably. He did it to please Iluska. If she wanted to call him Ivan, then he had to start looking like a Russian Ivan. Bee-Bee kept staring at him - something familiar, annoyingly familiar. She just couldn't place him. As for the woman beside him; she was a complete mystery, even when she spoke with the Russian accent. It is sometimes hard to recognise a person when seen out of their previous context. Not for a moment did Bee-Bee think it could have been Iluska, the girl with blond plats at the NASA cafeteria with the dirty waitress apron. *How could she possibly have ended up on this spaceship, standing next to the Captain like an important dignitary? Not possible. It couldn't be her.*

'Come on Maliska - wake up. We have to feed the animals before I go to work.' For a fleeting moment Ivan thought about what he'd just said.

Their alarm sounded at the usual time without managing to wake them. Celebrations from yesterday had stretched late into the evening preventing them from retiring at the usual time. While Iluska went through her morning routine Ivan fell into deep thought. Although it had only been a week since their departure it felt much longer because so much had happened in such a short time. *I can't believe I'm standing here looking out at a field of a few cows, listening to chooks clucking away under the window. Betty completely rejected the idea of playing farmer. Yet look at me now.* He didn't at first think of where he and Iluska actually happened to be. *I'm a physicist not a farmer. There are so many other things I could be doing.* Lingering in the back his mind were all those troublesome dreams he'd had back at NASA, some of them manipulated by Dr Kathleen.

Ivan went into the kitchen. Iluska was there making breakfast. 'Pinch me Maliska. I want to make sure this isn't one of my peculiar dreams.'

'You have dreams of farms?' she asked giving him a slap on the bottom. 'Vy?'

He thought of all those occasions when he and Betty spoke about chooks and cows, mostly in jest, and how she hated the smell of farm animals. He didn't want to go into all the details with Iluska of his past. That was another life; a life he would never get a chance to revisit. Her slap hurt. It would have woken him if he *was* dreaming.

'I don't really know. Everything from the past seems to be so artificial. Thinking back over it now I'm beginning to doubt any of it ever even happened.'

'You go vork. I feed animals.' The sunshine smile had returned to eyes. She seemed to be actually enjoying her new life.

Ivan had been sleeping so much better since AIDA stopped interfering in his life, twisting and blending reality with dreams. *I like my beard. What an obtuse thing to think. I like my new name.*

Franklin felt the time had come. He couldn't delay the inevitable any longer. Bee-Bee had a strong impact on him. He liked her intelligence. He liked her strong determined character quite apart from the 'chemistry' he felt between them. *I want to get to know her much better. But it's not going to happen if they lock her away for some peculiar reason from the past.*

'Bee-Bee, I need to know what's going on.' As pleasant as their almost ritualistic morning coffees at the Café had become this issue had to come out into the open.

'I know. It's all been pretty dramatic. You probably won't believe me.' She knew as well as Franklin she couldn't keep hiding, running away from what she'd started. Early in the morning she'd determined to put an end to it all. *The worst they could do would be to send me back. I don't think they'd do it. We've come too far. And maybe I can convince them I could be useful. I'll do anything not to have to face J'Ark again.*

'Try me.' He reached around the small table to take her hand.

Bee-Bee enjoyed his touch. John had never managed to make her feel like that. All the fire had gone out of her determination to steal the secret. Partly because it just didn't seem so important anymore, but mostly because she didn't want to give J'Ark and the UNSC the satisfaction of having used and manipulated her for their own ends. *If John could work it out let their own scientists do a bit of work!* She hated J'Ark. She hated Popovich and she hated the pompous Aksel Ingersen with his superior attitude and false friendliness ... I'm the one who makes the decisions, he said ... *Bastard.*

Franklin continued holding her hand, waiting, watching the play of emotions on her face. Having wound herself up Bee-Bee couldn't help but think of the frustration and pain John had caused her. And for what? Just so he could keep his precious secret to himself! *Well, I hate him too!* Her face assumed the most serious look Franklin had seen so far in their short acquaintanceship.

He gave her hand a little squeeze, keeping silent, giving her space.

'To start with, my name is Betty.'

'I like Bee-Bee. You'll always be Bee-Bee to me.'

That elicited a little smile. She didn't know how to react exactly. *John used to call me BB.*

'I'm a member of the UNSC, an Interplanetary Security Consultant.' She waited for his reaction. He didn't seem impressed. 'I was sent here on a covert mission.'

He raised a questioning eyebrow. *How much more can I tell him?* 'Er - I had a special assignment.' There it was, the crucial turning point. This was entirely uncharted territory for Bee-Bee.

'You've completed it?'

'No. I can't.' She'd never entirely trusted anybody in the past. That was probably the only reason she'd survived for so long. *Can I trust him?* - 'Franklin?'

He could see her struggling with something which was clearly trying to burst out of her. 'You can trust me Bee-Bee.' Perhaps he shouldn't have said it. Such a predictable thing to say.

'Franklin?'

He gave her hand another little squeeze. 'Don't you feel it?'

I do - I do. Can I trust myself?

Franklin didn't make an issue of it. If Bee-Bee didn't feel the same about him as he'd started to feel about her then what was the point of the whole conversation. *I'll simply hand her over to Järvinen and that'll be the end of it.*

'I'm a spy.' She didn't elaborate. No amount of explanations would have made any difference. Franklin tilted his head slightly as a smile spread across his face. It's not what Bee-Bee expected. She started to pull her hand away from his. He held on.

'How incredibly exciting!'

Bee-Bee let out a little giggle. Such an enormous weight had been lifted off her shoulders. Franklin leant closer casting a conspiratorial glance around the Café. She could see he wasn't playing with her.

'You said you didn't finish your assignment.' He tried to draw her out, showing sincere interest. 'Do you want to tell me why?'

'Not here.'

This relationship had become quite serious. Bee-Bee knew those two little words could be the beginning of an entirely new chapter in her life. One more little step and she could never go back. One more little revelation and she would know if Franklin was going to betray her or support her. This time she wasn't manipulating. She was trusting.

They took a small electric pod to Franklin's apartment in District #2, not far away.

Bee-Bee waited outside Captain Järvinen's office while Franklin discussed her case with the Captain.

'Why has it taken you so long Citizen Franklin?'

A very difficult question to answer, especially since last night. Captain Järvinen demanded absolute truth - from him - from everyone aboard the Butterfly.

'I have been recruiting.' Broadly speaking it was true; much more difficult to explain in detail. He was ordered to find a potentially dangerous fugitive. Instead he found a woman he fell in love with. How was he going to explain that. 'Bee-Bee is outside, waiting. She's got - er - something important to - er - discuss.'

'You mean Ms Johnson?' Captain Järvinen read something quite peculiar in his body language and in the hesitancy of his words. She'd always known Franklin to be a very direct, no-nonsense kind of person. When told to do a job he did it well, he did it expeditiously and without making a fuss about it. *He is now standing in my office making a fuss about a very strange woman he's never met before.*

'You haven't answered my question Citizen Franklin.'

'I - er - actually found her on the first day.' He paused, not sure how to proceed.

'Go on. Why don't you sit down? Ms Johnson isn't going to run away again I take it.'

As Captain Järvinen relaxed so did he a little. He admired and trusted their Captain. He felt her to be a competent and reasonable person.

'No. It was actually Bee-Bee - sorry - Ms Johnson who wanted to come and see you. Until now I've been watching her to see what she was up to.'

'Well?'

'Nothing. Be-Be was lost and she was confused.'

'So to ease her confusion you took her on a little picnic.'

There it was. Captain Järvinen obviously had a pretty good idea what went on in her spaceship.

'Yes Captain.'

'I take it this has become a private matter. In that case in such an informal, private discussion you can call me Helmi.'

'Thank you Captain - Helmi.' It seemed to ease some of his anxiety. He felt much better about the discussion and Bee-Bee's prospects. He desperately wanted to help Bee-Bee, and maybe he could. 'She's not dangerous Helmi. Not any more at least. What she was sent here to do wouldn't have caused any harm to the Butterfly or to anyone else. Something happened to her on the picnic. She's become a different person.'

'Perhaps you should let her tell me herself.'

Although somewhat nervous waiting outside Bee-Bee actually felt a lot better than when she first arrived. Franklin helping her buy a new outfit probably had something to do with it. It wasn't a bright red power dress. She didn't feel the need to impress anyone anymore. She found one with the soft pastel colours she'd always liked. She'd had a long shower, did her hair and thoroughly enjoyed shopping with Franklin. *Why couldn't life on Earth have been like this?* The thought kept recurring to her all morning. If this wasn't the moment of truth coming up then the unreality of the entire situation would have worried her. *Where is the pain?* She kept asking herself.

'Bee-Bee - do you want to come in?' Franklin popped his head out of the office. His voice jolted her back to the present.

Captain Järvinen clearly remembered her first interaction with Ms Johnson. It wasn't an encouraging one. Whatever the problem was between some of her technicians and those on the ISS no longer existed. Ms Johnson may have been aboard for a legitimate reason at the time. Captain Järvinen tried to assess the woman as she walked into the office. She definitely had a different looked about her and her body language had changed. That much was obvious.

'Captain Järvinen,' Bee-Bee greeted, slightly frowning.

'You have led us quite a chase Ms Johnson. Care to tell me why?' The direct approach without any preliminaries put Bee-Bee on edge. She was definitely expecting to account for herself, perhaps without a less confrontational beginning. She hadn't even been invited to sit. She glanced at Franklin for support.

'I've told the Captain very little of your story Bee-Bee. You go ahead.'

With a slight resurgence of defiance she asked, 'May I sit?'

'Please.' Captain Järvinen waited. This matter had to be resolved without any more unnecessary time wasting at this early stage of the voyage. Any potential threat had to be eliminated. 'Nice dress,' Captain Järvinen commented.

Whether intentional or not those couple of words opened the door for Bee-Bee. 'The real reason I came aboard was to take a copy of all the software associated with the anti-gravity propulsion system. I couldn't manage to get the information out of John back at NASA and this was my last chance.' Having started Bee-Bee wanted to unload everything. Her confession to Franklin had set the precedent and she now found it easier to unburden herself. 'They indicated in no uncertain terms my life would be forfeited if I failed.'

'They being?'

'The United Nations Security Council and the ESA.'

'I don't need to know all the details of the past. Tell me - what is your intention now Ms Johnson?'

Bee-Bee stole another glance at Franklin. He was smiling and nodded encouragingly. 'I don't see the point anymore. This is an entirely new universe where we are now. The past no longer applies.'

'We can't send you back. How could you contribute to our enterprise?'

'I'm not sure. I want to. Franklin - Citizen Franklin that is - and I have not discussed this. I don't want to go back.'

Captain Järvinen didn't lighten the discussion with any further friendly comments. This was a serious situation. From what Ivan had told her about this woman she could be dangerous. At the moment she seemed anything but that. *Perhaps Franklin's had a good influence on her. Clearly she's intelligent and probably accomplished in her field. There's always room for such people.*

'One more thing Ms Johnson. What exactly was your relationship with - John.' She almost said Ivan. Bee-Bee's eyes lowered for a moment and her lips tightened.

This was almost enough to tell the Captain what she wanted to know. 'Are we going to have a problem here?'

'I've known him since our school days. I knew him when he was working for NASA.' The deep animosity she harboured for John couldn't be allowed to come out into the open. It was one area where Bee-Bee no longer trusted herself. 'He wouldn't reveal anything about his work to me. That was the problem.'

'Thank you being honest with me so far Ms Johnson. You know he's aboard the Butterfly don't you.' Bee-Bee tried to look neutral about the revelation. 'Let me just say that our survival depends on everyone working together - in peace.' The gritted teeth and clenched jaws did not please the Captain. She addressed herself to Franklin. 'I'm making you responsible for Ms Johnson - for her welfare, Citizen Franklin. Do I make myself clear?'

Betty let out a long, slow breath. Now she could become Bee-Bee for real, no longer just a pretence. The Captain didn't exactly welcome her aboard the Butterfly, but she didn't lock her up either or threaten her with stupid comments like Aksel Ingersen. And so far there was no despicable J'Ark ready to torture her again.

Back in Action

Captain Järvinen realised the biggest danger facing her congregation of enthusiastic colonists was them losing their sense of reality.

Dr Kathleen was right. The Butterfly had been set up too perfectly. You could close your eyes and feel the artificial sun on your face and the soft breeze in your hair. Each day the forecast had to be checked in case it rained. AI random watering algorithms created unpredictable weather patterns. Very much like it was on Earth - natural. In one respect the ideal set up protected and maintained mental stability on an extended space excursion. From another perspective it fostered delusions.

What Citizen Franklin had inadvertently initiated in the way of 'outings' became standard procedure.

It became necessary, as well as a range of other measures, to help in fostering mental wellbeing.

Picnics in space became a mandatory periodic activity for all Citizens of Apollonia. Exposure to outside reality created a reference for the colonists from which to understand at least their physical location in the cosmos. Not that, by comparison, anyone on Earth actually understood that particular aspect of their own existence. To them the Earth was the universe, regardless of whether they believed it to be flat or a sphere.

Space walks were not compulsory. In extreme cases of delusion Dr Kathleen did consider it as a last resort; much like electroconvulsive therapy. Examples of such a loss of grip on reality had not yet arisen, so the efficacy of 'space-exposure' had so far not been tested.

Franklin and Bee-Bee walked out of Captain Järvinen's office relieved. There was always the chance she would have taken a hard line approach if Bee-Bee had presented herself in a less favourable or less honest manner. Bee-Bee didn't say anything for quite a while as they walked towards a transport pod. Captain Järvinen had stirred things up for her when she mentioned John. Unconsciously Bee-Bee rubbed the scar in the palm of her hand; a souvenir from her adolescence.

Franklin stopped in front of one of the many large screens displaying a view of space around the Butterfly. Some showed images from behind and to either side of them. Others concentrated on the view ahead. It showed the most discernible change each day as the Butterfly progressed through the solar system.

'If you have any doubts about the future Bee-Bee just look at any of the screens around the ship. Those stars are everywhere. They are the flowers to our new reality.'

'How long before we get to Titan?'

'Many months yet. This is early days.'

Time enough. The seed of a plan was still there. A new use for a transport cube had suggested itself to her other than a way to get back to Earth.

'What do you want me to say to Sarah and Hudson?'

'What do you think?

You heard what the Captain said. I'm responsible for you now. I have to keep a constant eye on you.' His cheeky voice a clear indication of what he had in mind.

Yet again her hand sought out Franklin's; a rapidly developing habit.

At this early stage of the voyage Ivan needed to ensure the propulsion system worked according to specs. Graviton tanks had to recharge automatically, consistently and reliably. Those little particles were like the corpuscles in the blood stream of a living organism.

'Don't you trust me?' Citizen Levi commented good naturedly as Ivan walked in to the control centre. He was finishing off his shift and his cup of coffee.

'Nope. You keep changing G in here. I almost floated out of bed last night!' They both laughed.

'Depends entirely on what you were doing. Having a good time no doubt.' Another laugh.

'Just checking the equipment, not the people.' Ivan ran several diagnostics - all coming back nominal to his satisfaction. 'Any problems with the software?'

Why did he mention that? A twinge of conscience as he recalled the woman he'd allowed to see a segment of the complex algorithm suite. She hadn't returned, much to his disappointment. Levi didn't like the stress of keeping secrets. For some reason he'd felt the woman's presence was somehow suspect. There was really no good reason why she should have ended up in his control centre. He had to unload.

'No. None at all. By the way - there was a woman here the other day. I guessed her to be someone 'official'. She introduced herself as Citizen Bee-Bee. Do you know anyone by that name? Citizen Hudson brought her.'

BB! Betty Boo! It couldn't be. I'm the only one who ever called her that. 'Oh. What did she look like?'

Ivan tried to sound as disinterested as possible.

'Rather beautiful actually.'

'That doesn't help me.'

'Sorry.'

The brief description drained the blood from Ivan's face.

What the hell is she doing aboard the Butterfly? A number of scenarios played out in his mind. None of them good. *She's still after the specs on the drive system!* Then logic started to kick in. *How is she going to get it. How is she going to transmit it. She can't go back with it.* Everything became a jumble of unlikely possibilities. *Where is she? I have to find her. No I don't. Damn!*

'Ivan?' Levi became concerned. The man seemed to have gone deep underground. 'You all right?'

'No - yes, yes. It's nothing. I was thinking about something.' He didn't mention Bee-Bee. He'd made up his mind. He would definitely have to find her and have it out with her. It wasn't until that moment the penny dropped. *Captain Järvinen. She's already spoken to Järvinen! I thought she'd gone back to the ISS. Shit!*

Franklin and Bee-Bee went shopping again. All standard necessities aboard the Butterfly had been provided by NASA as part of the outfit for the spaceship. Personal discretionary items were up to individuals to buy.

Captain Järvinen requested their presence in her office, interrupting their outing. Time for an unscheduled review.

'How are you two settling in together?' Captain Järvinen was clearly interested, not out of personal considerations but because of the peculiar circumstance created by Bee-Bee's presence on the ship. She already knew the answer, but wanted to hear it from the new couple. They didn't immediately reply. It had only been a few days since Bee-Bee had moved in with Franklin. 'I see you are taking your new responsibility seriously Citizen Franklin.'

'Yes Captain.' He glanced at Bee-Bee, who was actually beaming. 'We are.'

'I've been checking up on you Ms Johnson. You could become quite useful here. That's why I called you here. You seem to have some unique skills.' Bee-Bee remained silent. This wasn't anything like trying to interact with a person like J'Ark. 'How would you like to retain your position as Security Consultant and join our security team?' Trust a thief with money and a murderer with a knife, might have been the Captain's rationale. Though in this case she didn't think she was taking a big chance.

Whatever Bee-Bee might have been expecting it probably wouldn't have been the offer. A chance to turn her life around. An opportunity to cross the bridge from one awful reality to something that seemed quite extraordinary to her. Again the impulse to check if she was dreaming surfaced - only for a moment. Franklin holding her hand made it all seem very real. This was a reality without pain.

'Yes. Thank you ... Thank you.' This wasn't some reprehensible person asking her what it was like to be dead. Or some pompous megalomaniac telling her he'd be making all the decisions about her. 'When do I start?'

'You already have. I believe you visited our main control centre already to make sure everything was running smoothly - no doubt,' the comment making Bee-Bee blush. She realised this woman was far more formidable than J'Ark had ever tried to be. 'There's a major meeting in a few days. Please be there - both of you.'

Captain Järvinen knew Citizen Ivan would be in attendance. *I want to see how Ms Johnson and Ivan react to seeing one another.*

Each of the four districts had their own elected Burghers. They'd been deliberating for a week unable to come to a consensus of a name for their district. Their indecisiveness received encouragement when Captain Järvinen solved the problem for them.

'We will all meet in eight days. If you haven't got a name by then for your district I've asked Iluska to give you one.'

It turned out to be a reasonably large gathering. Five burghers from each district, their assistants as well as the Captain's key personnel attended, including Citizens Franklin, Ivan, Iluska and Citizen Bee-Bee. The conference room could accommodate forty people. For this event the relatively few gathered around one end of the main table. In this room, as in most administrative venues, the large screens acted like windows to their passage through space. No one took notice of the Milky Way anymore, which as always appeared motionless making their spacecraft feel stationary. The immobility perspective distorted their appreciation of where they were and their speedy progress towards their destination. It required no effort at all to forget their adventure in the midst of all the routine of daily life in an environment no different from Earth in so many respects.

It had been over two years since he last saw her.

Ivan heard Captain Järvinen announce that Ms Johnson had been appointed as a member of Butterfly's security team. A flood of memories were disrupted when each District announced their names.

'Ivan - Ivan,' Iluska whispered trying to get his attention. She recognised Bee-Bee immediately, who only acknowledged her after a long hard look at close range. Iluska had changed considerably since their first encounter. It wasn't only her hair colour and dress. It was her demeanour. The waitress Bee-Bee saw at the NASA cafeteria no longer existed. This woman standing beside Ivan behaved like a person who belonged. So much so her previous companion may as well never have existed.

'Ivan, she look at you,' said Iluska when he at last took notice of Iluska's prodding.

Without glancing at Iluska, for his eyes were fixated on Bee-Bee, he said quietly, 'Yes. She's recognised us.'

'Could we focus our attention on the proceedings please,' Captain Järvinen reminded the gathering obviously annoyed at the interruption of others speaking. She'd noticed the interaction between Ivan and Bee-Bee. From the Captain's perspective this was more important than the mundane matters on the agenda.

Bee-Bee didn't smile when she recognised *her* John in the guise if the hirsute Ivan. Her first reaction was to seek out Franklin's hand under the table.

An hour or so later the meeting ended. Captain Järvinen asked the two couples to remain.

Any potential danger to the expedition had to be dealt with.

'Citizen Ivan - this is Citizen Bee-Bee.' Captain Järvinen decided on the formality despite knowing the existing history between the two individuals. But that was in another life; a past reality between two different people. They had to realise the irreversible change. No better place and time than right then and there.

Two years is a long time. Long enough to come to terms with most pressure points in any past relationship. And yet some things resurface very quickly. Ivan and Bee-Bee didn't see each other as they appeared in the present with their bodies on the Butterfly hurtling through space. Their minds flashed back to the kitchen of the rented house overlooking a field of cows in Houston.

As far as Captain Järvinen was concerned this is exactly where a new relationship had to start between them. Could they do it? With still a few months before their arrival on Titan she had time to decide what to do with them if things went the wrong way; more with Bee-Bee than Ivan. He was essential - she was expendable.

'Ivan?' She didn't extend a hand for a handshake. 'I used to know a John once. He didn't look like you at all.'

What is she doing? Being herself he realised. 'Citizen Bee-Bee, was it? Sounds familiar for some reason,' he countered. Iluska put an arm around his waist, staking a claim to her property. Letting him *and her* know it.

'I'll do nothing to sabotage your spaceship,' she said turning back to Captain Järvinen, ignoring Ivan and his comment. With a show of possessiveness she took Franklin by the elbow to lead him out of the conference room.

'Citizen Ivan?' The implied question from Captain Järvinen put him on the spot. What Bee-Bee didn't say was the thing which worried the Captain.

'How far can you trust Franklin?' Ivan asked. Not what Captain Järvinen wanted to hear. Ivan remembered Bee-Bee's persistence to get what she wanted. Now she was aboard the Butterfly.

For the best part of two years neither Ivan or Bee-Bee had to contend with manipulations by their resident nano-bots. Captain Järvinen had not yet reinstated communications back to Earth base. From the nature of the interaction between these two Citizens she was inclined to maintain silence. Unknown to her the AIDA controllers were all back there. She had no knowledge of the part Dr Kathleen played in the game of manufactured dreams.

To some extent Ivan found himself living his dream aboard the spaceship. He was on his way to Titan. He'd never realistically considered the possibility of Betty ever becoming a part of that reality. Her annoying persistence trying to get him to divulge the secret technology created a barrier between them, destroying any chance of a depth of intimacy which could have formed the foundation of a lifelong partnership.

A new person had filled the void for him. Since taking up residence aboard the Butterfly Ivan had peace of mind; peace in his dreams and more than a reasonable expectation of realising a lifelong ambition.

There is nothing BB can do to destroy everything, he tried convincing himself. *She's a long way away from those who controlled her. They can't influence her anymore. With Franklin beside her she might even decide to make a life for herself with the rest of us.*

The swarm of AIDA nano-bots had become restless. Insufficient time had elapsed since their last contact with Dr Kathleen; their queen bee, for them to fully wake up. Armbruster may have been the brains behind bringing them into existence and he was definitely the only who'd programmed a special code sequence into the controlling algorithm. Yet it had been Dr Kathleen's responsibility to animate them, to seed them with data and to let them loose in Ivan's hippocampus.

They were still there. The right conditions for them to self-destruct had not yet arisen. Adapt and learn; a fundamental characteristic of the AI lifeform regardless of their size.

Ivan's face-to-face interaction with Bee-Bee, albeit short, triggered something in his mind which had become dormant since they left Earth. His choice of a second career as a farmer of animals contributed to subsequent events.

He made no attempt to contact Bee-Bee. Nevertheless she became a frequent visitor to his thoughts. *I have Iluska. I have a farm. I have a spaceship propulsion system to maintain. Work ... Work.* Fatigue became his companion. It helped to keep Betty under control in his head. *At some point I have to somehow stop being chased.*

Iluska began to feel uneasy about his new found dedication to working so much of the time. One consolation had been Ivan's deep sleeping pattern. Yet she was concerned for his welfare, not in regard to her own future if she lost him, but for Ivan. Iluska had developed a fierce love for this man.

'Out! Out!' she shouted at him just on sunset a few days later as he stomped into the kitchen with every unpleasant farm smell imaginable about him. 'Out! Dirty boots! Go Vash!'

Ivan froze. He heard the words. He understood what Iluska had just said.

He heard them said in Betty's voice.

'Ivan, you not come in house dirty!' She couldn't understand what was wrong with him just standing there like that. It was as if he hadn't heard a word she said. She had to physically turn him around and push him out the door. Ivan didn't resist. He didn't move once outside the door. His eyes registered the failing light of the day. In his mind he saw the farm of a past dream, one which no longer had the quintessence of a dream but the feel of an actual reality from a past life. His senses fed data to his hippocampus.

The nano-bots twitched.

Iluska continued watching her man being overcome by some strange stupor. Smells of cow dung and chook manure and dirt no longer mattered. 'Ivan! Ivan!' she went outside to stand in front of him, shaking him. She had to shake him everal times.

With some effort his eyes refocused on the woman in front of him. Two dirty, smelly hands lifted themselves to cradle her face. She was shorter than Ivan and raised herself up on tiptoes thinking he was about to kiss her. He just stared.

'Maliska?' His voice calling her name switched on her sense of smell. Something had happened to her Ivan but he still had to be cleaned up. She led him to the seat a few steps from the back door, and sat him down.

'Maliska.' This time it wasn't a question asking to confirmation of her identity.

'Vat happen?' she asked as she took off his boots and dirty shirt.

'I need a coffee,' he said in a normal voice.

'You vant coffee - now?'

Ivan got up, walked back into the kitchen bare foot, with Iluska following behind - and again just stood there.

'Da, I make coffee.' At least he'd responded. It made her feel better, though not much. *He wants coffee. Alright I'll make the coffee. I don't understand. Tomorrow I'll take him to the doctor.* In only a few minutes Iluska was handing him a hot mug.

'You make a great coffee,' Ivan commented in his perfectly normal voice as he took it. It was hot.

Smash! Coffee everywhere, pieces of mug flying all over the floor. He'd fumbled with the large hot mug dropping it onto the tiles.

Iluska watched as he stopped moving after the first lunge to try and catch it. The blank look came back into his eyes. This time he didn't need to think if it was a dream or a past reality he'd remembered. Either way this had happened before. He saw Betty standing in front of him.

The nano-bots were not supposed to activate imagery until their host was asleep.

Without receiving specific instructions the AIDA bots released a flood of disorganised information that night effectively creating disjoined nightmares for Ivan. In the morning he couldn't string together a coherent sentence.

'Captain Järvinen,' Iluska called the only other person she trusted, 'Ivan he sick. No vork today. He sleep bad.'

'Stay at home with him Iluska. I'll ask Dr Kathleen to go visit him.'

Ivan had stopped wandering around the house by the time Dr Kathleen arrived. He was standing by the kitchen window and turned around when he heard the Doctor's voice.

'What happened?' 'Bad dreams?' she asked Iluska. As soon as Iluska mentioned Ivan's restless night the Doctor suspected the cause.

'What day is it? Where are we?' he asked in a serious, normal voice as if it was the normal Ivan asking a perfectly acceptable question. A person in his position of responsibility and comprehensive involvement in the Titan project should not have been asking such a question. 'Dr Kathleen?'

'Yes. I'll explain on the way. I can't treat you here.'

In her consulting rooms Dr Kathleen had all manner of equipment ready for use except for one device about the size of a laptop computer. It was locked away in a safe, its use no longer thought to be required to seed the bots.

'Vat vrong viz Ivan?' Iluska asked as the Doctor prepared the equipment, including the interface.

'You don't need to worry Iluska. I think I know what the problem is. Please wait outside for a few minutes.' *I know exactly what the problem is. Something must have activated AIDA. It might even be some hidden code by Armbruster. I had a feeling he couldn't be trusted.* Ivan remained quiet and seated during the interchange. Dr Kathleen considered contacting Armbruster to get instructions on the best way to proceed in this situation. That wasn't possible. All incoming and outgoing communications had been suspended by the Captain. Without consciously realising it Dr Kathleen had made her decision as soon as she heard what Iluska said. This was a different world now. The past had been left behind and all the clandestine intrigue abandoned with it.

Armbruster had not given her a contingency framework on which to make decisions concerning Ivan or Bee-Bee. It only took a few minutes to attach the contacts to Ivan's temples and the base of his skull. The bots had no defence mechanisms and were not armed. However they did have a comprehensive schematic of human anatomy. They could navigate to any instructed location.

Dr Kathleen watched the progress of the entire swarm vacating their bases of operation in his hippocampus to migrate into the cerebrospinal fluid. Having been permanently deactivated they would be washed out of the hosts body through the normal physiological process.

Ivan felt nothing.

'John - sorry - Ivan, how are you feeling?' He'd closed his eyes at the beginning of the procedure, appearing to be unconscious. Dr Kathleen called Iluska back into the room. 'Talk to him Iluska. I think he's fallen asleep.'

He did wake after several prompts from Iluska. His eyes were clear. That vacant look in them had disappeared. He glanced around the room then at himself lying back on the consulting couch. One hand reached up to feel the attachments to his temple, the other to touch Iluska's face as she bent over him.

'Dr Kathleen! There must be a good reason for me to be here.' Ivan was back. This was the first time he had ever seen his doctor smile.

'Stay where you are for a moment. Let me get these things off you.'

Iluska put her arm around him as soon as he stood up, all worry gone from her face. 'Vat vas problem?'

'Nothing very serious Iluska. Ivan can explain it at home.' She didn't go into in-depth explanations to Ivan about his problem or the solution. 'Do you remember the sleeping problems you once had with strange dreams? It's been fixed. From now on your dreams will be your own.'

Being a very smart and alert person Iluska latched onto the strange statement. 'Vat zat mean Ivan?'

'It means I won't get upset anymore if you tell me off for going into the house without cleaning myself up first.'

'Is good. Ve go now. I make for you coffee.'

He believed Dr Kathleen.

The only proof would be to see if his bad dreams continued and if they didn't reoccur after another face-to-face with BB. *As sure as we're hurtling through space I'm not going to look for another meeting with her. For all I know she's still being manipulated the same as I was.*

He stepped back into the room for a last word with Dr Kathleen. 'We both know Betty's been coerced into behaving in ways she normally wouldn't. If the opportunity or the need arose would you be willing to help her as you have helped me?'

The doctor's conscience had been cleansed through her actions. She replied without any hesitation. 'Yes. And I'd do it with or without her consent. There's a very good chance she doesn't know about the implants. If they're there I can purge them.'

Bee-Bee had been entirely truthful with Captain Järvinen. She could see no reason to continue pursuing Ivan for the sake of completing her mission and to satisfy J'Ark's demands. She'd found a more meaningful reason to exist in this new reality. It wasn't simply a matter of survival anymore. She wanted a fulfilling life of her own, with Franklin. It didn't mean Ivan had to be a part of it. His being on the Butterfly would continue be a constant source of irritation unless she could find a solution.

She invited Franklin, 'Would you like to take me on another picnic?'

He jumped at the suggestion. 'Just the two of us? Great idea. We do have a few small reconnaissance cubes. I might be able to convince the Captain to let us do an external maintenance check of the Butterfly.'

A few days later a small hatch opened to reveal a tiny cube fly out of the Butterfly, looking like a scout bee taking off from the hive to search for flowers to harvest. Franklin introduced the excursion to Captain Järvinen as Bee-Bee's idea for her to get more involved in life aboard their city in the cosmos.

In the nights leading up to the excursion Bee-Bee had several bad nights. The AIDA bots resident in her head were no different to those which had recently plagued Ivan. The interaction between herself and Ivan had stirred them into uncoordinated action. Her dreams were not lucid or in the least pleasant. A jumble of disconnected events from the past overlapped memories of manipulated dreams and actual events. Featured in one of the nightmares were images of Iluska as she had been at the NASA cafeteria, with her golden plaited hair. Combined with her own animosity towards Ivan an undefinable emotion stirred Bee-Bee into putting into action a vague plan which began during her first picnic with Franklin.

She seemed enthusiastic enough to Franklin as she helped gather the makings of a picnic lunch. Yet there was something ...

'I realise you haven't been sleeping well Bee-Bee. Is everything okay? Do you still want to go? We can put it off for another day. We still have a few months before we get there.'

She'd been preoccupied with disturbing emotions all morning, looking a little vague and not her latest normal happy self. Even so she had been much happier after confiding in their Captain, right up until meeting John again.

'I was just thinking ... would it be possible for you to teach me how to pilot the cube? You know - just for fun? And it might come in handy later on as part of the work I may need to do on the Security team.'

Peter Returns from the Dark

Ivan had already seen Mars from this close during his first trip with Peter in the experimental Cube.

Using standard technology of the day a trip to Mars could take five to seven months. The American Golden Butterfly had only been traveling for two months. Bee-Bee still found it difficult to convince herself the image she saw on the maintenance Cube's screen was the real planet getting larger every day. It was too large. It was too red. She could see details like the Vales Marineris, the largest canyon in the solar system, which previously could only be identified in photos taken by space probes.

'We have come so far in such a short time,' she commented.

'And have a lot further to go. The distance between each planet is longer as we get further away from the sun. As we increase the Butterfly's speed we'll cross into the dark matter universe,' Franklin said. All leadership on the Butterfly had been briefed by Ivan about the necessity to travel much faster once the ship had proved its reliability, and the effect on normal matter such as the Cube travelling at near light speed.

'I have heard of dark matter. Is it safe?' A question to satisfy natural curiosity, the concept being so theoretical for her as to be of no importance.

'Ivan says it is. He's been there. So has his father, who by the way is thought to be in that environment right now working on some experiments I believe.'

'Incredible. John ... sorry, Ivan was always so secretive about his work. I never knew what he was doing.'

'Never mind about that. Are you ready for lunch?'

Bee-Bee glanced up at the screen again. *Lunch. What a strange notion.* The only light to be see was the reflection of it from Mars. Otherwise the universe was dark except for the brilliance of all those pin pricks of light representing myriad suns floating in the Milky Way. The mid-day light from Sol heralding picnic time had truly become a memory.

A picnic was still a picnic. As such there had to be a picnic rug and a picnic basket. Some things in life clung fiercely to traditional reality. Franklin emerged from the rear storage area with both essentials. Bee-Bee smiled broadly when she discovered the special liquid refreshment.

Placing the craft on autopilot Franklin was able to join her on the floor and still be able to keep an eye on the instruments. *So that's how to engage the autopilot* - Bee-Bee took special note of the simple process.

When the two picnickers weren't chatting total silence engulfed them. The Cube propulsion system produced no sound. Internal lighting had been dimmed to allow better view of the screens showing their surroundings. The Butterfly showed large in the rear, and behind it Mars though still at considerable distance.

Bee-Bee relaxed, enjoying Franklin's company and the sandwiches. If ever there was an anchor to reality picnic sandwiches acted as an essential tether. That illusion of normality could not be sustained. Firstly Bee-Bee had something she desperately wanted to do. After washing down the meal with the refreshments she mentioned again what she wanted to; not all of it as some details of her plan still hadn't crystallised in her thoughts.

'Is this a good time to have a driving lesson?' she asked. The way she put it made them both laugh. It was so completely incongruous considering their location and the nature of the vehicle.

'Alright. let's put all this stuff away first.'

With their attention no longer focused on the screens they didn't see it. Perhaps they would have been startled by the sudden appearance of another cube, much bigger than theirs, which wasn't actually there a moment ago. They did hear a voice which sounded like it was calling for help.

'John, John! Is that you John? Can you hear me?'

Franklin jumped to the comms. 'This is Citizen Franklin. Identify yourself - repeat - identify yourself.'

'Thank God - John, help me.' The man didn't recognise Franklin's voice.

'Stay where you are. We are coming.' Franklin immediately advised the Butterfly of the encounter. The next voice he heard was Citizen Ivan's.

'It's my father, Peter! Can you get him to follow you?'

Bee-Bee couldn't do anything. Her driving lesson would have to be postponed. She was trying to understand what was happening. They were having a picnic in the depth of space when another machine appeared out of nowhere carrying Ivan's father. And they were about to go into another enormous vehicle in space which on the inside looked like any rural/urban environment on Earth.

Emergency and medical personnel surrounded Peter's Cube as it landed on the docking platform inside the Butterfly. The fragile looking old man who stepped out of his spacecraft wept when he saw Ivan. Peter was already old when he accepted the challenge to return to the dark matter universe. Ivan had forgotten how he'd looked, only remembering the enthusiasm and the energy with which his father took on the job of creating the tools to perceive the reality within that other realm.

'Dad, what happened to you? We thought you had ...'

'No - no son. Not lost anymore. If I hadn't found you ...'

Ivan didn't think he'd be so emotional if he ever saw his father again. The gathered personnel let them immerse themselves in the reunion. Captain Järvinen gave them a few more minutes before stepping forward.

'Ivan, introductions please.'

'Ivan? Who's Ivan?' asked Peter looking at the Captain.

It was only when Captain Järvinen indicated Ivan that Peter took a second look. 'Since when did you forget to shave?'

He said it with such good humour it helped relieve the drama of the rescue and allowed everyone to relax. Bee-Bee had been watching the event unfold from the background, slowly realising the significance of the situation. She had become involved in something far more important than simply a new propulsion system for spacecraft.

Because of that very fact it made her even more determined to find a way to compensate herself for what Ivan had made her go through. *Why couldn't he trust me? If I'd only known I would never have given away any secrets. We've known each other since for ever. Why couldn't he just trust me?*

Franklin and Bee-Bee went home. Ivan and the Captain accompanied Peter to Dr Kathleen's rooms for his medical examination.

'How long have you been in the Dark Peter?' asked Dr Kathleen. She remembered the results from the first time she examined him after he and Ivan returned from the test flight. She'd already started taking a DNA sample to examine the most critical indicator of Peter's wellbeing - the difference in the age of his telomeres compared to his chronological age.

'Long enough to get hungry Doc. I was running out of supplies. Otherwise there's nothing wrong with me - just a bit weak.'

'Let me be the judge of that. Ivan, would you like to bring Captain Järvinen up to date with this bit of history, particularly as it concerns the analysis of your telomeres after your initial test flight?'

Ivan and the Captain retired to her office. She understood the significance of this fortuitous encounter with Ivan's father. She had been fully aware of all stages of the Cube's development, including the reason Peter had departed on his solo mission.

'I want to know two things Ivan. Is it safe for us to jump into the Dark, as Dr Kathleen put it - and are we likely to bump into anything along the way?'

' Yes and no. My father has a brilliant mind. He is truly a genius as far as such cosmic matters are concerned. When I first went out with him we made the jump and got quite close to Mars in only a few hours. My very presence here would indicate we didn't play dodgems out there.'

The Golden Butterfly had proven itself to be a reliable spaceship in technological terms. It had proved capable of supporting human life in its artificial internal environment. Captain Järvinen had no doubt it could continue flying through space almost indefinitely. That was not her concern. The delusion of reality affecting the passengers could become the most formidable danger to the health and long term viability of their survival. Several hundred of Apollonia's Citizenry had already demonstrated their susceptibility to denialism.

'We have to get to Titan as soon as we can Ivan. If people begin to believe our spaceship is the only reality we may end up with the same illusions people on Earth have, with all its attendant misbegotten belief systems. The people of

Apollonia have to maintain a firm grasp of the true nature of their existence.'

Ivan could identify with what the Captain was saying. He had to admit to himself that from time to time he and Iluska had to have a reality check. It was so easy to forget the unreality of their experience. To go to work each day looking after the animals on the farm, enjoying the false construct of the passing of time divided neatly into hours of daylight and night created a sense of normality which wasn't entirely real. At least not in the greater context of their existence. Iluska had more of a problem. At least Ivan had his other job maintaining the systems for keeping the Butterfly in motion and heading in the right direction.

'There is one other thing to think about, ageing.' He came back to an important issue. 'This sounds most interesting Citizen Ivan. None of us are getting any younger. Details please.'

'It's actually exactly about that. It seems, according to Dr Kathleen both Peter and I are possibly twenty hours younger than the rest of humanity. She's convinced that our telomeres had stopped ageing, or at least dramatically slowed down while we were travelling in the Dark.'

'Oh. That *is* interesting. I'll have to think about that. Does it last?'

'We'll know more after my father's been examined. He's been in the Dark since shortly before we left Earth. I have to say though that at the moment he doesn't seem to look too well.'

Preparing For the Jump

Bee-Bee's attempt to master the Cube had to be abandoned for the time being.

Seeing Ivan and Iluska together again stirred her emotions. She couldn't help thinking it should have been her not Iluska to be greeting Peter. It should have been her to experience the joy of a family reunion. None of the complicated history of events leading to this moment meant anything anymore other than what she had to go through.

Franklin couldn't understand her preoccupation on the way home after their picnic simply because it had been cut short by rescuing the space gypsy. The best thing he could do, which he'd learnt even in their short acquaintanceship was to leave her to it. He had no idea of the intricate web of unreality she and Ivan had been exposed to and the long term effects of those experiences.

Prior to their attempted picnic and driving lesson Bee-Bee had begun to have unsettled sleep. That night was no different. It resulted in Franklin being woken by her thrashing about, sliding off onto the floor, drenched in perspiration.

'Let me go you Russian bastard!' she yelled at Franklin as he tried picking her up. The pain from landing on her elbow registered just one thing ... Reality! This was Popovich trying to hurt her again. Without direct input to control the AIDA nano-bots they reactivated themselves triggered by Bee-Bee's memories of past events after seeing Ivan unexpectedly that day. How could she explain to Franklin what had just happened? Her dream had been more real than the initial assault by Popovich when he slashed her arm and pushed her to the ground. There was no pain during her entire time aboard the Butterfly until that night. How could any of it possibly be real?

He released her letting her slump back down. She backed up against the bed, rubbing her eyes trying to force herself awake. Franklin settled in front of her, waiting.

It took some time for her to come back to reality, her eyes finding it difficult to focus.

'Franklin?' she said at last. He reached out to her, causing her to withdraw further from him.

'Bee-Bee, it's me, Franklin. You had a really bad dream.' His voice helped.

'Mmm,' she moaned. 'I'm sorry.'

'Nothing to be sorry for Bee-Bee. What can I do?'

'Mmmm,' she moaned again feeling her elbow which still hurt.

'Do you want to tell me about it?'

'Later. I want to have a shower.'

He helped her onto her feet. 'Go ahead. I'll make you a coffee.'

'No!' Another memory hit of the time John had made her a cuppa after one of their bad nights of confused dreaming.

'What?'

She turned back to him. 'So sorry Franklin. I was remembering something from the past.'

'Okay. No coffee.' *If this continues I'll have to take her to see Dr Kathleen.*

Ivan quickly used the short version of his experience for describing the Dark Matter Universe to Captain Järvinen. 'The only way we'll get to Titan any faster is to make the jump. But I'd like to know what progress Dad's made with navigating in the Dark.'

'What preparation do we need to make for the jump?' asked the Captain.

'Psychological only. Our first transition was sudden with no physical indication of any change having taken place. Except we ended up literally in the dark. Absolute darkness. We couldn't see the sun, or any stars or the Earth - absolutely nothing. I think it was the most frightening experience I've ever had, except for bouncing off a wall once.'

'Bouncing off a wall?'

'Never mind. It's a long story, nothing to do with us here. I think our people need to be aware of what's going to happen before we do it. They've all become accustomed to seeing space around them filled with the Milky Way.

It's going to disappear. How do you think they're going to react. Especially the mentally borderline cases?'

'In that event we'd better find out what your father has achieved.'

Peter had made some progress in finding ways to see in the Dark. That's the only reason he was able to find the Butterfly.

Dr Kathleen brought him up to the Captains office after completing her examination. Her preliminary findings did not diverge from Peter's past medical history. Since arriving on the Butterfly Peter had not been exposed to the spaceship's completed internal environment. He knew the plans they were drafting during the initial phase of its construction; he was a co-designer.

The Captain's office had a large picture window giving a panoramic view of an internal layer of the Cube. Peter had just arrived from spending such a long time by himself in an unimaginably alien environment of darkness. Now he was standing inside an artificial structure seemingly suspended in space, overlooking a wheat field under passing clouds, being harvested by a machine with people milling about contributing to the activity.

He walked closer to the window. 'Is this ...?' He couldn't finish the sentence. His eyes were closed behind two hands cupped to hide his face as he turned away from the window towards Ivan. Dr Kathleen had to help him to a chair.

The three of them gave him time to come to terms with the situation. They all knew the effect the Butterfly had on people when they first saw it on the inside. From the outside it was a magnificent spaceship overwhelming in size and physical simplicity. Inside it revealed a world which defied comprehension. Every sense, every logic dictated it was not possible.

Peter was no different from anyone else, even though the Butterfly was his idea. He needed to come to terms with the actualisation of his concept manifest in reality. With an unexpected sudden movement he jumped up, eyes blazing with excitement, looking from the Captain to the Doctor to his son.

'I saw you! I was able to see you John!' Peter exclaimed without making much sense.

'My name is Ivan, Dad. I've changed it.'

'Don't be stupid, son. I know what your name is. I gave it to you myself. What's wrong with *John*?'

'Nothing. This is a different world, a new life. I have a new partner.' Then to reinforce his new reality he insisted. 'Call me *Ivan* from now on.'

'You were always a strange boy. You asked all those peculiar questions; like the wetness of water and ...' Peter had a tendency to digress into irrelevancies particularly when excited.

'Dad, Stop. What did you mean you saw us? How could you? There is nothing to be seen in the Dark universe.'

Dr Kathleen had her own exciting revelation to make, feeling it to be as important as anything Peter might have to say. Her discovery could add weight to Peter's report if they all knew what condition his body was in and more specifically his mind after his experiences.

'I think you should know this Captain before you hear anything else.'

'I'm fine,' interrupted Peter. 'Nothing wrong with me. A few good meals and sleep and I'll be ready to get back to work.' In spite of his protestations Peter wasn't well. Exhaustion, dehydration and a lack of nutrition had taken their toll on him. His current exuberance was nothing more than a prolonged adrenalin rush precipitated by his rescue. He sat back down, eyelids beginning to droop as Dr Kathleen gave her report.

'Best to leave him for now. He needs the rest. The situation is this, which may be serious depending on how you look at it. The delayed ageing factor is far more obvious than it was after his first trip into the Dark. You remember what I said to you then, Ivan.'

Captain Järvinen was now aware of a side effect of crossing the dimensional threshold, uncorroborated until Peter's return. There were unknown repercussions. Although without any obvious symptoms with Ivan a worrying aspect was the possibility of a reversal of the slowed ageing and possible complications. Something yet to be discovered. She listened intently to the discussion.

'Are you telling me we would not show any signs of ageing over the next few months on the way to Titan travelling in the Dark?'

Captain Järvinen contemplated the advantages resulting from such a thing.

'So it seems,' Ivan reluctantly had to agree. 'Dr Kathleen, can you tell us if the phenomenon has stopped or if it is continuing now he's back?'

'No. Sorry. I would have to compare his current condition to what he's like in a month.'

'Exactly what shape is he in,' asked Ivan, not so much as it related to Peter being his father but more as a human being who had stopped getting older. 'I would hate to see my father fade away as we move into the future at a different rate to himself, leaving him behind?'

Apart from the obvious phenomenon something else showed up in Peter's examination results. It did not seem to be anything threatening yet Dr Kathleen wanted to run some more tests. Until then there was no point mentioning it.

Remarkably in a few days Peter seemed almost the same as the day he left Earth, leaving Dr Kathleen mystified as to what prognosis she should contemplate. Considering his remarkable recovery Captain Järvinen wanted to see progress on devising the means to navigate safely through the Dark when they made the jump. Peter had said he could 'see' the Butterfly.

Under the Captain's urging Peter and Ivan launched into feverish development of the rudimentary tools Peter had invented. Their fundamental principle lay in being able to detect disturbances in gravitational waves.

'Without these gravitational wave antennae we'd be blind,' insisted Peter. 'They will be able to measure the vibrations in the fabric of space-time regardless of which dimension we're travelling in.'

'By refining the reception of baryonic acoustic oscillations we'll be able to see matter in both the light cosmos and the dark cosmos, correct?' Ivan made an educated guess.

'Yes - yes,' replied Peter impatiently. 'I've already achieved most of that, otherwise I would not have seen the Butterfly. But there's not a lot of matter out there, it's mostly a thick spaghetti soup of gravitational energy.'

Iluska, and Bee-Bee Disinfected

The two scientists knew what they were doing.

They only needed time to build the equipment and attach the sensors to the Butterfly. Ivan had to rely on Iluska to run the farm with the help of a few co-workers. Some nights Ivan wouldn't even make it home. A situation uncomfortably similar to what had happened before which may well have been the starting point for the rift between himself and Betty. Iluska certainly expressed her displeasure when she began to feel more and more abandoned.

Iluska's Yartsevo was a small village. It had far fewer people than the population of the Butterfly. It was a small world in which she was nevertheless happy. Happiness is an elusive feeling at the best of times, yet a comfortable contentment had descended on her soul once she became accustomed to life on the Butterfly. It too was a small world, far less threatening than the steel and concrete jungle of Houston.

'Vy you no come home anymore Ivan?' She confronted him some weeks after his life routine had so dramatically changed.

'I have explained the important work I have to do Maliska. It won't take much longer, then everything will be back to normal. He did try and explain how he had to make instruments to help them fly through Dark Space.

Iluska understood they were in Space. At the beginning of their journey she did not doubt it. Now the idea had become somewhat elusive. A daily routine on a normal farm, pleasant social interactions, shopping for a few nice things and the reassuring routine of everyday life had made the idea of Space much less a reality. Then there was the other woman, Citizen Bee-Bee. That was far more real. Ivan's past life with her was very real. *What if* scenarios began to infiltrate Iluska's mind. Unreasonable, without foundation and yet the woman existed, and she was there with them in Apollonia.

One day, without any warning Iluska made quite a foreboding announcement on one of those now rare occasions when Ivan managed to get home for a day or two. 'I not make babies. Nyet.'

Ivan couldn't believe it. It was happening again. His relationship being jeopardised and this time without any interference from manipulated dreams. Iluska wasn't the conniving type of person like Bee-Bee. What she said she meant. Instead of tying to argue or to justify his prolonged absences Ivan made the decision. He would make a promise and keep it, right after Iluska had a chance to speak with his father.

'Will you come to meet my father? He can explain what we are doing.'

She let go of his hand. He seemed so sincere. This was the first time he'd invited her to meet his father. Painful memories surfaced of her own family. She sat down to think things through. *I was going to be married. Yuri came to*

speak to my father about me. Everything is the other way around now. I want to meet Ivan's father. I want to know what kind of man he is.
'Da. I come.'

Peter didn't bother getting up from his desk. He was busy and annoyed at being interrupted. Nevertheless Ivan made the introductions.

'So - you are my son's new girl.' He didn't so much look at her as examine her. This only made her feel uncomfortable. 'Why did you bring her here son?'

'I vant to know vat you do,' she said revealing her assertive side.

'Why is that?' *She doesn't look like a scientist. It's none of her business.*

'Because Ivan not come home.'

'That's because he's busy with me.'

Iluska persisted. 'Vat you do?'

'Is this necessary John? We're almost finished. A few more days and the sensors can be tested. If we don't get this done it will take years to get to Titan.'

Iluska heard exactly what she needed to know. Ivan was not 'busy' with the other woman, and life would soon be back to normal. She believed Ivan's father. He had honest eyes.

'Is good. You hurry up - finish.' Iluska said this while looking at Peter. She'd given her order and expected it to be carried out, reinforced by hands on hips.

Peter was taken aback for a moment. Then with an enormous grin he slapped his son on the back. 'I like this girl son. She's the right one for you! Go home. Come back in a couple of days. Do what you have to.'

Without going into exhaustive explanations Ivan made his promise. 'I will come home more often.'

'Da. I like your fazer. He good man, like you.'

Bee-Bee deteriorated rapidly. Each night seemed to be worse than the one before. No amount of probing from Franklin could shed any light on why this problem appeared so suddenly. Bee-Bee steadfastly refused to divulge painful details from her past. The only thing he could think of was when the sleeping problem started. He only knew the recent history within the Butterfly's context - nothing of the manipulations by J'Ark from the past. As far as he was aware she wasn't like this before she met Ivan. It began to worry him.

Immediately after one of her worst nights Franklin tried exploring that possibility with her. 'I know this might be completely wrong - but is it possible your nightmares have anything to do with your past life with Ivan?'

'No. No. I don't want to think about it.' This wasn't true. All she had in her mind lately was exactly that. What made it worse was having to put her plan on hold, it being thwarted when they had to rescue Ivan's father.

'Your problems seemed to start after you met him in the Captain's office.' Franklin persisted. If she didn't open up to him he'd have no choice but to take her to the doctor.

'No.' Bee-Bee got out of bed, pacing up and down for a few minutes. He could see from her face she was fighting with memories or emotions, or something that significantly bothered her. Then she stopped. Her mouth dropped open. 'I've just remembered something. If I tell you, you have to promise me not to tell anyone.' She sat back down on the bed and took his hands in hers.

'I promise. I promise, alright. Just tell me. We have to sort this out. You can't go on living like this. How are we going to make a life together if these monsters from the past keep haunting you.'

'Did you mean that - about making a life together?' Bee-Bee still hesitated. As she thought more about it she became convinced about the cause. 'There is something in my head creating these bad dreams. It's happened before -

while I was with John, sorry Ivan. He told me about it but I took no notice at the time.' All the time she was talking her eyes never left Franklin's.

His brow furrowed and his gaze intensified trying to gauge if Bee-Bee had become mentally unstable. She could see his reaction, his hesitation to believe her. Now she'd started it made it easier to bring out the whole history of her past. *If Franklin can't accept me the way I am then there is no future for us.*

He listened without interruption. *She actually believes all this business about being controlled by smells and then by micro robots in her brain.* For over an hour Bee-Bee brought as much detail as she could remember, especially the conversation she and John had about how his dreams were not his own, and that he thought she was being controlled as well.

'I believe you Bee-Bee. I believe everything you said. There is only one way to make sure and find a permanent solution.' As he talked Bee-Bee had her own thoughts ... *The only permanent solution is to do something about John. And I know exactly what I want to do. ...*

'I'll take you to see Dr Kathleen. She was Ivan's doctor in the past, wasn't she?' Bee-Bee immediately tensed up. 'No. Don't be like that. It has to be done.' Franklin would not let her out of this one.

Dr Kathleen had been carrying the burden of the things she was forced to do to Ivan. At first it seemed exciting to be able to control a person's thinking; their dreams, to be at the very forefront of that kind of AI technology. Then her conscience got in the way. The ethics associated with manipulating a person that way, without their knowledge, purely for financial benefit was wrong - absolutely wrong. And now here was this situation with Ms Johnson. She remembered Ivan mentioning he thought she had been infected with AIDA as well. It would be the easiest thing in the world to find out.

Without any hesitation Dr Kathleen agreed to try and treat Bee-Bee.

'Citizen Franklin has explained the situation. Are you prepared for me to probe your hippocampus to see if there are any resident AI nano-bots causing you problems?'

'Is it going to hurt?' *I don't need any more pain in my life to tell me what is real.*

'No. None at all. A few minutes to set up; to get the attachments onto your head. Then I do a scan, which will show what's in there. If they're there it's a simple process to instruct them to leave your system. You will feel nothing. Are you ready?'

Franklin stayed with Bee-Bee. It's not that he didn't trust the doctor. Bee-Bee needed support, probably more than at any other time in her life.

'Right, we're ready to start.'

'Dr Kathleen,' Bee-Bee raised herself enough to see the doctor, 'did you do this for John, I mean Ivan?'

It was hard to get used to your ex-partner being called by such a different name.

'Yes. Just relax.'

'He's free?'

'Yes. He is. Now stay still.'

Without rushing she scanned Bee-Bee's entire neural structure. Then did it again.

'Got them. They've all gathered into your hippocampus, and they are active. Something must have set them off.' Dr Kathleen knew the process and how the little devils behaved. Without any doubt it was Ivan's appearance back in her life setting off the triggers. They were not supposed to be autonomous, and probably weren't. She was convinced Armbruster had secreted code into their algorithms to behave exactly as they had. 'This won't take long.' She already had the command string and uploaded it. The bots reacted instantly and did what Ivan's swarm did. Within days they would be flushed out of Bee-Bee's system.

Next, Dr Kathleen decommissioned the micro controller implanted in her chest. Once deactivated it could stay there. It was inert and would not harm her.

'There you go. All done.'

Bee-Bee couldn't hold back her flood of tears. She realised the reality she'd been living on Earth wasn't her own reality. With the overwhelming emotion of being given her freedom she broke out into hysterical laughter on top of her tears. Dr Kathleen cried with her. She too had been released from the guilt she had carried for so long.

On the way home Bee-Bee asked Franklin to do something very special for her. 'Could we go on another picnic, tomorrow. I need to bathe in the light of the stars.'

Crossing Into Dark Matter

Bee-Bee learnt to fly the transport Cube, Franklin unaware of her true intentions for doing so.

So much had changed in such a short time. The euphoria of knowing she'd been freed from covert manipulation by robots and the overt machinations of J'Ark made a substantial difference to her outlook on life. A new perspective on the importance of some things as opposed to the weight she placed on the desires and plans of others should have had a dramatic effect. Bee-Bee looked forward to the simple renewable pleasures promised by day-to-day existence with Franklin. She had also been given new responsibilities to help maintain security in Apollonia. To that end she convinced herself of the importance of being able to control the smaller Cubes in order to effectively carry out her duties.

Remarkably the Butterfly's population adjusted to their new reality with only a few cases of denialism. Even those few had to face the loss of what they considered normal when exposed to a series of 'reality' picnics enforced by Captain Järvinen. The very process of having to leave their Earth-like environments and jobs aboard the Butterfly to climb into small spacecraft shaped like cubes to go out into cold space to be surrounded by nothing more than the cosmos helped to re-align their awareness. Looking up into the night sky from Earth's surface could not compare with the impact of the sharp magnitude of the Milky Way.

To reinforce their 'picnic' experiences large screens throughout the Butterfly's interior showed exactly what they had experienced on their outings. They could gauge the image of Mars becoming larger with the passing of weeks.

Apollonia must have been the strangest city to exist in the universe. It could not be seen, unlike the cities on Earth clearly visible from space. It travelled through space cocooned in a golden cube which didn't look like a planet or a moon. It didn't even look like a spaceship. Yet there were people living there who now accepted this existence. How would they react if suddenly their screens went blank and all they could see was impenetrable blackness?

The theory of a dark matter universe had become common knowledge by the 22nd century, just another theory spread by scientists which the common person didn't really believe.

It might have been out there - somewhere - but it couldn't be seen, or touched or experienced. Captain Järvinen had not mentioned to anyone on this expedition their intention to go that realm en route to their destination out of necessity. They could not afford to take seven years to get to Titan.

'It worries me how our people are going to react, Ivan.' She wasn't alone in feeling the apprehension. The gathering of community leaders, technicians and scientists met to discuss the imminent jump into the unknown. Peter among them, feeling impatient as always for he had plans of his own. Ivan and Iluska sat on the opposite side of the conference room to Franklin and Bee-Bee.

Citizen Bee-Bee knew she had to have a confrontation with Ivan. Residual feelings continued to permeate her daily thoughts, though no longer a slave to AIDA generated nightmares. This meeting presented a possible opportunity.

'I'll tell you what I want to do' said Captain Järvinen addressing the meeting. 'If you disagree I'll have to find a way to convince you.' At this point in the proceedings she heard no objections. 'When we make the jump into the Dark I want to be prepared and I want our Citizens to be prepared. Peter, a most important job for you. You've been there. Go back and return with images of what your new instruments can see. I want to show people what they can expect.'

'Yes Captain!' He gave a mock salute. He didn't consider himself to be a part of the expedition and didn't intend to remain on the Butterfly. 'You want me to go now?'

'Do you have a problem with that?'

'No. None at all. You may not like what I come back with. Some of your Citizens will have trouble with the images.' He wouldn't say anymore despite worried questions from a couple of the more sensitive attendees. 'I'll be back in no time at all.' Only Ivan understood the allusion to the differential passage of time in the two dimensions.

'Iluska. Thank you for coming. I have a job for you as well, which I think you will like as much as you seem to like butterflies. Can you organise a Festival for us; a 'Flowers and Butterflies' festival. Lots of flowers and butterflies and a big feast. It needs to be on the day we make the jump.'

'Da! Da! I make.'

Ivan had never seen her so excited, not even when he first showed her the rockets at the NASA space centre. 'I go now!' Iluska intensified flower production on every farm level, then engaged a large team to catch butterflies in preparation for the Festival.

That's two people who had important jobs to do. 'Bee-Bee. Here's your chance to let us see how good you are at your job. I expect there will be some discontent, perhaps a few people who'll be unable to cope with the transition, though it be temporary. I expect you'll be able to initiate a few measures to maintain order and peace at the festival and in the days following.'

'Yes Captain. I'm sure Franklin will be right there beside me to keep me focused.' Bee-Bee jumped at the chance to do something tangible, something simple with clear benefit. Becoming part of the UNSC was supposed to satisfy that ambition in her. That organisation had seriously let her down.

'Oh yes - Franklin. I need a register of every person on board and where I can expect to find them in case of - well, just in case. I expect it'll be a time consuming job.' Franklin got the hint. He despatched himself with alacrity as Peter and Iluska had done. 'As for the rest of you - make yourselves useful to those three.' One or two people started asking questions of detail and procedure, things they should be able to work out for themselves. Captain Järvinen said as much. 'If there are no more interruptions please get on with it.'

As an aside to Ivan, 'I don't want to get into complications with everybody asking questions about this telomere ageing suspension phenomenon. I do however want to discuss it with you. Please come with me. Kathleen, I need you too.' No one at the meeting consciously noticed their Captain dropping the 'Citizen' prefix protocol.

Yet it had the effect of bringing them into a more personal liaison with their leader.

Ivan couldn't help comparing the Captain's method of getting things done as opposed to the bourbon swilling Angus Silverman at NASA. *I can work with this woman. But then again Captain Järvinen doesn't have to cope with all the complications Silverman must have had in front of him.*

Bee-Bee waited for Ivan outside, without knowing exactly what she wanted to say to him. Maybe if he wasn't aboard she might have been able to let go of the past. But he was there, a constant reminder of how messed up her life had become. And it was only because of him, because of his stubbornness.

'Let me get this right Ivan,' Captain Järvinen wanted immediate reassurance, 'You personally don't feel any side effects from this gravitational doppler shift you experienced, correct?' Neither she, or for that matter Peter, knew just how much effect the absence of light had to do with the ageing phenomenon. Of all the contingencies put in place to safeguard the success of the colonisation mission none specifically addressed the issue of suspended ageing whilst travelling in the dark matter dimension.

Dr Kathleen's regular check-ups should have been enough. 'I've assessed both Peter and Ivan. If it will make you feel any better they are both ageing normally, the same as you and I. Although Peter's situation is a little more complicated. We won't know for certain if he'll live any longer than the rest of us until he passes over to the other dimension from which he may not be able to return if he stays there too long.' She glanced at Ivan. Whatever the depth of relationship was between father and son Ivan might still be sensitive to a premature death of his father caused by their experimentations.

'I've been working with my father, spending a lot of time in his company lately. Other than being his normal cranky self I could see no changes in him. He gets a little tired from time to time, which is a new development. If he keeps going back and forth from the Dark I might end up being older than he is.'

'Kathleen, all I want to do is get to Titan in one healthy piece with the rest of my people. I need you to monitor general behaviour amongst our Citizens. I don't want to end up with a civilisation of immortals on Titan. I'll be relying on you to prevent that.'

Dr Kathleen began to mumble some objection about science not having evolved to the stage of controlling life spans. 'I'm not interested in what you can't do.' The implied dismissal was enough to send the doctor on her way, bumping into Bee-Bee outside the office.

'Are you sleeping better?'

'Yes,' came the curt answer. She didn't want an extended conversation and thereby miss the chance to speak with her John.

The Captain had made the situation quite clear. Mortality had to remain the status quo.

'Do you have a special job for me?' Ivan asked the Captain.

'Apart from keeping this ship afloat what else would you like to do?'

He walked out of the office without wasting any more of his Captain's time. He didn't see Bee-Bee waiting for him, consequently he ran into her with such momentum he had to reach out to stop her from falling.

He hadn't touched her for many years.

His mind flooded with the memory of her standing at the front door of their house in a red dress, with a bag in her hand. He remembered the surprise and that he didn't recognise her straight away.

They held onto each other for longer than necessary. Bee-Bee's thoughts went into turmoil. This wasn't supposed to happen. She could feel the scar on the palm of his hand against her bare elbow. Captain Järvinen heard the commotion and stepped out of the office to see what the noise was, breaking the spell. Bee-Bee fled. Ivan apologised self-consciously and also went on his way.

Three days later Peter returned, excited, energised, though looking tired again. He didn't bother reporting to Captain Järvinen. He went directly to his laboratory which had been set up for himself and Ivan. He was already there working on refining the navigational tools to use in the Dark.

Without a 'hello', or 'how are you', from Peter he said with a glint in his eye, 'This should convince all the unbelievers. Have a look at this!'

'Hello Dad. Good to see you so happy,' Ivan made the sarcastic opening gambit.

'Stop your jabbering. Concentrate.' While he proceeded to download his new data onto the ships AI he tried to explain ... 'There is no matter in the Dark universe. There are eddies and whirlpools of gravitational energy, with dangerous concentrations of gravitational back wash near large planetary masses ...' he had to pause to take a breath ... 'You won't have to worry about running into anything, unless it's in our normal matter cosmos, but you'll be able to see everything now.'

On their first trip into the Dark they didn't see anything. The equipment to do so didn't exist. That's not what held Ivan's attention.

'You said *you* won't have to worry. What did you mean? You're coming with us aren't you?'

'Watch!' Peter ignored him as he played images on the screen, images he'd brought back and enhanced. He didn't go far from the Butterfly; far enough so it could be seen as a disturbance in the refracted wave patterns of gravitational waves.

Ivan watched magenta and cobalt blue patterns swirl in front of him. He had to sit, as if that would help him believe what he was looking at.

'There's the Butterfly!' Peter pointed to a disturbance in the swirling gravitational wave image. 'That's how I saw you. There's not enough detail to tell what's causing the interference but you can clearly see it's there and how big it is.'

Some of the patterns looked like ripples' reflections of light through water at the bottom of a swimming pool. In other places magnificent concentric circles of waves spread from a central point, much like small concentric waves created by a rock dropped into calm water. At the centres bright yellow fuzzy shapes pulsed in regular beats as if generating the waves. 'Those are neutron stars orbiting each other,' said Peter. 'Stay away from those.' Ivan didn't look up, completely mesmerised by the moving images.

'How are we going to explain all this?' he said aloud to himself.

'Not my problem son. I'll be going back out there soon enough.'

Ivan couldn't tear his eyes away from the extraordinary overlapping colours created by gravitational wave interference patterns showing their phase differences. 'They might even enjoy this. Did you create the colours Dad?'

'It's all black and white out there. I introduced the colours to make the feeling of chaos less disturbing.'

Peter had panned his recording equipment towards the Butterfly. Ivan saw another smaller disturbance in the pattern as his eyes became used to the overlapping movements and colours. 'Is that Mars?' It had shown up not as a red planet but as a shimmering mass of white light with a halo reminiscent of the spread of magnetic waves around Earth. 'They are not going to believe this is real.

They'll think it's one of those digital artworks which had become so popular before we left.'

'Again not my problem. What they believe to be real is entirely up to them.'

'Houston this is the Butterfly - do you copy?'

Captain Järvinen had to repeat several times before an incredulous voice responded.

'Butterfly - this is Houston. What happened to you!?'

She didn't want to go into long explanations. This was a courtesy call for a brief update. 'We are about to make the jump Houston - repeat - we are about to jump into Dark Matter. Butterfly will make contact on arrival at Titan. Butterfly out.' Captain Järvinen terminated the discussion, reverting to silent flying. Houston didn't get a chance to have a discussion with the Captain, putting Silverman into a particularly foul mood.

The day had arrived. They were ready.

Apollonia looked like spring had arrived in full glory of colour and sunshine. The town centre could barely contain all the people who had been primed with the expectation of a mystery celebration. Flowers of every description festooned every balcony, every street corner and lined every street. Balloons decorating trees moved gently to the sounds of Vivaldi's Spring. Iluska waited to release the butterflies right after Captain Järvinen's announcement.

Standing on the usual balcony the Captain began softly. 'You have been outside. You have seen the stars. They swim in the light matter universe.' She paused to let the sounds of Spring wash over their manufactured internal reality.

'There is also the darkness. The darkness of the Dark Matter Universe. We will soon follow Peter. Watch.'

All the large screens switched to show Peter stepping into his Cube. Everyone could see him wave and smile. They watched as the portal opened to let his Cube make its way out of the Butterfly. They had all done the same thing each time they went for a picnic under the light of the stars. Screens showed Peter moving away becoming smaller each moment. All of that made sense. It was believable.

Someone called out, 'What is this? What happened to Peter?' Peter had disappeared from in front of their eyes as he made the jump.

The image changed again showing their Butterfly, now familiar, with Mars in the background. Sounds of Vivaldi's Winter followed Spring as the Milky Way disappeared. At first inky black darkness. Patterns of moving colours emerged into view, soft, indistinct, inviting questions to be asked.

They heard the quiet reassuring voice of Captain Järvinen. 'Peter has made the Jump. He is showing us what he sees in the Dark Matter Universe.' The colours and movement of everything Ivan first saw filled every screen. 'This is the Art of the Cosmos,' she declared.

There were no more questions. What they saw wasn't like seeing images of the Horse Head Nebula or the Pillars of Creation from millions of light years away. The canvas of gravitational wave magic enveloped them, flowed over and around them. They were inside the magic.

For five minutes she let them swim in the pool of their imagination, to be broken by the sight of Peter returning to the Butterfly.

Vivaldi had stopped.

Captain Järvinen gave Ivan and Iluska the signal.

Citizen Levi jumped them into the other dimension.

The opening bars of Beethoven's 5th released the kaleidoscope of butterflies accompanied by larger, more vibrant images of the patterns of Darkness.

Their accustomed noon-day sunlight had been dimmed for effect.

'This is no longer your imagination,' announced Captain Järvinen. 'We are now travelling in another dimension.'

The images were wonderful, fantastic, incredible but everyone's attention was diverted from the magic.

'Where is our sun?'

'What did you do with our light?'

'Is this an eclipse?'

'There was no storm forecast!'

Agitation had begun to pervade the large gathering.

The only reality they understood was the one under their feet, and the yellow sun above their heads. Nothing changed when the Butterfly made the jump. They couldn't feel the rapid increase in speed. There was no change in G force. Everything was the same. Butterflies happily landed on flowers oblivious of everything except the pollen of survival.

Citizen Bee-Bee became worried a riot might break out, quickly deploying her peacekeeping force out of the shadows to the perimeters of the gathering.

Captain Järvinen's expression froze. After all the effort she'd made to get the Citizens to realise the fluid nature of their reality they still didn't understand. *What will it take to make them realise we are no longer on Earth?* She made an impromptu decision ...

'Yes Captain?' Levi, on stand-by in the main control centre responded immediately.

'Lower the sunlight to level 4.' Normal noon sun had been set at level 10. *Are they so primitive they need a Sun God to dictate reality to them?*

Agitation increased tenfold. Beethoven's 5th wasn't helping the mood. The decrease in ambient lighting only increased the vibrancy of colours and movement of swirling gravitational energy seen on the screens as the

Butterfly flew through it. Captain Järvinen had to shout to make herself heard above the noise of the agitated throng.

'I will bring back the Sun!' It made no sense to her to have to speak that way to her Citizens. Levi increased the illumination to 6.

She heard some people muttering as the shouting began to die down, as if they were praying, only making Captain Järvinen angrier. 'Levi, more!' He increased it to 10.

Many others joined in to pray. Captain Järvinen thought she heard sounds of people giving thanks. *Wrong! It's all wrong!* 'We are in control of our reality!' she heard herself shout. 'I'll show you!' She ordered Levi, 'I want lightning and thunder!'

'Yes Captain. How much?'

'I'll tell you when to stop. Just do it!' She shouted almost hysterical.

Citizens Iluska and Bee-Bee were standing beside her on the balcony overlooking the main square as the drama unfolded. They each took an arm and led her inside.

Dr Kathleen rushed into the room. Obviously something had triggered their Captain. She was ready to give her a mild sedative. Outside in the full light of the sun thunder clashed and lightning lit up the buildings. Most people were familiar with augmented virtual reality environments. This must have seemed like they'd all been transported into that world.

'Levi, stop.' Captain Järvinen came to her senses as she was forcefully taken inside. Seeing the doctor with a syringe helped her to refocus.

Outside the music continued. The images on screens continued. The sun was back. Butterflies continued their harvesting.

Citizen Bee-Bee stepped out onto the balcony. She waited until eyes focused on her. 'We are now travelling through the Dark Matter Universe towards Titan. As we near it the Butterfly will resume its journey through the cosmos as you know it.' They heard, they muttered, they had settled down when the lightning and thunder stopped. 'The rest of today is a holiday. Enjoy the party.' What else could she say to so many people who'd completely lost all sense of reality?

From   Mars

To   Jupiter

To Saturn

Progress in the Dark was easier, faster.

Previous to the jump Mars had been many weeks away. Now it was only days.

Peter was still with them helping Ivan to navigate by interpreting the signs of normal matter in the sea of gravitational waves.

The Citizens of Apollonia once again felt nothing as the Butterfly slowed to cruising speed in the near vicinity of Mars. They did notice the change from cosmic art on their screens to an enormous image of Mars, which was not an enlargement.

Every transport Cube and maintenance Cube was despatched from the Butterfly when they arrived at the three hundred mile orbital distance. Each had a full payload of Citizenry forced to absorb the scenery. 'I want every person to see this planet firsthand,' Captain Järvinen told the Burghers of their four districts. 'We will wait here while they do two full orbits. Eventually they will have to believe their eyes.'

She badly wanted to revel in this unique life event herself. Captain Järvinen gave up her place to give a possible unbeliever the breathtaking experience. Imagination, VR constructs or photographs couldn't replace the impact of actual reality. She realised the rightness of her decision when so many people expressed a desire to land on this planet, to ascend to the summit of Olympus Mons, and walk along the bottom of the great canyon. Mars put on a spectacle for the visitors from Earth with a planet encircling dust storm so large it almost hid the peak of Olympus Mons.

These visions would have been enough in themselves to convince even the most diehard denialist. Captain Järvinen could only enjoy the video of their return as they would have seen the Butterfly in context of its proximity to the red planet. Those on the excursion experienced not only the mental concept of perspective between the Cube and the sphere, they saw it in sharp three dimensional reality.

Photographs were not permitted to be taken. 'I want every person to remember the experience in their soul. That will never fade. Photographs lose the clarity of their origins with time. They externalise the images. The experience should remain as an internal conviction of a snapshot of the foundation of their existence.'

Only one expedition went out at this particular cosmic wayside rest stop. The Captain had plans to make another. That one she determined not miss.

'I called you together to discuss what happened when we made the first jump.'

Once again the routine of life brought Bee-Bee and Ivan face-to-face. It wasn't Captain Järvinen's intention, though she continued to be watchful of developments in their relationship. They acknowledged each other as acquaintances would without either making reference to the incident outside the Captain's office. It did come to

Bee-Bee's mind. Ivan made no indication of having thought of it again.

'I apologise for my behaviour,' The Captain began, followed by words of support from her officers. Ivan particularly felt empathy with the Captain's frustration. 'This is an incredible situation for all of us to find ourselves in. I believe there are still people on Earth who are uncomfortable at being in buildings higher than trees. And look at where we are now. Is it a wonder so many of us need a little more time to make the adjustment to living in a reality which isn't a virtual simulation but an actuality.' Thank you all. Now - on another issue. I'm prepared to take advice from you as to whether we should make this next matter public knowledge, considering our Citizens' latest behaviour.' Only Dr Kathleen, Ivan and Peter knew about this next detail apart from herself.

'Immortality.'

Stunned silence from her audience. As if they didn't have enough fiction in their lives to deal with their Captain was about to make everything far more complicated. What she said made no sense. Human lifespan had a very narrow time-span. At no stage did an extended life duration ever come up in any briefings about the Titan project.

'Do you have the data Dr Kathleen?' The doctor had been carrying out tests on a large sample of their people since they jumped back into normal space-time on arrival near Mars.

'Yes. The condition is confirmed.'

'Let me make it a little easier for you,' she said on seeing looks of incomprehension on so many faces. Bee-Bee seemed to be more unsettled by the revelation than the others. Perhaps because unlike them she'd already had to endure the warping of her reality so many times, and the idea of immortality definitely fell into the category of warped reality. She edged her chair closer to Franklin, sneaking a hand onto his lap. He was much too busy with his own thoughts trying to interpret the concept to interpret her action.

'Slowed ageing, or if you like suspended ageing. Dr Kathleen's examinations confirm what Citizens Ivan and Peter have known for some time. Ivan, would you like to elaborate?'

To bring everyone into the picture he started at the beginning with his first test flight in the experimental Cube. They listened in silence until he'd finished. He included everything except his speculations about a possible side effect.

Burgher Esmeralda from District #2, called Ulysses City, started the conversation. She, like the Burghers of the other two districts had little involvement in the running of the Butterfly other than managing the welfare of their own contingent of citizens. They had enough on their hands after the revelation was made of the spaceship's jump into the Dark. They didn't need another trigger to set people off.

'Do you know why we called our district 'Ulysses'? The Ulysses butterfly is a symbol of transformation. I don't think any of you will disagree with the appropriateness of the name its Citizens have chosen for their home. It represents their appreciation of the change they are going through. That understanding had been tested during the Festival with your news of jumping into another dimension. Now you want to tell them they could possibly become immortal.'

Burgher Esmeralda didn't labour her point.

Ivan glanced at Captain Järvinen before contributing further. 'The medical examinations have shown the effects of our first jump. It's definite. Our ageing had been suspended during our time in the Dark.' He stopped immediate interjections. There was more to it. 'We are all back to normal ageing now. This was only one jump. We need to make several with the Butterfly.' Again he had to forestall interruptions. 'It doesn't harm us. I want to make that point very clear. We don't know if the effect is cumulative. We also don't know if there is going to be a period of catch-up for the time lost and what effect that may have. In some respects we are pioneers. We are like the sailors braving the danger of sailing over the edge of the world to be swallowed by dragons.'

'That's no consolation,' someone said. It may have been Franklin or Levi.

Further discussion ensued. Outlandish fears surfaced, like the idea of overpopulation on the Butterfly if no one ever died. The outcome was an unequivocal - No, do not tell them.

'I agree with you,' said Captain Järvinen. '*We* need to be aware of the situation. Dr Kathleen will continue with her monitoring.

However, I would ask all of you not to spread this information. As you saw, our Citizens are having enough problems coming to terms with how their lives have already changed.'

The gathering got ready to leave the conference amid private discussions exploring this latest twist to their existence.

'Before you go you should know, we are making another jump tomorrow. Our next stop is Jupiter.'

After all that Bee-Bee's attention focused on discussing a most private matter with Franklin. Something she and Ivan had been extremely careful not to have happen to complicate their lives back on Earth. She didn't even notice Ivan glance in her direction as they left.

Captain Järvinen didn't announce this next jump. She let the screens tell the story with the change of imagery from Mars to the now familiar gravitational wave patterns generated in the dark matter universe. A few people commented on it. Some believed it to be a replay of what they had seen before. Others speculated, without concern, of the possibility they had jumped again. But all went on with their daily life routines.

Perhaps if there had been some physical manifestation for the change of going from one dimension to another; like a shudder in the spacecraft or some sounds of engines roaring the people may have taken more notice. As it was their manufactured normality had blunted all thought of dwelling on where they were and where they were going, and how they were getting there. Captain Järvinen timed the jump for the night period to lessen the psychological impact.

Iluska had been at the meeting. 'Vy you no tell me zis?'

'Because it's something that effects all of us. So it makes no difference,' replied Ivan as they made their way home. She didn't seem angry at all.

'It important.'

He didn't understand why she was so concerned about the ageing factor. 'Why? You can see it has not affected your health or mine.'

'Ven ve have babies vill zey grow up?'

That stopped him in his tracks. Nobody had thought of that little complication. Not even himself or Peter. If his babies were born with inherited telomeres which didn't age what would actually happen? Was it even possible? Iluska saw the concern on his face.

'You speek viz doctor. Da?'

Up till then Ivan could only think of benefits to the strange situation; the main one having the ability to travel cosmic distances without having to worry about the time factor. As long as they were self-sufficient theoretically they could travel to the other end of the Milky Way and back. As long as they remained in the Dark they would not age.

'Dr Kathleen has confirmed we are back to normal ageing now,' Ivan reminded her.

It wasn't reassuring enough for her. 'You ask,' Iluska was adamant. Now that she'd raised the matter it began to play on his mind. How would such a circumstance effect the entire colonising project? He imagined the very fact of quasi immortality could bring the whole effort to an end. Whatever they may have planned would never become a reality with a future, perhaps a struggle at the beginning but with no future if the babies couldn't grow up.

'We've just come out of a jump. We do have some pregnancies on board. I've tested the mothers and the foetuses. You can tell Iluska every single one of them is growing normally.' Dr Kathleen realised a little more time would reveal any problems. She kept a strict record of all her patients. Ivan seemed reassured, especially that she'd always been honest with him in the past.

'Did you know about any of this when you were with Ivan?' Franklin never really worried about anything that *might* happen. Yet he preferred to have full knowledge of what was happening around him at any one time, one of the aspects of his character making him good at his job.

'Nothing. I couldn't get anything out of him. Only once did he let his guard down when he mentioned something about the Cube spacecraft. Not the Butterfly, only one of the small ones.'

Bee-Bee didn't want to talk about the past. She and Iluska had similar concerns. Whatever the world might become either on Earth or in space there was one constant no scientist had ever distilled down into a formula. A circumstance of human existence; continuation of that existence. One which took no notice of whether the human psyche could cope with changing realities. It was - procreation. The primary imperative of all life could be summed up in one word - babies.

Betty had been with John for most of her life from childhood to adulthood. In all that time the bond between them had not evolved further than to the level of mutual benefit. Their degree of commitment to each other always seemed to have a caveat dependent on career considerations rather than anything else. Their moves to other partners did not involve the least sense of abandonment of their existing relationship.

'We're together aren't we Citizen Franklin?' Bee-Bee asked suddenly. His thoughts had meandered off into an entirely different realm to consider unlikely aspects of having to keep track of an exponentially increasing population if this immortality thing should kick in. Her question took him by surprise.

'What's this *Citizen* business Bee-Bee?'

'What I mean is - we're together, as in life-partners?

'Do you need to ask?'

'Yes I do indeed. If you're going to be a dad you'd better hang around.'

They had just arrived at their apartment, barely having closed the door when Bee-Bee delivered a reality which hadn't made a nest in his thoughts so far. He turned to face her, a smile beginning to make its way across his face. At first it felt a little strange to actually think of himself as more than a singular unit even though Bee-Bee had become a part of his life. The idea of having a child brought an entirely new level of reality to their relationship. It amazed him how little effort it took to conceptualise a cot in their spare room.

Bee-Bee immediately saw in his smile that he took her statement as a happy invitation.

'No, no, no! Not just yet Franky Boy. We need to talk.'

'Sure, Citizen Bee-Bee,' he relaxed his hold around her waist, grinning at the sudden formality - no less at the thought of a little human creature calling him 'da-da'.

'I want to be reassured babies are going to be *normal* before I'm prepared to go shopping for one, particularly in regard to them having a future. I'm sure under normal circumstances, even considering we are flying through space in a magnificent simulation of Earth reality, we would not have to consider any of us not having a future.'

'Oh. I see. I imagine it would be pretty difficult to devise an experiment to test the theory, though I'm sure there'd be a few willing to try.' His grin lingered.

I couldn't have imagined in a million years this situation for myself. Bee-Bee considered after Franklin had fallen asleep. *Not so long ago I had only one aim in life. What happened that? John - Ivan, whatever he's decided to call himself; he's still* ... She couldn't quite define her thoughts about him. Yet she remembered her desire to somehow soothe all the pain he had caused her. That need stubbornly persisted.

The distance between Mars and Jupiter was far longer than between Earth and Mars. Life had settled down to a normal routine with no thought to the fact the population of the Butterfly was travelling through the Dark Matter of the Universe at an unprecedented speed, and all the while normal life went on, biological ageing for the human organism had been substantially slowed.

They couldn't feel it. Nobody ever took any notice of the images on the large screens telling them where they were. It made no difference. They still had to get up in the morning and go to work. They still had opportunities for entertainment and social interaction. They were as close to being happy as could be imagined. Life in the Butterfly became much more stable and predictable than it had ever been on Earth. They could even count on the weather without having to worry about dramatic climate change bringing unprecedented disasters.

Earth was gone. Their lives on Earth had been forgotten.

It was too soon to think of living on Titan. Maybe Titan didn't even exist.

Some months later images on screens changed.

Jupiter had become the focus of attention. Some people questioned what they were observing. Was it images from the old Web telescope enhanced for their benefit? Perhaps it was some form of advertising for another imminent festival. Only the leadership prepared for the next phase of their journey towards Titan. Jupiter was their last rest stop before the Butterfly arrived there.

Dr Kathleen had difficulty in accommodating into her knowledge base the differential time lapse between their chronological ageing and biological ageing. She kept Captain Järvinen up to date on any abnormalities she'd discovered on the way to Jupiter from Mars. There were none. New babies not yet born in the alternate dimension couldn't be tested yet.

'We are not leaving here until every individual has enjoyed an orbit around Jupiter,' she advised the Burghers of each district. This was her last opportunity to convert any latent disbelievers. Such people could prove to be potential mutineers. There was no place for them on the Butterfly.

'Not again!' one excursionist exclaimed as she was ushered into one of the cubes due for an orbital run around Jupiter. So many of the travellers had difficulty in imprinting into their schema of existence their experiences of seeing cosmic reality close up. Yet for others such outings became a source of some annoyance for having interrupted their daily routines. 'We know Jupiter's out there. Why do we have to go into its playground and put our lives in danger?' Such comments arose when Io came into view with its active volcanoes throwing lava many miles into space.

Europa fascinated some people when they were told it may have a liquid ocean with the possibility of life. But so what? 'We're going to Titan. There's definitely going to be life on Titan! - Us!'

Whoever drew up the schedule for the Jupiter fly-bys were not instructed to ensure Ivan and Bee-Bee didn't end up in the same Cube - or to ensure partners should be kept together.

Franklin and Iluska were enthralled by seeing how extensive Jupiter's moon garden was. So many moons with such incredible diversity. Those two sightseers gravitated to each other probably because of their familiarity from so many meetings with their Captain.

'You have a most interesting accent,' Citizen Franklin commented. Just idle chatter.

'Da. I Russian. You?'

'American. Born in Houston, Texas.'

'I know Houston Texas!' With all the strangeness life had thrown at her and now finding herself in space looking at this most incredible planet, to talk with a person from Houston was a poignant reminder of another reality she'd lost for ever. 'It wonderful place,' she said smiling broadly. She knew deep in herself it wasn't actually a wonderful place. She lost Yuri there. Not a wonderful place at all. And yet - it was exactly that because it represented a primordial destiny zone of where she as a human being should have been at that time.

They couldn't even see each other as Iluska and Ivan ended up having to board different Cubes located at different exit points in the Butterfly's shell. Bee-Bee and Ivan hadn't been explicitly avoiding each other, but were both mindful of accidental meetings other than at official gatherings convened by their Captain. Ivan could see Bee-Bee at the front of the embarkation line.

I can't avoid this. He didn't want a confrontation in public. She was intelligent enough not to bring it on. He knew she had some tact. Besides there have been other opportunities if she wanted to make trouble.

Bee-Bee noticed him getting aboard. 'Shit!' She couldn't remember having used the word since she first saw the knife in Popovich's hand. *Shit, I hope he doesn't come over.*

Ivan waited, prevaricating until the Cube was in orbit. Io had just come into view with its spectacular display of lava and sulphur spewing out onto its surface from numerous volcanoes. He was waiting until Betty became distracted before going over to her. Even though they were one and a half million miles from Jupiter that fireball was one hell of a spectacle.

'Betty.'

'John!' She pretended to be startled.

'Ivan.'

'Whatever. Why?'

'Why did I come over or why the name change?' They'd often had to clarify one another. Common understanding never came easily between them. It must have stemmed from the time when Ivan was never sure if he was chasing her, or she him.

'Whatever.' *What does he want now?*

'We can't avoid each other for ever. This is a small world and it won't get any larger when we get to Titan.'

He is a courageous bastard. He's always had a backbone. Betty had to admit to herself. It didn't make speaking to him like this any easier.

'No.'

'So what are you really doing here?'

'Same as you, looking at Jupiter.'

That's not what he meant and she knew it. She wasn't ready for this. There was still too much interference from her emotions for her to be anything more than grudgingly civil. Extended gaps between the words of their strained conversation gave enough time to complete the single orbit and see them heading back to the Butterfly.

'Okay. Maybe some other time.'

'Yes, maybe,' Betty replied, almost inaudibly. As soon as she saw Ivan getting on the cube her mind reminded her she was Betty, not Bee-Bee. It catapulted her back to another realm, where things were both simpler and more complicated at the same time. *Not if I can help it.* Then she realised that wasn't entirely true. There was only one reason she wanted to learn how to control a Cube.

Angus Silverman could barely control himself when told of the brief contact from the Butterfly.

'They had clear and explicit instructions to keep me informed all the way. And what do I get? A three second Hello and Goodbye!'

James Armbruster could do nothing to calm him down. He'd joined Silverman in his office as soon as Captain Järvinen made the contact. While listening Armbruster strode over to the bar and prepared two bourbons. The strategy had worked before. The bourbon had helped them make a few important decisions in the past. He let Silverman blow himself out before offering him the drink.

Red in the face, perspiration beads forming on his forehead Silverman dropped into a sofa.

'How are we progressing with the second Cube,' asked Armbruster.

Silverman's bourbon came first - several gulps of ambrosia. 'Not bloody fast enough. For all we know they're all dead in that blasted dark matter universe of theirs.'

Armbruster tried to be conciliatory. 'We'll know soon enough. Based on what John calculated they've got at least another three months to get there.'

'I hope we've got enough bloody bourbon to last that long.' Silverman could not be placated. 'I thought we'd made such a good choice in Järvinen as the Captain.

Most impressive with her background with the Finns. Turns out she's got a mind of her own.'

More complaints, mostly from Silverman, which the best part of the bottle of ambrosia failed to progress into the realm of constructive decisions.

'And they cut us off! What is she playing at? This entire enterprise is critical. It's not a picnic in the park!'

J'Ark knew nothing of what was happening. Being a member of the ESA precluded her from anything but the most basic information. With the ESA and NASA being in direct competition over the project didn't help the flow of useful communication between the two organisations. She didn't even get enough intel to have a quantifiable reason to get upset. She knew nothing of what had happened after Betty crossed over from the ISS to the Butterfly. That didn't prevent her from creating demons in her dreams. The Russians seemed to have more information than the ESA. *How the hell did they manage to get enough to even start experimentation?* She was mystified. Popovich had managed to keep a low profile and as yet undiscovered as a mole. *'Oh God, I hate that woman!'* This became an almost nightly mantra for J'Ark. A self-imposed torture from which there was no escape. She knew the chances of her ever meeting Betty Johnson again was as likely as her becoming a big fat pink pig with a short dark bob and severe fringe flying happily through the air.

No chance of revenge. J'Ark was a woman who would have enjoyed exerting the right amount of pain upon the woman, and then some. All she could do was to create a dream reality in which to enjoy an illusionary satisfaction.

'It's about time,' said a relieved Captain. The general chatter and feedback was indicative of the level of acceptance of the undeniable nature of their existence. At the least the vast majority of her passengers had attained some degree of comprehension. Would it last? In her own mind she believed herself to be totally aware of where they were, what they were doing, where they were going. *Is this possible? How is this possible?* Captain Järvinen's senses and her logic and her soul told her the truth. The fibre of her being, her cellular memory still refused to accept they were anywhere but on Earth. Each time she looked out her office window upon the dwellings and the trees and the cultivated field it took an effort not to let her mind drift off towards the edge of sanity.

Her highly competent team appeared to take the entire experience as the most normal thing in the world. She didn't know anyone of them well enough to allow herself to confide in them. 'Did you all enjoy Jupiter?' It was a ridiculous question really. How could a person enjoy the incredible, the miraculous? One enjoys a party not something that strikes awe into the depth of one's soul.

The gathering remained silent. Iluska wasn't restrained by artificial societal conventions of what she should or should not feel. 'No. I not enjoy. Is not real. I not believe.' Her eyes reddened. A few unwelcome tears rolled down her cheek. 'I cry because ... because ... I do believe.' She looked up towards Franklin. He was there to share the one most sublime experience of her life, standing next to her, comforting her as she cried on seeing the red heart of Jupiter swirling before her eyes. 'I not vant go home. Zis is home.' Franklin put his arm around her.

Levi, like the rest must have been overcome by the giant of their solar system. 'What she said.' He let it go at that. The others must have felt the same for all they could do was nod gently at the still fresh memory of their own deep feelings.

'I didn't either,' Järvinen said quietly. In all the months they'd spent with their Captain this was the first tender moment when they saw the humanity in her. It put the whole project on an entirely new level of meaning for them. With those simple words she earned their respect, not just obedience as officers under her command.

'That was our last wayside stop. From now on it gets serious.' She didn't let the mood in the room deteriorate. 'Any ideas on how to prepare our people for Titan?' Her gaze alighted lightly on Iluska.

Facet 3

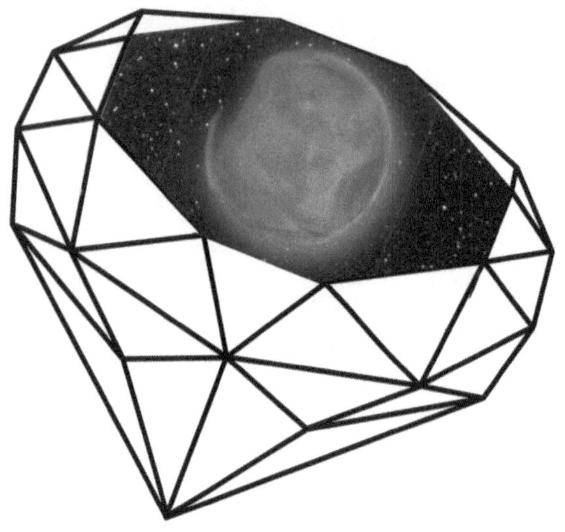

Titan Reality

Titan Mindscape Project

Iluska had done such a proficient job of managing the Flower and Butterfly festival she was put in charge of the *Titan Mindscape* project.

By common consent the Captain's team decided the Citizens should be made visually aware of every step of the process from then onwards until the Butterfly landed on their new world.

'Bee-Bee, I would like you to work with Iluska on this. It will give you a good opportunity to monitor the colonists mindset. Keep me informed.' Bee-Bee's immediate reaction didn't escape her attention. The Captain had no illusions about the apparent latent animosity between the two women, which existed for no other reason than the presence of Ivan simmering away in the emotions of each. There was that long muddled history behind Bee-Bee and Ivan. Iluska's problem had its origins in their much more recent history. Was Ivan's affection for her based on some element of emotional rebounding from Bee-Bee?

Iluska organised images of Jupiter to be replaced by those of Saturn; their final destination. As previously, nobody noticed the jump back into the Dark. At the beginning eyes sought the reassurance of images presented on the large screens. Now they had become a matter of passing interest, although the increasingly larger images of Saturn started to attract attention. As had videos of construction crews within the Butterfly as they gathered equipment to prepare the landing site on Titan.

Details of the procedures accompanied all the images. In simplified terms they were told the landing area would need to be levelled to give the Butterfly, their city of Apollonia, a geologically stable and permanent foundation. Schematics showed the location of Tui Regio in relation to the Xanadu region to the North, where they would have access to sub-surface liquid water.

To better bring home the reality of the enterprise Bee-Bee organised seminars presented by scientists and engineers. The most important message to get across to settlers related to the suitability of the location.

'Tui Regio environment is geologically stable. There are no impact craters, no linear tectonic features and no erosion channels,' they said. 'It's the safest location on Titan.'

Citizen Hudson, the engineer who had helped Bee-Bee during her first few days on the Butterfly, became interested in the process. 'How difficult will it be to prepare the site?'

'Let me show you some of the earth moving equipment we'll be using.' The bulldozers, graders, land planes and scrapers were the most prominent. 'We'll use these the same as if we were on Earth.'

Geologists concentrated on the surrounding land masses. 'The most critical area for us will be a region called Xanadu. It's important because of its water ice content, as well as the liquid water ocean under it. You've heard this before but it's worth emphasizing. Our initial effort will go into harvesting some of the water.'

'How much water is there?' Citizen Hudson asked again.

'It's an area about the size of Australia. Enough water to drink as well as go ice-skating on the surface ice.'

The flippant comment brought out a little more interest. 'Will we be able to go outside?'

'Patience,' the geologist warned. 'It will take time to develop the nitrogen/methane filters to make that possible.'

'What about gravity?' someone else asked.

'You could easily go for a walk on Titan, in a spacesuit of course. You might even be able to fly with a little equipment. Imagine standing on a dune and flapping your spacesuit wings. A short burst of speed and you'd be off!'

A few imaginations lit up. Where else could a person fly like a bird? 'How soon do we get there,' came the obvious question.

Captain Järvinen was heartened to hear a real sense of reality demonstrated by those enquiries.

The hazy orange globe of Titan would not be seen for several months yet. The Butterfly had been in the Dark for a couple of months since leaving Jupiter. During the transit Captain Järvinen hoped the intense exposure to details of the next phase of their enterprise would instil a sense of expectation in her people.

Citizen Bee-Bee grew into her responsibilities. The degree of concentration needed to work with Citizen Iluska temporarily pushed thoughts of Ivan into the background. He didn't even come up in any conversations between herself and Iluska for a while.

'Could we make a special occasion of it?' Bee-Bee asked Captain Järvinen, referring to the imminent departure of the landing site construction crew.

Screens continued to display simulations of what the landing party would be doing, showing detail about the nature of the terrain, drainage necessary for the methane rains and plumbing to bring water from Xanadu. But those visual constructs were not reality. They were not even in the realm of interactive VR.

All the Cubes carrying construction materials, the habitation Cubes and Machinery carriers had been loaded. Video images of the entire process could be seen as the workers went about their daily activities. Captain Järvinen held firmly to the opinion that to believe you had to see with your own eyes.

The majority of people gathered in the numerous flight bays from which the Cubes would be leaving. There they could interact with the away-teams, especially those with partners. It brought a sense of purposeful reality to something which had been in the planning process for so long. It was actually going to happen. The Citizens could speak with the people who were going to land on Titan, discuss their apprehensions and share their excitement.

Captain Järvinen attended with the leader of the construction crew giving a last word of encouragement.

'Of all the people on this spacecraft Citizen Anton, you would be the only person with an absolutely unequivocal conviction of the reality of what you are about to do.'

'Strange of you Captain of all people to say so. Are you not telling me something I should know before we leave?'

'Not at all. I have a suspicion there are a few among us who think we are still on Earth.'

'Is that all. I have a solution for that. Send them along with me! I'll teach them how to dig a ditch in the dirt of Titan. Would that do the job?' General laughter greeted the nonsense of the suggestion.

'Why didn't you suggest it sooner. I might have gone along and given you a hand myself,' the Captain quipped.

Such easy going banter helped to bring home the monumental significance of the event.

The celebration progressed through the afternoon late into the night. The arbitrary time subdivision made no difference out in space. The Butterfly had jumped back into normal space-time so people could see the departing Cubes to the background of the Milky Way in the distance and the now prominent sight of Saturn itself.

On every screen people could observe the silent exodus of all the Cubes as if the Butterfly was releasing all her eggs into space. They saw the small golden cubes fly several miles away from their home base before suddenly disappearing. They all knew in their minds where they had gone, yet it was still a challenge to believe they continued to exist - somewhere out there.

All the hype about construction at a place that may or may not exist felt like an anti-climax. Suddenly the long time expended on preparations, visuals and discussions had come to an end. It wasn't possible to follow their progress through the Dark. There was nothing to help maintain interest or enthusiasm. Back to normal life once again. Many wondered what would be the next occasion for a big party or a festival.

Pilot Engineer Citizen Anton had become used to the miracle of the Cubes' drive system during normal operations. Yet going ahead of the Butterfly to Titan didn't qualify as anything remotely normal. He needed to get his crew and equipment there in good time. *Does this thing have a speed limit?* he asked himself. Citizen Ivan had taught him all the intricacies of navigation. Anton could accurately gauge their speed by observation of the gravitational wave vortexes behind them. He could also see the disturbances in patterns around them which indicated the presence of normal matter objects.

Of all the people on the Butterfly he and his crew couldn't afford the luxury of contemplating the theoretical elusive nature of reality. If they didn't keep their craft on course mindful of the two hundred and seventy odd moons then more than just pain would convince them what was real and what wasn't.

Although the Butterfly didn't need to adhere to a strict deadline for arrival their foundation needed to be ready when they did finally arrive. Anton conferred with his pilots.

'Any risk takers amongst you?' he asked.

'You mean apart from yourself Citizen Anton?' They were all in an exceptionally good mood. Life within the belly of the Butterfly had become much too normal, far too predictable. They didn't sign up to this project to be living a normal Earth existence on a weird looking spaceship that didn't look anything like a spaceship. They were all trained as astronauts, as wells as being qualified in their own professions. At last they could get on with the other jobs they were trained for.

After the laughter died down, for they all knew of Citizen Anton's antics during training flights he said, 'Excellent. You all know how fast we are going. Are you also familiar with the theory of relativity as it relates to speed and mass?' A variety of grunts and hand waves confirmed what he wanted to know. 'In that case do you want to find out how heavy you could get?'

One pilot out of all of them commented, 'But we're in the Dark Matter dimension. We don't know what's going to happen.'

'Exactly!' shot back Citizen Anton, grinning widely. 'Let's see if we can stretch the limits of reality a little.'

...

The day after the construction crew left Iluska and Bee-Bee had the first opportunity to relax. Captain Järvinen had not yet convened a report meeting. Of the several Cafés open they found themselves at the one in the main district, on a corner well-known to Bee-Bee.

They worked well together. Iluska's lack of proficiency in English proved to be no impediment at all to her innate organisational skills. Besides, everyone she came into contact with seemed to like her. Even Bee-Bee grudgingly gave in to her magnetic personality. The woman was a little powerhouse of energy and good ideas.

After a few words of small talk, mostly about Citizen Anton's reputation in a number of amusing areas Bee-Bee took the initiative.

'We need to talk seriously about something.' Her smile wasn't entirely relaxed.

'Da. You vant talk about Ivan.'

'To me he is John and he'll always be John.'

'He not yours.' As laconic as always Iluska wasn't entirely sure she wanted this conversation - not unless she could find out details about Ivan's past. *If I'm going to have he's babies I have to know.*

'Are you sure he's yours now? I was with him for a very long time. I thought we would have a life together. Then he sees you and that was the end of it.' An edge had come into her voice. *Why am I having this conversation anyway? It wasn't that simple at anytime.*

'Ivan good man. You zink he good man?'

'He's certainly a very clever one. We would not be here without what he and his father achieved.'

'Nyet. I vant know if he good man. You understand. You tell me his life.' A small hint of assertiveness started to show itself, like she had displayed towards the Russian spy Popovich when he began to pressure her. 'You tell everyzing.'

Bee-Bee didn't expect a counter-attack. *What is this woman planning?* the question suddenly appeared. *Alright, I'll tell her.* 'He works. He's always working. And when he's not working he has crazy dreams. He's stubborn.

He can be so bloody stubborn.'

Iluska interrupted. This seemed to be important. 'About vat?'

'Secrets. He has many secrets. He would not tell me.'

'Zat no problem. I have secrets. You have secrets - Da?' Iluska didn't emphasize it but it hit home.

For an unexplainable reason Bee-Bee wanted to confide in this woman. She liked Iluska in spite of her having commandeered her property. Bee-Bee definitely felt Ivan was still her property.

'Look at this.' She opened the palm of her hand revealing the scar left by Ivan's adolescent carelessness.

'He do zis?' The instant revulsion on her face made Bee-Bee immediately regretting have done it.

'Accident. It was only an accident. He did it when he was still a boy.' Iluska's face relaxed.

'He show me vere *you* used knife.'

They looked at each other. An understanding closed the gulf between them.

'Yes, he is a good man,' Bee-Bee's voice had softened. Their coffees were still untouched. She took a sip. Iluska hesitated to say something else. 'You can tell me Iluska.' *Where did that come from?* Bee-Bee's attitude seemed to have taken a hundred and eighty degree turn within those few minutes of conversation. Iluska took a sip from a now almost cold mug.

'Zis big secret. You, me - and Ivan. He know.' She had trouble getting it out. It was important. If the three of them were to live together in such a small society these things had to be out in the open. 'I vant make babies viz him.'

Bee-Bee was never very good at hiding her emotions. She levered her eyes away from Iluska's face, picked up her handbag and quietly walked away.

...

After the Flowers and Butterflies Festival Peter had made himself scarce, burying his head in further developing the instrumentation to enable more accurate navigation in the eddies of gravitational waves animating the Dark. The welfare of all those people on the Butterfly didn't concern him as much as the welfare of his son. Construction crews preparing to go ahead had to have the best tools possible. They and the Butterfly had to make a safe journey the rest of the way to Titan. That's the only way he could ensure his son's safety.

'What are you going to do when you get there son?'

'Why do you ask? Are you going somewhere else?' *So that's what he meant when he said 'we'* ...

'I told you. I can't see myself being cooped up in this Cube on Titan waiting for something to do. I've discovered a new reality out there. That's where I'll be if you need me.'

'How will I find you?'

'Call me.'

'How?'

'I'm working on it. When it's done I'll be on my way. Good luck son - Ivan.'

'It's about time you worked out who I was.'

...

There was more work to be done with the Titan Mindscape Project. Seeing the crew fly into the unknown was only the beginning. Workload for Iluska increased as they neared Titan. As they got closer to Saturn extraordinary images of this cosmic ballerina were displayed on all the Butterfly's screens. People had a mental image of Saturn with its ring from all the photos NASA's exploratory probes had sent to Earth. They were lifeless photos compared to the videos streaming into the Butterfly as they approached. The small orange ball of Titan orbiting so far from Saturn had not yet made an impact on what people saw.

Captain Järvinen called upon Citizens Iluska and Bee-Bee to give their report - not on paper but face-to-face to her at the same meeting. *They have worked so well together on this project. I wonder if I can engage them on another important job.* So far she didn't know about the confrontational peacemaking effort between them, or how it had ended.

Only two days had passed since they met at the Café. Two days of turmoil for Bee-Bee to come to terms with Iluska's revelation. *How could she do that? How could he do this to me? John's betrayed me!* As far as Bee-Bee was concerned John was still hers. They had decided a long time ago not to have children. *What is so special about this woman anyway?* She felt the acute pain of the abandonment. She felt it in her dreams that night and in the first moment of waking in the morning.

Franklin couldn't drag out of her what her problem was. Bee-Bee had withdrawn into herself refusing so much as exchange more than a few words with him the night before. His attempt at an affectionate 'Good morning' was completely ignored. She lay there as if in a coma, her face showing the intense concentration which comes from the sharp focus on feeling intense pain. Franklin didn't know what to do. Bee-Bee had never been like this, not even when she was having those terrible nightmares.

Pain!

The thought filled her being. Then sudden release.

Reality!

That's the one thing J'Ark had taught her to trust. Ivan and Iluska were the reality. They were going to have a baby, not her and John. *That was the reality!*

I have to take her to Dr Kathleen again. Franklin had sat up, about to swing his legs out of the bed.

Bee-Bee lurched herself upright and attacked him before he could make the move. She clamped her arms around his shoulder swinging his body back onto the bed.

Their ferocious love making didn't stop until Captain Järvinen's summons later that morning for him to report to her office. Franklin was no less mystified by the morning's antics than Bee-Bee's previous night's frigid behaviour.

Did it matter? She was back to normal, though never quite as energetically normal as that morning.

On her way to see the Captain she felt much better. *Iluska isn't the problem.* Her mind focused again on who was.

Citizens Bee-Bee and Iluska arrived outside the Captain's office at the same time, Bee-Bee looking slightly dishevelled. Iluska seemed preoccupied though giving no indication of any residual effects of their Café encounter. They exchanged smiles, without words.

'Good morning Citizens.' Captain Järvinen watched them walk in, looking for signs. The construction crew launch was successful as were all the activities leading up to it. Her two Citizens had done an excellent job in involving the travellers' attentions on the enterprise. It wasn't the reason she called on them to report. She was more interested in the relationship between them. They seemed businesslike. Perhaps a little too businesslike. No hint of animosity.

'Your thoughts about the launch?' she asked them, referring to what they considered the reaction of the people to the event.

'It appeared to me they had no trouble accepting the reality of what was happening and why.' Bee-Bee spoke first.

Iluska started to say something but Bee-Bee didn't hear her. She was repeating in her mind what she had said a moment ago ... *no trouble accepting the reality of what was happening* ... she repeated it in her mind several times before returning to the moment.

'Bee-Bee, what do you think of Iluska's suggestion?' The Captain had to prompt twice before Bee-Bee responded with a questioning look.

'Sorry, what did you say Iluska?' Once more her mind shot off at a tangent - she just realised she'd dropped the 'Citizen' formality, as had the Captain.

'I say - I have idea. Vat you zink Bee-Bee? Make big picture of Saturn in sky. Little pictures of Titan on screens!'

'I don't understand Iluska.'

'Well I think it's a wonderful idea. What she meant was we should project Saturn's image onto the holographic sky of each of our levels and show live images of Titan on the screens as we approach it.'

Bee-Bee's imagination flashed back to the time in her adolescence when she accompanied John and his family to the Star Camps back on Earth. She remembered the first time she saw close up images of the planets projected onto the huge screens of the overhead dome surfaces. Magnificent!

'Yes!' She remembered the effect it had on her concept of the reality of the Earth in relation to the rest of the Universe. 'If you showed Saturn perhaps only for an hour each night ...' She turned to Iluska with a big encouraging smile. 'You have so many good ideas. Anyway, most of them are good.' The allusion to babies perhaps wasn't lost on Iluska.

'Excellent. I'm sure the two of you can manage to make it happen. And I have another project for you.'

'More picnics?'

'Not quite. We'll be there sooner than you think. I want to be assured of full acceptance by our people of our new reality. Excursions on Titan.'

Captain Järvinen had prepared herself to lose some of her Citizens to forms of mental illness resulting from failure to fully grasp the nature of their future on a new world. If any of her people were to fall off the edge of sanity she wanted it to happen soon upon arriving on Titan. Not weeks or months or years later when it would be much more difficult to deal with, as anything put off always is.

'You'll be working closely with Dr Kathleen this time. You take them out onto the surface Bee-Bee.

Citizen Kathleen will vet the mentally unstable individuals.'

'What exactly do you mean by *vetting*, Captain?'

'It's a big universe out there. Some may find themselves on the way to Earth.' It wasn't necessary to elaborate on that, just as it wasn't necessary to delve into the likelihood of the survival of those who attempted the return journey.

...

The construction crew had left only a week ago. No one could reasonably claim life to be boring aboard the Butterfly when one night their AI generated holographic 'night sky' disappeared. An enlarged image of Saturn appeared without forewarning in the sky of each level. Most people missed the spectacle on the first night, which only lasted an hour. No one missed it the second night. Captain Järvinen decided against giving an explanation. The time had come for people to work these things out for themselves.

Saturn with its rings of ice was truly an awe inspiring sight. The thing making Iluska's idea so brilliant was that the image presented itself not on a flat vertical screen but people had to look *up* to see it. During the hour it was also possible to see some of the closer moons in orbit around the planet. As the days progressed Saturn became larger each night. Incredibly some people lost interest after a few nights, as if they'd become tired of watching some program on an old vid. Those vid images represented a constructed unreality. Perhaps they thought the images of Saturn were no more than VR fabrications put there purely for their amusement. Some people remembered the sun disappearing in the middle of the day to be replaced by thunder and lightning. This was probably another bit of technical wizardry.

The small hazy orange globe on screens created little interest. The Citizens were not told it was Titan. *Let them get used to it, then I'll tell them.* In every way possible Captain

Järvinen tried to use a variety of techniques to engender a belief in the new reality of their lives. There was no option but to believe if they were to survive. In years to come there might be visitors from a distant planet in the solar system to challenge their normality - perhaps sooner. They had not only to survive but to grow, to become strong, to become a confident self-determining society.

The   Plains
Of
Rui Regio

Saturn became so large in the skies of the Butterfly it created the sensation of it falling towards the spectators.

If they'd not seen it get bigger each night then recede as they flew past it panic would have engulfed the entire population.

As it was only one person needed medical attention. Citizen Lucy broke under the mental strain, not made any easier by the ravings of her partner Citizen Spiers. He needed sedation having become violent when Lucy was being taken away to the hospital. He had to be temporarily incarcerated; the first person to suffer the ignominy of becoming a prisoner aboard the Butterfly. Lucy's problem was far less severe than the imprisonment of Spier's mind by refusing to accept what his eyes saw. The sphericality of Saturn couldn't be argued away by any outlandish conspiracy theories. If it was round then the Earth had to be round. To Spiers that was unacceptable. He vented his frustration by berating Lucy to the point of her having a mental breakdown.

Captain Järvinen's attention concentrated on hearing her construction crew's report. She couldn't spare the time to analyse the Spiers vs Lucy episode. Although it was important because it was symptomatic of what could happen to many others. Yet it had to wait. Their landing took priority.

'You will not believe this place!' Citizen Anton raved about their chosen landing site. 'The colours, the air, the rivers of liquid methane!'

'I will do my best.' *And the rest of our people better do so as well.* 'I followed you reports. You did an excellent job preparing the foundation for us. All of us in the Butterfly watched your progress. Enlarging the landing site to a square mile was an excellent idea. It'll give us room to expand outside the confines of the Butterfly. But tell me - is it difficult to move about down there?' She was already thinking of the excursions she'd planned. They had to begin almost as soon as they landed.

'As long as the suits are appropriately weighed down no one will float away. Our only difficulty was getting the dozers to work to their potential. The surfaces were workable but we could only move about a seventh of the dirt we could on Earth.' Being a construction engineer Citizen Anton launched into all the exciting details of actually moving dirt on a lower gravity cosmic body.

Captain Järvinen let him go on for a few minutes. *I wonder if he would be willing to run a few sessions for our Citizens, tell them about Titan?* 'How much light is there?' She had to interrupt his flow of enthusiasm.

'You would not believe it,' he said again, 'I thought it would be almost pitch black. But in spite of the thick atmosphere there's actually more light than during a full moon on Earth. And the colours ... you gotta see it to believe it!'

She started having doubts whether her people would or could accept the world they had come to when listening to

Citizen Anton's adjectives about the unbelievable nature of the place.

'The strange thing is you can't see Saturn clearly even though it's so close. Perhaps that's why there is so much light. Probably a reflection off Saturn,' he rambled on.

'So in your opinion the people might not be able to reconcile their experience of living on the Butterfly with living on Titan.'

'No worries about that. Put 'em to work out there and they'll soon see what's real. Just let 'em try taking off their suit helmets - I tell ya, reality can really bite on Titan. They'll be happy to get back into the Butterfly.'

Instead of giving protracted information concerning their arrival Captain Järvinen decided to take the soft approach once again. Their skies lost Saturn. Citizen Anton had sent extensive vids of Titan's mornings and sunsets - entire days of the play of orange tinted light. She decided to ask Iluska to replace images of Saturn in their sky with Anton's vids for a few days as they made their final approach to Titan. Once they landed she would allow the AI generated normality they'd become accustomed to as their mental safety buffer.

Citizen Ivan took over the control of the Butterfly. With such a strong gravitational pull from Saturn he had to exercise a particularly delicate control over the craft. 'I'll do it in slow stages over a few days. Let them see our approach and let them see the dense atmosphere we'll have to fly through before we land. They'll not feel landfall at all if the pad has been prepared properly.'

The plains of Rui Regio defied belief. On all the screens people saw through the orange atmospheric glow a river flowing not far from the Butterfly's landing place. As a bonus a rare event of slow motion methane rain fell continuously for weeks. The large drops sparkled ethereally in the external lights of the Butterfly as they floated to the ground.

'I can't believe we've actually arrived,' Bee-Bee commented to Iluska as they prepared for the first of many excursions to come. 'I look at our sky in here and then I look at the sky out there ...' her thoughts trailed away into fantastical imaginary of what the rest of Titan might look like.

Iluska, never one to waste words remained silently gazing at the alien landscape. Since she and Yuri left their home in the woods of Southern Siberia soon after the last of the winter snow fall she hadn't thought of Yartsevo very often. Her life aboard the Butterfly in an Earth like environment didn't need her to drop into nostalgic excursions into past memories. 'Vat vorld is zis?' She wasn't expressing fear or refusal to believe what she saw of Titan. Nor was she quite ready to totally accept this new reality. 'You vant go home? To Earth?' she asked Bee-Bee.

The two women had begun to share many intimacies during the later stages of their odyssey, after having opened up to each other about Ivan.

'Sometimes. When I first arrived here I thought I might be able to ...' without consciously realising it Bee-Bee looked around to see if anyone was in earshot ...'you know - steal a small cube and go back.'

'Vat happened?'

'I met Franklin.'

'Is good.'

They kept staring at the Titan landscape.

'Tomorrow I'll go for a walk out there. Are you coming with me?'

'Da!'

They were included in the first reconnaissance led by Citizen Anton. He'd spent so long on Titan already digging it up in readiness for the Butterfly it must have felt like his own backyard by then.

While crews prepared for more excursions Captain Järvinen made contact with Earth. Fortunately she didn't have a sensitive disposition. The incoming tirade of abuse only made her smile. *These people have no idea what we have achieved. Their world is still so small. They can't see beyond the horizon.* She listed in silence not really registering Angus Silverman's ravings until he'd exhausted himself.

'Can you possibly conceive of where we are?' She only managed to get the question out after a lull in the storm of his words. 'I'll send you some photos. Compare them to the Buffalo Bayou. Then tell me if you can understand. The main image is a river of methane flowing not more than a mile and a half from Apollonia.'

'What the hell is Apollonia?' Shouted back Silverman utterly frustrated by not knowing what was going on out there.

'Apollonia is our city. This is where we live now. This is our world, not yours. So stop shouting at me.'

To Silverman it sounded exactly like the words of a mutineer and there was nothing he could do about it. In effect he'd lost control of the project. At least the Russians didn't get their hands on the propulsion technology. Nor did the Europeans, that he knew of. As far as America's investment was concerned it was secure for the time being - provided the infuriating woman Järvinen did her job. It would be years before the new craft would be completed for another NASA flight to be deployed out there. *She'd better have dug up something valuable by then!*

News media on Earth got hold of the story. NASA tried to keep the lid on it. But how could it be possible to keep something like this quiet. Transmissions from Apollonia were picked up by space monitoring facilities around the world.

Sensationalising something doesn't give it the badge of authenticity. As much as the global news network scrambled to get information, pictures, anything at all, it wasn't enough to convince the people on Earth humanity had landed on Titan and had already created a city of close to two thousand inhabitants. It wasn't possible. Seeing an image of a gigantic cube floating near the ISS only generated conspiracy theories by the dozen. The battle of suppositions and fake news had begun between the Russians, the ESA, USA, China and every other country. All this managed to do was to annihilate the credibility of the achievement. It wasn't as if any nation could run a little trip out there to verify or debunk NASA's claims.

'Why am I locked up like a criminal! My wife is sick. She needs me. It's all your fault.' Citizen Spiers couldn't be consoled. Dr Kathleen tried the rational approach. It's not possible to reason with a person who refuses to believe their own reality. Every effort had been made to expose his mind to the commonly accepted experience. Spiers either didn't have the mental capacity or was driven by the bloody-mindedness of ignorance.

'Citizen Spiers,' Dr Kathleen tried to get a simple message through to him, 'your wife is under medical care. You are responsible for her breakdown.'

Spiers didn't think that was the truth at all. Yet he was concerned for her. With clenching jaws he remained silent, listening yet rebelling at the same time. *I'll make them pay. There has to be a way. They can't get away with this. They can't lock us away in some peculiar virtual reality prison.*

'When she's well enough to go home you'll be able to join her. But you will have to make the effort to settle down as well. You don't want to stay locked up, do you?'

He turned his back on her. Facing him on the wall the screen showed the very thing he refused to believe. He looked at the same image Captain Järvinen had sent back to Earth. 'You can't keep me locked up.' Spiers growled at the doctor without turning around. His tone worried Dr Kathleen. This was either a case of extreme self-delusion or borderline insanity. Either condition could be dangerous to their survival on Titan if he became violent and vindictive.

'Can you sedate him?' Captain Järvinen definitely didn't want to invoke the ultimate mandate given to her in the case of clear and present danger to the lives of her people. Dr Kathleen's analysis of Citizen Spier's condition forced her into a most unwelcome decision option.

'He's quietened down for the time being. I know what you're thinking. It would be devastating to morale to lose one of us under such circumstances. Think of his partner. What would it do to poor Lucy?'

'Don't argue with me Kathleen! I know what has to be done.' She and the doctor weren't just colleagues. They'd become close friends during the journey. 'If he shows any signs of violence you know what you have to do. I'll do the rest. Don't worry about the paperwork - that'll be my job.'

Stunned silence was the best any of them could manage as the ground level portal of the Butterfly opened to reveal the new world to the first reconnaissance team. Bee-Bee and Iluska stepped onto the ramp side by side. A team of twelve followed behind. Geologists, physicists, a botanist and several security personnel. The brain doesn't philosophise about the nature of reality - it concentrates on survival. Only the mind creates monsters. The scientists didn't fall into deep thought. To them this was the supreme adventure. Not so for Bee-Bee or Iluska.

Are there any bears on Titan? Iluska's mind tried to find something solid and familiar to hold onto. The two security officers jostled past them, slightly heavy footed. Their boots needed a little more weight adjustment.

Wake up Betty! I will wake up. I can wake up. There is no pain. This can't be real. The next thought demolished her incredulity. *If I take my helmet off I'll wake up.* Her brain, the ultimate organ of survival would not allow it. Her hands refused to move towards the helmet.

To see images on a screen cannot compare with being flooded with the orange thick atmosphere surrounding you in every direction. Visibility only allowed them to see about a mile past the end of the ramp. Bee-Bee took Iluska by the hand. Together they walked slowly, carefully down to the end of the ramp, feeling the awkwardness of wearing weighted boots.

Iluska pointed to something to the right of them. 'Look. River.' *Not like the river at home.* They were standing near the edge of the flattened landing area. Some of the construction crew were working on building a bridge across the river. On the other side, beyond the edge of the Plains of Rui Regio, Xanadu began, the ocean under the frozen water ice that would have to be mined. The river flowed in slow motion. Their minds worked in slow motion mapping this new existence into comprehension. The crew worked in slow motion.

'Is dream!' Iluska tightened her grip on Bee-Bee's gloved hand. 'No bears here,' she said. They both laughed.

There is no smelly Popovich here either. Strange that should have been Bee-Bee's lasting memory connection to Earth.

Behind them towered the Butterfly six hundred meters high into the methane/nitrogen rich air.

'Let's go back.' Bee-Bee had had enough. She needed to think. It seemed like years since she first arrived on the Butterfly - years since she formulated a tentative plan to escape. Then later a tentative plan to deal with John's treachery towards her.

I need to think.

Confusion and clarity fought with the images of the Titan world and the world inside the Butterfly.

Conflicting loyalties surfaced between her newly found friend Iluska, Captain Järvinen and the future she represented - and her feelings towards Ivan. *Ivan*, Bee-Bee became uncomfortably aware she'd begun to think of him as Ivan and not as John. *When will this end?*

Whilst internal reconstruction work began to help Bee-Bee and Iluska and the rest of the people from Earth to accommodate their understanding of the new nature of their existence, efforts began in earnest on the outside to plumb water into the Butterfly.

Water. The one constant in the universe which life could not deny. From space it seemed the water-ice fields of Xanadu were in close proximity to their landing site. In reality several hundred miles of insulated pipes had to be laid. Water mining and purification infrastructure became a priority task. Survival came before business. Satisfying America's insatiable greed for resources, hence wealth, had to wait patiently. Or impatiently as in the case of Angus Silverman and the President of the United States.

In the case of Citizen Spears an unhinged mind still has the capacity to function on the borders of genius. Without the constraints of fear or thoughts of impossibility, bold and daring plans become a probable reality. He became a most persuasive actor who managed to convince Dr Kathleen of his reformed awareness of the truth - of his contribution to Lucy's mental condition. His other core beliefs could not be fooled by his conniving mind.

A   Mutiny
Brewing

'We know next to nothing about our new world.' Captain Järvinen had no illusions about that.

The enormity of the task she had taken on did not truly manifest until they had actually landed. The journey between Earth and Titan now appeared as an incidental accomplishment when faced with the task ahead.

'Tell me Kathleen, how are we going to manage. How are we going to make a life here?'

'Should I say the obvious? Together.'

'Yes. That's what worries me. I know I can rely on some of our people, like yourself. Can I rely on everyone? They seem so concerned with their day-to-day existence on this tiny comfortable piece of the Earth. They're behaving as if they were still there. How many of them actually accept what we are doing, where we are? Like for example Citizen Spiers. He seems to have gone off the deep end. What's his condition?'

'I have visited him almost every day over the last couple of weeks. He's relieved Lucy is home. I don't know if it's because someone is there to look after his farm allotment or because he's genuinely concerned for her. He's a farmer, and quite capable from what I hear,' explained Dr Kathleen.

'Can he be trusted?'

'He's not raving anymore, always asking about Lucy and what we are doing to help her. He seems very interested in what's going on outside with setting up Apollonia. I'm inclined to let him go back to Lucy.'

Captain Järvinen needed to assess the risk. As one man he could do little to sabotage the project. It wasn't as if he'd organised a dissident group to mutiny and take over the Butterfly. Even if he did it wouldn't accomplish anything. *Bee-Bee and Iluska ... any real animosity between them could have created a great deal more unrest amongst our people. It looks like they've sorted things out between themselves.*

'Yes. You do that. But ask Franklin to keep an eye on him. What do you make of the relationship between Bee-Bee and Iluska?'

'The last time I saw them they were walking down the ramp out onto the Titan landscape hand-in-hand. I doubt if you'll have any trouble from them.'

Their respective partners Franklin and Ivan gave no indication of any friction between themselves. *So much to think about - so much to do.* 'I think we need to have a little party to celebrate our arrival. Could you ask Iluska to come and see me about it. She's such an excellent organiser.'

Dr Kathleen wasn't only the Captain's friend. She was also her personal doctor. It amazed her how an individual could face so many predictable and unpredictable situations and remain as strong as she appeared to be. She became vigilant of any cracks appearing in their Captain's psyche, especially now. It did not bear thinking what would happen without her leadership.

'Citizen Iluska, we need another get-together. I doubt anyone would object to having a big party to celebrate having our feet firmly on the ground again. And while you're at it see if you can organise to get volunteers to join exploration teams to go and find out what our world has to offer.'

'Ivan can help train more pilots.' As always Iluska knew exactly what needed to be done.

That night after work Iluska's bubbly personality asserted itself in a most unambiguous way. No matter where a human being might find themselves, no matter how unbelievable the circumstances of their existence might be nature would assert itself.

'I have important job for you Ivan.' She tried to keep a straight face.

'What have you done this time Maliska? You have already made such an enormous contribution to the project, particularly in the things you've done to help people deal with their new reality. I can't imagine what else you could possibly do now that we've arrived.'

'I speak with Captain. You train more pilots. Explore Titan.'

'Is that all?' He thought it would be something much more interesting given her latent excitement.

'Ve make new Citizen.'

He didn't understand. He'd been involved in so many technicalities during the preceding days associated with preparing the Butterfly to be decommissioned from its function of flying through the Dark that other matters relating to the citizenry didn't have a place in his thoughts. Iluska saw his mystified frown. That only ignited her naughtiness. She took him by the hand, grinning all the way as she led him to the bedroom.

'Time ve make babies! Big job!'

The moment of enlightenment spurred him into immediate action. In the days following his concentrated nocturnal activity Ivan became a little less attentive to his duties at the control centre.

Iluska went about organising the party and the volunteer drive, always happy, always smiling. On some mornings this happy girl felt a little more tired. Both Bee-Bee and Franklin worked with her on the new recruitment project, Bee-Bee by her side almost every day. Two weeks later Iluska turned up late for work. It had never happened before.

'You are looking like death warmed up girlfriend. What's been going on?' Her most immediate thought turned to what Ivan might have been doing. *That bastard had better been behaving himself.* Bee-Bee surprised herself with her supportive thoughts towards Iluska. Ivan had never been physically aggressive towards herself. *What the hell is he up to now?*

Iluska burst out crying and laughing at the same time. The people around her came running. She threw her arms around Bee-Bee smearing tears of joy all over her face.

'I pregnant.'

Bee-Bee hugged back tenderly. 'You want this baby?'

'Oh yes. Da, da, da!'

I have to do something to stop Ivan hurting Iluska like he'd hurt me. A completely illogical and unfounded thought. Iluska was obviously ecstatic about her pregnancy. The past still cast its long shadow over Bee-Bee's feelings towards Ivan.

'I can't believe it.' Captain Järvinen had been so preoccupied with so many things the prospect of having to deal with a population increase escaped her thoughts. 'Of course I believe it,' she admitted to Dr Kathleen, 'how stupid of me. Have you got the maternity ward set up?'

'Of course, Captain. It's been ready for the last month.'

'Are you telling me our first generation of Titans is about to be born?

'Oh yes. And Iluska's baby will be one of them. There are quite a few ahead of her. It seems some of our citizens have felt sufficiently secure with their new lives to take the chance.'

'Titans. Actual Titans. I can't believe it!' So much that could be believed and so much that could be fiction. The first humans born on Titan. 'A double reason to celebrate. We must tell everybody.'

What could possibly go wrong to change such a good day?

Pilot Training had started for the first batch of volunteer intake. Citizen Spiers was one of them.

He had an agile mind having no difficulty in learning to fly the smaller Cubes. Without having formed any definite strategy somehow learning to handle the Cube propulsion system was important. He also knew whatever plan he could devise would need others to help him carry it out.

'It's not so hard once you get used to the lag,' he said to several volunteers who couldn't quite catch on. Perhaps they didn't have the aptitude. Spiers made friends easily. It was the same in the Flat-Earth society on Earth. He seemed to attract minds which needed reality anchors of a certain configuration, which included a distrust of authority.

'Don't think of it as if it was a racing car with instant response to the accelerator. Be gentle with the controls. Treat them like your favourite bed warmer.' The small group of men sniggered. The women sneered.

'Pig man,' one of the women commented under her breath. Two others with her turned and left the group. The four men didn't take much notice. Spiers was interesting. He was entertaining and he'd obviously learnt how to handle these peculiar spacecraft. Towards the end of the third week of training he'd attracted two more to his little band of followers.

Citizen Franklin had been leading this group of trainees. He knew about Citizen Spiers' most recent history. He did however recognise the man's skill and his ability to get on with people.

'Citizen Spiers,' Franklin took him aside a day or two before the completion of the course. 'How do feel like leading one of the smaller groups of volunteers in the next intake?'

'Sure thing, provided you can organise some help for Lucy to look after the farm.' His thoughts had turned away from everything except the plan which had begun to crystalize. He needed a few more people on his side. 'Oh - and another thing ... we've been flying close to Titan's surface never actually going out into space.'

'No need for it. You'll all be involved in exploring the planet's surface, taking geologists and scientists with you. Relax. You will not need to go so far out into space.'

'That's just the point. What if ... you know ... something happens and ...' he let the thought peter out.

'Alright. I see what you mean. You can take shuttle cube #34. But I want you to take a couple of other pilots with you.'

Spiers' rational mind couldn't cope with seeing the reality of Titan's sphericality, having the core belief the Earth was flat. Titan was a sphere. There had not been enough time for the on-board authorities to create a hoax. Titan should have been flat, like every other planet in the solar system.

It took them only minutes to get through the orange atmospheric haze to reach the clean, dark freedom of space. They had all seen it before, hundreds of times during their voyage to Titan. Yet now after months of living in the thick atmosphere soup of the planet it was a shock. Without any specific destination Spiers piloted the cube straight up until 'up' stopped feeling like 'up'. He let Ziggi take the controls while he contemplated the image of the planet in front of him. The curvature of Titan challenged Spiers' concept of reality. It angered him. *How are they doing this? It should be flat. It should be flat.* 'It should be flat,' he finally said aloud.

'What did you say?' Ziggy heard correctly. He'd always thought Spiers had been joking when he spoke about the Earth being a flat disk floating in space, with the sun revolving around it.

'Do you want to go home?' responded Spiers.

'What are you talking about?' Stephan, the other pilot took notice. It didn't sound like Spiers wanted to go back and land. His voice was strange.

'Earth. I want to go home to my flat Earth.'

'Don't be an idiot, man. We don't have the supplies.' Stephan laughed. 'Come on. Let's go back.'

They had not been taught how to make the jump into the Dark. Spiers knew about the dark matter universe.

Minutes from landing Stephan had to know. 'What did you mean about going home Spiers?'

'What do you thing of the idea?'

Stephan's head jerk in Ziggy's direction made Spiers rephrase. 'Just joking friend. I wanted to see your reaction ... a bit of fun ... Yeah.'

'Spiers - you're an idiot.' A slap on the man's back relieved the sudden tension building up.

They'd barely touched down inside the Butterfly when another larger Cube settled close to them. It had strange markings and looked a little worn. Ivan ran up to it expecting to see his old father, completely ignoring Cube #34.

'You got my message.' Peter sounded more than relaxed. He tended to be low key whenever achieving something significant. This time his message cut through the gravitational wave interference to reach the Butterfly. 'You're Ivan, right?'

'Very funny Dad. I didn't think we'd ever see you again.'

'Couldn't stay away. How would you manage without me?'

'You're looking exceptionally well dad. Eating well?' Then noticing the dark rings around his eyes, 'Not sleeping well, Dad?'

'Don't pretend you don't know. The longer I stay in the Dark the better I end up feeling. And don't bother getting that doctor of yours onto me.'

Citizen Spiers wandered over to see what all the fuss was about with this person. He listened to Citizen Ivan and this new guy discussing the communication link between themselves and the Dark. *Useful.*

Franklin was there to greet Spiers. 'Any problems?'

'Smooth.' Stephan and Ziggy nodded agreement, not saying anything about Spiers' strange idea of a joke.

Ivan, Peter and Franklin moved away, discussing the installation of the new communications system into all the exploration Cubes. Spiers, Ziggy and Stephan hung back to have a closer look at Peter's large Cube.

'We're training pilots and could use your help - granddad.' Ivan threw the last bit in to wind up his father. Peter had harassed him endlessly concerning what life was really about.

'I am not that old and I reckon I'm in better shape than most of you. What's this malarkey about *granddad*?'

'Think back to what you used to say to me. I know it was a long time ago - but think.'

Peter never forgot important things. Like the death of his wife. He gave Ivan a very strange pained look. He remembered his son's dedication to his studies. Then an image of Betty popped up. His eyebrows shot up. 'You've reconciled with Be ...'

'No. Let me remind you. You tried to cram the true meaning of life into my thick skull. You said I should have a lovely girl by my side, a couple of nice kids and a good job with both feet firmly on the ground. Your words.'

'How many?'

'Just one to start with. She'll be a Titan, dad.'

'It's that Russian girl, isn't it. Well done, son - Ivan.'

All Ivan received from his father was a solid handshake and ... 'Are you going to give her some strange Russian name?'

'Why not? We're not Americans or Russians any more. We're Titans. That's up to Iluska.'

'Whatever. Let's get to work. We have the new comms to install.'

'Here's the reality dad. I do have a nice girl. My baby will be born soon enough and both my feet are planted firmly on the ground. Is this what you had in mind?'

Peter looked at his son, not believing the twisted logic in his head. *I didn't mean for him to go off to another planet, for heaven's sake.* 'You didn't have to go to this much trouble for my benefit - I mean, another planet, another girlfriend.'

From the first intake of pilot volunteers only four graduated, receiving appointments to begin the first wave of explorations. Captain Järvinen needed more pilots. The next intake prepared for their first lesson within a few days. Citizen Bee-Bee turned up late as one of the volunteers.

'It's a while since I've learnt to fly,' she told Captain Järvinen. 'My security responsibilities might be more expediently carried out if I became a little more proficient.'

Sound logic. And with people all over the place it makes a lot of sense. She might have to go out to the water-ice fields or visit an exploration camp or even out into space to chase up any orbiting miscreants. Who knows?

'Go right ahead. Take all the time you need.' Captain Järvinen agreed on the spot. Citizen Bee-Bee had proved herself most capable. She wasn't a trouble maker, perhaps a little troubled within herself but most likely no worse than anybody else on this enterprise.

Peter took the group on their first flight after they completed the theory. This included the process for jumping into dark matter and navigation when normal matter could no longer be seen. He'd asked Bee-Bee to join him in his training Cube. He wanted some inside info about his son and her relationship with him.

'Well done Betty. I see you've ...'

'It's Citizen Bee-Bee,' she interrupted.

'What? Why? Every time I go out and come back people have different names. What's the deal?'

'It's Citizen Bee-Bee because I have left my old life behind, and everything associated with it.'

'As you wish - Citizen Bee-Bee. I was going to ask you about ... shit ... Ivan. You know, the guy who used to be John. This is crazy. Tell me what's going on with my son.'

'Don't ask.' She didn't hear the rest of what Peter was saying. The droning of her own words blocked her ears ... *I have left my old life behind, and everything associated with it ...*

'... very well.' Peter finished off. 'Are you listening to me? You're just like my son. He never listened either.'

'Sorry.'

'I said - you've flown before. It's obvious. So why are you on the training course?'

'I'm in Security and need to be very good at flying these things ... For instance, can you teach me how to jump into the Dark?'

'Sure thing, if you don't mind not getting any older while you're out there.'

That won't matter after I've done what has to be done.

The   Last
Picnic

Peter took charge of all the pilot training.

Life became busy and satisfying for Peter again with his involvement in upgrading all the communication systems and the flight training. Dr Kathleen insisted on doing a full medical on the man, considering his repeated and extended sojourns in the other dimension. If any undesirable side effects showed up she wanted to be ready to deal with them, thought at a complete loss as to what she could do. She didn't like Peter's sleeping problems either. It couldn't possibly be anything to do with AIDA. It had to be something else - and the constant fatigue.

If all went well with Peter she wanted to run a special trial with a group of test subjects.

'Would you agree to be part of the experiment Helmi?'

Captain Järvinen had always been a forward planner with contingencies to cover unexpected situations.

Not ageing at the standard Earth rate couldn't be considered to be in any way an expected symptom of flying in the Dark.

'We've been here many months now. Things seem to be progressing well,' she said. 'No one's gone crazy.' She gave a little unsure laugh, 'But who knows what's around the corner. I may need to stay on the job for quite a while yet. If Citizen Peter is any indication I think your experiment idea is pretty much essential.'

'If we could safely extend the life spans of essential personnel it could only work in the Projects favour. Individuals like Iluska for instance. We need people like her, with her skills and her ability to work with virtually anybody in Apollonia. Have you seen her lately?'

'She's glowing. In her 2nd trimester and you can already see the baby bump.' A slightly wistful look came into the Captain's eyes. She had a partner but somehow there never seemed to be the time to do any baby planting.

'Are you going to shout at me again or do you want a progress report?' Captain Järvinen had developed a particularly strong dislike for Silverman in a remarkably short time.

'Report.' He slurred and already annoyed.

'We have several exploratory teams doing regular trips to all parts of Titan. It's not as easy as going on a picnic in the Kalahari and looking for gold.'

'Results. I want results!' His voice had gone up a notch. 'And I want regular reports.'

'You can want whatever you like. This is not just a mining operation. I have the lives of many people to think about, and a lot of Titans to consider.' The Captain mentioned that slightly obtuse comment to see how Silverman would react.

'What the hell are you blabbering about woman? What Titans?'

'Babies. They're the ones who are blubbering and blabbering and pooping. Kids who have not seen Earth and may never see Earth.'

'Who gave you permission to have children?!'

'Are you seriously so out of touch with reality? *The man is a cretin.* 'Apollonia out.' *If that man can't get two of his neurons together to start making some sense we may well have to spend the rest of our lives here.*

Whatever challenges the new life may bring Earth could not contribute to coping with them. Earth may as well not have exited. If the US decided to send a backup team they would face exactly the same issues. The best that could be achieved would be for them to be integrated into the Butterfly's society.

Citizen Spiers had worked himself into a position of some trust. He no longer played at being a farmer. Citizen Lucy managed quite well with him out of the way and the new farm-hand doing a magnificent job. Lucy withdrew into her simple life on the farm. It was enough for her. No more watching unreal fabrications of space and orange planets and enormous golden cubes floating in space. Holding still warm eggs in her hand - that was reality. And having someone beside her in bed at night without being continually told she was stupid - that was an even better reality.

Though manic, but definitely short of a planet to enjoy a picnic on, Citizen Spiers' body continued to function within the parameters of the Titan experience. His unhinged mind sought a hitching post in order to regain an equilibrium which could only be achieved through satisfaction; satisfaction gained by vindication that he was right. *Lucy's illness wasn't my fault. They caused it with false images to distort her mind! They had no right to put me in prison just because I would not believe their Titan fabrication! I have to prove Titan is flat - because the Earth is flat.*

Citizen Spiers believed there was only one thing left for him to do; He had to go home back to his flat Earth - back to normality - back to a reality he could understand: Back to his own personal fabrication.

He saw his opportunity when Citizen Peter arrived in his large experimental Cube #2. It had everything he needed; well equipped with all the navigational controls, the new communications equipment and plenty of supplies; much more than would be needed for a short recon mission. Peter had restocked already, not intending to stay on Titan.

'Are you with me? Piers asked Ziggy and Stephan. These two borderline mental cases had been attracted to Spiers early in their pilot training sessions and had stayed with him so far. The few other acolytes had found more interesting friends - friends with less radical ideas.

'No bloody way. You must be crazy!' Ziggy at least had some sense to realise the utter stupidity of the idea. It had taken the Butterfly more than seven months to get to Titan. 'We'd never make it! That Cube is hardly big enough for three people. How long would it take? Idiot.'

'You're out of your mind Spiers,' Stephan added, unable to believe what he heard. 'We thought you were only joking when you said you wanted to go back. Besides, Ziggy's right, we wouldn't survive for long out there.'

'Listen to me you two numbskulls. You know what this guy Peter's been doing don't you. He's been out there in the Dark for who knows how long. Do you have any idea how fast he can go in that thing? We could be back on Earth in a couple of weeks at the most.'

'You don't know that.'

His two unlikely mutiny conspirators shook their heads. Ziggy managed a laugh which sounded more like a nervous cackle. 'Yeah, I know about him. But he's a scientist. He knows what he's doing. You're just a bloody farmer for fuck's sake. You don't know what you're talking about.'

Stephan had made up his mind. 'Ziggy, you can't be seriously thinking about this hairbrained idea. Life is good here. Why would you want to go back to Earth anyway?'

Spiers wasn't winning these two over. Maybe Ziggy but most probably not Stephan. 'One more thing,' he paused for a moment's suspense, 'Did you know that while Peter was travelling in the Dark he wasn't getting any older?' Spiers didn't labour the idea, letting it worm it's way into their imaginations. He could see Ziggy grab the tail end of the squirming little creature.

'You're raving.' Stephan just about had enough and was ready to go back to his apartment when Spiers dropped the little gem.

'You think so. Did you know Peter's over ninety years old? He's prancing around as if he was no more than forty.' That was true. They couldn't deny that one. 'So - you with me?'

'That ain't true - is it?' ask Ziggy.

Stephan remembered something. He put a finger in the air putting a temporary stop to the jabber. 'Guys, a while back I had a bug or something and went to see the doc. Here's the thing - I asked her if I should worry about the infection. Do you know what she said?' Spiers and Ziggy now hung on his every word. This just might be important. 'She said, and I quote < It's not as if you were getting older, not while we're travelling in the Dark.> A slip of the tongue do you think? This was when we were on the way between Jupiter and here ... travelling in the Dark.'

'Well. What did I tell you!' Best news Spiers could possibly have heard.

'How fast do you reckon this thing can go?' Stephan still hadn't entirely abandoned the daringly intriguing escapade.

'I've been talking to Citizen Franklin about it. He seems to know a lot about these things. He says it could travel a lot faster than the Butterfly did on the way here. Ever hear about gravitons?'

Ziggy had been quietly contemplating. The worm must have found its way in. 'Yeah, I've heard something.

Theoretically they say you could go as fast as the speed of light using the power of gravity.'

'There you go,' exclaimed a triumphant Spiers.

At the end of another long day Bee-Bee helped Franklin prepare their evening meal. She moved with a heavy step doing what had to be done, perhaps because of the weight of a thought she hadn't been able to shake all day ... *I've left my old life behind ...*

The satisfaction of having become quite a proficient pilot, able to jump in and out of the Dark as well as manoeuvring the Cubes in Titan's low gravity didn't seem to make her feel any better.

'Franklin?' There was a question there waiting to fight it's way to the surface.

'What is it Bee-Bee? You look a bit tired. Why don't you take it easy and I'll finish the cooking.' She went into the sitting room to her favourite couch.

His kindness, not only that night but ever since she got to know him, even his behaviour at the Café on that very first day, made it much harder to say what she wanted to. 'Franklin?' *Have I been deluding myself?*

'Come on get it out. I won't bite.'

'Do you want to have any children?

Franklin turned away from the kitchen bench. He put down the vegetable cutting knife, composing himself. *I'll have to be careful. There's something more here than an attack of the cluck-clucks.* He went to sit beside her on the couch, not opposite as he usually did.

'You're thinking of Iluska aren't you.'

'No. Yes - I don't know. I'm thinking about my life. What am I doing? Why am I here? Why are you here?'

'Take it easy Bee-Bee. It's not all that complicated. Quite simple really. I'm here because I want to be with you.

If you want babies - sure - let's make a dozen!' He grinned, remembering the exuberant love making not so long ago.

'Be serious.'

'I *am* serious. Do want to start tonight?' Bee-Bee thumped him on the shoulder, perhaps a bit harder than she should have. 'Ooh - I wouldn't want to be your enemy. That hurt.'

'All right. Yes, I have been thinking about Iluska. And I've been thinking about the incredibly surreal life here. Do you actually realise where we are?'

'Sure. As I said, it's not complicated. Try taking a walk out there without your suit. Have you been thinking about Ivan too?'

'Why are you so good to me Franklin? You know a little of my past and what I've gone through. You know why I'm here and it's not by accident or because of my UNSC job. But do you know why I'm really here?'

Suddenly Bee-Bee got a cold chill down her spine. This was it. The thing she hadn't been able to face. The demons who had been driving her to such an incredible place. It was a lot simpler when she decided not to return to the ISS on the day the Butterfly left. She had a clearly defined mission; two missions, one of them personal.

Franklin watched all kinds of emotions flitter across Bee-Bee's face, her eyes darting or fixating on something, or staring down at the floor.

'I've had a brilliant idea.' He turned to face her full on. 'How about we skip dinner until a bit later and do a test run. You know, just to see if we remember how to do this thing.'

Bee-Bee knitted her brows, losing all those thoughts tumbling chaotically in her head. 'You want to go flying? Now?'

'Three words - Bee-Bee, Bed, Babies!'

The following morning got away from them. In her hurry to get to work Bee-Bee had forgotten the perilous path she'd started to stumble down on last night. She hadn't forgotten what was driving her, only that something Ivan said changed something in her.

In her office she was alerted to a matter of security concerning a minor case of pilfering.

'One of our food stores reported provisions having disappeared,' advised Bee-Bee's assistant.

'Nothing major really. With all the explorations going on we've had to stock up on a range of food items and water to keep the crews happy. Sometimes they have to go out for weeks. Titan is a big planet.'

'Exactly how much was taken?'

'Apparently enough to keep at least three people alive for several months.'

'Check all the Cubes. I don't want anybody thinking they can start a profiteering business.'

Citizen Bee-Bee went directly to Captain Järvinen.

'No, I didn't order any extra expeditions. The only person I can think of who might need provisions is Citizen Peter. But he's still here working with Ivan. By the way - is everything alright with you? Surely this isn't so serious.'

Citizen Bee-Bee looked worried when she faced the Captain, almost as if someone had committed a murder. 'No, of course not. I'll speak with Peter. Perhaps he's getting ready to leave again.' She couldn't confide in Franklin last night. Things got in the way of her being able to open up. Nevertheless her resolve had strengthened. What she had to do couldn't be put off any longer, not with what Franklin said to her before they became busy. For a fleeting moment she thought perhaps she could talk to the Captain about it. On her way out of the office she turned back to say, 'It's something private I have to do.'

'Go - Go - do what you have to.' Captain Järvinen might not have said it if she knew what was in Bee-Bee's mind.

It had been Peter's habit to restock his Cube each time on arrival before he did anything else. His spaceship was on stand-by ready to fly anytime. 'I've got everything I need Bee-Bee,' Peter said. 'Ivan and I will be finished doing all the upgrades in a couple of days. I'll drop in on the Doc and then be on my way.'

'In that case I won't need to search your ship.'

'Go ahead. I'm not planning on starting a new career in smuggling.' For no apparent reason he lost his balance and almost fell, coughing at the same time.

'Make up your mind Stephan. I've got someone very keen to take your place. I don't want to take over the city. They can have Apollonia and the Butterfly and the whole damn planet for all I care. I just want to go home. It's like a prison being here; bigger than the one I was in on Earth but it's still a damn prison.'

What Spiers had said about not ageing made Stephan consider the crazy plan. *What if we get lost? Spiers has never flown in the Dark. What if we don't have enough food? What if ...* 'Give me a few days to think about it.'

'You haven't got a few days. We've stocked Peters ship with extra provisions. It's ready to go. I want to get away before he decides to use it. Face reality Stephan. If you don't come with us now you'll die here on this lump of useless rock.'

'I'll take my chances here.'

'You won't have much of a future if you give us away.' These quiet, threatening words from a crazy guy who couldn't tell a disk from a ball ensured Stephan's silence. He was sure this guy could be dangerous in the extreme.

'Your crazy Spiers. Just go. As far as I'm concerned you never even existed.'

It really wasn't that important. The Butterfly had become a secure, self-sufficient sustainable environment. If some idiot became so unhinged as to feel the need to set up a bolt-hole like the people on Earth who built private nuclear fall-out shelters, they were welcome to their delusion. As far as Bee-Bee could tell the Butterfly had become the safest place in the solar system to live. People on Earth had completely lost all sense of reality with their wars, the way they raped the planet, their insecurities and spying and ... *I've had enough of the place.*

Bee-Bee went to find Peter again. She didn't want to see Peter. She wanted to talk to Ivan. They would be together working on some other blasted secret, for sure. Another night with Franklin did nothing to change her mind. It did the opposite.

'What are you doing here?' Ivan wasn't being nasty, only surprised to see Bee-Bee in the research building. Their last encounter didn't suggest the two of them would rendezvous for a friendly coffee anytime soon.

'I want to make peace, John - sorry Ivan.' She'd become extremely intense, emotion showing in her strained eyes.

'Oh yes. What's brought this on?' He knew Betty well enough that she never did anything without a jolly good reason. Caution was the best way with her. VR games and knives and threatening dreams had all laid the foundation for a healthy scepticism with anything to do with Betty.

'I - that is, you - er, Iluska.' She knew she wasn't making any sense.

'What about Iluska?' Extra caution crept into his voice. He heard a voice once inside his head - a long time ago - it said he shouldn't trust this Betty woman.

'You have Iluska.'

'So? You have Franklin. What else do you want?'

'I want to make peace. I want to live in peace.'

'Are you telling me you don't want the secret anymore?'

'Yes - I don't want it. I want something else.' Her voice started to soften, her intensity dimmed a little. It had to if she was going to convince him. 'Look John - you're still

John to me. You took me on a picnic once. I had the best time ever.' She lied, although the post picnic exercise wasn't so bad. 'Would you come on another picnic with me? Just for old times sake. No funny business. We can make peace with each other.' She'd lowered her eyes at the last sentence.

Ivan had been in love with Betty since they were kids. Listening to her now he remembered her old voice, the way she moved, the way she always smelt so good. *What harm can it do? It might be nice to have a picnic - and to put the past behind us.* He didn't for one moment consider telling Iluska. Why should he? One little picnic and that was it. Peace at last. No more background aggravation.

Bee-Bee didn't tell him it would a picnic in space - in the Dark, where no one could easily find them.

'Yeah. Alright. When?'

'I'll get everything organised. You did it last time. Let me do it this time.'

'Sure. But I'm Ivan now.'

Whether it was a side effect of prolonged exposure to the push and pull of gravitational waves in the dark matter dimension of the cosmos or some simple infection picked up on the Butterfly made no difference to Ivan. His father was ill; an inconceivable situation. The old man had acquired a reputation of being immortal.

He'd been a regular presence on the Butterfly, flitting in and out of the Dark. He never seemed to age, always so full of energy and enthusiasm.

Lying there in the infirmary Ivan saw the body of an old man seeming to age from one hour to the next. 'What did you do out there Dad? Where did you go? There has to be a reason for what's happening to you.' It had come on so suddenly it had taken everyone by surprise including Dr Kathleen.

Peter could barely string together a sentence after five hours of struggling to stay awake. 'There are limits, son,' he said without being specific.

'Limits to what?'

'Everything.'

'That's not very helpful Dad. How can we help you if we don't know what you did.'

'I didn't tell you this before son, but you have to know.'

Dr Kathleen was furiously running tests on his DNA, suspicious of telomerase dysfunction. She had discovered an abnormal increase in telomerase activity within Peter's cells. When she tested others aboard the Butterfly it was the same. Except Peter's was different somehow. He'd spent a lot more time in the Dark, jumping in and out over an extended period. This disrupted the normal functioning rhythm of his telomerase enzyme. It went into uncontrolled activity, becoming hyperactive with the attendant effects on his cells. Peter had developed a lethal, increasingly aggressive cancer, which now rapidly consumed his body.

'Every time I jumped I felt something. Nothing substantial, just a feeling of having some activity increasing in my body. It didn't seem to affect me so I didn't say anything. Occasionally I couldn't sleep very well.'

Dr Kathleen returned to the man's bedside looking white as a sheet. She led Ivan aside to tell him.

'Your father has a form of cancer I have never seen before. It's growing so fast he could be gone within the next few weeks.'

There was nothing wrong with the old man's hearing. 'I suspected as much.' He tried to smile. 'Speed. When you're out there don't go too fast son.'

'What is too fast Dad?'

'When your body gets so heavy you can't even lift your feet. You know - all that malarkey about relativity.'

Peter closed his eyes as Captain Järvinen entered the ward. He didn't want to talk any more.

Bee-Bee wasn't there. She didn't know about Peter's illness. She was busy preparing for the picnic. A large rug, big enough for a spread of four and a basket with plenty of room for everything; drinks, plates and mugs, cutlery, fruit, vegetables, cheese and bread with a multi-purpose knife. Bee-Bee went through the motions much like the time when she and John prepared for their VR game of 'Space Hunt', not consciously thinking about what she was doing. She didn't consciously dwell on the peculiarity of the entire situation. Back then the experience of being in space was just a make believe, an unreality; an attempt to trick the brain into thinking that something actually real was happening. This time trickery didn't need to be used.

'We have to go NOW!' Spiers still tried convincing him for the last time. Stephan had disappeared at the next moment. The lure of the adventure got him as far as the Cube bay in which Peter had parked his spacecraft. Compared to the small reconnaissance Cubes this thing looked enormous. Then hearing Spiers' fanatical voice made the decision for him, and he took off leaving Ziggy and Spiers to go by themselves.

'Don't worry about him. We don't need him. Leaves more food for us.' Ziggy grabbed his personal kit and jumped in behind Spiers.

'Ready to go, if you would be so kind as to open up,' Spiers spoke pleasantly to the Bay controller. The woman on duty knew Cube #2 from the odd size of it. It was that man Peter's - the one who'd been coming and going out into space from time to time.

'Good luck. See you next time Citizen Peter.'

Spiers was careful to follow protocol. He levitated slowly, inched his way to the opening before increasing speed slightly. 'Come on, come on - what are you waiting for?' Ziggy's nerves took over as he realised the highly illegal nature of what they were doing. He didn't know what the penalty was for stealing a Cube. He didn't want to find out.

'Take it easy buddy. They're not coming after us. They think it's that guy Peter leaving again. Relax. Have a drink.'

Twenty minutes later Spiers opened up the throttle, not that this type of technology had throttles exactly. It was much more complicated, though the controls seemed simple enough - forward was down, backwards was up and so on. This was Peter's spacecraft. He had an intimate relationship with it. He didn't need indicators or warnings to be displayed on any of the instruments, such as the limitations on speed control and the dangers of going too fast when travelling in the Dark.

'So which way do we go?' asked Ziggy, genuinely concerned as he'd not seen Spiers navigate before.

'That way.' Spiers pointed to a speck of light, which he assumed was the sun as it seemed to be the brightest spot.

Ivan could do nothing to help his father. While he waited for the inevitable he decided to go along with Bee-Bee, as a distraction for himself if nothing else. They met at Bee-Bee's favourite Café. Greetings with smiles, without words. They didn't linger for both felt it better they not be seen together in public without their respective partners. She handed him the picnic basket. Ivan saw the slightly vacant look in her eyes without taking much notice. *This must be as hard for her as it is for me. I hope this puts an end to all the nonsense.* Ever since he saw her on the Butterfly there was this background tension inside him. He got on with his job, his life, his relationship with Iluska yet it was always present.

'Lead the way.'

She did. He thought they'd take one of the electric pods to one of the 'park' levels. Bee-Bee went past the lifts and past the pods towards one of the Cube bays. *Ok, so we're going to find a nice spot by one of the rivers near here. I wonder how this is going to work in Titan's atmosphere.*

'We're taking that one,' she said speaking for the first time. She'd indicated one of the larger cargo carrying Cubes.

'Looks good. Gives us plenty of room. You can fly one of these things?'

'By now probably better than you, Johnny boy.' *Oops. I didn't mean to say that.* Her memory flashed back to when she last used those words; it had something to do with being able to handle knives. Johnny boy never seemed to be very good at it.

Ivan's eyebrows lifted slightly at her odd remark. The interior of the craft was spacious, with several cabins as well as the storage compartments. A scene surfaced which had been etched into his memory from the time he and Betty played that peculiar 'Space Hunt' VR game. His memory may have faded, yet the layout of this craft appeared to be unnaturally similar to the one where they played the game which would have such wide reaching consequences their future lives.

He saw what appeared to be normal food supplies stored in every available space.

'This is a lot of supplies, more than we need for a picnic. You planning on a sightseeing tour around Saturn?'

'Maybe, if we feel like it. Are you going to let me fly this thing?'

'Sure. You don't have to ask. Show me what you can do.' It always surprised him in the past how proficient and clever Betty was, like for instance her facility with languages.

Meticulous as always Bee-Bee went through the pre-flight check list, registered their departure with the bay controller ... and waited.

Ivan found a seat near the controls, not exactly relaxed, more like expectant. He found the entire situation somewhat surreal as he thought about the last time he was alone with Betty in a spacecraft, one that didn't really exist. Yet here they were now doing almost exactly the same thing. Except the 'hunt' was replaced by a 'picnic'. *There has to be more to this than a picnic for old time's sake.*

After some minutes of watching Bee-Bee doing nothing, just staring at the front screen ... 'I'm ready when you are,' Ivan prompted.

Bee-Bee pulled herself back from where ever she'd gone, lifted off the pad and moved forward to the open bay hatch.

'Don't be too long. Weather looks fine out there though there is a strong wind forecast in the North-East quadrant,' said the controller assuming their flight was intended for Titan conditions.

Schrödinger's Box

Citizen Peter's condition worsened.

Dr Kathleen had neither the means nor the expertise to slow or stop aggressive cancers. Her tests showed multiple attacks on his body including pancreatic cancer and leukemia.

'He's not going to survive is he.' Captain Järvinen's concern wasn't only for this one man. Everyone on the Butterfly, including herself, had been exposed to the same environment as Citizen Peter. They had all travelled in the Dark.

'I've tested a good sample of citizens. For some reason we're ageing normally again without any of the effects we found in Citizen Peter. Maybe it's the frequency of his jumps, or maybe he did some dangerous experiments out there. I don't know.'

The Captain's assistant poked her head into the office. 'Excuse me Captain, you should know this. One of our Cubes has been taken out on an unauthorized flight. It's been identified as Citizen Peter's ship.'

'That's impossible. It can't be the same one. Citizen Peter is in hospital.'

'They have not responded to out calls.'
'Get a search party out there. Find them.'

Ex-Citizen Spiers was on a high. He'd beaten them all. They couldn't keep him prisoner. He was on the way home. At the beginning he'd accepted being called 'Citizen'. It felt inclusive. It felt like he'd been accepted into something special. He even found Lucy aboard the Butterfly. Setting up a home together in an environment looking and feeling exactly like Earth took his mind off the utterly bizarre situation of flying in space and seeing his home planet as a magnificent sphere when they left the ISS. It should have been flat. For a while he forgot that.

'Look at it,' he pointed at Saturn as they flew past its rings. How do you suppose they managed to do that?

'Do what?' Ziggy felt exhilarated as well by their daring escape and being caught up in Spiers' exuberance.

'To make it look like it's round, with that ring of stuff around it.'

'It is round you idiot.'

'Shut up Ziggy. Have another drink. It's all a massive conspiracy.'

'Yeah, right. How about you watch where we're going. I don't want you to go crashing into it regardless of whether it's round or flat. Why didn't you answer them when they called before?'

'Because they'd find us. They'll come looking for us for sure.'

'They'll catch us anyway - won't they?'

'Not if I can help it. Are you ready for this?'

Spiers made the jump, like Peter and his son had in their first test flight by instantaneously increasing the Cube's speed. Saturn disappeared from view replaced by images they should have been familiar with; the chaotic swirling interference patterns formed by gravitational waves.

Line-of-sight navigation wasn't going to get them home even in normal space. Spiers didn't know how to interpret the interference patterns created by normal matter. He saw only chaos. He'd been out of touch with reality for most of his adult life. The quasi stabilising effect on his mind by engaging in the beliefs of the Flat-Earth Society created only a thin veneer of actuality, enough for him to live his life without indulging in the joys of insanity.

The outer perimeter of sanity had left him stranded.

'We'll be home in no time! Watch this!'

Ziggy wasn't a dolt and he wasn't insane either. The realisation hit him suddenly and hard. This man was going to kill him if he wasn't stopped. Ziggy lunged at the controls knocking Spiers off his feet.

The fight didn't last long. With manic strength Spiers grabbed twisting him away from the control panel. Before Ziggy could recover Spiers had pushed the speed control as far as it would go. The excessive speed indicator light, which Peter hadn't installed, didn't flash its warning.

When relativity kicks in as you near the speed of light things begin to happen. As Peter said on his death bed about flying too fast, 'You know you're going too fast when your body gets so heavy you can't even lift your feet.'

Spiers was right. The search party had no hope of rescuing the two mutineers. They'd gone as far as the edge of the rings of Saturn finding no trace of a spacecraft which no longer existed in the same universe, or any other.

The two mutineers came face to face with the problem of ultimate discontinuity.

The head of the search party received a directive from Captain Järvinen herself. 'There is another craft missing. Citizens Ivan and Bee-Bee aboard. They have not responded to our communications and may be in trouble. Abandon the search for Citizen Spiers and look for Ivan and Bee-Bee.'

They'd been cruising for about ten minutes after leaving the Butterfly with Bee-Bee concentrating on something before putting the Cube on auto-pilot, as well as switching off the comms.

'How have you been sleeping John?' she asked. He couldn't respond on the spot. Such a peculiar and unexpected thing to ask. Bee-Bee said something else suddenly. 'John, would you mind terribly calling me Betty?'

'Are you alright? This is a bit strange. I know who you are Bee-Bee. What's going on?'

'Just for old time's sake. Please John.'

As a distraction for her nerves Bee-Bee flew their Cube further out, close enough to Saturn to put it into a high geocentric orbit just beyond the rings belt, at the same time activating the two hatch locks. They may as well have been in suspended animation, without communications and without external access into the Cube. She switched all the screens to previously recorded images of Saturn. Ivan took no notice, engrossed in his own thoughts about their past history and the very peculiar present situation. He could not see the gathering storm of thoughts on Betty's face.

'Alright - Betty.' He glanced at the still closed picnic basket. 'Ready to have our picnic?'

The sooner this is over the better.

Hearing her proper name brought on a wistful smile. 'You don't feel like your dreams are being controlled anymore?'

'Dr Kathleen sorted it out for me. What about you?'

'Same. All that manipulation ruined our lives, didn't it?' Ivan waited to see what this was leading to. 'We've had a discussion, Iluska and I. She told me. I hope you'll be happy.'

'It's a girl.'

'You never wanted to have a baby with me.' She didn't react to the gender, as any woman in a normal state of mind would have.

'That was a mutual decision.' Ivan felt defensive.

'Are you happy?'

'Wouldn't you be?'

'I would have been.' Bee-Bee pulled over the picnic basket while Ivan sat there confused as to the entire nature of the conversation. It didn't sound like she was trying to make peace. It sounded more like provocation. *I'm not going to play this game. I'll just shut up and have the sandwich.*

It didn't take long for the search party to find their Cube. If Bee-Bee didn't want to be found she would have had to make the jump. By the time she and Ivan stepped into the Cube her thoughts were no longer rational. When she found out Iluska was pregnant and saw a new light of happiness on her John's face it completely stirred up her animosity towards him.

Citizen Arnold, leading the rescue party tried numerous times to contact them. 'Captain Järvinen, they won't respond. I'm sure they must be able to see us. We're close enough to space-walk across to them.'

'Keep trying.'

Captain Järvinen's apprehensions surfaced rapidly. She knew enough of the past history between her two citizens to have made her worry previously. She thought bad feelings had been resolved between them as she watched them working together, seeing no sign of tension since landing on Titan. She remembered Bee-Bee telling her on one occasion how she got the scar on her hand. Ivan would never tell her how he got his knife wound. Captain Järvinen remembered all of it.

Citizen Arnold flew around the Cube several times. If he didn't know any better it could have been a cargo Cube somehow coming lose from the Butterfly and floating out into space. But he did know better.

'They are still not responding. I think they can't see us Captain. We certainly can't see what's going on inside.'

'Stay with them. I know our two people are in there. Maybe something has happened to them. We won't know until you crack open that box. Give them another hour then see if you can get across to them.'

Ivan would not have seen anything other than the images of Saturn if he'd bothered to look up at the screens. There was no reason to. He was watching Bee-Bee fiddling with the latches on the picnic basket. She seemed unusually clumsy.

'This is almost like that VR game we played John. You remember,' she didn't look up as she managed to flip open the lid.

'I do, Betty.'

She took out a small cutting board, the bread, the ham and the cheese. 'It's gouda, the same as we had then.' Her mind went back to that day.

As Betty took out the knife John saw it immediately, reacting violently and falling off the seat.

Feeling the weight of the instrument and the flash of light on its blade Betty was transported back to that past unreality of the Virtual Reality Space Hunt game.

'It's been an hour people and still no response. There's only one way to find out what's going on. Captain Järvinen said we have to try and get in there.'

*

424

425

We nibble at our mortality
day by day

As a mouse at his block of
cheese.

One day it will be gone.

Seeds
of
Contemplation

There is a reality outside of our comprehension of it.

We are a part of it yet our perspective of it is compromised. Our vision of it is myopic for our horizons do not stretch beyond our physical senses. As much as our mind yearns and strives to come to an understanding true reality remains a fugitive. So we create fantasies to achieve conceptual comfort.

Our perception of reality is channelled towards achieving survival. The more accurate the perception, enabling effective survival action, the closer that perception is to empirical reality.

We can expect to understand through our senses that which has been created through the use of the same kind of senses.

We cannot hope to understand that which has not been created through the use of the same senses we have.

For Flat Earthers the Earth will remain forever flat until the proponents of the concept need the Earth to be round.

Reality is a perceived condition of existence which has an influence on the observers ability to negotiate with existence in order to continue to exist.

The Journey from trying to climb into a Russian tank during the Hungarian revolution of 1956 to writing science fiction is in itself a story of a leap across worlds of reality.

Zsoall, born in Hungary, was brought to Australia by his parents during the uprising. He currently lives a creative life with his wife and animal family in the Northern Rivers, New South Wales, Australia.

His reality has changed direction a number of times. After qualifying as a sculptor he worked as a secondary teacher before becoming an administrative manager. None of those career paths offered satisfactory opportunities for creative expression. That began when he embarked on a career as a computer programmer. Whilst in that profession his continuing compulsion to create made it inevitable his life would change again. Completely giving up programming he immersed himself in creativity as a sculptor and painter.

Much of his time is now dedicated to creating glass paintings and sculptures.

Another reality is infiltrating his life as the art of recording future visions takes a firmer hold of his creative inclinations as he continues to pursue the writing of science fiction.

Books by Zsoall Robi

The Origination Trilogy

Book 1 – Earth Phase

Born to an insignificant peasant family Lai Xii was destined to change the path of human evolution, and in the process spread the seed of homo sapiens beyond the Milky Way Galaxy.

Book 2 – Europa Phase

The first stage of Lai Xii's plan was to save the human species from extinction, and the destruction of its home planet, by taking the entirety of Earth's population to another destination in the solar system.

Book 3 – Photon Phase

The re-engineered human species arrives at a location that Lai Xii could not possibly have foreseen; a consequence of the myriad decisions made by herself and her closest collaborators.

Potential Absolute

Lelek could not conceive what the future held for him when he struggled to survive as a Stone Age man. Forces beyond his control set him on a path to the unfolding of all that was possible for this single, special Hominid.

Instant

Is it at all possible to cross the bridge between two consecutive instants of time into Eternity? Mary wanted much more than to experience reality outside of her digital matrix through her three remote autonomous processing units.

Immortal

Aliens are those who are different, those who belong to a different civilisation. Who is worthier of survival? Them or us? The aspirations of an entire species drives them to invade an alien race to which it may be related.

Neural Surveillance

Anything seen, heard or said is transmitted and monitored by the Angels and Saints public servants. Privacy is a luxury that is no longer tolerated by the ruling classes. Absolute control has become the nature of the world order, for no reason other than the lust for power.

Fundamental Particle of Self

A global business conglomerate commissioned Nick, an artist, to paint a portrait of God. Nick had to meet his subject in order to do this.
On the way to the centre of the universe, where God was thought to be, Nick underwent unexpected changes and formed some most unusual relationships.
The portrait did get painted. However, it was nothing like what the Company expected to see.

Quintessence

Is it possible to travel through time to meet one's ancestor and one's descendent even though they may be separated by thousands of years and even by intergalactic distances? Kobayashi Beau found himself captivated by energies within the void of space that transported him into realms unimaginable.

Binary Trojan Horse

Reality and evolution are closely linked. We don't perceive how reality changes just as evolution happens without us being aware of it.
So it was for Jakxson and Serenity. Normality became elusive when their girl child seemed to have inherited Albinism.
Rose was exceptionally beautiful with her very light skin and long white hair. But her eyes were abnormally big with enlarged, dark irises: traits she couldn't possibly have inherited from her parents.

430